Almost

DEFINITELY

mostly

FINE

Amy grew up with a lifelong passion to be a writer, despite her dad's best efforts to make her a dentist. She is now based in Brighton and works as a freelance journalist, which she juggles with her other writing. Her work has appeared in national newspapers and magazines. *Definitely Fine* is her debut novel.

Almost DEFINITELY *mostly* FINE

AMY LAVELLE

ORION

An Orion paperback

First published in Great Britain in 2021
by Orion Fiction
an imprint of The Orion Publishing Group Ltd
Carmelite House, 50 Victoria Embankment
London EC4Y 0DZ

An Hachette UK Company

1 3 5 7 9 10 8 6 4 2

A CIP catalogue record for this book is
available from the British Library.

ISBN (Mass Market Paperback) 978 1 3987 0363 6
ISBN (eBook) 978 1 3987 0364 3

Typeset at The Spartan Press Ltd,
Lymington, Hants

Printed and bound in Great Britain by Clays Ltd,
Elcograf S.p.A.

www.orionbooks.co.uk

For my mum, Dawn

How to Cope When You Definitely Can't

I was standing in front of the fridge, spooning hummus into my mouth with a slice of bread when it happened. I'm not thrilled that's the way this all started: with the fridge door resting gently against my bum, but nevertheless, that's where I was when my phone buzzed and I got the news. Then I dropped the hummus.

One of the first thoughts I had after all this happened was: what now? There was also: how could this happen, what am I going to do and how are we supposed to survive this (and then bigger questions involving a cruel God and funeral plans). But *what now* was the main one. That was the one that kept coming up. After all, what are you supposed to do when it feels like your world has just disintegrated? I used to have an answer to that: it was call my mum, which I did, after every bad break-up, failure, or eruption of teen acne. But calling your mum is no longer an option when the whole reason your world is now disintegrating is because she has suddenly died. So you see my point. In situations like that one, what now becomes an important question. What exactly are you supposed to do?

What happened was, I got that call that everyone dreads. The one that wakes you up at three in the morning and lets you know that something awful has happened to someone you love and the last vestiges of life as you know it are quickly swept away. Only it wasn't a phone call at three in the morning, it was a text from my younger sister, Laura, in the middle of the day. And it was actually saying that our mum was completely all right, but she'd fallen over and was in the hospital and could I tell Dad, because her signal was rubbish. Which she then repeated over about seven texts, while I tried to pry the name of the hospital out of her, which she had forgotten to mention. Then I tried to make that phone call to my dad, to let him know his wife was in hospital, but it was okay, because she was okay. 'Dad, Mum's had an accident,' I would tell him, calmly, so he would know not to panic, but with authority, so he would listen and not immediately start talking about the golf and holes, or whatever happens in golf. 'Now, don't panic, she's going to be okay. I don't know the details, but Laura's with her and she's in the hospital . . . No, I don't know which hospital.'

I took a deep breath, grabbed my boyfriend Ollie's hand tightly and rang my dad. He didn't pick up. I tried the house phone. Still no answer. I called my dad's good friend Nigel to see if he was with my dad. He wasn't. We drove over there to tell him in person. He didn't open the door: he was watching the golf. Only when he realised no one else was home to do it did he let me in.

'Hannah, what's going on? The phone's been ringing off the hook,' he said.

'I know,' I said. 'That was me.' I restrained myself from upping the list of casualties to two and explained.

When we made it to the hospital, we found Laura, bright red and crying. Things weren't all right, after all. For starters, we had lost Mum.

'She's gone,' Laura said, tears running down her face.

I grabbed at Ollie's arm. 'She's dead?' My legs crumpled underneath me and I sat down on the floor.

Laura shook her head. 'No. She's gone missing.'

Slowly I got back up again.

'She was here, but they took her away to do some tests and now no one seems to know where she is,' Laura said. 'She's disappeared.'

I looked down at Laura's T-shirt, which had the word 'beast' written on it in bold neon letters.

She crossed her arms over it.

'What happened?' I said.

Laura shifted her feet. 'We were on a run.'

Laura had moved back home the year before, after she finished her degree, and was now working nearby as a secretary for a local firm, while she saved money. This meant that she and Mum had been spending more time together. Running was the latest hobby in a list that included art classes and pottery painting. Every now and then, I would join them, but this tended to be for the more sedate activities. Running wasn't one of them. I was beginning to regret that.

3

'She tripped on a tree root, or a broken paving stone or something and just went over. I think she knocked her head on someone's garden wall as she fell, but not that hard. And she was fine. She seemed okay. You know, more or less. They sedated her, just in case. Then they took her to do tests and now, she's disappeared.' She dropped her arms again. 'She's missing.'

My first instinct regarding Mum's disappearance was to blame Laura. Laura is one of those people you never want to lend anything to because she can usually be counted on to lose it. She once lost her skirt whilst she was still wearing it. Still, losing our mum felt like a new low. After all, how do you misplace a whole person, especially when that person isn't in a position to walk off under their own steam? My dad pointed this out to the staff at the emergency room, while they checked their systems and repeated that Mum wasn't there.

'But where is she then? We were told she was here. She should be here. Look, it's Jennifer Kennedy,' he said, before he began to slowly spell her name again.

'Sir, for the last time, we'll let you know when we hear. Now, please sit down, there's a queue.'

So we sat and waited on brittle plastic chairs in a corridor, vaguely listening to the nearby doctors who were discussing a particularly hopeless patient they didn't know what to do with.

Ollie leaned forward. 'I think they're talking about your mum,' he said. 'Extensive cranial bleed ... They are. They're talking about your mum,' he said, looking rather triumphant until he noticed that Laura had

4

put her head between her knees and was beginning to hyperventilate. 'Oh...'

It was another six hours before we found her, at a specialist unit she had been rushed to. The news wasn't good, which is the kind of stupid thing people say when actually they mean it couldn't possibly be worse. That locusts raining from the sky might be a welcome distraction for you right now because *hoo boy*, is this news bad. Which, by the way, it was.

We were standing in the waiting room next to the ward. Dad made us sit down, then sat down as well.

'The doctor says she is unlikely to live through the night,' he said. 'If she does, she's unlikely to live for much longer. Her brain is bleeding and there's nothing they can do.'

'Are you joking?' Laura croaked. 'You're joking.'

'Of course I'm not bloody joking. Why would I be joking?'

'I don't know. To lighten the mood. She was fine. She can't be dying.'

'Well she is. She's going to die. She probably won't last till morning so you should go say your goodbyes now, because it's probably the last chance you'll get,' he said, although he didn't so much say it as shout it.

It should probably be said at this point that my dad, second generation Irish, was raised to believe emotions are for *The Archers*. You might have them, but that doesn't mean you have to talk about them. I knew all about his emotional repression and I'd met my aunt Iris (who I'll get to later, but who makes our dad look

5

well-adjusted), but I still couldn't help but wish he'd dug a little deeper this once and pushed through his irritation at having to cope with his feelings. It felt unfair that this was how we were finding out, next to a stack of *OK!* magazines with a Kardashian on the cover. Dad picked up a copy and pretended to read it, which would have looked more convincing if he hadn't been holding it upside down.

I looked up at the ceiling in the way that I do when I'm really trying to eye-ball God, like He exists somewhere on the floor above me and will really pay attention when He notices my hard stare. (Over the next few days, God would come to look like a hospital ceiling tile to me. *Please make this better. Please save her. Really, God? You're leaving me with this lot?*) Come on, God, I thought. Let's agree this is just some bad mistake, okay? After all, they've already lost her. This isn't that big a stretch.

Then we got to the ward and despite my best efforts at denial, in the face of reality, everything began to feel utterly hopeless. Especially when that face no longer looked like reality, or the face of my mum as I knew it at all and in fact, looked a lot more like Jocelyn Wildenstein. If Jocelyn Wildenstein was in a medical coma that doctors had to induce to prevent any further damage to the brain. Her swollen face still had dried blood on it from where she'd fallen. Lying there, her auburn hair pulled off her face and exposing her greying roots, she looked more like her own mother than mine.

I tentatively took Mum's hand and gripped it tightly, her soft skin broken by cuts from where she'd fallen. I whispered into her ear, 'Please don't die, Mum. We can sort this out in the morning. These things always look better after a good night's sleep. I just need you to make it through the night, first. Just. Don't. Die.'

I don't remember how I got back home that night from the hospital, only that we all ended up there together and at some point, I collapsed into bed and curled into a ball, with Ollie's arm thrown over me. I slept the kind of sleep that doesn't really feel like rest at all, but more like your mind begrudgingly submitting to your body's will, after it refuses to remain standing, functioning and conscious any longer. My last thought was Mum. It had to be a dream.

Of course, it wasn't. The next morning, we headed straight to the hospital's Neuro-ICU. Every time we walked to and from the hospital, I tried to keep my eyes fixed on the sea. The sea wasn't something I usually gave much thought to in my everyday life. Living in Brighton, you tend to neglect the beach until those few days a year when the sun finally shines and then you, along with everyone else within a thirty-mile radius, rush to it to claim your small patch, which you then proceed to determinedly sit on for hours, drinking cider and gradually burning, declaring it a wasted resource and one you won't continue to neglect. But during that time, I focused on the water as if I was suffering from motion sickness and that wedge of blue on the horizon was all that could save me. This often proved difficult, as the hospital was in the opposite direction, but it was necessary, because once we were inside, we spent almost all of our time in the family room.

'Family room' was a deceptively welcoming name for what it really was: a tiny, windowless box without any source of natural light, that was so depressing, you began to wonder if it had purposely been made that way to better prepare people for the misery of grief. 'This is how crap it's going to be for the upcoming months, so you might as well get used to it now' could have been stamped on the door as you walked in and it would have looked perfectly in place and actually, quite considerate. Over the few days we spent there, we never saw another family come near it, which was a relief, because they wouldn't have fit.

Anyway, that's where we were when the consultant came in, followed by his aftershave. He looked like a man who is often told he looks a bit like Richard Gere; a man you suspected might try out leather trousers and refer to his hands as 'the money makers'. This was supported by the flaccid handshake he gave us that seems to be the preserve of all surgeons (it's as if they're told at medical school that too firm a grip could be the end of their career), before he draped himself on the sofa.

He threw one arm across the back of it, like he was a guest on *Graham Norton*. 'I don't have any good news for you, unfortunately,' he said, before glancing down in what looked at first like a practised moment of solemnity and concern, until you realised he was actually checking his reflection in the surface of his shoes. 'Your mother's fall caused an extensive bleed in the brain,' he said, repeating a combination of facts we'd already gleaned from eavesdropping on the other doctors and from what Dad had shouted the night before. Then he said some other things, which basically boiled down to 'there's no hope'.

'Even if she did somehow survive, she would be in a vegetative state for the rest of her life.' He paused. 'The best thing to do would be to turn off the machines now. It's the kind thing to do. If it were my mother, I would.'

This, for the record, is a completely stupid thing to say, because you can't know what you'd do with your mother unless it is your mother. And what's more, no one cares what you'd do with your mother, because it's not your mother, it's their mother. Or in this case, our mother, and that word means something.

'You don't understand,' I wanted to tell him. 'She's not just another patient; she's our mum.' I wanted to tell him she was the focal point of all our lives; the person that pulled us all together. I wanted to tell him that we didn't have one of those difficult mother/daughter relationships that people describe as 'complex' if they're in public and 'strained', 'fraught' or 'toxic' when they're not; we had always been very close. She was the one that I went to whenever something happened to me and, more often, when nothing at all happened to me. The kind of mum you'd call your best friend, if it wasn't completely naff to call your mum your best friend (but who was still, when it came down to it, my best friend). I wanted to say that none of this should or could be happening, because

9

none of us knew how to function in a world in which she didn't exist.

It had only been fifteen hours since we had heard she'd fallen over (something she did quite a lot, anyway and usually, with a lot less fuss). We weren't ready to give up all hope. We hadn't been given any warning.

When I ended up in counselling a couple of months after this all happened, I recounted this story to my counsellor and she nodded and said, 'This sounds like anger,' which was not the breakthrough moment she seemed to think it was.

I shifted my attention to the triangle of chest hair that was making its way out of the top of the consultant's shirt and the three buttons he hadn't done up that morning, probably while looking his reflection in the eye and humming Hot Chocolate songs.

'But she made it through the night,' I pointed out.

'Yes,' the doctor said.

'You said she wouldn't,' I said.

'There aren't any assurances.'

'But she didn't die when you thought she would, so couldn't she still live?'

'No.'

'I thought there weren't any assurances.'

'That one is.' He shifted on the sofa. 'I know this is all a shock to you, so I will give you some time to think about it. Ultimately, however, this is our choice, not yours and our duty is to the patient. Either you give us the go-ahead, or we turn the machines off ourselves.' And with that, he got up to leave.

'Thank you for all your help, Doctor,' my dad said, in such a deferential tone that I was convinced he was about to march into the ward and unplug every machine Mum was hooked on to. Then the door swung shut.

Dad turned to us. 'Right, well, bollocks to all that. We're not turning anything off. We'll get a second opinion.'

I went outside to call everyone that needed to be called, but who we'd avoided calling up until that point in the hopes that, eventually, we'd have some good news to tell them. Waking people up in the middle of the night to tell them you might have some bad news, but you still weren't 100 per cent sure felt inconsiderate. I was really hoping we could bypass all of that and go straight to the 'bring flowers' one, instead. At this point, I couldn't put it off any longer, though. So I called everyone on Mum's side of the family: her brother and sister, my cousins, her best friend, most of whom then turned up and crammed themselves into the family room like a protective shell, until running out of oxygen no longer felt hyperbolic and more like a genuine concern. At which point, they spilled out into the corridor, where they proceeded to patiently sit and wait, instead. Luckily, the nurses were unceasingly easy-going and kind and after a quick glance, gave up all pretence of maintaining visiting hours or the correct procedure involving number of visitors at a patient's bed.

I loved the nurses. I might have hated the doctors, the ones telling us there was no hope, but I loved the nurses. They were wonderful. They would brush Mum's thick hair and clean the nails that she always kept short, because she played the piano and listen every time one of us would tell them how special Mum was. That you couldn't really tell through the coma, but it was really true. They would turn a blind eye every time someone convinced Laura or Dad to eat something, even though you weren't supposed to have food on the ward. And every time we got bad news from a doctor, they would hug us and murmur soothing words and sometimes, well up along with us. They didn't even say anything when it began to seem like Dad might be considering making one of them his next wife, if this didn't work out. If he had, we might even have understood – they were that good.

Roughly every few hours, a cousin would go home for a break and be replaced by someone new and we would go through a ritual: they would squeeze Laura and then me, they would pat Dad reassuringly and ask if he'd eaten, then they would go and sit with Mum for a bit and cry. Finally, they'd come back to us and ask what we knew.

'It's looking fairly bad, if you believe the doctors. But we've stopped doing that now and things aren't looking as bad as they could be. When you look at things our way, they're looking all right,' we told them, nodding and smiling earnestly in that way you imagine cult members probably do when they're trying to sign up new members. 'After all, Mum's still alive. That's crucial. They keep telling us she will die at any minute, but she hasn't yet. We're getting a second opinion. Hopefully, from someone who shares our opinion,' we said.

As everyone else wanted there to be positive news almost as much as we did, this was easily accepted. They were quick to reassure us.

'Nina fell, split her head open and she was eighty-six. They stitched her up and she lived for at least another few years.'

'Bill was twenty stone, legally blind and had an aneurysm. The doctors cut it out and now, he's lost five stone, has the vision of a twenty-year-old and never even misses the part of his brain they removed.'

'I knew someone who was told he had a rare and incurable disease. He lived the next year like it was his last, which he thought it was: he quit his job, said goodbye to everyone he loved, squeezed in every life experience on his bucket list. Then it turned out, the doctors had mixed up his file. He was perfectly healthy all along.'

'Miracles can happen,' they said.

This was almost as gratifying as if we already had the second opinion and that opinion was that the doctors were just overly pessimistic. We had already been think-ing that. It all felt extremely reassuring.

Or at least, it was, until we actually got the second opinion and that doctor agreed with all the other ones we'd already spoken to. And those first doctors then insisted on showing us the scans of Mum's brain to show us just how hopeless the situation really was, thanks to a bleed the size of a potato. It was becoming pretty clear that this wasn't going to be one of the miracle suc-cess stories, after all. Then the people that were once cheering us on, complicit in our denial, were suddenly very keen that we faced up to the facts.

'Bill's aneurysm was in a different part of the brain . . .'

'Nina never really was the same after that, you know . . . And her hair didn't grow back over the stitches.'

The rare and incurable disease story, for what it's worth, remains the same.

I went outside and sobbed. I did this a lot over the next few days. I became a harbinger of doom, not unlike the people you see vomiting outside a Burger King. I'd stand by the front of Brighton General Hospital and call everyone that needed to be kept up to date who wasn't currently sitting inside, and when that was done, I would give in. Patients and visitors who were probably only coming in for some minor ailment, like a broken toe or chesty cough, would notice me shaking my fist at the air and hurry past, looking as if they were newly convinced they were on their way to their own death sentence.

That first night, I went back inside and prepared to say a final goodbye, just in case the doctors were right and she didn't make it through the night.

I like to believe that on some plane (hopefully not the physical one where she could overhear us talking about a fate that she no longer seemed to have a say in, but a nicer, metaphysical one), Mum could see everything that was going on. Really, it would have been a shame for her to miss one of the only times that anyone could remember ever having seen Dad cry. Laura and I were so surprised, we almost forgot to cry ourselves for a minute, until the realisation that things must be really bad crept in and then we went off even harder than before. So we said goodbye. We wept and told her what an amazing mum she was, that we would be okay and not to worry about us. We told her there were no spiders in the room, which might sound odd, but makes more sense when you understand that that's something she would say to Laura and me in turn each night growing up, in order to get us to go to sleep, and had since become a ritual. Then we shuffled out of the hospital, tightly holding on to each other, and began to make our way in a group back to mine and Ollie's house again, as it was the closest one and no one really wanted to leave anyone else alone that night.

Laura and I clung to each other and listed everything we would never get to do now Mum was dying.

'We'll never watch *Funny Girl*. She always tried to get us to and now we never will.'

'We'll never have another birthday card. Dad never remembers.'

'We'll never again eat her roast potatoes.'

'Actually, I know how to make her roast potatoes. You need semolina powder,' I said.

'It's not the same. I'm never eating another roast potato,' Laura said, the thought of which was such a bleak and dramatic sacrifice, I began to wonder if she cared more than I did and we both burst into tears.

'You can't stop eating roast potatoes. Mum wouldn't want that. What about Christmas?' I said.

15

'All right, maybe just at Christmas. It won't be the same, though. Nothing will ever be the same.'

When we made it home, we collapsed on the sofa and watched *Grand Designs* (feeling a particular kinship with every blown budget, collapsed roof and couple whose marriage was visibly disintegrating) until we fell asleep. There was something deeply soothing in seeing someone else's life fall apart, even if those crises didn't come close to what we were going through. A botched tiling couldn't really compare. As far as clusterfucks went, ours was catastrophic.

How to Communicate
with Doctors

There was more good news the next morning: Mum was still alive. Never underestimate how cheering this news is in situations like this. While Dad made his way back to the hospital to check, Ollie went off to buy breakfast to celebrate, coming back home with an armful of pastries and cupcakes covered in Disney characters. He is committed to the idea there isn't a problem that can't be solved by food, which is part of the reason we work so well together: we're both firm supporters of cupboard love. If we ever get into an argument, we know that the way to resolve it is usually with a cup of tea and a biscuit. I dread the day we have a fight so bad we can't fix it with a snack.

That morning, though, even I was having trouble forcing down more than a croissant, especially since Laura (who couldn't eat at all) was watching every bite accusingly.

She poked at a bright pink cupcake topped with a picture of Pumbaa and burst into tears. 'What if she dies?' she wailed.

I got up and hugged her as she sat there, wooden and

unresponsive. 'She won't die. Mum's strong. She's going to get through this,' I said. I stared at Ollie over her head. 'Ollie, can I see you upstairs for a second?'

He raised his eyebrows at me.

'Now,' I said.

We went up to the bedroom and I shut the door carefully.

I turned to Ollie. 'What if she dies?' I wailed. I heaved into his chest. I dribbled on my hair. I wiped my face on his T-shirt. Then I pulled myself together again and walked downstairs and pretended I hadn't been doing any of that.

Laura looked at Ollie's T-shirt, which now resembled an Edvard Munch painting, then at me and took my hand.

'You don't have to be strong for me, you know, Hannah. We need to be there for each other,' she said.

'I'm not being strong. I don't need to be. Mum's going to be fine. You'll see,' I said, giving her another quick squeeze. 'Let's go. I'm sure there'll be better news today.'

Staying strong and keeping positive are the emotional taxes on firstborns. Even so, for the most part, I meant this. Really I did. When I wasn't hysterically weeping, I remained resolutely optimistic. I wore my positive outlook like body armour that blocked all reason. If I had been more clear-headed, I might have thought of my friend Louise. Louise read about the Law of Attraction on Wikipedia one day and became a sworn devotee, convinced that she could manifest anything in her life by instructing the universe and talking to herself in the mirror. When her boyfriend broke up with her, she refused to acknowledge it and would instead tell anyone that asked after him that he was on a work trip away. Once, she even dressed up an inflatable doll that she had bought for her sister's hen do in one of his T-shirts, so she could better visualise his return. I was a bit like her. I truly believed that if I refused to give up hope, the universe would hear me and bring Mum back. It turns out, I'm quite good at denial. It probably comes from my Catholic upbringing. I haven't even mentioned the fact that I wore the same jumper to the hospital every day because something nice happened to me once while wearing it and ever since, I have considered it lucky.

Months after this, my counsellor suggested I was still in denial, which I largely pish-poshed. After all, I knew perfectly well my mum was dead. I was hardly denying that. Looking back, though, she might have been more insightful than I ever gave her credit for.

But at that moment in the hospital, I really did believe there was still hope. After all, that was the second time the doctors had been wrong. It was very encouraging.

I gleefully pointed this out to the surgeon when he came in to meet us. It was a new one, this time, who looked kinder and more sympathetic than the last one. He greeted us in the family room, still wearing his scrubs, which gave him an 'everyman' appeal, sort of like when Obama wears jeans. He even threw years of medical training to the wind and squeezed our hands. I thought we might have one doctor willing to see things my way. Until I launched into a practised diatribe about medical miracles, that is.

He rubbed his face. 'You're asking me the same question, but I can't give you a different answer,' he said. Then he told us that they were going to turn off the ventilator and as they didn't expect her to survive, we might want to say our goodbyes, again.

Dad looked so glum at this news that for a moment, I felt a true emotional connection between us, a shared experience of misery and heartache over what the doctor had said. Then he waved his phone and announced that his sister, Iris, was coming. Admittedly, this was awful news. To make things worse, it was my fault.

'Bloody hell. How did she know we're here?' Dad asked.

I bit my lip. 'Ah,' I said. 'I texted her. To let her know. About Mum. But I didn't think she'd see it. I thought Iris didn't believe in mobile phones?'

'Of course she does. She's just texted me from one to say she's coming.' Dad gave me a baleful look. 'I'll be with your mother,' he said and walked back into the ward, leaving me, Ollie and Laura alone in the family room, staring morosely at each other.

Iris is the sort of maiden aunt you usually find in an Austen novel, whose sole purpose seems to be to pose an obstacle between the romantic leads, but who you assume died out in real life sometime around the 1980s — the remaining few becoming Thatcher supporters. She and Mum had one of those relationships that gets turned into a joke on greeting cards. She had spent the first year of my parents' marriage referring to Mum as 'That Woman'. She thawed only when I was born, calling to announce, 'Not to worry, perhaps the next one will be a boy,' which all things considered, marked a step forward.

She was not a woman you wanted around in the aftermath of a crisis, when the emergency was over and you were tentatively counting survivors. She would berate them for being careless. I wished I had remembered all that before I invited her to our crisis.

'This feels like the time we played with Hayley from next door's Ouija board and a week later, we all got food poisoning and thought we'd summoned the devil,' I said.

Laura looked at me. 'I'd have preferred the food poisoning.'

'Don't be silly,' Ollie said. 'You didn't have a choice. You had to let her know: she's family. You both just need to eat something. Laura, you've barely had anything today. You'll feel better if you've had some food. I'll go downstairs to the shop.'

'Forget it, Ollie,' I said. 'The shopkeeper probably felt the wind change and closed early.' Service staff live in fear of Iris.

'What if she gloats? What is she says it's Mum's fault?' Laura said. 'She once told me I was too careless to keep hold of my virginity.'

'She won't say that,' Ollie said. He shifted his feet and looked away. 'Probably.'

We walked out into the hallway. The hermetically sealed ward door slid open with a hiss and Iris emerged. Iris was a woman you suspected might be hermetically sealed under her tweed skirt and sensible shoes. If you ever thought about what was under there, which I'm not sure anyone ever has. At that moment, her perm firmly set, all five foot two of her frame properly erect, she looked like the human embodiment of a hospital corner. I braced myself for a comment about Mum's clumsiness.

Instead, she hugged Laura and me tightly.

'Girls. I won't pretend to understand God's plan. It's not my place to do so. Rest assured, there is one, even if we can't for the life of us work out what it could be and sometimes, it can seem unthinkably cruel. I must say I'm really quite annoyed with Him this time. Now, where is your mother?'

Laura pointed and Iris marched into the ward, us following behind, where Dad was hiding out, talking to the nurses.

'Patrick, stop flirting with the nurses. Your wife is in a coma, for heaven's sake. It's unseemly.'

Then she walked up to Mum's bed, took her hand and said loudly, 'Jennifer, wake up. Wake up now, Jennifer. Jennifer, it's time to wake up.'

When she didn't wake up, Iris turned back to us.

'Well, you never can tell. Sometimes, people just need a stern talking-to.'

There was another reason why Iris's arrival was the Worst Possible News (which is the kind of thing you only really have the right to say when the actual Worst Possible News has already happened) and that was because of my mum's sister Cathy, who had blown in in a flurry of scarves a few hours before Iris arrived, after the travelling theatre she worked for had dropped her off. No one knew what exactly she did for the theatre; it was one of the mysteries of Cathy, like where she found her unending supply of kaftans or why her lipstick line was always half a centimetre over her actual lips. Cathy was nothing like Iris. In fact, this was true of the rest of the in-laws, which makes me wonder if their differences were part of the attraction that brought Mum and Dad together in the first place. Whatever it might have meant for them, though, it didn't always translate to their families, who tended to treat each other with a bemused but distant acceptance. Having one of your family members lying on their deathbed, though, was exactly the kind of situation that could make things feel strained. With Iris and Cathy in the same place, it would only be a matter of time before Cathy said something zany and Iris said something caustic.

As it was, Iris had barely settled onto the small sofa back in the family room with us when Aunt Cathy, who had gone outside for some fresh air, burst in, slinging around an IV drip bag attached to a stand. My uncle Dan sidled up behind her, making an apologetic face and shrugging, before going back to take his turn sitting with Mum.

'Oh my God. Cathy,' I said.

'Where did you get the IV drip?' Dad said.

'You didn't steal it from someone, did you?' Laura, who looked ashen, said.

Cathy bristled. 'Of course I didn't steal it. I found it

23

in the corridor outside next to an empty bed. Someone must have left it there. Anyway, it's lucky I did. You wouldn't believe what they fill these things with in the name of science.' She looked meaningfully around the room. 'Drugs.'

This was not the answer we expected; it seemed a bit too obvious.

'Mind control drugs,' she continued, which was more like it. 'Big conspiracy to cover it up. They want to make you more placid, you see. Docile. So you don't question what they're doing to you. I noticed they have Jenny on one.'

We all collectively held our breaths and looked at Iris, except for Cathy, who was squinting at the bag.

Iris nodded, slowly. 'Yes, Cathy and clearly it's working. She's in a coma.'

'Exactly. It's terribly upsetting.' Cathy grabbed at the folds of her clothes. 'Where are my reading glasses? There are all sorts of ingredients listed on the bag, here.' She waved at Laura. 'One of you girls come and read these out to me.'

'Will they put the names of the mind control drugs on the outside of the bag, though, Cathy?' Dad said, hiding a smirk behind his hand. 'Would they not want to hide that information?'

'You'd be surprised.' She tossed her flyaway hair out of her face. 'Just look at how many people die here. It's because their bodies can't handle the medication.' Cathy eyed Dad. 'What are they feeding, Jenny? I've brought some unpasteurised yoghurt. She'll need plenty

24

of natural foods to counteract all the harmful things they're pumping her full of.'

My phone buzzed. It was Evie: she was waiting outside.

Evie was my oldest friend. She and I had met at playgroup and had basically grown up together.

I walked out of the ward and into the corridor, where she was waiting with her eight-month-old son, Harry. As she regularly texted me to tell me she could barely find the time to go to the loo any more, her arrival at the hospital felt like a real testament to our friendship.

I hugged her tightly and brought her into the ward and the family room. 'Evie came to see Mum,' I said.

Iris eyed the two of them up. 'Really, Patrick. A hospital is no place for a baby,' she muttered.

Dad ignored her. 'Thanks for coming, Evie,' he said.

She smiled. 'Well, Jennifer practically raised me, too. I wanted to be here to say goodbye. If that's okay?'

Dad nodded.

Cathy jumped up. 'Of course, dear child. Here, let me take this beautiful boy off you.' She grabbed Harry, who looked slightly shocked.

Evie looked from Cathy to me.

I nodded at her. 'It's okay,' I said. 'We don't want to traumatise him with the sight of Mum, hooked up to all those machines.'

I didn't think about the trauma we might have done to him with the sight of Cathy.

She smiled uncertainly, then stood up and left the room.

The door had barely closed behind her before Cathy started cooing over Harry, squeezing him so hard I began to wonder if it was physically possible to burst a baby, while covering him in her lipstick.

'And still, her lipstick line doesn't budge,' Laura whispered to me.

Harry, for his part, responded equally quickly by bursting into tears. This in no way helped save him from Cathy, who simply pressed him closer to her.

'There, there,' she said. She looked up and round at us. 'Babies are very sensitive to negative vibes, you know. No doubt he can sense the presence of death,' she said, whispering the last word.

Laura and I looked at each other.

Iris watched her. 'Cathy, you'll smother him. A child needs space. Give him to me and I'll put him outside. If you coddle him, he'll never learn.'

Cathy held him tighter and jiggled him. 'Nonsense, Iris. A baby needs to feel closeness. The power of maternal warmth can't be overestimated. He just needs to feel the contact of human skin. Hannah, hold him while I undo my blouse.'

I took a step backwards. I've never been good with confrontation.

Iris closed her eyes. 'Really, Cathy. I think that's quite unnecessary.'

Cathy studied her and nodded. 'Jenny always said your mother was a cold woman. It's such a shame when the basic, fundamental needs of a child aren't met; it makes for such unhappy adults, I've always found. Iris, have you considered opening yourself up to a visualisation exercise. You picture your mother and let loose all your repressed emotions towards her. I think it could really help you move past some of your issues with emotional closeness.'

Evie came back into the room ten minutes later to see Cathy, her blouse worked down to her midriff, holding on to a distraught Harry, while Iris tried to wrestle him off her.

'Iris, you don't understand attachment parenting,' Cathy was saying over Harry's wails, tugging her thick bra strap back up her shoulder.

'Um,' Evie said. 'I should go.'

This was how the consultant found us – not the nice Obama consultant this time, but the Richard Gere one, again – with a nurse in tow, when he came back to make sure that we were really clear, once and for all, that there really was no hope now and keeping Mum alive was actually a disservice to her. And then Laura was crying and the nurse was passing out tissues, Dad looked quiet and sombre, and even Cathy and Dan were gently explaining to me that this was it now and we had to let her go.

Doctor Richard Gere cleared his throat. 'We know you'd like to bring a priest in to give the Last Rites,' he said, 'so we're willing to wait for that.' He glanced from the corner of his eye at the nurse who was hovering behind him. 'How's that going, by the way?'

She spread her hands, apologetically. 'We're looking for one, but they're all on holiday.'

'What? All the priests in the area? Together?' Gere asked. 'Oh for God's sake,' he muttered. He glanced at Dad. 'Sorry.'

'The bishop's down. There's some kind of convention...' the nurse said.

Behind me, Iris snorted. 'How absurd, all of them fawning over him at once. Patrick, you should write to him. People's mortal souls are at risk — unlike his ego, clearly.'

Quietly, I smiled to myself. This felt like a sign, if not from God Himself, at least His henchmen. No priest; no Last Rites. No Last Rites and we'd bought ourselves — and Mum — some more time.

They found a nun instead.

There are lots of times when religion, faith, or some general belief in another power can be of great help to you during the really hard times in your life. This was not one of them.

The nun was a gnarled, shrunken woman who looked like she'd been carved from wood.

'Do you regularly deliver the Last Rites, Sister?' Dad asked.

'I am a vessel of God,' the nun announced, manoeuvring us into a circle around the bed and clasping our hands together. For one horrified moment, I thought she was going to make us sing 'Kumbaya'. We looked at each other, until we noticed her sternly eyeballing us and bowed our heads. From a battered satchel, she brought out a prayer book and bottle of water. Then she shuddered, threw her arms in the air and began what felt like a dramatic reading of the Book of Revelation. If you've ever watched one of those evangelist preachers in America give a sermon, you might have an idea what this was like. Her prayer book jerked around in her hands. She called on the Spirit of the Lamb and warned off Satan. At one point, she began describing the beginning of the endless night, which felt a little too on the nose. Just as she was beginning to lose her audience, she produced a bottle and liberally threw holy water around like she was trying to physically wash off our sins, causing the nurses to look round in alarm. She even danced a little jig (although in retrospect, this might have just been arthritis).

'Bless you child,' she finished, making the sign of the cross, before declaring loudly, 'She is with God now,' which caused a collective intake of breath and a moment of mass alarm, until we all looked at the heart monitor and realised it was still recording beats. Then she walked round to me, grabbed my hands and told me it was time to be strong. It was my duty to look after the family now.

I stared at her in alarm. 'Actually,' I said, 'I don't know if . . . You see, Dad . . .'

It was one of the most unsettling experiences of my life. I felt short-changed.

I glanced at Iris who was watching the nun, her mouth pursed so tightly her lips had turned purple and almost disappeared entirely. Iris was raised by nuns and had never really forgiven them for it.

Dad cleared his throat. 'Thank you, Sister,' he said. 'Let me walk you out.' He escorted her out of the ward, leaving the nurses to mop up the worst of the holy water.

As the ward doors closed, Cathy, who had made a strategic exit before the ritual, wandered back in.

'You can see why she became a nun, can't you?' she said. 'Poor dear, with a face like that, what choice did she have?'

When Dad got back, the nurses walked over to us and, with a hand on Dad's arm, asked if we were ready to say our goodbyes. We looked at each other. We should have been ready. We had had our time. But we all agreed that wasn't really good enough and none of us had warmed to the nun, had we? And when someone's mortal soul is at stake, you really need the thing to be done properly, with an actual priest, right? So there was no other way: we had to do it again and with a priest this time. We were giving up on her body, but we were going to do the best we could for her soul. It was the least we could do.

While we were calling every parish in the county looking for a spare Man of God, the doctors were quietly bringing Mum's life to a close. They reduced the medication keeping her in a coma and when she didn't wake up, she didn't die, either. Then they turned off the ventilators that were helping her breathe. It felt like they had turned my oxygen off, too, until I realised I was holding my breath, waiting to see if she would take one by herself. When she did, I quietly clocked this up as another triumph.

I sat by her bedside, gazing at her. At school, people would always tell me how lucky I was to have a mum like her (she with her high cheekbones, youthful complexion and wide mouth that I'd always regretted not inheriting), before looking dubiously at me and deciding I looked like my dad. I stared at her, mentally willing her to wake up. She stayed resolutely unconscious. So I whispered into her ear to keep breathing, keep going, keep living. This was in her hands now.

When they had done all they could, the doctors waited for us to drag a priest out of retirement so we could deliver the Last Rites all over again.

So we wheeled in a priest, who was even smaller and older than the nun had been.

'Thank you for coming, Father,' Dad said. 'We appreciate you coming out of retirement to do this for us.'

'You interrupted karaoke night at the home,' the priest said. 'I'm glad to be here.'

Laura grabbed my hand. 'If he's retired, will his powers still work?'

The priest turned to her. 'My dear, I'm a priest, not a genie.'

He pulled a little black book from his jacket and quietly read the words and prayers that absolved Mum's soul from all of her earthly sins, anointed her with holy oil and made the sign of the cross. With that, he was done and we had completed the last task we could ever do for Mum. After the nun, it was wildly anticlimactic.

And then there was nothing left to do but say goodbye.

There's really no way to say the next bit without sounding callous and uncaring. I've tried, opening up in deep talks with friends and tentatively admitting it. But then they all, without fail, got the same look of alarm and vague sanctimony on their faces, before muttering that they wouldn't find it such a task. So I gave up on trying to make it sound any better and have reconciled myself to the fact that, the chances are, I'm going to sound completely heartless.

So here goes: there are only so many times you can say goodbye, properly, in a short space of time. After all, you only have a limited number of emotional reserves to draw on and to be quite honest, once you've said your heartfelt, ending of *Casablanca*-esque speech (which you secretly tell yourself would be worthy of some kind of award, in another context), then revised it and delivered it again a second time, you really do feel a bit exhausted. By the time you get to your third go at it, there's really nothing for it but to hope that you were heard the first time, when you really said it best and that they got the message then. Which was the point we were all at by the time the priest had left. Even then, it didn't really matter, because it still wasn't really the final goodbye, we told ourselves. It was more of a 'see you later', because we were just popping out to have some dinner. Then, we'd come back to sit with Mum again into the night, or however long we had left with her, which would leave plenty of time to come up with another, really final this time, goodbye. After days of being told she could die any moment, only to find she was still alive, we were fairly confident she would wait another hour or two. So everyone cleared out until only Dad and I were left with Mum.

'Go eat, have a rest. I'll stay here,' he said.

'We're just going to get some food, then we'll be back,' I promised. 'I'll see you soon, Mum.'

Of course, I didn't.

Laura, Ollie and I walked out into the night, barely having seen natural light that day, and to the car. I looked back at the hospital block towards where Mum was lying. Invisible hands reached up into my throat and squeezed so hard I could barely breathe. I felt like I was suffocating under a wave of homesickness that was made worse because I knew now it was permanent: I could never go home. Home was lying upstairs in a hospital bed, dying and there would be no overcoming this. Home was gone for good. I pushed myself into Ollie.

'I don't want this to be happening. I want my mum. I just want my mum.'

He held me and shushed me until I could control myself again and then he, Laura and I piled into the car and headed back to our house, with Iris following behind. Iris had wisely decided Dad needed some space and time alone with Mum. She hadn't thought about the fact that we might have liked some space as well. (We did.) So instead, we all sat in front of *Grand Designs,*

33

chewing on pizza while Iris made comments about Kevin McCloud's wardrobe.

'Is he wearing lederhosen? . . . A man of his age has no business wearing sunglasses . . . Good Lord, leather trousers? How frightful.'

She was so immersed in it, that when it came time to go back to the hospital, Laura and Iris both stayed behind. So I was alone in the car with Ollie when the phone call came from Dad.

'That's it. She's gone, Hannah.'

We had missed her. My final go at a farewell was gone. She was gone and I wasn't there. I wailed so loudly that Ollie reacted like a spooked horse. He slammed his foot onto the accelerator and drove off so fast that I had to start shouting that I didn't want to die, too, before he slowed down again. There wasn't any point by then, anyway: we were too late.

We arrived at the hospital at the same time as Uncle Dan. Dad met us at the door and we all huddled together and hugged and cried. Then we stopped crying and went back into the family room for one last time, where some kind member of the hospital staff brought us a tray of tea and biscuits. We ate and made jokes and even managed to laugh, the relief of not having to wait any more for the worst to happen was so great. It was the most British thing I could have imagined.

How to Plan a Funeral

There needs to be a 'What to Expect When the Thing You're Not Expecting Happens Anyway' how-to guide to grief. We have one for when a life is beginning; why hasn't anyone suggested one for when it ends by now? The majority of people are very unhelpful on this subject.

The fellow bereaved clutch your hands and stare deeply into your eyes, all too eager to welcome you into the club – because you are, undoubtedly, in a weird club now. It's as if you've been marked with the silvery grip of the Grim Reaper. They mean well, but can come across as a little intense. 'You'll never get over it, you know,' they tell you urgently, as if there's a chance you might get over it after all, unless they stop you in time. 'People say you will, but I miss so-and-so every day and it's been ten years now,' they say of their mother, father, or sometimes even pet. This is quite depressing. You might not even know how you feel yet, but you're sure as hell clinging on to the idea that you're not going to be feeling that way forever. About all you're clinging on to at that point, in fact, is the hope that it will get better at some point and life will stop feeling like a bowl of soggy cardboard. (You might not know how you feel, but you are clear on this.)

It's equally unhelpful, though, when people declare it will get better 'at some point'. This will either make you want to throw yourself on the floor and declare it impossible: colour has left the world and nothing can bring it back, or desperately cling to them and ask for a detailed schedule of when, exactly, this might be. When will the fug that has descended on you lift?

Of course, you won't actually do either of these things at all. You'll smile and nod and thank them for their insight, which hasn't got you any further. So you see, a how-to guide is essential.

I was sitting at the kitchen table at my family home, mulling this over as I realised we had a funeral to plan and I had no idea what to do, but I also knew that that didn't matter and I had to be the one to plan it, anyway. I couldn't leave Laura to do it – she was wafting vaguely in and out of rooms, stopping only to pick up a snack every now and then – and Dad was accruing the national debt of a small country catering for the wake.

He walked into the kitchen holding a menu. 'I've ordered three boxes of wine and a hundred miniature chicken kormas. Do you think that will be enough? The caterer said they go quickly. Maybe I should add a few more on...'

'The caterer's lying. And you don't even like curry.'

'It's not for me, it's for your mother.'

'She's not going to eat them, either. She's a vegetarian. And this is her funeral.'

'I've also ordered three hundred mugs. Don't start fussing about this, too: they're bringing their own hot water. For a very reasonable price.'

I might not have known what I was doing, but it was clear no one else did either.

The problem, I have realised, is that no one talks about these things. It's a bit like having sex: you can only learn by going through it and I hadn't ever been through it before. Before this happened, my experience of death had been limited to my grandparents, whose funerals I'd been too young to attend and the memorial I had held for a particularly vicious pet rabbit I had named Fluffy, who, in life, I had done my best to avoid. The service was conducted largely out of guilt that it had been dead for a week before I'd noticed.

The closest I came to anything like this was the funeral I had staged for Laura when I was seven and she was two and I was trying to convince my parents how much better life would be without her. I made her hide in a cupboard, then went downstairs and calmly told my parents that she had moved on to a better place and not to worry, I had already taken care of the messy part and buried her. I rarely tell that story; it doesn't make me come across in the best light.

If I ever thought seriously about losing someone really close to me, I had always vaguely assumed that time would stop, the world graciously slowing down while you burrowed under the duvet and stayed there, sort of like when you're going through a particularly bad break-up. But it turns out, there's no time to be self-indulgent. There's a body to bury and a funeral to plan and these things can only be put off for so long before the authorities get involved. What's more, it's boring and tedious and there's tons of admin, but it's also really important you get it right. You can't pay lasting tribute to someone's life by just slapping the only Dylan Thomas poem you remember from your GCSEs onto the Order of Service. Luckily, Dad, who was increasingly seeing his social circle play out on the obituary pages, came prepared with armfuls of Order of Services and snide comments about the correct type of buffet tables (there aren't any). It was like a more solemn Pinterest.

By the time I'd had a stern talk with the caterers and bought a lot more wine, I was beginning to feel more in control, like perhaps I did know what I was doing after all. Then our priest did a runner and disappeared (he showed up again at the worst possible moment, but I'll get to that). This was actually fine with us, because none of us had liked him anyway – he giggled, which I realise doesn't sound all that bad, but it always came out at the worst moments, like the time he forgot the name of a parishioner, repeatedly, while giving his funeral mass. As Catholic priests have done a lot worse, no one listens when you talk about giggling, so you're just going to have to trust me on this one: no one likes a giggling priest. But even if we were quite glad we escaped him, that still meant we had to find another one to conduct the funeral instead.

This didn't leave time to do any of the things I wanted to do, like sit in the bottom of Mum's wardrobe and sniff her clothes, or surround myself with her things, stroke pictures of her and have a good cry.

Still, even when I was explaining to Dad that we had our own hot water and didn't need to pay someone else to bring it, things were more or less manageable. This is nothing I can't handle, I told myself. This is really fine, I thought. Until I agreed to give the eulogy. The problem was, someone mentioned we should do one.

Laura, Dad and I were all sitting round the kitchen table.

Laura looked pale. 'I couldn't do it,' she said.

Dad looked pained. 'I wouldn't be able to get through it,' he said.

I felt sick. No, I thought. That's going too far, I thought. I can't do it, I thought. 'I'll do it,' I said.

Dad looked at me. 'You? You can't do public speaking. You once vomited on stage in the middle of a school play. You made five other children vomit, too.'

'I was ten,' I said. 'Besides, someone needs to do it.'

Dad crossed his arms. 'That doesn't mean it has to be you.'

'Are you sure, Hannah?' Laura said. 'Maybe we could ask someone else to do it.'

'This is for Mum. She needs a good send-off. It's the least I can do,' I said, with the bloody determination that was beginning to settle on me.

This was one of the last things I could ever do for Mum. I had to be the one to do it. A part of me was also beginning to envision a moment in the spotlight, during which I would deliver a speech so powerful people

39

would bring it up at all the future family funerals, like they do with best man speeches at weddings. 'That was a lovely send-off for Martha. You know Paul overcame his stutter to give that reading,' I imagined them saying. 'Still, it wasn't like Jennifer's funeral, was it? Hannah's eulogy practically brought her back to life.' I will admit that this did not bring out the best in me.

When Ollie got home that night, I gave him the news.

'Are jokes okay? What if no one laughs at my jokes? Will they applaud? Applause might be nice . . .'

'Hannah, you don't like public speaking,' he said.

'I'll be fine. This is for Mum,' I said, feeling noble. 'Besides, if I get stuck, I'll give you the nod and you can jump in and finish it for me. I'll have it all written down; you can just read it.'

'Hannah, I don't like public speaking. What have you got so far?'

'Nothing, yet. I'm waiting for inspiration to strike.'

He rubbed his eyes. 'Maybe we can ask someone else to do it.'

'That's what Laura said.'

'Well of course she did. The last time you tried to give a speech, you threw up.'

I love Ollie. There are a lot of reasons we work well together, including the fact that he's rational and practical and I'm not really either of those things. He's also taller than me, which I've always seen as important. He's not all that imaginative, though and at this point, it was becoming clear he couldn't see the bigger picture. I told him so.

'. . . It's about paying lasting tribute, you see. Something that people will always remember.'

'Isn't this supposed to be about your mum?'

'It is. You just don't understand. You have no imagination.'

Ollie gave me a look. I knew this look: he uses it quite a lot. It's the one he gives me when he thinks I'm being irrational, right before he gives me a sandwich.

'Hannah, I think you might be in denial. You're not acting like yourself. You hate public speaking.'

If you ever find yourself in this situation, desperately clinging on to any small activity or supposed gesture as a means of getting through one of the most difficult experiences in your life, while still feeling vaguely connected to the person you've lost, I can only say this: don't do it. 'But you just said it yourself,' you say. 'A tribute, honouring their life.' And that's true, I did. I recognise your dreams of an homage worthy of Hemingway, but – and this is crucial – this will all disappear the second your face starts to uncontrollably leak, which it probably has already been doing since your loved one died. When this happens, all your carefully held dreams will fall apart and you will wonder what on earth possessed you to get up in front of a congregation-full of people on one of the worst days of your life. It really doesn't matter how beautiful your send-off: no one will be able to hear it when you throw yourself onto the coffin and demand to be buried with it. Trust me on this one. I know.

Naturally, I didn't realise until it was too late and I was staring at a blank sheet of paper with nothing remotely profound or moving to say. And of course, I couldn't tell anyone this, because then they would know that they had been right all along and I should have listened to them in the first place. Only now, it was too late to find someone else to do it and besides, I really did want to honour Mum and if I couldn't do it, who would? To make things worse, I realised that I had swallowed superglue at some point. I couldn't remember doing this and it didn't really seem like something I would do in the first place, but nevertheless, I must have done as now the insides of my throat felt firmly stuck together and were stopping me from forming sound. Even if I did have something important to say, I wouldn't be able to say it. So instead of saying anything remotely poignant or insightful, I instead just wrote down how Mum was the best part of all of us and how impossible it was that we didn't get a chance to tell her that. Then I added a lot of clichés that probably make up 90 per cent of eulogies, because no one's doing their best work under such conditions and threw in a couple of jokes for good measure.

I read it to Ollie.

'It's good,' he said.

'It's not Hemingway,' I said.

'It shows how much you love your mum and how important she is to all of you.'

42

'Maybe we should develop a signal in case I start to fall apart and throw myself on the coffin.'

'I think throwing yourself on the coffin would be a good enough signal,' he said. 'Shall I make you a sandwich?'

I went back round to my family home the next day. I spent a lot of time there in the days leading up to the funeral. I both dreaded going and felt desperate to be there.

Dad opened the door this time. I gasped. He had a tampon wedged up his nose.

'I've found another priest,' he said, ushering me in. 'Father Ray. He's coming round later. Nice chap, sounded devout, not at all like that idiot Thomas. He drank more communion wine than the parish ever saw. He might even be Irish. I thought I heard a twang.'

Proximity to Ireland is the highest compliment my dad is able to pay someone.

'Wasn't Father Thomas Irish,' I said.

He ignored me. He hurried me through to the dining room, not once mentioning the repurposed feminine hygiene product, the string of which he'd tucked behind his ear as he talked. He stopped in front of the dining-room table, where a selection of bottles had been lined up. 'Wine or whiskey?'

'Neither, I'm driving,' I said.

'Not for you, for Father Ray. What?'

I gestured at his face. 'What have you got in your nose?'

'Oh,' he touched it, gingerly. 'Laura gave it to me. Kept getting nosebleeds. I was blowing it too much. I'll take it out before he gets here,' he huffed, picking up a bottle of Pinot Noir and carrying it off to the other room.

I retreated into his study at the top of the stairs, as I have been doing for years. When I was little, I'd hide under his desk and read. At this point, its main attraction was that it had few reminders of Mum. I sat at his computer and printed off the eulogy.

Laura appeared in the doorway behind me, wearing a pair of fluffy teddy bear pyjamas that were too short in the leg, and chewing on a chicken nugget.

'Dad wants you. The priest is here.'

Dad and Father Ray were sitting on the sofa, both holding a glass of whiskey.

'Hannah,' Dad said when he spotted me. 'Come and say hello to Father Ray, a good Irish man himself.'

Father Ray looked at me and smiled. 'Hello, Hannah. I'm terribly sorry about your loss.'

'Born and raised in the same county as my old dad. Can you believe it?' Dad said. 'Maybe you knew him, Father: Francis Kennedy. Sure, most of my family's still out there, generations of us. I'm the first raised out here.'

My dad is the kind of Irish that is only really Irish on certain occasions – usually, when watching certain sports, when confronted with someone else Irish or when he wants to complain about the English. The rest of the time, he's, for all intents and purposes, English. But when any of these things happen – the sports, the

44

complaining, the other Irish person — he stops being the Englishman he pretends to be in his normal life and reverts to his true self, one that just happens (via a cruel twist of fate and his English mother) to be living over here. You'll know this has happened because he'll start to mourn the 'good old days, back home', occasionally in an Irish brogue. Sometimes, he will sing. Once, when he was particularly plastered, he taught me a decent approximation of Riverdance, although he didn't remember this or how to dance when he woke up the next morning, English again. As much fun as that birthday was, you usually don't want to be around to witness this.

I watched as Dad took a sip of his whiskey and winced. He doesn't actually like whiskey, but he feels obliged to drink it, as part of his patriotism. 'You should have seen the turnout for my old dad's funeral. Half the town was there. The procession held up the roads. Of course, that was partly because there was a sheep blocking them, but you should have seen it. Nothing like the one for my mum. Of course, she was English.' He eyed Father Ray meaningfully.

Father Ray took a sip of his drink.

'Jennifer was English, too, of course. But I never held that against her.'

'I should go,' I said.

As much as I pitied Father Ray and strongly felt someone should be there to rescue him from what could be a rousing rendition of 'Danny Boy', should Dad be allowed to get that far, I had realised something much more important that took precedent: I had a funeral to attend and nothing to wear to it, especially when part of the day was going to be spent on stage and all of it was going to be spent wishing I was somewhere else. If you're going to have to face down one of the worst days of your life, you can at least do it in a good outfit, which is an important lesson I learned from my prom. I had to go shopping. Shopping would distract me. It would cheer me up. So I marched into town with the grim resolve of a parent walking into a children's birthday party armed with only a wet wipe, determined to find the Perfect Dress.

A lot of women will, at some point, have had to find their version of the Perfect Dress and will have their own definition of it. Mine was that it would look fantastic (and, by extension, I would look fantastic in it), it would cheer me up and it would have pockets. You might think this is a lot of pressure to put on a single dress and if you do, I can only imagine you wear trousers a lot.

I applied myself to this with a military precision and skill that should really have a place on my CV. The only problem was, I couldn't find anything remotely approaching what I wanted. This had nothing to do with what was actually on sale and everything to do with my disintegrating mental state, but I wasn't going to admit that to myself. I decided that the problem wasn't me but what was on offer: nothing in polyester was ever going to make me feel better. I needed to regroup. So, I walked into the kind of shops that usually make me feel as if I have my bank statement stapled to my head, meticulously picked out every evening gown they had in stock and stalked into the changing rooms.

One of the women that worked there hovered nearby, like they tend to do when you're thinking about spending large amounts of money and they're working on commission.

'This is lovely,' she said, firmly, when I stepped out of the changing room. 'And so wearable.' She pulled out the foot-long lace train with a flourish. 'Is it for anything special?'

'Yes,' I replied, examining my reflection. 'My mum's funeral. Do you have this in black?'

I frowned at the mirror. My reflection was looking suspiciously sad and drained. I gave myself my hard stare. I told myself I was treating myself. I told myself that treating myself made me feel better. I told myself I needed to buck my ideas up and get behind the huge amount of money I was about to spend.

I sighed. 'This isn't working,' I said and flounced back to the changing room. I was beginning to seriously question capitalism.

I threw off the first dress and wriggled into another that had seven petticoats and a tiny row of buttons up the back. It was the kind of dress that seems to have been designed to make anyone that doesn't have someone to help them get dressed feel bad about themselves. I stuck my head out of the changing room and looked for my former helper, but she was at the other end of the shop and determinedly ignoring my gaze. I looked back at my reflection, which had gone a bit pink around the eyes and puce in the cheeks. I decided I wouldn't let the dress get the better of me. I contorted myself, grasping at the buttons, panting. I was coming dangerously close to overheating. There was a stab of pain that confirmed I had almost definitely sprained something and I toppled over, landing on the floor with my head sticking out from underneath the changing room curtain. I gave up and started to cry, kicking my feet in frustration at the dress, the day and myself.

A woman wandered over to me and looked down. 'We have jeans that offer more stretch,' she said.

I needed to get out of there, but I couldn't leave without buying something, so I got the dress and stomped home.

When I got back, I threw myself down on the sofa where Ollie was sitting, playing on the PlayStation.

'I've bought a dress and you're going to have to help me get in and out of it because the patriarchy hates women.'

How to Adult

I never thought I'd end my mum's funeral on top of the dining room table, dancing to the 'Tequila' song. But looking back on it now, I don't think I can be the only one to have ever done this. Funerals are weird: they're somewhere between a birthday party and a popularity contest, only without the person you're meant to be honouring. And we didn't even go down the route of having the deceased 'attend'. I don't mean in the open coffin sense, but there, propped up in a chair, with their eyes open, surrounded by some of their favourite things, which the funeral director assured us was a thing and quite popular, while we sat in the lounge and felt uncomfortable.

'It's like they're there, you see, watching over everything. People find it comforting. Like that.' He pointed to a stuffed owl that sat on a bookshelf in the lounge.

We obediently turned to look at the owl. My parents had found it in a flea market abroad. Or technically, Laura had. She spotted it from her pushchair and became so attached to it, my parents felt they couldn't leave it behind and brought it home. We named it Bert. It had become a sort of family mascot.

'Did ... did you shoot it yourself?' he tailed off.

Funerals are the only times when you're so deeply sad you might wipe your nose on a crust-less cucumber sandwich, yet are still expected to work to a dress code and make small talk. And if you're the one in charge, you have to welcome a crowd of people into your home and provide them with food and drink. You're having a wretched time, just doing your best to get by, but are also aware there's a right and a wrong way to behave and everyone's watching you closely. If you behave the wrong way (either too sad or not sad enough; it's a very thin line) then you'll be judged. Suspected murderers have been tried and convicted in the court of public opinion on their behaviour in the immediate aftermath of the death alone. 'Of course he did it. You can tell by the way he's acting. You just don't behave that way when someone you love dies,' people will sniff. To which I reply that yes, the fact that he's wearing his dead wife's face as a hat looks bad, but maybe that's just his way of feeling close to her again.

We behaved the wrong way. Or at least, I did.

The problem was, the one person that would have known exactly what to do wasn't there. Mum was the consummate host. She loved having people over; it combined two of her favourite things: seeing the people she loved and feeding them.

Growing up, dinner parties were a regular occurrence at our house. Mum would swan from the kitchen to table in platform heels, dressed immaculately and serving course after course, while Dad would be constantly refilling glasses, until people eventually left, around one in the morning, completely plastered and barely able to walk. The annual New Year's Eve party was always the worst. One year, our next-door neighbour Barry tried to go swimming and dived into the outdoor pool, crashing through a layer of ice in the process. I only found this out the next day, when Mum got off the phone with Barry's wife, who was calling from the hospital.

'He's absolutely fine, but he's not allowed to drink any more, according to either the doctor or Cheryl. Cheryl wasn't clear which,' she said.

Laura had a very sanctimonious attitude towards parties and houseguests in general for years, for which she blamed the overexposure from our parents growing up.

When Ollie and I first started dating, we went round one evening for dinner.

'What does Ollie like? Is there anything he doesn't eat?' Mum asked me.

'He eats everything. Don't go to any trouble. Spag bol would be fine,' I said.

She thought about this. 'I'm making a roast. Would four courses be too much for a Tuesday night or do you think you'll be able to manage cheese after?'

Mum was known for her roasts. When I was growing up, I was convinced her cooking was half the reason anyone wanted to hang out with me, so I would cunningly bring them home as soon as I could, to ensnare them with Mum's food. This worked so well that my friend Matthew would show up every Sunday just in time for lunch, retire to my bed afterwards for a nap and then leave. When he heard that she had died, he wrote me a letter. A real letter, handwritten on paper and everything. That's how good her roasts were. It's part of the reason I love to eat but hate cooking; I get frustrated, after a lifetime of being spoiled, that nothing quite matches up. Laura was the one that got her flair for cooking (though she rarely bothers); I got her flair for shoes.

If Mum had been there, she would never have let the caterers get so far with the mini curries. 'It's simple, Han,' she would have said. 'You just need to make sure you've got plenty of little things that you can eat with your hands and go down easily, that people don't have to think about. And lots to drink. And put on some music. Just because it's a funeral, it doesn't mean it has to be all doom and gloom.' Then she would have stuck some music on and started cutting the crusts off sandwiches, because that's all you really want at a funeral after all: white bread that you can eat with one hand and that will soak up some of the drink.

I thought about what she would have said if she'd known it was her own funeral. Most of the time, I try not to do this. People always say how terrible it is that we didn't have any time to say goodbye, but I am always grateful she had no idea what was coming. She would have worried too much about us, probably because she knew how quickly we would fall apart without her there to organise us. But still, I can hear her advice on this one. 'Try not to be too sad, darlings, I'll always be with you. Try and have some fun. And make sure you eat something.'

On balance, I think she would have been quite happy with how it all turned out. It could have been a lot worse.

That morning, all of the aunts and uncles and a cousin or two descended on my family home before the funeral. This was ostensibly so we could all band together, but really it meant there was a lot of flapping. Everyone tried to make sure everyone else had eaten something, so pieces of toast with only a bite taken out of them littered every flat surface. Then the hearse turned up and everyone dutifully trooped outside to look at it and remark on how nice the flowers looked. Except for me. I was resolutely ignoring it in case I started crying again. I couldn't cry until I had got through the eulogy. Then it was time to go and we all had to squeeze into the two limousines we had hired. But it turned out, there were too many of us to fit in and the process of trying to decide who would take their own car descended into a weird contest of 'who was closer to Mum'. Even when we thought we had worked it out, everyone still tried to squeeze into the two limos and we had to start all over again. And because I refused to look at the hearse, I was doing all this with my back turned, which meant I kept bumping into people, until Ollie picked me up and put me into one of the cars.

'You're her daughters. You're definitely close enough,' he said, herding Laura in next to me.

Laura looked at me. 'Nice dress,' she said. 'I bought mine for a fiver from Primark.'

'Maybe you could wear it for work,' I said.

Laura looked down. 'I don't ever want to wear it again after today.' She plucked at it. 'I wish we could do this in pyjamas.'

'When do you go back to work?'

'Next week. I'm almost looking forward to it. It will be a good distraction. I'll have to at least pretend to be okay.'

'Mm.' I nodded. I thought about the freelance writing I did, from home, occasionally from bed and often, in my pyjamas. I didn't have anyone to pretend to.

Laura exhaled. 'Has Ollie just taken today off?'

'Yeah. He's managing a new marketing campaign, so he needs to go back.'

Laura looked at me. 'What about Dad? He's retired. Without Mum, he's just going to be knocking around the house by himself the whole time.' She hugged herself. 'It's so depressing.'

I chewed my lip. 'I can pop in and check on him some days while you're at work. I'll just do my work from here, instead.'

Laura nodded. She looked out the window. 'I suppose after today, life is just going to go back to normal.'

Dad got in the car. 'Cathy wanted to travel in the hearse. She said she didn't want your mum to be alone. I finally persuaded her to get in the bloody car.' He looked accusingly at me. 'I told you I should have opened the whiskey. A little drop wouldn't have hurt anyone. It might have helped.'

It was almost a relief to get to the church.

Grief makes me glad I was raised Catholic. I definitely have not always felt this way. Growing up, I would rather have been a part of any religion or even loosely organised group that meant you could have sex and not feel guilty about it for the rest of your life. I probably would have been fairly open to joining a cult at that time, if they had said the right thing, so it's a good job no one asked me to. Especially in the very early days of having sex, when it's barely worth having any at all and definitely not at the cost of your mortal soul. When I first tried it, it was over so quickly I didn't realise it had happened. I'm not exaggerating, either. I asked my boyfriend.

'When does the sex start?' I said.

'We've had it,' he said, looking confused. Then he awkwardly told me he loved me, rolled over and went to sleep.

I could barely walk into a church after that without worrying I was going to be struck down by a bolt of lightning.

But all of that felt like a decent trade-off at that moment, sitting in a church and having the comfort of knowing that wasn't It. Mum wasn't gone forever. There's Heaven to think about and she was probably going to be looking down on us and having a good laugh, while relaxing in celestial nirvana. Sometime after she finished agonising over what we were serving and before I got on the dining room table. And I needed that at that point: the belief in Heaven. Even if I was never going to get there myself, because I had sex.

I filed into the church with Dad, Laura and Ollie, past a crowd of people.

'We generally ask the other guests to wait outside until the family have arrived,' the funeral director murmured. 'But as it's raining, you might want to hurry.'

It was a lovely church: very old and ornately decorated. It was filled with impressive-looking mouldings, stained glass and other things people mention when they know something about architecture. Dad had been thrilled when we had managed to book it.

'It's a very big get,' he had said. 'People have been impressed when I've told them where the funeral is. Make sure you get it for me when it's my funeral.'

Laura nudged me. 'Everyone's staring at us.'

I glanced around. Behind us, people were subtly jostling to get inside, while still trying to look respectful. For the most part, this meant giving us pained looks, although some were also making elaborate signs of the cross, staring up at the vaulted ceiling. I spotted Evie, who had worked her way to the front of the crowd holding Harry, who was waving at me.

I turned back to Laura. 'I know. Look sad. But don't overdo it. It will make people feel uncomfortable.'

'My friend Sara said when her dad died, she got so tired of people staring at her and asking how she was doing, she got blind drunk.'

'Sensible woman.'

'This was in the car back to the house. When she got to the wake, she just wanted to avoid everyone. So she started body-crawling into the front room to get more drink or something to eat, then she'd body-crawl back out again so no one could spot her and make her chat.'

'And no one saw her do this?'

'Oh yeah, everyone did. Someone tripped over her. She pretended to be a carpet. But she said it's hard to argue with someone who's mourning. They probably thought she had gone mad with grief. She said she was so drunk, she had to be carried to bed. She woke up the next morning with a carpet burn on her face.'

I snorted loudly. From the corner of my eye, I saw Evie look at me in alarm, elaborately mouthing at me. I grinned and waved, then remembered where we were. I glanced at the stained-glass windows that showed Jesus' final moments playing out, and genuflected.

'Her basic advice,' Laura continued in a whisper, 'was that today, anything goes; do whatever you feel like doing. And also, that whatever you're feeling is completely normal and okay.'

For what it's worth, this remains some of the best advice I have heard about grief.

As we shuffled into our pew, we saw him.

'Oh God,' Dad said.

'No,' Laura breathed.

Father Thomas, the giggling priest who had completely disappeared when Mum had died, had chosen this moment to reappear. He was sitting fleshily at the altar. He looked over at us and smiled. Triumphantly, I thought.

'What's he doing here?' Dad muttered. 'The whole reason we came here was to get away from him.'

'Maybe he heard Mum died and followed us,' Laura said.

'He does look a bit vindictive,' Ollie said.

'Does this mean he's going to be doing the ceremony, now?' I asked.

'He better bloody not be.' Dad crossed his arms. 'If he forgets your mum's name and starts laughing again . . .'

Laura pointed. 'Father Ray's here too. Maybe Father Thomas is just here to watch.'

'That's a bit passive aggressive, isn't it?' I said.

I glanced over my shoulder at the pews that were being steadily filled. Behind us, I could see family members, friends and vaguely familiar faces from my childhood finding seats, exchanging tissues and squeezing each other's hands. Barry and Cheryl had slipped in at the back. Across the aisle, Dan helped Cathy into a pew, as she covered her face with a scarf. It's what I imagine the green room must feel like at a screening of *This is Your Life*. Dad had turned in his seat and was graciously nodding and smiling.

'At least Mum's got a good crowd to send her off,' I said.

Laura looked sharply at me. 'Hannah. Do not vomit during the eulogy.'

As the last guests sat down and the doors closed behind them, Father Ray stood up and cleared his throat, waiting for everyone to settle down and pay attention. The congregation obliged, hushing obediently and looking expectantly at him.

'Dearly beloved,' he began.

And with those words, he spelled it out: that was it. It was the beginning of the end. There was no more ignoring it, no more pretending that it wasn't really happening. We were at our mum's funeral and after this, we would be expected to go on with normal life without her. Next to me, I could feel Laura holding her breath.

Father Ray was welcoming everyone to the church.

'As he's Jennifer's parish priest, I have invited Father Thomas to be here, today,' he said.

Dad sighed. 'I wish you hadn't.'

'And he's going to start today's ceremony with a reading.'

Father Thomas ambled towards the altar and smiled smugly.

Ollie leaned over. 'He looks like a boiled ham with eyebrows. Has he always looked like that or is that new?' he whispered.

Father Ray offered the other priest the prayer book and pointed out the passage.

'Dearly beloved,' Father Thomas began.

'No, I've done that bit. From here.' Father Ray pointed.

'We're gathered here today—'

'No, Father, from here . . .'

'As Jennifer's parish priest . . .'

Dad put his head in his hands.

This really set the mood for the rest of the service. Looking rather desperate to move on, Father Ray called for a reading we had asked Uncle Dan to do, then launched into it himself. Dan shot me an aggrieved look across the aisle.

'I'd been practising that for days,' he mouthed.

Father Thomas did the wrong reading, again; Father Ray visibly gave up. After the homily, Laura started crying. To avoid joining in, I stared with my eyes wide open at the altar, until they started drying out. When it came time for a hymn, the organist (who was almost as old as the church) started playing so gently and respect-fully that no one realised she was playing anything at all, until the second verse. Then they all launched loudly into it to make up for it and startled the organist, who was so thrown off, she gave up a full verse before the end of the hymn. This didn't stop the congregation, who staunchly carried on a cappella.

Then it was my turn.

'Oh, God. I hate public speaking,' I said. I stood up and moved past Ollie. 'Remember the signal,' I said, nodding pointedly in the direction of the coffin, before tottering up to the pulpit.

I took a deep breath and looked at the coffin. I moaned and looked away. In the front pew, Laura, Ollie and Dad visibly clenched.

I tried again. 'People keep telling me what Mum would want.' My voice sounded like a cracked plate, but at least, I reasoned, I had a voice. 'They mainly mean we should eat and look after ourselves, but . . .' I took a breath and ramped up to my big opening. 'I'm pretty sure Mum would absolutely have wanted me to buy an expensive dress and matching shoes for today.' I waited for a laugh. There was silence. I cleared my throat and ploughed on. Thankfully, my voice steadied the further through I got. 'It feels so cruel that she's been taken away from us so soon. There's so much she's going to miss out on seeing. Weddings, children . . . Or so she always hoped. She had been teasing us about getting on with it for years. It was kind of inappropriate – I was fifteen when she first started mentioning it . . .'

Towards the end, I began to wonder if I'd get a round of applause, which by that point, I felt was really my due.

'She meant a lot of things to a lot of people, but first and foremost, she was always our mum. And she was the best one we could have asked for. I hope I can be to my children what Mum was to us,' I finished.

The applause didn't come. I felt a little bit aggrieved. I was sweating under seventeen petticoats and surprisingly bright lighting for this moment. But then, not many of the congregation had been present for my last on-stage appearance so they couldn't know how badly it could have gone. I made it back to my seat.

Ollie squeezed my hand. 'And you didn't throw yourself on the coffin once.'

'No one got my jokes,' I said.

'You made a lot of people cry, though.'

I can't tell you the specifics of what happened after that because, with the pressure of my on-stage performance over, the rest of the service passed in a wet blur. Soon, we were walking back down the aisle and then we were back in the car, waving vaguely at the people peering in through the window and making sympathetic faces at us.

'There's wine at the house,' Dad mouthed at them. He turned back round. 'Well, that was all right, wasn't it? Good turnout.'

Back at the house, I was stupidly grateful I hadn't talked Dad out of hiring a full catering staff as a waiter with wine greeted us at the door.

'Would you like a—'

'Yes, please,' Dad said, grabbing three glasses and handing one each to Laura and me.

You might think by now that we were relying on alcohol a lot at the time to get us through and you would be right: we were. I could blame this on my Irish roots – something my dad often did, toasting it while cracking open a bottle of something new, by the way – but really, it's because alcohol was necessary, especially because it fell on me to host everyone in Mum's absence. Dad also had a part to play in this, of course, but his role largely seemed to involve getting handed tissues and being swept along towards the food. Laura, meanwhile, was swallowed up by a gaggle of friends doing their best impression of the witches in *Macbeth*. So it was my responsibility to welcome everyone and pretend to recognise the distant relatives and family friends who would offer their condolences and then tell me how much I'd grown.

I put my wine glass down to hug someone and instantly regretted it when one of the caterers whisked it away.

I was enormously relieved when my friends Sophie and Lou emerged from the crowd. I had met them both at Fresher's Week at university, during an awkward evening that had involved standing outside for hours at the local dog track. That had been the night we discovered snakebite. We had since disavowed the snakebites, but never each other. I grabbed them. 'Thank you for coming.'

'Han, I loved the eulogy. You did so well,' Sophie said. 'And that dress.' She nodded. 'Your mum would definitely approve.'

Sophie is the kind of person who always notices the details of what you're wearing, perhaps because she is usually immaculately turned out herself. She was the first of our friends to start regularly dry cleaning things. Lou, on the other hand, reminds me that it's okay to still wear tops that cost a fiver from H&M that you bought three years ago and sometimes play 'find the small hole' with. Despite her best intentions, she is rarely on time for anything and even when she does turn up, she has often forgotten something vital. We once lost each other for an hour in a Topshop during the January sales after we got separated, because she'd forgotten to bring her phone that day.

'How are you doing? Is that a stupid question?' Lou asked.

'I lost my wine,' I said. Over their shoulders, I saw my dad's friend Alan walking determinedly towards me. 'Oh God. Here we go again.'

Lou hugged me tightly. 'We've got you covered,' she whispered in my ear and marched off to get me a fresh glass, Sophie on her heels.

Alan came up to me and squeezed me. 'Hannah. Your mum was wonderful. It's such sad news.'

Alan used to watch sport with my dad. You could always tell when he was there because all natural light would be shut out, the lounge door would be tightly closed and no one was allowed near it until whatever game Ireland was playing in was finished. Every now and then, the whole house would shake as the two men would start yelling over the top of the television that had already been turned up to full volume. On those days, Mum would look witheringly in the direction of the lounge and open a bottle of wine, then she'd go out and apologise to the neighbours for the noise. I learned my best swear words from Alan.

He took my hand. 'The last time I saw you, I was chasing you round this house. I used to pull you over the sofa and tickle you until you cried. You probably don't remember,' he said. 'None of that today, of course.'

'Well, you never know,' I said. 'The night is young. Have you got a drink?'

His wife came up behind him and took his arm, 'We

have to be going, now. Sorry for your loss,' she said and they walked off.

Lou came back, brandishing a large glass. I took a deep gulp.

'I'll keep those coming,' she said.

Sophie followed her, holding a plate of food. 'Yes, wine's good, but I really think you should eat as well or it'll end up like that "dinner party" you threw that time,' she said, emphasising the words dinner party with her eyebrows. 'And Han, I won't let you end up half-naked on the bathroom floor in front of people you haven't seen since you were two.' After that, she followed me around with a plate, determinedly shovelling food into my mouth whenever she could until she was satisfied I'd had enough.

When we had been planning the day, we had been convinced that everyone would be gone by six at the latest, at which point we could settle in front of *Grand Designs* in our pyjamas with a takeaway. But then it got to six and most of the people were still there, some that had left had come back again and it was beginning to feel more like the New Year's Eve party that had ended with Barry embracing a new life of sobriety than a funeral. There was a pile of men's ties on the floor and the caterers in charge of circulating the wine were looking increasingly harassed. In fact, the only person I could be sure had left was Evie and that's because she had to take Harry home. After days of constant crying and suffocating grief, it was a huge relief to be able to let go.

I walked into the kitchen where Uncle Dan was standing, staring at the cooker.

'It's a terrible day, Hannah. I need to get hammered,' he said.

'Fantastic idea. I think everyone else already has. Let's drink up.' I raised my glass.

'I can't. My wife stole my whiskey.'

Laura ran through the kitchen, her friends in a line behind her, cackling and slopping wine on the floor.

Dan rubbed his face. 'Is it me, or are there four of her, today?' He refocused his eyes on me. 'You'll need to take care of her you know, Han: Laura. Without your mum here, it's your responsibility now. Your dad, too. You'll need to make sure they're coping without her. It's what your mum would want. She wouldn't want to have to worry about them.'

I thought about this and nodded, slowly.

'That's what you do as the oldest. Take care of your younger siblings.' His face began to crumple. 'It's what I should have done. For your mum. As the older brother.' He looked dangerously close to saying it should have been him.

'I'll go find you a drink,' I said.

He pulled me into a hug. 'Bless you. Your mum would want that, too. Don't let your aunt see.'

I followed Laura's dribble of wine into the lounge. Across the room, my friend Mark was sitting on the sofa, with Cathy draped over him. I walked over.

'You have the loveliest thighs,' Cathy was saying, punctuating each word with a pat on Mark's leg. 'Hannah, Hannah, Hannah, darling, tell him. Doesn't he have.' Pat. 'The.' Pat. 'Nicest.' Pat. 'Thighs?'

Mark cleared his throat.

'A tragedy has occurred,' she continued, wiping at her eyes with one of her scarves. 'Our sweet Jenny is gone. My darling Jenny. Can you believe it, Hannah darling?'

I shook my head.

'I'm so sorry for your—' Mark said.

'Have you ever worked in the theatre, Marcus?' she interrupted.

'It's just Mark,' Mark said. 'Actually, I work in IT.'

'What a waste. Such a nice face, like yours. And those thighs. I tell you, Mike. If I was a few years younger...' She laughed.

Across the room, someone shouted my name. My cousin Paul was brandishing a bottle of Baileys in front of the small crowd that had formed.

'Hannah, you like Baileys, right? Great. We're doing shots,' he said.

By this point, we had already consumed so much wine that later, after we took out the recycling, someone slipped a pamphlet on alcohol abuse through the letter-box. Even so, it's probably safe to say that this was the point where the evening took a turn.

I took a glass off Paul and downed it, as everyone around me cheered.

By that point, people had stopped coming up to me to give their condolences. Unfortunately, I then started going up to them, pumping their hands and enthusiastically telling them how glad Mum would be that they had come.

'She loved parties,' I exclaimed.

This also led to me having a long conversation with

my former piano teacher, whom I hadn't seen since I was eleven, but to whom I solemnly swore I still practised every week.

I extricated myself just in time to see Laura grab Cathy and Iris and tell them that, although they didn't get along, it was wonderful that they could be there together.

'There are more important things, you guys. Iris, stop looking at me like that. Life's too short to not get along. So I hope now your differences can be in the past. Like that: poof,' she said, gesturing as if she was releasing a dove into the air, whilst releasing more wine from her glass.

Cathy put her hand on her chest. 'Iris, I know you're uptight and we've talked about that, but I have always liked you.'

Iris looked murderous.

Dad opened another crate of wine and the people that had looked like they were going to leave, took their coats back off and called for another toast to my mum.

Then, when our playlist finally ran out, Cathy announced she would perform. Calling for accompaniment, she attempted to climb on top of the piano and then gently slid off again. Ollie put a CD on.

This seemed to boost everyone's spirits again. One of my dad's friends, Philip, who had been staring at Lou for most of the evening, took the opportunity to try and dance with her (something I don't think he'd ever done before). Completely ignoring the beat, he launched into a helpless rendition of the Sand Dance and zagged around her, shouting, 'Here we go Looby-Loo.'

Lou swiftly shimmied back to me.

'You know, I really think that was his way of trying to flirt with you,' I said.

At one point, he slipped over and landed heavily on the floor. I leaned over to help him up.

'You should have kids, now,' he said. 'You'd make a great mum. And the family needs one now — a mother. It's your time.' He pulled himself up, breathing heavily. 'Lovely girl, that Lou.'

Sophie fell asleep on Mark's lap.

Then Paul unearthed a bottle of tequila and once again, called loudly for shots, dashing into the kitchen for the table salt.

He lurched back into the room and looked at me, gravely. 'Life has given you lemons, Hannah,' he said, swaying slightly. 'You need tequila.'

We poured ourselves large measures and knocked them back, with a shudder. This was enough to tip me over the edge. I grabbed the bottle, climbed onto the table and started singing the 'Tequila' song, flinging my layers of petticoats in the air and performing a stunted version of the can-can, while those left gathered round the table and clapped.

Afterwards, Laura said to me, 'It was so strange: it was the worst day of my life and there you were, dancing on the table.' Which I think ignores her part in the whole thing.

*

By two in the morning, Laura had collapsed into bed with her friends squeezed in around her, Ollie had carried me off the table and Mark was getting ready to drive us home.

I left Dad and Philip settling down on the sofa with a fresh bottle of port.

'Don't worry,' Philip winked (or at least, I thought he did. It's possible one side of his face had just fallen asleep). 'I'll make sure he goes to bed soon.'

When I next saw him, he had no memory of this, leaving, or falling into the bush he then woke up in the next morning.

Dad patted me goodbye. 'All things considered, I don't think your mother would have wanted it any other way.'

How to Move On

One of the biggest problems with my mum dying is that now I can never have a nose job. I've always wanted a nose job, in a vague but constant way. Not enough to actually have it done, but still committed enough to the idea to form a long list of celebrities whose noses I would rather have. After one particularly bad break-up with someone who didn't realise we were dating, I even went so far as to cut pictures of people's noses I liked more than mine and stick them onto photos of my face. There's a very strange album of this that at one point, I started calling my vision board. Ollie found it when we first started dating and this might be why he now adds my nose when he lists things he loves about me, with a pointed look for emphasis.

Now, though, I'm stuck with the same old nose for the rest of my life, because my mum gave it to me and I can't get rid of something my mum gave me.

It wasn't just the nose. Ollie came home from work one day to find me sitting on our bed, staring into space, wearing a hoodie that I could barely fit into.

'You were never a Newquay lifeguard,' he said. 'Have you done any work today?'

'It was the early noughties, Ollie,' I said, without breaking my gaze. 'Besides, it's research for an article I'm doing on the return of noughties trends. For *Vogue*.'

Ollie raised his eyebrows. 'Wow, really? *Vogue*?'

I glanced at him. 'No. Mum got it for me.' I dug my hands into the pouch and pulled out a tissue. I held it up. 'Look,' I said, reverently. 'I bet I used this when I was with Mum. She probably even gave it to me.'

This too I would have kept, if Ollie hadn't plucked it out of my hands and thrown it away.

'That's really gross.' He eyed me. 'Perhaps spending all this time at home alone isn't good for you at the moment. Maybe you should think about working from a café sometime. You know, for a bit of human company. It might be helpful.'

'I'm fine, Ollie. I'm comfortable here. I have a hoodie, now.'

He launched himself on the bed next to me and plucked at my hoodie. 'I had one a bit like this. But mine said "body inspector".'

'Wow.'

He grinned. 'That's what the girls would say.'

'Is it?'

Ollie looked down. 'No. But I can inspect your body.' He threw himself onto me, flattening me into the mattress, kissing my neck and tugging my hoodie up.

I laughed and pulled it back down. 'Ollie, get off.'

He nuzzled into my neck, then rolled himself onto his back, pulling me on top of him. I looked down at him and patted his chest. He put his hands on my bum and twitched his hips up towards me.

'Not now,' I said, rolling off him.

He sat up. 'Why not? It's Friday. We haven't got anything on tonight. Come back.' He pulled me back towards him.

I pulled away. 'Because. I'm not in the mood right now.'

He sat up. 'Okay, but when do you think you might be, again? I feel like you haven't been that interested in me recently.'

'Sometime,' I murmured. 'Maybe later. Tonight.'

Ollie rolled off the bed. 'Yeah, it's just . . .'

I put my hands on my hips. 'What if Mum's up there, like, watching us? Have sex. That's what I keep thinking. I mean, it's hard to be in the mood when you think that, right? Your mother, watching you have sex? Didn't that happen to you before?'

Ollie recoiled. 'She wasn't watching, Hannah. She walked in on us. Those are two very different things.' He held up his hands. 'It was a very traumatic moment. I was fifteen. We had to discuss my respect for women, after that. You know I don't like talking about it.' He shuddered. 'But I mean, you can't think that about your mum. Or we'd never have sex again. I mean—'

I pulled the hoodie up over my head, his words getting lost through the fabric. I folded it, carefully putting it into my jumper drawer.

Ollie watched me. 'You're keeping that?'

73

'Of course. Mum gave it to me. Come on, let's go make dinner.'

The nose, of course, is the most important thing.

I'm telling you this to show how, at some point, I decided I needed to be able to joke about my loss. Joking about it is how you show people you're not going to be a depressing bore for the rest of your life. It reassures them that actually, you're probably fine and even if you're not, you're going to pretend like you are to make everyone feel more comfortable. This was important to me. After the funeral, I felt like I was sort of expected to get better. No one said so explicitly, of course, but I was aware of it nevertheless. I wasn't particularly happy about this (then again, I wasn't particularly happy about a lot of things at that time. Including the nose issue.) I didn't feel like I'd started grieving at all. In fact, I was mainly walking around under the thick fug that had settled over me and that was effectively blocking everything that had happened. Every now and again, the fug would clear a bit and I would catch a glimpse of the full horror of what had happened. But this would only ever last for a moment, then the fug would ensconce me once again and I wouldn't be able to see through it at all.

I desperately wanted to get on with grieving, so I could get better again. I was terrified it would strike me at the worst possible moment, like how you imagine getting your period on your wedding day might be – in the middle of the ceremony and in full view of everybody.

I believed I had an allotted mourning period when people would be patient with me and when that mourning period ran out, I would be expected to be better.

I would clutch at Ollie's hands. 'I'm not grieving yet. Not properly. I generally feel okay. What happens when I stop feeling okay and too much time has passed and people expect me to be okay and I'm not okay? What then?'

So I started joking about it. In fact, I think this might need to be added onto the general list of stages of grief you're meant to go through. Not that I put much stock in them. Who was I supposed to bargain with, for example? I didn't think God was listening.

Anger was the only one I could understand. Anger I could get on board with. I had plenty of it: great vats of irritation simmering away below the surface that I was ready to unleash at any given moment. I was worse than the time I was jet-lagged after a fifteen-hour flight and came home to house guests who were planning on staying for a month. And let me tell you, I was furious then, too. The sound of the toaster going off was enough to have me grinding my teeth and pacing. I once found my desk chair had been adjusted and I had to leave the house and couldn't go back for hours.

I was angry then, but even at the moments when I truly thought I must be losing my mind, I had nothing on the kind of emotion I felt after Mum died. The problem was, it wasn't at Mum for dying, or even at God for taking her away. It was mainly at my friends. I was irrationally, illogically yet completely furious with them.

I'm not proud of this. I've been in their position and believe me, I was completely useless in the face of other people's grief – worse than useless. I am ashamed of just how ineffectual I was when people I knew were suffering. I said things like, 'I don't want to remind them that so-and-so died,' when debating whether I should say something to them, as if they could have forgotten.

My point is, I know how hard it is to say the right thing. Especially because there is no right thing to say. The only right thing would be if someone suddenly announced, 'Hey, you don't know this about me, but I'm a necromancer,' and no one ever says that. Or at least, they didn't to me.

That didn't make me any less angry at them, though.

I sat looking at my phone or laptop, watching the messages that came flooding in in the immediate aftermath.

'Jack didn't even know my mum,' I hissed. 'Why is he leaving a sad face and crying monkey emoji on my Facebook. What does a crying monkey even mean?'

'It generally means something sad has happened.' Ollie stroked my hair. 'He doesn't have to know your mum. He knows you and wants to be there for you. People care about you.'

I growled. I mean this literally. 'Oh and this from Natalie,' I continued. '"Come over and meet the new boyf". The new boyf! I don't care about her new boyf. Why would I care about her new boyf? My mum just died. And speaking of useless men, where's Anthony? He knew my mum. He broke bread with her.'

Ollie raised an eyebrow. '"Broke bread"?'

'How could he not have been in touch? When his dog

died, I wrote him a really heartfelt message. I never even met his dog.'

It was around this time that Ollie floated the idea of going to counselling.

'I think it might help.'

I turned so quickly I slapped myself in the face with my hair, which might as well have stopped being hair and become hundreds of snakes, instead. Ollie flinched.

'I don't need counselling,' I said. 'You only think I do because your mum's a therapist. You've been indoctrinated.'

'I think it might help if you had someone to talk to. Besides me. My aunt saw a grief counsellor after Boris died and she said it really helped.'

'This is my mum. Boris was a cat.'

'Yeah, but they were very close. She was a wreck when he died.'

I spread my hands. 'Fine. But I'm not even grieving yet.'

He waited a beat. 'Er, yeah. Well, that's sort of the point. It's just to make sure you're coping properly with everything. You know, make sure you're not repressing anything. And maybe you could talk about this whole, "watching over you while you have sex" thing.'

I thought about this. 'Thank you,' I said, squeezing his arm. 'But I just don't think I need counselling.'

A couple of weeks later, I went to counselling.

I was dubious about counselling. My counsellor was also dubious about counselling. It didn't help that I'd been referred to a 'proper hospital', where people with 'real problems' (air quotes featured heavily in my thinking) went. It was the kind of place that isn't called a hospital at all, but a facility, that looked very smart and upmarket – a lot like my old girls' school – but still required you to sign in and out, carry a security pass and be buzzed through two sets of heavy doors with reinforced glass before you got anywhere – a lot like the places where girls from my old school would frequently end up. I couldn't even put on a good show of being depressed. It didn't help that I'd managed to use private care to get here, tagging myself onto the health insurance Ollie got through work. I'd basically skipped the queue. I imagined the long line of people that were also suffering, probably more than me, that would have to wait months to get anywhere close to where I was and felt even guiltier.

I looked at the self-assessment form that was asking if, on a scale of one to ten, I'd ever felt violent urges towards others. Everything was on a scale of one to ten. I considered how I felt every time someone cocked their head, widened their eyes and whispered – whispered! As if grief had made me so fragile, I would shatter if someone dared speak to me at a normal decibel – 'How are you doing?' I thought about the uncontrollable waves of irritation I felt every time someone did this. I put myself down as a three.

The doors buzzed. Someone came through, called my name and ushered me into a room for a proper assessment with one of the head counsellors, who was sitting with his legs crossed, watching me from behind a pair of thick-framed glasses.

I sat down in an armchair opposite him. He eyed me over a clipboard. I felt desperately anxious that I was wasting his time, and soon he would realise that and tell me off for taking him away from the other patients who really did need his attention. I cleared my throat and shifted my weight.

He asked me what had happened to bring me there; I told him.

'So, how do you think you've been coping?' he asked.

'Um,' I said.

He made a note. 'Are you able to get the time off work, should you need it?'

'Actually, I work for myself from home. I'm a writer,' I said.

'Hmm,' he said. He made another note. I imagined that he'd seen my type before and didn't like it. I pictured a frowny face and a few words underlined. It was the same reaction my dad had had when I first told him what I wanted to do.

'Have you had any inclination to self-harm?' he said.

'No, definitely not.'

'Drugs?'

'No. And I would tell you if I did do them, honestly. But I really don't. I'm very boring.' I went for a light laugh, but I don't know how convincing I was.

'Drinking? More than you usually do?'

'If anything, I'm drinking less. I just find it makes

me feel worse, now.' I didn't count the funeral. Nor did I feel the need to tell him about the table dance or the extreme aversion I'd felt to alcohol ever since. Although perhaps I should have done – he might have found me more interesting. I had the distinct impression he was wondering why I was there.

He sighed and put down his pen. 'So why is it you're here? Why do you think you need counselling?'

My boyfriend made me come didn't feel like the right answer. I thought about how alone I sometimes felt. My friends said they'd be there, but sometimes I swore I could see looks of relief when I changed the subject. My family wasn't any better. Laura refused to talk about it and Dad had already mentioned clearing out Mum's wardrobe.

I shuffled in my seat again, then stopped, in case this revealed something about my personality. 'Well,' I said, 'I thought it might help to talk to someone about it. I don't feel like I'm grieving properly, at the moment and I want to make sure I deal with it now, that I'm not repressing anything.'

He slotted his pen back into his clipboard. 'Well, you seem to be coping very well. There is no right and wrong way to grieve.' He put the clipboard away and clasped his hand over a knee. 'You might not grieve at all. Some people don't.'

'Oh,' I said. 'I . . . Right.' I wondered if that only applied if you hadn't really liked the person in the first place. It sounded a little too easy.

'If I'm going to be frank, I don't think you need counselling,' he continued. 'And even if you did, there's no real proof that grief counselling works anyway.' He waved a hand, vaguely. 'Some people say it's useful, of course. But there's no way of knowing if the same results wouldn't have been achieved without counselling.'

'Ah,' I said. 'I see. Well, okay.' I felt like I'd failed a test. I had begun to look forward to having someone to talk to, after all. 'Thank you, Doctor, for your time,' I said and scurried out, feeling a little shamefaced.

I walked outside and called my dad.

'I've just been to see a counsellor,' I said.

'A counsellor?' Dad thought *One Flew Over the Cuckoo's Nest* was a documentary. 'You don't need counselling. Why did you see a counsellor?'

'For grief counselling,' I said. 'To talk about Mum. I thought it might help.'

Dad moaned. 'You sound like something off *The Archers*,' he said. 'Tragedies happen, that doesn't mean you have to talk about it; that's not the way we do things. If you must talk to someone, go speak to Father Ray. He'd be happy to talk to you. You don't need to see a counsellor.'

'That's what the counsellor said,' I said.

'Well!' He sounded a little too triumphant given he had had no part in this process. 'What did I tell you? No need at all. I'll make an appointment for you with Father Ray,' he said.

Ollie was less pleased. I came home to find him making dinner, carefully stirring his special sauce as I repeated what had happened. This was Ollie's signature dish, one he perfected over years and made roughly once a month, during which time, I would be banned from entering the kitchen.

'Stirring is crucial,' he'd say, whenever he made this sauce. 'It's all in the wrist.' He had this entire routine down to an art. He'd even made a special playlist that he said gave the right beat to stir to. It was all hip-hop.

This time, though, his rhythm was off.

'Grief counselling doesn't work?' he said, the spoon moving faster and faster. 'That's ridiculous. My aunt found it so helpful, she went back four times. How does he know if it works or not?'

'Well,' I said, 'he is the head counsellor.'

Ollie ignored this. He was so annoyed with what the doctor had said, he didn't even notice when I got out a tub of hummus from the fridge and started eating from it with a spoon.

'How can he say you don't need counselling after one meeting? It doesn't matter if you "need" it, anyway.' A bit of mince flew out of the pot and landed on the wall. 'The point is, you want someone to talk to. And,' he said, waving the spoon and flicking a tomato onto the cupboard, 'you're paying for it. It's a private hospital. This isn't a free service he's performing.'

'What if I don't need it, though? He said I didn't,' I said.

'Hannah, you told me how much you want someone to talk to. That's what grief counselling is. You need it.' He started ladling the sauce aggressively into bowls. 'Bloody doctor,' he muttered under his breath. 'Telling you what you do and don't need.' He threw the spoon into the pot. 'Well. This is ruined.'

I went back to counselling.

I got buzzed through the doors, sat back in the armchair and stared at the doctor.

'I'd really like grief counselling,' I said, firmly.

'We'll set you up with a counsellor,' he said. 'I think you might benefit from it.'

How to Be a Good Patient

I still wasn't entirely convinced about counselling. Part of me — the part that chided me for having sex and just happens to have my dad's voice — was still saying that I was overreacting. I was just wasting everybody's time. The other part of me, though, was feeling quite hopeful that this could help. I thought of my friends who regularly saw a counsellor and who raved about it. 'It's helped me work through all my issues with my parents. I barely feel any guilt about them any more,' they said. Even the ones who probably should have felt some guilt as they had very nice parents they were terrible to — or so I thought from my sanctimonious new position of being down a parent.

I felt quite optimistic. I pictured a wise older woman with grey hair who wore a muumuu — but a chic one — and would impart her life's wisdom to me. She would be somewhere between Joan Didion and Oprah. I had purposefully forgone mascara that morning in anticipation of all the healing tears I would no doubt be shedding later that day in the soft comfort of her office. And maybe her arms. I felt excited about all the progress I had, in my mind, almost made already.

I heard someone call my name. A young woman in a pencil skirt and cropped jumper came up to me.

'Hannah? Wow. My name's Hannah too,' she said, widening her eyes. 'My first patient and we're both called Hannah. Can you believe it?'

This was not what I had imagined. This wasn't the wise older woman I had pictured. This woman was my age, maybe younger. She wasn't even wearing a muumuu. How was she going to impart a life's-worth of wisdom at twenty-five?

'No,' I said.

She ushered me back through the doors and into a room.

'Losing your mum,' she said. 'That must be so hard. I can't imagine it. I'm so close to my mum.'

'Mmm,' I said. 'You said your first patient. Of the day?'

'No, I'm so new. You're one of my first ever.' She smiled and waved me into a seat. 'So, how are you doing?' she said.

'I'm fine, how are you?' I said, then felt instantly stupid. I had been in counselling for two minutes and had already proclaimed that I didn't need to be there.

'Yes, I'm fine, thanks,' she said.

Silence. I looked down at her shoes. 'I like your shoes,' I said.

She also looked at her shoes. 'Thanks. I got them from Office.'

'It's hard to find a heel that's wearable for the day,' I said.

She nodded. 'So true.'

I nodded back.

She cleared her throat. 'We should probably talk about why you're here. What do you want to get from these sessions?'

'I just want to make sure I'm dealing with my grief now and get it all out of the way, so it doesn't come up again at some terrible moment later on. Like at my wedding or if I had a baby.'

Her face brightened. 'Are you engaged?'

'Well, no,' I said. 'But, you know, it could happen . . . One day. I'm dating someone . . . I want kids.'

'That's very organised,' she said. 'But it's not like trying to schedule a dentist appointment.'

'Oh I know, I never get around to doing that,' I said.

'Oh-kay,' she said.

She said this a lot, the oh an octave above the kay, which she added five extra 'a's to. I later told a friend who had done her own time in counselling about this.

'Oh yes,' she had said, sagely. 'The counselling "okay". There are lots of oh-kaays and mm-hmms. I got an och aye once. I think she just wanted to try something new.'

Hannah cocked her head. 'So how have you been coping? Do you find yourself breaking down a lot?'

'Actually,' I said, 'I've stopped crying completely. And that isn't like me. I cry a lot. It's sort of a problem, actually. I feel as if my body is going through a drought. I've been drinking a lot of water to make up for it.'

I'd only managed to cry properly twice since the funeral and one of those was at a video online when I

86

had PMS. The other time was when I tried to go swimming, only to find my costume soaking wet at the bottom of my gym bag where I'd left it the last time. This was enough to leave me face-down on the sofa. I cried so hard that Ollie had tried to fix things by blow-drying the swimming costume, which was enough to set me off all over again. I take it back: I had cried, just not properly, over something that actually mattered.

'Oh-kay,' she said. 'It's important you think about your mum and really feel the emotions this brings up. Is there anything she would say to you a lot? Something that makes you think of her?'

'Like a catchphrase?' I said.

She leaned forward. 'Anything she would say that really stands out?'

I wanted to say no, because Mum was a real person and not a game-show host, but she seemed so invested in this, I didn't want to disappoint her, so I tried harder. 'Well, she used to say life was too short. And it turns out, she was right,' I said.

'Oh-kay,' Hannah said. 'Well, you can think about it, anyway.' She leaned in even farther. 'I want you to try and access your emotions. Really focus on your mum. Think hard about her. We can talk about how you get on with that next time. Can you bring in some photos of her too? Great. Good work.'

I left feeling robbed. I hadn't wept once.

I pulled out my phone and called Evie. 'Can I come over?' I said.

*

Evie greeted me at the door, holding Harry, who was chewing on a book.

'We think he's teething,' she announced and walked back into her flat.

I followed her in and sat next to Harry on the floor.

'How is Harry?' I cooed at him.

He dribbled.

'He's learned how to use his hands properly and has developed a pincer grip,' she said, her fingers pushed into her eyes. 'We're thrilled he's developing properly.'

I remember when Evie found out she was pregnant. She had called me and wailed down the phone, 'I'm pregnant.'

'Is this good news?' I had asked, tentatively, which was the polite way of asking if she was keeping it or not. When you hit a certain point in your early to mid-twenties, there's a crossover where that news can either be good or absolutely terrible and you really won't know until you ask. It requires a lot of tact.

'It's awful news,' she practically shouted. 'I don't know anything about children and now I'm going to have one. I'm going to be a *mum*.'

I watched as Harry knocked some toy bricks over and clapped.

'So, what's going on?' Evie asked me.

I started restacking the bricks. 'I've just been to my first counselling session.'

'And? How was it?'

'She's younger than me, we have the same name and she has better shoes.'

'Bitch,' Evie said.

'And she says okay a lot.'

'Okay.'

'Yes, but not like that. I didn't cry once. It was awful.'

'If you don't like her, you should ask to see someone else. Counselling's personal and sometimes there's a clash of personalities. Like the time I saw that man who picked his nose and would flick it. I spent the whole session subtly dodging.'

'That wasn't your counsellor, that was your driving instructor.' I held up my hand. 'And I don't care how vulnerable you were, or that you never passed your test after that and now have to get the bus everywhere, it's not the same thing. Anyway, I can't dump her. I don't want to hurt her feelings. I have no choice: I'll just have to keep seeing her forever and it will be rubbish and I'll have to resign myself to the fact that I'll never grieve.' I picked up Harry and sniffed his head. 'Can I have Harry?'

Evie sighed. 'It was your first session, Han. What did she actually say to you?'

'She wants me to think about Mum and "access my feelings",' I said into Harry's scalp.

'Well, that actually sounds sensible. I think about Jenny a lot. Especially now I have Harry. She was really there for me when he was born, you know.'

I sniffed.

Grief made me very self-involved. I'd love to be able to tell you that, in that moment, listening to my best friend talk about how my mum had been there for her when she had a baby of her own, I felt proud, that I was marvelling about motherhood and the whole human experience. But I can't, because I wasn't. All I was thinking was how unfair it was that Mum wouldn't be there to do any of that for me when I started my own family in the way I had always envisioned her being. And how good Harry's head smelled. To be honest, I felt very sorry for myself.

I clutched Harry.

Evie watched us. 'Feeling broody?'

I smiled. 'Always.' I thought of Mum again and how she wouldn't be around to see my children, then I squeezed Harry so tightly, he went red and was sick on my hand.

Evie gently extricated him from my grip. 'It's probably bath time,' she said.

I wiped my hand. 'I should go.'

It would have been a lot easier if I hadn't been thinking about my mum, and doing so was the radical advice the counsellor thought it was. But it wasn't. I thought about Mum a lot. It just didn't do anything. Nothing therapeutic, anyway. Take the nights, for example. They were the worst. I spent most of them berating myself for everything I had ever done wrong in our relationship. It was like a preview of what Saint Peter shows you at the pearly gates before he tells you you're not getting in. When I finally did drop off, I would dream about her. Only, these weren't the lovely comforting dreams other people seemed to have, during which they would have a cup of tea and catch up with whoever it was that had died. In mine, I would tell Mum her new jeans made her look frumpy or her roast chicken was dry and then I would spend the whole of the next day feeling guilty about it. And it was no use telling me that hadn't actually happened, either. That's the problem with being Catholic: we're encouraged to think the worst about ourselves. It was exhausting.

Lying in bed that night after seeing Evie, I decided I had had enough. I rolled over and looked at Ollie. I plucked his phone out of his hands, threw it over my shoulder and dramatically took off my bra. If you want to know how you dramatically take off a bra, I can tell you that in this case, it involved me straddling Ollie, lots of meaningful eye contact and a shoulder jiggle that looked a little bit like I was doing a sexy dance, but without music and without being particularly sexy. Then I leaned over and sort of waved my breasts in his face. Despite this, Ollie grinned and grabbed my hips. I leaned over and started kissing his neck. I might have gyrated a little, but honestly, it's embarrassing enough remembering this much.

He pushed some of my hair out of his face. 'You're really wet,' he said.

'Mmhmm,' I said.

'No, your face. It's leaking.' He sat up a bit and looked at me. 'Are you crying?'

'No,' I mumbled. 'Maybe,' I sniffed. 'I just really miss my mum,' I wailed.

We decided to spoon, instead.

*

I was back in my counsellor's office, watching as she pored over the photos of my mum I had brought in.

'She was so pretty,' she gushed. 'Do you . . . look like her?' She looked up at me, then quickly looked back down. 'I can never tell.'

'No,' I said, trying to be helpful. 'I look more like I've been carved from a potato.'

I crossed my arms. The purpose of these sessions, as I was discovering, was to find something that would upset me and once she had worked out what the something was that did it most effectively, to keep doing it as much as she could, to get me to feel something. She had already asked me to bring in the eulogy. It was very tiring.

Occasionally, she'd wave a photo about and sneak a look at me to see if I was crying. I never was.

I pointed to a photo she was holding. 'That's my mum's best friend, Charlotte.'

She smiled. 'Aw, Auntie Chaz.'

I thought about Charlotte, who was very decidedly a Charlotte. She had never been anything but a Charlotte, except to her mother, who had occasionally called her Lottie. I thought how she would react if someone called her Auntie Chaz.

'Sure,' I said.

She shuffled the photos and handed them back to me. 'Let's talk about your week.'

I crossed my legs. I wondered if I should tell her that

I had managed to break down, but that it happened in the middle of sex and quite frankly, put me off both.

'I don't feel like I'm any closer to grieving,' I said.

'Oh-kay,' she said. 'Do you talk to your friends about her?'

'Sometimes,' I said. 'But it's quite difficult.'

She nodded. 'Because you feel so sad?'

'No, because I get so angry. They do this thing when they tilt their head and widen their eyes.' I mimed the expression, opening and closing my mouth like a fish.

She leaned back in her seat. 'They're probably just trying to be nice.'

'I know. It's very annoying. It's hard to understand if you haven't been through it.'

'Would you rather they didn't ask?' she said, a bit frostily, I thought.

'No, that wouldn't work, either. I'm terrified that they will stop asking, because when they do it will mean that they expect me to be over it and that will be right when I feel like talking the most.'

She gave me a look that suggested she was re-evaluating her choice of career. 'What about your boyfriend?'

'Ollie,' I said.

'Ollie,' she said.

'He's easier to talk to. But I don't want to talk to him too much about it.'

'Because you feel so sad?' she said, hopefully.

'In case he gets bored of me always going on about it,' I said.

I know this is a deeply unfeminist thing to say and I already have a lot of guilt in this area. Sometimes, I feel if I spent less time getting angry about Ollie leaving his dirty socks by the front door (he takes them off with his shoes when he comes through the door; by the end of the week, there's a little pile), I'd have a better career; other times I don't want to get angry about it in case I come across as a nag. But grief – the kind that leaves you unable to leave the house, unable to walk, unable to get out of bed in the morning – felt like it could put a real strain on a relationship.

'It's quite depressing, isn't it?' I said. 'I feel like I'm asking quite a lot of him. Maybe he won't want to take that on.'

I looked at her as she stroked her chin. I like to think that even if she didn't entirely agree with me, she could at least understand the conflicts of trying to resolve fourth-wave feminism with the realities of life and dating as a millennial woman.

'Oh-kay,' she said.

Ollie and I had been together for three years, since we had met at one of Lou's parties. Lou had been trying to pair him up with our friend Izzie and was quite cross when she saw how well we were getting on. It was only when Izzie left with someone else that she stopped trying to distract me by asking me to do the washing-up.

He was kind and easygoing, emotionally and physically sturdy. He didn't suggest I was mentally ill every time I went through PMS, like some of my past boyfriends. I don't want to sound too shallow here, but he also bought me really good presents – never things I actually wanted, but thoughtful gifts he thought would lead to interesting experiences we could have together. I woke up one year to a canoe. That doesn't mean he didn't have faults, because he did, like the sock thing. He could also be dismissive of my emotions and tended to think that every time I was upset about something, it wasn't anything to do with what I was upset about, but was actually a sign of low blood sugar (which might have been right some of the time, but definitely wasn't the rule). But it was generally accepted that something really terrible would have to happen to break us up. And then something really terrible did happen: this. And I worried that, despite a really great few years together and the shared trauma of capsizing a canoe and almost drowning, we wouldn't be able to get through this. It would be too much – I would be too much – and he would find someone who was easier to get along with. Like Izzie.

I sighed and looked at my counsellor. 'I just wish I could skip all this and be better already.'

Ollie picked me up after my session. 'How was counselling?' he asked.

I thought about telling him what I had told her: that I worried I would lose him, too. 'She wants me to write a letter to Mum,' I said.

'She knows your mum's gone, right?' He grinned. 'Maybe you can write it on the way to my parents' this weekend in Dorset.'

I thought about spending the weekend with Ollie's parents. Usually, I enjoyed staying with them. I'm not just saying this because there's a chance they may read this one day, either. We got along. They made gin cocktails every Sunday and had other drinks other days of the week. In that respect, they were a lot like my family. I was having complicated feelings about families, though, and I hadn't seen them since it had happened, which meant there would be probing looks, sympathetic faces and an awkward period when we all worked out how to behave around each other. Besides, you know what they say about family: other people's can be exhausting.

'Hmm,' I said. I kicked the car floor mat.

'What?' Ollie said.

'Maybe I shouldn't go,' I said.

'Why not?'

'I don't know if I should be around happy families right now. It might be . . .' I thought about the best way to explain myself. 'Triggering,' I said.

'My family's not *that* happy,' Ollie said.

'Also, your mum will be there.'

'You like my mum.'

'I know, but that was when I had a mum. Now, it might feel like it's rubbing it in a bit, you know?'

'No,' he said. 'You're coming.'

Ollie's mum, Anne, is a brisk woman. Not brisk in the way people say Iris is brisk, when they're actually thinking of another word entirely. She was a therapist, until she retired. Now, she occasionally gives bracing advice over the internet to her former clients (and some strangers). She's popular on Twitter.

As we drove up to their house, she walked out to meet us, straightening her mauve wool skirt and matching jumper.

'Welcome, welcome.' She hugged Ollie. 'Hannah, dear, I didn't know if you'd feel up to coming. You look tired.' She patted my back.

Ollie squeezed my hand.

'Come inside. I've been arguing on Twitter all morning. John, they're here. Put the kettle on.' She said all this as she walked us into the house, steering us towards the kitchen.

'Hello, you two,' John said. He hugged Ollie and kissed my cheek. 'Tea? Or something stronger?'

'Tea's fine,' Ollie said, glancing at the clock. 'Where's the dog?'

'Oh dear.' Anne sighed. 'We had to send him back to the farm.'

I gasped.

'He's dead?' Ollie said. 'What happened?'

'Dead? No, he's not dead. He went back to the farm. The real farm, where we got him. He bit the postman.'

'Oh,' Ollie said.

Anne sat down at the kitchen table and patted the chair next to her. 'Oliver, how's your sister? I'm still not sure about that new boyfriend.'

'Lucy's fine, Mum.'

John put a mug in front of me. 'Stop worrying, Anne,' he said.

'I'm their mother, I'm supposed to worry. And I don't do it very often. John, the biscuits.'

I stared into my mug and slowly sipped my tea. I had really liked their dog.

I was washing up after dinner that night when Anne finally cornered me. Up until then, I had been doing a good job of silently nodding and smiling along with the conversation, without actually contributing anything.

She turned off the tap, passed me a tea towel to dry my hands and handed me a gin and tonic. 'John can do that in the morning. Come on, sit down. Have a drink.'

I looked around desperately for Ollie to come and rescue me, but I could already hear him arguing with John in the front room about John's new car. I sat down and clasped my drink.

'How have you been coping?' Anne said.

'Fine,' I said. I swirled the gin around my glass.

She gave me an assessing look that told me she didn't believe me. In fact, what the look actually said was, 'You may say you're fine, but I can tell you've been wearing bikini bottoms for three days now, because you can't face doing a wash.' I know that's what the look said because I was there when she gave it to Ollie's sister, once, when she was going through a break-up. She said the underwear bit out loud that time.

'I'm washing my underwear,' I said.

Anne raised her eyebrows. 'Always important,' she said. 'Oliver said you've tried counselling.'

I shrugged. 'I feel silly telling you that. You must have seen people with real problems. Everyone loses their parents. It's not like a child or a spouse. I wasn't even a tragically young age, either.'

'What nonsense. There's no shame asking for help. We all need it some time.'

'I don't think it's helping much, though. Most of the time, I feel fine.'

Anne leaned back in her chair. 'And that's no good?'

'Well, yes. But I feel I should grieve first. And I haven't.'

'But you want to?'

'Not really, no. But I need to. I'd feel guilty if I didn't. It would be like I'm betraying Mum. Like I didn't care enough about her to be upset. And that isn't true.'

'I see.' She crossed her arms. 'Well, you have to give these things time. What does your counsellor say?'

'She wants me to write Mum a letter.'

Anne threw back the rest of her drink. 'Solid tactic. I'm sure she knows what she's doing. You might find it helps. Fancy another? John, the gin,' she shouted and marched through to the next room. I wondered if I'd have better luck with her on Twitter.

That night in bed I prodded Ollie. 'Are you awake?'

'Yes, but I don't want to be and I'm trying not to be, so sshhh.'

'Your mum cornered me, today,' I said.

'Did she?' he asked into his pillow. 'Was it helpful?'

I sat up. 'Is that why you left me alone with her while you talked to your dad about his car? Is that why you made me come here? Did you ask her to talk to me?'

'No. I made you come because I wanted you here. But I thought she might talk to you. What did she say?'

'She thinks I should write the letter, too.'

'So maybe it's not as weird as it sounds.'

Ollie took my silence as an excuse to fall asleep.

I started thinking about the letter on the journey home, making notes on my phone. Anne had waved us off with the promise to check in with me later and I didn't want to be told off if I hadn't done it. I thought about how grateful I was I had been born with my mum and not, say, Ollie's, which I was allowed to say even if I did like her. I wrote that down. I sniffed. Ollie glanced at me. I rubbed my temples. I thought about the time I had gone home with a hangover so debilitating, Mum had put me to bed and had made Dad tiptoe around me, even though I was in my twenties and had brought it on myself, anyway, as Dad pointed out. 'You booked us into a health clinic in Switzerland on a hangover,' she had reminded him. 'I cancelled it,' Dad had said, but he had been very gentle with me after that.

I wrote that down, too.

I squeaked.

'You okay?' Ollie asked.

I waved him off. I thought about the time Mum had bought a set of knickers as a birthday present for a girl at school's party and how everyone had thought I was weird. I thought about how guilty I had felt for getting upset with Mum about it. I started crying quietly.

Ollie looked at me, a bit alarmed this time. 'What's going on?'

I took a great, shuddering breath. 'I take back everything bad I ever said about my counsellor,' I said. 'I think she might be a genius.'

'This is your last session, can you believe it?' My counsellor smiled at me. 'If you think you need more, I can always recommend you for another set of sessions, but I think you're coping well. You were resistant at first — I don't think you were on board with some of my ideas; you probably thought I was a bit out there at times.' She laughed. 'But I think you're showing real progress. So, the letter?' She beamed.

'I think it was helpful,' I said. 'I think it unleashed something.'

She nodded and put a box of tissues in front of me. 'Just in case,' she said. She took one for herself. 'If you don't mind, I might get tearful, too.'

I smiled back at her, but inwardly, I was sceptical. I had yet to shed a single tear in these appointments. I'd even started wearing mascara to them.

I cleared my throat and smoothed out the letter. 'Dear Mum,' I began. I talked about the hangover and the knickers and Anne. I said how grateful I was for her and I hoped she knew that. I said I hoped she wasn't worrying about us too much. And then I started crying and I looked up in embarrassment and saw my counsellor was crying, too, which made me cry harder and we both sat there, with tears running down our faces as I tried to get the rest of the letter out.

'I miss you so much,' I wheezed, 'and I just hope that you're in Heaven,' wheeze, 'and can see that we're all okay,' wheeze, 'but still miss you.'

And so it went on, until I had finally finished and I sat, quietly, sniffling over the paper.

My counsellor dabbed at the corners of her eyes with a tissue.

'Wow. Well done, Hannah. That was so moving.' She put her hand on her heart. 'Do you feel better?'

I nodded.

'That's great. Right, that's all the time we have today. Great work. Really, you did well. Remember, if you want more sessions, just get in touch.'

We stood up to leave. 'You might want to . . .' She gestured around her face. 'Okay, bye Han.' She swanned off.

I shuffled out towards the loo, smiling and nodding wanly at the people that walked past. I locked myself in and looked at the mirror. I started, which is one of those things people are always doing in books and never do in real life, to the point where you begin to wonder what it means. So I will say that in this case, my head shot back on my shoulders so quickly, I cricked my neck.

'Gah,' I said, loudly.

My mascara was all over my face. It was everywhere, except where it was supposed to be. I think there was some in my ears. I looked like the missing member of a Kiss tribute band.

'Damn counsellor,' I muttered as I went to work with a piece of wet toilet roll. 'She really is a genius.'

How to Christmas

In the immediate aftermath of Mum's death, I spent hours obsessing over the milestones. Not even the big ones, like moving house and getting married and having children. Just the things that come along every year that I would now have to face without her. This might be natural and understandable, but it's also a complete waste of time. Take Halloween, for example. I agonised for days about the first Halloween. Oh God, I thought, how on earth am I going to make it through Halloween without her? I decided it was impossible: time would just have to stop moving until I was ready to face such important events again. Then it passed without me even noticing, until one day, I realised it was November and I had made it through Guy Fawkes Night, as well. It was only then that I remembered that I never cared about Halloween in the first place and we hadn't been to see fireworks together as a family since I was a child, when I picked up a sparkler at the wrong end and swore off the day entirely. It was then that I realised that all that agony was a total waste of time. What I really should have been worried about was Christmas. Christmas would be coming up quite soon and is a holiday actually worth agonising over. What the hell was I supposed to do about Christmas?

'What the hell are we going to do about Christmas?' I said.

Ollie looked up from his computer. I was standing in the middle of the lounge, clutching a handful of baubles in one hand and paper chains in the other. I waved them at him.

'I don't know how to do Christmas without Mum. None of us know how to do Christmas without Mum. She did everything. I don't even know where the turkey pan is.' I dropped a bauble. 'Oh my God, we're not going to have any presents.'

Ollie stood up and put his hands on my shoulders. 'Hannah, it's November. We have plenty of time to worry about Christmas. But you don't need to worry,' he said, quickly, when he saw my expression. 'It's going to be fine.'

It wasn't.

'We'll help your dad,' he said. 'Between us, we'll make sure it's just like your mum's Christmases.'

'What about Father Christmas?' I sat down on the floor.

Ollie opened and closed his mouth. 'He knows where you live.'

I gave him a look. 'Mum always made us stockings. Laura has to have a stocking.'

'Okay, then we'll make her a stocking,' he said.

I got to my feet. 'I'll have to take over. Dad won't know what to do. Besides, it's my job to take care of him and Laura now, without Mum here. They need me. I'll have to do everything. I'll have to cook,' I said, rather bravely, I thought.

'Laura is also a good cook,' Ollie said. Subtext: Laura is a better cook.

'I'll have to cook.'

'We'll both cook,' Ollie said.

'What about your parents? We're supposed to be spending Christmas with them this year. They'll be upset if we don't spend Christmas with them.'

'Maybe we can invite them? For Christmas Eve; they can spend Christmas Day with my sister. Your parents are always inviting people over for Christmas Eve.'

'You're right.' I started nodding. 'People depend on us for Christmas Eve. We can't let them down.'

'I don't know if they depend on it,' Ollie said. 'Don't put too much pressure on yourself. They probably have their own—'

'We can't let them down,' I said. 'We'll have to go ahead. It's what Mum would want. Wait. What if Dad doesn't agree? What if he suggests we just go to a pub?'

I handed Ollie the decorations. 'I need to call Dad,' I said. I pulled my phone out of my pocket and dialled his number.

'What the hell are we going to do about Christmas?' he said, when he answered. 'I think we should cancel it this year. No one will feel up to it anyway without your mother. It's for the best.'

'Cancel? We can't cancel Christmas. People depend on us for our Christmases. I depend on us for our

106

Christmases. What about Christmas Eve? We can't leave people out in the cold on Christmas Eve.'

'They do have their own homes,' Dad said.

I ignored him. 'That's practically blasphemy. We're not cancelling Christmas. That's not what Mum would want.'

'Well, we can't do it without her. I don't even know where the turkey pan is.'

'I'll do it,' I said. 'I'll do everything: the shopping, the decorations, the food. I'll take over Christmas.'

'You?' Sometimes I suspect my family has a real lack of faith in me. 'No, that's too much for you to take on, Hannah. It would be easier for everyone if we just left it this year.'

'I don't mind. I want to do it.'

Dad went quiet. I held my breath. I was one step away from bringing up Jesus. We couldn't cancel Christmas. The only thing more depressing than our first Christmas without Mum would be no Christmas at all.

'I suppose if we all chipped in, it could be nice. Your mum would want us to celebrate. And Laura could cook . . .'

'I'm cooking,' I said. 'It will be fine. No, it will be great. It will be just like Mum's Christmases.'

'So I should invite people over for Christmas Eve, then? I suppose if we fill the house a bit, it won't feel so empty. You know, without your mother.'

'Invite everyone,' I said. 'It's what Mum would want. We'll do it in her honour, just as she would do it.' I took a deep breath. 'I'm going to need your credit card.'

I hung up the phone and smiled triumphantly at Ollie.

'It's going to be okay.' I said. 'Dad wanted to cancel but I convinced him not to.' By this point, I could almost hear trumpets sounding in my honour. 'I've saved Christmas,' I said. 'I am the saviour of Christmas.'

'Well—'

I grabbed the decorations and went to walk out of the room, then turned in the doorway and gasped. 'What about New Year's Eve?'

My triumph evaporated when Dad called me back a few days later to tell me he had now invited twenty-five people to our sit-down dinner on Christmas Eve. One that I would be cooking. On our first Christmas since Mum had died.

I tried not to drop the phone as I stood in my kitchen, staring into the fridge, listening to him.

'Twenty-five?' I thought about this. 'Twenty-five?'

'Yes,' Dad said. 'What's wrong with your voice? You sound hoarse.'

'I'm having a reaction.'

'To what?'

'The thought of cooking for twenty-five people. Dad, twenty-five?'

'Yes. When are you going to stop saying that?'

'When you realise we can't cook for twenty-five people.'

'You told me to invite everyone. You said you could handle it.'

I shut the fridge. 'I meant enough people to sit round

the table, fill up the house a bit. Not so many that it's standing room only.'

'What do you want me to do about it? I told Iris not to come, but she insisted.'

'That was when there were only going to be twelve of us. That's thirteen people ago.'

'Well, I had to ask the Peters. Your mum always liked the Peters.'

'Mum once called her a pernicious troll.'

'Yes, well, he's all right.'

'And they have five children.'

'Do you think they'd want to bring them all?'

'Of course they would, it's Christmas.'

'Well, we have to have the Wilkinsons. You used to love their daughter.'

'That was before she put gum in my hair and Mum had to cut it out. I had a lopsided bowl cut for months.'

Dad sniffed, something that, I can tell you, can be extremely passive aggressive when done correctly. 'Your mum wouldn't complain. She always had time for everyone. She would have said "The more, the merrier."'

It's hard to get angry at a parent when you've only got one left and are suddenly all too aware how vulnerable you all really are; that death could be lurking round every corner (which is a cliché you really come to embrace after someone dies). I thought about how upset I would be if Dad died and how guilty I'd feel if I had yelled at him about Christmas Eve. Then I decided that under the circumstances, it was completely justified and I would understand. I might even be able to work the whole story into a touching anecdote in the eulogy about his generosity. I took a deep breath. 'Well I'm not Mum. She's dead. And I'm not cooking for twenty-five people on our first Christmas without her. It's going to be hard enough without having to serve the girl who got everyone at school to call me Ringo.' I slammed the phone down. Or I would have done, if I wasn't on a mobile. There's no way to really slam a mobile, so I hung up and dropped my phone on the floor instead (which was only partly accidental).

Later that day, I got a text from Dad. 'Maybe you're right. I've cancelled the Peters and the Wilkinsons. I've told them to pop round on Boxing Day instead.'

'Twelve people,' I thought. 'Twelve people I can handle.'

I tried to focus instead on the Magical Family Christmas I was now fully responsible for. I planned a frenzied attack on the Black Friday sales, where I was almost certain I'd be able to find the Gift of Christmas, purchase it and present it to my family on Christmas morning, with me and the present bathed in a beautiful golden glow. You don't need two shopping stories, here, but let's just say, I came home with more bags than I remembered buying and blisters on my hands.

I showed them to Ollie when I got home.

'Yeah. Maybe you should let your dad do some of this and try and get back to normal life, a bit. Get back to work and stuff,' he suggested.

'You don't think this is work?' I hissed.

'Well, no,' Ollie said. 'Work is what you do for a job. What you get paid for, so we can pay our rent. Your work,' he continued, in a helpful tone, 'is writing. Maybe you should focus on that a bit, instead of . . .' He gestured at the shopping bags. 'This. Let your dad do all of that.'

I puffed up my chest. 'Clearly, Oliver, you have no idea how much effort and energy is involved in being a parent.'

'You're not a parent.'

'I know that. But right now,' I said, dramatically throwing open my arms, 'I am working like one to provide my family with a Magical Family Christmas. That you will also be enjoying. So, you look at my hands and tell me this. Isn't. Work.'

Ollie dutifully took my hands in his and studied them. 'It's not work,' he said.

I didn't have to see my dad again until Ollie and I went over to help decorate the Christmas tree, as was our family tradition. Every year, we would put our favourite Christmas CD on and make a batch of mulled wine, which we would drink while we danced around the tree, singing loudly and strewing the house with Christmas lights. This might be why our decorations usually ended up looking a bit crooked.

By the time Ollie and I got there, the music was on and there was a strong scent of cinnamon and orange cloves coming from the kitchen. I walked in, dragging a sackful of presents and huffing slightly under the weight.

Dad watched me, his eyebrows raised. 'Are all those for us?'

'Yes.'

'Hm. Quite a lot, aren't there?'

'Well, yes, but it's Christmas. Presents are crucial to Christmas.'

'Did I pay for them?'

'Yes.'

'That explains why the bank's been calling, then. What did I buy?'

I looked pointedly at Laura across the room. 'I'll tell you later.'

'Did you get anything for yourself?'

'No.'

'Well, who's going to get your presents?'

I squared my shoulders. 'I just won't have presents this year.' I felt courageous, magnanimous and selfless. Presents are crucial to Christmas, after all. I'd just said that. This subtext was clearly lost on Dad, though, as he just shrugged and handed me a glass of mulled wine. I walked over to the tree.

'I always forget how weird your decorations are,' Ollie said. He pulled a piece of cardboard out of the decorations box. 'Is this a toilet roll? In my house, these go in the bin.'

'Ollie,' Laura said, plucking it gently from his hands, carefully sticking pieces of tinsel and cotton wool back on. 'This is the Yule Log. It's very important and special.'

'Right. And why is that?' he said.

'Because I made it.' She stuck it on a branch.

Ollie laughed. 'Okay, and what about this?' He held up a few pieces of coloured paper.

'That's just some rubbish Hannah made,' Laura said, draping more tinsel over the tree.

'That's not rubbish. It's one of the first things you brought home from school,' Dad said, looking at me. 'See, you wrote "Mummy" on it. Your mum insisted we put it on the tree. I don't see my name, on the other hand...'

I knelt down and rummaged through the decorations box. 'That's the last of them.' I looked up. 'Where's the Christmas angel?' The others looked at me blankly. 'The Christmas angel. The one Mum knitted. It always goes on top of the tree.'

Dad frowned. 'Didn't we have a star?'

Laura looked over my shoulder. 'It's not in there?'

'No.' I upended the box and sat back on my heels. 'This is terrible. How can we have Christmas without the Christmas angel? It's not Christmas without the Christmas angel.'

'You still have the Christmas toilet roll,' Ollie said.

'Could it be in the loft? Did you miss a box?' I looked round at Dad and Laura.

'No, this was everything,' Laura said. She looked around the tree, like it could be hiding on a branch at the back and she hadn't noticed.

Dad crossed his arms. 'I'm sure we had a star.'

I lifted the decorations box over my head and shook

it. Tissue paper wafted out and landed on my head. 'We can't have lost it. It was Mum's. She made it.'

'I've got it.' Laura ran out of the room.

'It was a very nice star. It had lights on it,' Dad said.

Laura came running back in, brandishing a Barbie dressed in a fluffy red mini skirt and red sequin bra. It looked like a miniature model from the Ann Summers Christmas collection. 'Here,' she said.

I stood up. 'That's not the Christmas angel,' I said.

'I know, but we can use this instead. Mum bought her for me.' Laura climbed up the ladder next to the tree and placed the doll on top. 'There.' She smiled round at us.

We stared at it, dubiously.

'And her name's Angel,' Laura said. 'See, it's perfect.'

'Because she's a stripper?' Ollie said.

Dad crossed his arms. 'You can't leave that there. It doesn't look like an angel, it looks like a tart. You can see right up that skirt.'

Ollie tilted his head. 'Why is its hair wonky?'

Laura shot me a venomous look. 'Ask Hannah.'

Ollie looked at me. 'What happened?'

'It was Christmas, 1997.' Laura put her hands on her hips. 'Hannah decided she wanted to be a hairdresser . . .'

'Are those fluffy knickers?' Dad said.

'Hannah always ruined my dolls,' Laura said. 'You know, she tried to bury me once?'

'Hannah?' Ollie said.

Dad put his hands on his hips. 'I'm going to find that star myself.'

114

'She wanted to be an only child,' Laura said.

I held up my glass. 'Who wants more mulled wine?'

The doll stayed put.

Then it was Christmas Eve and Ollie and I were standing outside my family home, holding extra bags of potatoes, waiting to be let in.

Laura opened the door. 'We found the turkey tray. Dad's put everything in the fridge, except for the turkey, which is soaking in brine in a bucket outside,' she said as we followed her in.

'Don't your neighbours have a cat?' Ollie said.

'Yeah, why?' Laura said.

Ollie dashed outside.

'Let me know if you need any help,' Laura said, walking out of the kitchen.

'I don't need any help. I have this all under control,' I said.

I stood in the kitchen and looked around. My counsellor had told me to spend time in the places that reminded me of Mum to get in touch with my grief. I thought of the endless Christmas Eves I had sat on the counter and watched her in this same room, preparing and cooking this same meal we were about to make. And now it was my turn. It felt like a rite of passage. I was absolutely positive I was going to cock it up.

Ollie walked back in, hauling the bucket with the turkey in it. 'I had to fight off a huddle of angry cats, but I saved it from the jaws of death.' He looked proudly at me.

'It's already plucked and missing a head,' I said.

'All right, so I saved it from the jaws of your neighbours' cats, then. Can we keep the food inside, now?'

I waved my phone in the air, trying to find a signal. 'Charlotte's supposed to let me know when she's arriving.' I started pacing. 'I don't know how she's going to find it, today; she hasn't been here since the funeral and she's Mum's best friend. And your parents are coming. They're going to be meeting my dad.' I stopped. 'They're going to be meeting my dad,' I said, slowly. 'For the first time. Oh God.'

Ollie dropped the turkey bucket. 'Are you just realising this?'

'No. I've thought a lot about how they're never going to meet Mum. I just hadn't thought about the fact that they would be meeting Dad. Okay.' I clapped my hands in the way I had seen Mum do hundreds of times. 'Let's get on with it. We have a lot to do and it needs to go perfectly. The future relationship between our two families could depend on this going well. No one wants fighting in-laws, Ollie. I saw a film about that once that went very badly. We can't let anyone down. This is Christmas. Peel potatoes, chop the veg, preheat the oven. We only have eight hours.'

By five o'clock, I was beginning to feel more relaxed. The food had been prepared, people weren't arriving until seven and the turkey was on track to be ready by the time we sat down to eat at eight. I had also had some mulled wine.

116

'This is actually quite easy,' I said. 'It's all about being organised. I really think I'm quite good at this. Maybe I should have filmed it and put it on YouTube so others can learn from me. Is there any more mulled wine?' I waved my glass.

Laura came into the kitchen with a fistful of Quality Streets in each hand. 'It all smells good, guys. Let me know if there's anything I can do.' She put a chocolate in her mouth and chomped on it. 'Who's that?'

I looked out the window. There was a taxi turning into the drive.

'Oh my God, it's Iris,' Laura said.

I gasped. 'What is she doing here? She's two hours early.' I'm not above admitting I might have screeched this. Ollie put a hand on my shoulder.

Laura looked panicked. 'I'm not ready to see people yet. I'm not even dressed yet. She's going to want to talk about Mum. Hannah, I'm not ready.' She grabbed my arm. 'She's getting out of the car. Quick, hide.'

'We can't hide, we're cooking,' Ollie said as Laura and I ducked beneath the window.

'Oh God, oh God. I'll never get back to my room in time. I'll be trapped.' Laura ran out of the kitchen, just as the doorbell rang.

Ollie and I went into the hallway as Dad walked up to the front door.

'What is she doing here?' Dad muttered. He swung the door open. 'Iris. You're early. We didn't expect you till seven.'

'Happy Christmas to you, too, Patrick.' She stepped

inside the hallway. 'I came early to help, obviously. That is what family does. Hannah, Oliver, nice to see you both.'

'Happy Christmas, Iris,' I said.

Ollie bowed. I glanced at him; he shrugged.

'Well, now you're here, let me take your coat,' Dad said. He turned towards the coat cupboard, opened the door and Laura stepped out.

'Iris, hi. Nice journey? Let me take that for you,' she said, hanging up Iris's coat in the cupboard behind her and ignoring Dad's face. 'So,' she clapped her hands. 'Shall we have a drink?'

'Yes,' Dad and I said, simultaneously.

We trooped into the lounge.

Iris looked around. 'Well, it all looks very nice in here. Well done, girls. Except...' she looked at the tree. 'Good Lord, what on earth is that on top of the tree? It looks like some kind of prostitute. Really, Patrick, what were you thinking? You have guests coming round. If they could see this back home...'

'Drink, Iris?' Dad said.

'Patrick, I told you: I'm here to help. You can have a drink if you feel you need one.' She looked at her watch.

Dad pulled out a bottle of wine.

Iris turned to me. 'Now, what can I do to help?'

'Really, Iris, nothing,' I said. 'We have it all under control. You just relax.'

'Yes. Let us get back to it,' Ollie said.

We turned and walked back towards the kitchen.

118

'Send in that drink when it's open,' I muttered to Laura on the way out.

Iris's voice carried through as we left the room. 'Honestly, Patrick, I thought it was Jennifer who insisted on being so ridiculous about presents. How many can the girls possibly need? When we were their age, we got fruit. And we were glad of it.'

The wine cork pulled out with a pop.

After an hour of terse conversation with Iris that Ollie and I managed to largely avoid, and glares from Laura every time we came into the lounge, it was a relief when Charlotte arrived at six. I opened the door this time.

'Hannah, sweetheart. How's it going?' She gave me a big hug then pulled back and examined me. 'Gosh, you look so like your mum in that apron.' She dug into her bag and pulled out a bottle. 'I brought this. I thought we could do a special toast to Jennifer, just us.'

I grinned at her. 'Thank God you're here. Iris got here an hour ago.'

'Oh God, really?' Charlotte whispered. 'Well, it's a good job I brought a bottle of Baileys with me, too, then.'

Laura came edging out of the lounge backwards. 'No, no, Iris. I'm not planning on spending the evening in my pyjamas, of course not. I should go get ready,' she called. 'Before everyone gets here.' She turned and bumped into us. 'Charlotte,' she said, giving her a hug. 'Thank goodness you're here. Hannah, stop hiding in the kitchen. I have been talking to her for hours.' She put a hand to her head. 'Dad and I are quite drunk.'

Charlotte put her bags down. 'Don't worry,' she

rubbed Laura's back. 'I'll go.' She picked up her bottle and strode into the lounge. 'Patrick, Merry Christmas. Oh Iris, hello.'

I walked back into the kitchen. 'Right, the carrots need to be sautéed and I have to make a start on the cheese sauce . . .'

Ollie gestured towards the stove. 'The carrots are on already. And the sprouts are ready to go. Go spend some time with your family. I can do this.'

'What? No.' I took a deep breath. 'No, thank you, but no. This is my mum's meal. I need to be here to cook it. It's my job, now. I can handle this. Go and say hello to Charlotte.'

Ollie raised his hands and stepped out of my way, rolling his eyes and edging out of the room. 'Okay then.'

Philip arrived next, marching into the lounge with another bottle of wine in his hand, then Evie turned up, with her partner, Jake, carrying Harry. I hugged them all.

Evie grimaced at me. 'Sorry we're late. The baby was napping.' Harry looked pleased with himself and waved. 'I wanted to get here early and help out. How's it going?' She looked over my shoulder into the kitchen.

'Fine,' I said firmly. 'Everything's in the oven. We have it all under control. Dinner should be ready soon. We're just waiting for Ollie's parents to arrive.'

'Oh, that's great. When are they getting here?'

'Should be any minute now.'

'Great. Well, I brought some snacks to tide Harry over until dinner. You know, just in case . . .'

I ushered them into the lounge, then went back into the kitchen.

'That just leaves your parents. Have you heard from them? I thought they'd be here by now . . .'

Ollie pulled his phone out of his pocket, then looked at me.

'What?'

'They've just left.'

'*What*?'

'Mum had some crisis with an old patient, apparently. It was an emergency. But they're on their way now.'

'Forget the patient. I'm having a crisis. Ollie, they live hours away. It's seven bloody thirty. This is a nightmare.'

I let out a shrill scream that I thought was inside my head, until Charlotte popped her head into the kitchen and I realised it wasn't after all.

'Um, Hannah?' she said.

'All fine, all fine. Ollie's parents are just going to be a bit late. We'll come out and sit down.'

I grabbed my glass and we walked into the lounge. Charlotte was talking to Philip, who kept looking over at me and winking.

'Everything under control in there?' he shouted.

Charlotte looked concerned.

Laura was taking Harry off Evie, as Dad procured extra glasses for her and Jake.

'You can have one and still drive,' he was saying. 'Come on, it's Christmas.'

Iris walked over to us.

'I hear we're waiting for your parents to arrive, Oliver,' she said.

He cleared his throat. 'Yes, they're on their way now. Mum had a crisis with a patient,' he said.

Iris raised an eyebrow. 'A patient? Is she a doctor?'

'A therapist,' Ollie said. 'Or she used to be, she's retired now.'

'A therapist?' He might as well have told her his parents took turns chewing food. 'Well. That's very good of her to think about her patient at Christmas. Especially when she already has dinner plans.'

Ollie looked nervous.

'Excuse us, Iris,' I said, pulling him away. 'We should mingle.'

Dad was still talking to Evie and Jake. 'You can have a drink and breastfeed,' he said. The brogue was beginning to come back out.

'Dad,' I said.

He gestured at me. 'Hannah used to love a bit of drink as a baby. It runs in the Kennedy blood.' He does nothing to help cultural stereotypes.

I pulled Ollie back into the kitchen at the next opportunity, in the pretence of checking the food.

'Anything?'

'They're stuck in traffic.'

'Maybe we should turn the oven down, so nothing burns.' I opened the door and looked inside. 'Why . . . Is the oven off? The oven's off. Ollie, the oven is *off*.'

Laura tottered in, emptying her glass. 'Harry's so cute,' she gushed. 'I want a baby. And also a boyfriend.

I should probably get one of those first. What's going on here?'

'The oven's off.'

'Noo,' she gasped.

'It's fine,' Ollie said. 'The turkey's cooked. That oven was on. It's just some of the vegetables that aren't. And most of those we can do on the stove anyway.'

I clutched at my head. 'Okay, we can still save this. It will all be okay, just. Don't. *Panic*.' I patted the air with my hands to emphasise each word. 'We need to stall people until we can get the oven back on and everything cooked. Ollie, your parents aren't even here yet, so we have time. No one can know what's happened.'

'Don't worry,' Laura threw back her head. 'I've got this under control. I know what to do.' She winked at us, then stalked back into the lounge.

Ollie and I watched her go.

'Everyone,' she called out. 'Hi. The oven's off. The oven is off. But don't panic. Dinner is just going to be a little bit late. But it's fine. I've been in there. It smells great – the cooked stuff, anyway. Everything is going to be okay.'

Ollie and I looked at each other.

'Why did they say they didn't want my help?' I heard Iris say.

'I'm going to kill her,' I said. I turned back to the stove.

'Iris?' Ollie said.

'Laura,' I said. 'Crank the oven up. Let's get everything cooking quicker.'

Fifteen minutes later, I was circulating around the group, offering nibbles and strategically topping up glasses.

Dad raised an eyebrow at me. 'Is everything . . . ?'

'Fine, it's fine. Just keep people drinking.'

I walked up to Evie and Jake, who were jiggling a grizzling Harry and looking tense.

'Everything okay here? More drink? It is Christmas, after all,' I said, with all the forced jollity of a career shopping-centre Father Christmas.

'Hannah, how soon do you think we might eat?' Jake asked.

Evie glared at him.

'Soon,' I said. 'We're just waiting for Ollie's parents. Besides, it's only—' I glanced at the clock. 'Oh. Nine. Right. Yes, any minute now, I'm sure.'

As I turned away, Charlotte swiftly came up to me and took my arm. 'If you need anything, I can help,' she said.

'It's fine, really,' I said. 'Can't chat. I've got to hand these around.'

Philip was sitting on the sofa next to Iris, watching me. He waved his empty glass.

'How are things going in there?' He raised his eyebrows, meaningfully, at me. 'You and Ollie fighting yet?' He laughed. 'Where's that nice girl, Lube. From the funeral. She coming tonight?'

'Sorry, no,' I said, offering him a stuffed olive. 'It's just us, tonight.'

Across the room, Harry suddenly wailed.

Iris glanced at him. 'I don't know why people insist on

bringing their children to things like this. Why bring a baby to a dinner party if he won't behave? She brought him to the hospital too, didn't she? The same baby.'

Evie and Jake looked over at her. Jake carried Harry out of the room.

Iris took a sip of her drink. 'Your mother was the same. She practically took you girls everywhere. It spoils a child terribly.'

Philip laughed and slapped Iris's back.

I practically ran back to the kitchen.

'How are the potatoes doing?'

Ollie stuck a fork in them. 'They're not cooked yet.'

I walked over. 'They look burnt.'

'Only on the outside,' Ollie said. 'On the inside, they're still raw.'

I clutched my head. 'This is a nightmare. Can you call your parents again?'

'No, Hannah,' he said, slamming the oven door.

'Why not?'

'Because I just called them five minutes ago and I don't want to hear Mum make pointed comments on stress management again.'

I opened the oven door. 'I need to fix the potatoes.'

'They just need to be put on a lower heat. Here, let me.' Ollie picked up the potatoes.

'It's fine. I can do it,' I grabbed the tray, burning my hand in the process. I yelped and dropped it again.

'Hannah, will you let me do it? I can cook a bloody roast.'

'No, you don't know what to do. I have to do it.' I willed myself not to start crying. I'd ruin my make-up.

Ollie started tugging his hair. 'For God's sake, Hannah, I'm trying to help—'

Evie stuck her head into the kitchen. 'Hannah?'

'No problems, here. Go, sit down. Have you got a drink?' I said, waving her back out again.

She looked uncomfortable. Possibly because my voice was coming out an octave higher than its usual range. My cheeks were beginning to burn from the force of my smile.

'Actually, Han, I'm so sorry but I'm going to have to go. It's Harry. It's getting late and as he hasn't eaten, he's getting really fussy. Jake's taken him outside but he won't stop crying. I'm going to have to take him home. But Jake can stay. Sorry, Han. Merry Christmas, Ollie.' She ducked back out.

I turned to Ollie. 'That's it. My perfect Christmas is *ruined*. Everything's going wrong. Half the food is going cold. The other half isn't cooked. Now my guests are leaving.' I wiped my face. 'And my make-up is melting. It is melting right off my face. This never happened to Mum.' I picked up my glass and drained it. 'And where are your bloody parents?'

The doorbell rang.

'They're here,' Ollie said.

John and Anne were hustled into the house and handed a drink each before they'd had time to take their coats off.

126

'I think everyone might have had one or two already.' I laughed nervously as I shepherded them into the lounge and over to Dad, who was talking to Philip and filling up his glass.

'This is my dad, Patrick. Dad, these are Ollie's parents. This is John and Anne.'

'You made it.' Dad spread his arms. 'Fantastic. We thought we'd never get to eat.' He laughed.

I closed my eyes.

It was ten o'clock before we were finally ready to sit down.

Dad came into the kitchen as we were serving the food.

'Where's Evie?' he said. 'She's not at the table.'

'She had to go,' I said, forcefully dumping carrots onto a plate.

'But we haven't eaten anything yet.'

'I know.'

Dad glanced towards the dining room table. 'So why's he still here?' He jerked his head towards the door and rolled his eyes, dramatically.

'Jake,' I said. 'That's Jake. Evie's boyfriend, Jake. Jake is staying and eating.' I thrust a plate at Dad.

'Without Evie? That's a bit weird, isn't it? We don't know him. Why couldn't he have gone and let her stay?'

Iris's voice came wafting through. 'You can always tell when Patrick's had too much to drink. He just starts shouting. Patrick, do stop shouting,' she called. 'We don't all need to be privy to your every thought.'

I glared at Dad and handed him another plate. He had the grace to look guilty as he carried them through.

We plonked the plates down on the table with none of the aplomb I had envisioned when I had planned this night. But then, a lot of things I had imagined hadn't panned out the way I had hoped. No one was audibly wondering how I did it, while I glided in, infused in a rosy glow, either.

'Better late than never, eh?' Philip laughed. 'Patrick, is there more wine?'

Charlotte smiled at me as we sat down. 'It looks great, you two. Well done.'

Dad stood up. 'Shall I make a toast?'

'To Jenny,' Charlotte said.

John leaned over to Ollie. 'Who's Jenny?' he said.

Ollie glared at him. 'Dad.'

'It's fine, it's fine,' I said, brightly. 'Jenny's my mum, John. She isn't here tonight. Because she died.'

'Right, of course. Sorry,' John said.

Iris turned to Jake. 'So your wife had to leave. Did you not want to be with her and your child on Christmas Eve?'

Jake cleared his throat. 'Well, we thought someone should stay and eat, as we told Hannah we'd be here . . .'

Anne looked at Jake. 'Your wife had to leave? What a shame. What happened?'

'We're not actually married.'

Iris looked appalled.

'We have a baby. He was hungry. It was getting late,' Jake trailed off.

Iris placed her napkin on her lap. 'It's remarkable this new trend to take babies everywhere. When Patrick and I were children, we barely saw our mother.'

'We're thrilled to have you, Jake,' I said, firmly. 'Wine?'

Philip waved his fork at Ollie and me. 'When are you two going to get down to having babies?'

I glanced at Ollie.

'Um,' Ollie said.

I took his hand. 'Well, I think we'd probably get married—'

'And what about you, Laura? Got a boyfriend yet?'

Laura shoved a bit of turkey in her mouth.

Charlotte leaned across the table. 'So Anne, I hear you're a therapist?'

'Remarkable what people will pay for these days,' Iris said.

I consoled myself with the thought that it was only Christmas Eve. We still had Christmas Day. That would be perfect.

No one mentioned the potatoes.

I can tell you exactly how Christmas Day would have been if Mum had been there. On Christmas morning, we would wake up to stockings, which we would open before we went to Mass. Then once we got home from church, there would be more presents and champagne. Christmas lunch would always be late and would go on for what felt like hours, which was the amount of time you would need after eating before you could ever imagine being hungry again. We would wait for half an hour and then start discussing pudding. There would be a Christmas film in the evening, during which Mum and Dad would open the advocaat and concoct the sort of disgusting cocktails that could only have been thought up in the seventies, but to which their loyalty verged on the devout.

Mum was central to our Christmas; without her, it all fell apart quite quickly. One year, she was stuck in bed with the flu and by the end of the evening, it had all gotten a bit *Lord of the Flies*. Dad had tried to cook, but had only taken the chicken out of the fridge an hour before we usually ate. Then, he put the potatoes on at the same time as the chicken, which meant they were burnt before anything else was even slightly cooked. By eleven at night, Laura and I had gone feral, fighting over a bag of raw peas, while Dad stood in the kitchen and shouted at the oven.

When we woke up on Christmas morning that year, Ollie lying on top of me because I only had a single bed in my childhood bedroom, I could already feel her absence.

Laura came in, rubbing her eyes and holding a stocking aloft. She pointed at the end of our bed. My heart leaped. I looked for a stocking; there wasn't one.

'You could have at least taken your shoes off,' she said.

In the kitchen, Dad was bent over the sink, looking at the stack of dirty plates.

'Iris didn't leave until three,' he said, hoarsely. 'She seems to think we're not coping. She said the house

130

hadn't been hoovered properly in months. She found a lot of dust. She was talking about moving in. I practically had to carry her into a taxi. Still, could have been worse last night, couldn't it.'

Laura took half a roast potato off someone's plate and started to eat it.

'Merry Christmas,' she said.

Ollie poked me. 'We should probably put the oven on, now,' he said.

I sighed, heavily. I might have groaned, even. As much as I love Christmas – and I do love Christmas; I love everything about it: the food, the festivity, the gluttony; I'm a big fan of the gluttony – at that moment, I really wished it was January. Cold, bleak January when no one wants anything heavier than a soup.

Ollie was still poking me. 'Hannah? The oven? If we're going to get this roast cooked on time.'

I didn't want to cook a roast. I wanted to sit on the floor and kick my feet and wait for Christmas to be over. After four hours' sleep, I was ready to give up. All of my carefully thought out plans for that weekend had already gone wrong. It no longer felt important to me to do Mum's Christmas. I could no longer remember why I cared so much. It wasn't going to bring her back; it might just remind us all that she wasn't there doing it herself.

Dad eyed me. 'We could forget about doing a roast today. It is Christmas. I think what your mum would want most is for us to enjoy it.'

131

This felt blatant, even for Dad, but then again, it also meant I wouldn't have to do any more cooking.

Ollie and I glanced at each other.

'There are plenty of leftovers,' Laura said.

'We wouldn't have to cook,' Ollie said, hopefully.

'We can have turkey sandwiches,' Dad said, nodding enthusiastically.

'Can we skip Mass?' Laura asked.

Dad frowned. 'No. Go get dressed.'

So it was agreed. We had given up. It felt okay.

We reconvened after Mass in our pyjamas. This felt decadent. It felt subversive. It felt a little odd. We came together in the lounge and stood looking at each other, grinning madly. We were full of our newfound status as rebels. And we didn't have a clue what to do next.

Laura shuffled her feet. 'Presents?' she said.

'I'll put some music on,' Ollie said.

'Some drink,' Dad said.

We were off.

I handed out the gifts I had bought, feeling benevolent and gracious. I probably look like a young Mother Theresa, I thought to myself. Julie Andrews in *The Sound of Music*.

Laura and Ollie pushed a pile in front of me.

I looked at them in surprise.

'I didn't think I was going to have any this year,' I whispered. 'Without Mum.'

Laura rolled her eyes. 'It's Christmas, Hannah,' she said. 'Presents are crucial to Christmas.'

We spent the rest of the day curled up in front of

the television, watching Christmas reruns of television shows and Christmas films, eating leftovers. When we ran out of those, Laura made a big pot of mashed potato and we ate that, instead.

Ollie and I decided to stay for another night.

Dad even got out the advocaat, because there are some traditions that you can't do without.

It wasn't my mum's Christmas, but sod it. Sometimes, you need to start your own traditions.

How to Make a Scene

In a way, Christmas was easy. It was chaotic and dramatic and drama and chaos are very distracting. We had a cause. Even if that cause was avoiding Christmas, which, as far as causes go, isn't a particularly strong one.

Take Boxing Day, for example, when the Wilkinsons and Peters were due to come round and we were due to cook for them. Or we would have been, if we hadn't given up on the idea of doing anything like that.

If Mum had been around, there would have been lunch. There would at least have been a selection of nibbles. That's probably what Dad had had in mind when he invited them, with the promise of a 'good Christmas drink and something nice to eat'.

'Much better than coming on Christmas Eve, really, anyway,' he had said. 'Hannah's cooking.' Then he had laughed.

Then they turned up and Dad was welcoming them at the door with half a plate of mince pies and some mulled wine. The rest of us stayed slouched in the lounge, hardly moving. We had barely managed to get dressed; Laura hadn't.

'I expect you were thinking you'd be sitting down to

champagne and a plate of food.' Dad chuckled, slapping Mr Wilkinson on the back as he walked in.

To which the Peters and the Wilkinsons laughed lightly, looked away and said of course not, while mentally calculating just how far gone Dad was now without Mum.

'That poor man,' Mrs Wilkinson whispered in her husband's ear, not particularly quietly, as Dad offered the mince pie plate to the Peters.

'We're doing something different this year,' Dad said, cheerfully. 'It's been quite marvellous. I spent all of yesterday in a robe. Wouldn't have got dressed today if Hannah hadn't made me. Have you seen *Home Alone*? It's on now. Why don't you pull up a cushion and have a seat?'

After which he resumed a running commentary on the plot, pointing out the different characters and what was going on, while the two families stood awkwardly in the doorway, drinking their mulled wine and jostling each other slightly.

The Peters were the first to leave, with the Wilkinsons following soon after.

Dad waved them off at the front door and came back into the lounge. 'Well, that wasn't so bad, was it? Do you see, Hannah? It's important to socialise. I told you it was what your mum would have wanted.' He looked at me, accusingly. 'You told me not to invite them at all. Mince pie?'

That was Christmas, though. As everyone tells you after someone dies, it's when life goes back to normal, when you no longer have the drama and chaos, that you have to worry. Christmas was fine. It was that murky time after Christmas that was difficult. The post-Boxing Day, pre-New Year's Eve period, Betwixtmas, when everyone's with their families still and no one's really doing anything more than eating leftovers and watching TV. For the truly energetic, there might be a walk, but that's it. Even Ollie was with his family, having finally given up on trying to sleep in a single bed with two people in it around the twenty-seventh.

We were with family, too. Only, a quarter of our family wasn't there any more and we were trying to ignore it. And since we'd already spent our Christmas eating leftovers and watching TV, we had been forced to move on to microwave meals I picked up from the local supermarket.

It was in those days when the full reality really set in: the emptiness of your first Christmas when your mum is no longer there. The days passed sluggishly in front of *The Vicar of Dibley* reruns and episodes of *Blackadder*. Days that used to fly by in years before were now broken up only by naps and offers of crisps and more Baileys, before everyone gave up and went to bed at ten. I began to wonder how other families were managing to cope during this time, how we had ever done it, before. How had we managed such an interminable length of time? We even resorted to going for a walk, tramping over the frozen grass that would snap underfoot and making observations about the cold, while furtively glancing into other people's homes and the happy families inside.

I went out walking the next afternoon, too, when the dark outside had prompted everyone inside to turn their lights on. I picked up my parents' heavy torch, pulled on some old wellington boots that my feet sloshed around inside and left Dad and Laura splayed in front of the television, mindlessly eating some mince pies I had picked up from the shops earlier.

I walked down the road and towards the fields that neighbouring houses backed onto, shining my torch onto the ground in front of me. I crept up as close as I could to the garden fences, turned off my torch and looked into all the houses that hadn't yet drawn their curtains. I spied on the families who were sitting together on the sofa, watching the same film my family were watching at home. I stood there, the cold air making my chest hurt, until someone looked out towards me, someone else got up to close the curtains, or until the cold forced me to start moving, again. Then I would walk on a bit further and look into the next house, where I would find an elderly couple sitting together, or a man reading a book by himself under a lamp, or teenagers splayed on the floor, looking at their phones. I did this until I ran out of houses and by the time I turned back, most had drawn curtains and shut blinds, closing themselves off from the outside world and my prying eyes.

By the twenty-ninth, the forced jollity of watching *Father Ted*'s Christmas special for the third time that day was proving too much. I went into the kitchen and pretended you could wash up microwave meal containers.

After a few minutes, Laura followed me in. 'Oh thank

God.' She dropped down on a chair. 'Dad's asleep. I couldn't take it any more. It was getting suffocating in there.' She picked up a tea cloth and started towelling off the plastic trays I was washing. When we finished with the trays, I picked up a few of the glasses and mugs we had been using and abandoning on the surfaces and dropped them into the soapy water, too.

'I just don't think I can take any more Christmas specials,' Laura said. 'At some point, you begin to start questioning reality. Like, what even is Christmas?'

We kept washing and drying in silence for a while.

'It's quiet, isn't it,' Laura said. 'I don't remember it being like this before.'

'That's because it wasn't.'

Laura nodded. 'I used to love Christmas. Now, it just feels like it's never going to end. I'm almost looking forward to going back to work.'

I patted her with a soapy hand. 'I know.'

'It's been nice having you here.'

'Mm. I'm going to have to go soon, though. Probably tomorrow.'

Laura nodded.

'Are you going to be okay here, just with Dad?'

She shrugged. 'It's not like I ever left. And it's not forever. Hopefully. Can you imagine if it was forever? Just me and Dad living together?' She shuddered.

I pulled out the plug and watched the drain suck down the water. I turned to Laura. 'How about a Baileys and a round of Snap?'

By New Year's Eve, I was longing to be back in that safe cocoon of boredom and familiarity. I wished I had never left.

I was conflicted about New Year's Eve. But this goes without saying, because I am always conflicted about New Year's Eve. Who isn't? It's the one night of the year you can almost believe you're going to become a completely different person in the morning. It doesn't matter that this transformation never happens (nor that the night itself is almost always a complete let-down); there's symbolism involved and symbolism is very heady. Surely the only people who aren't conflicted about New Year's Eve are the ones who refuse to buy into it at all. As I am not one of those people, I was feeling conflicted.

But that year, it was worse still because there had been a death. Everything, you find out, gets more complicated after a death. I'm almost certain I could work out a one-woman routine about the difficulties of going to Tesco when you're grieving, but I'll save it for another time.

New Year's Eve means you're casting off a year that has not been good to you. On the other hand, you're also leaving behind your loved one in it, to enter a year that they will never know, never see, never be in. It's as if a veil is coming between you and them, separating you permanently – even if there's already the arguably much thicker and impenetrable veil that exists between life and death separating you. Still. When we were in the same year, I always felt that it would almost be possible to reach out and touch my mum. A new year separated us completely.

There was also the new and compelling issue of whether my dad had a date (wondering if your dad is going to be copping a snog being the ultimate complication). Laura, you see, had texted me.

'Dad's got plans tonight for New Year's Eve. With a woman. Do you think it's a date?'

My stomach dropped. I pulled out a chair and sat down at the kitchen table. Dad was dating? How could Dad be dating? Mum's body was barely cold. It was too soon for him to be dating. 'Brazen hussy,' I muttered under my breath.

My phone beeped. Laura had sent another message.

'If it is a date,' it read, 'do you think it's bad Dad has one and I don't?'

I resisted the urge to call and interrogate her and typed out a message instead (very reasonably, I thought, given how I was feeling). 'No, men are rubbish. You're fine. You're living your best single life. What woman?'

'Someone called Susan,' came the reply. 'Dad knows her from church.'

'Oh thank God,' I said to myself. I made the sign of the cross and let myself start breathing again. 'No need to worry. Church means not slutty. She's probably some good soul doing missionary work by taking pity on him.' I dropped my phone and walked through to the next room, where Ollie was standing on a ladder, stringing up fairy lights from the corners of the wall.

'Dad's got plans tonight with some woman called

Susan,' I called as I went. 'But they met at church so that's fine right?'

He pinned a nail into the wall and turned round to me. 'What did you say?'

'Dad's got plans tonight.'

'Great, now we don't have to feel guilty about not seeing him.'

I hugged myself. 'It's with a woman he knows from church. That's not a date, right?'

Ollie climbed down off the ladder and walked over to me. 'No, she's probably some lonely old spinster and he's doing her a favour.' He leaned down to kiss me and squeezed my bum. 'Stop worrying. I want you to enjoy tonight. I'm going to clear the house up before people come over.' He gave my bum a parting smack and walked out of the room.

I sighed. I still felt conflicted. But then, it was New Year's Eve. I always felt conflicted.

I had thought seriously about spending the night at my family's house, with my dad, wrapped up in some of Mum's things. But Ollie had talked me out of this ('there's no way you're doing that' were his exact words). He had persuaded me it would be better to be surrounded with friends who could take my mind off things. He was probably right. My plans had involved some weeping, after all.

Ollie came back into the room holding a mop. He put some music on. 'Look, I know you weren't sure about having a party, but I'm going to make sure you have fun tonight, Han. It's what your mum would want.' He slopped the mop onto the floor, singing 'Auld Lang Syne' off-key under his breath.

I went into the kitchen and pulled out the packets of crisps and dips we had bought for the evening, putting everything into bowls. On the side, Ollie had lined up a selection of bottles. I could hear him singing to himself as he mopped the floor. I smiled. I went upstairs and started running a bath.

That evening, when everything was ready but before anyone had arrived, I wandered about the house in my dress and heels, holding a glass and touching the surfaces lightly, before moving on. I walked into the kitchen, where Ollie was standing, shovelling a handful of crisps into his mouth and stared out of the window into the dark. I looked at my reflection and took a deep breath. The doorbell rang.

I filled two glasses with Prosecco and carried one out into the hallway, where my friend Maria was standing inspecting herself in the mirror. Maria and I had also met at university, where I was studying English and she was doing a Media degree. She now works in PR, which is her natural calling – she's the kind of person who can make you believe your own hype. She is also almost alarmingly attractive and very aware of it, which can make it hard to hold her attention. I handed her a glass and she took it without turning away from her reflection.

'Ah, darling, thank you. I'm gasping,' she drawled, in her studied accent. Maria watched a documentary on

Princess Margaret once and was very influenced by it. Now, when she goes on holiday, she doesn't say she's going to Milan, but Mil-ehn. Even if she's spending the week in Ibiza.

She kissed the mirror and winked at me. 'Gorgeous,' she said. It was unclear which one of us she meant.

I leaned against the wall and sighed. 'I need to perk up, Maria. I'm feeling a bit sad.'

Maria widened her eyes until she looked like a cartoon deer. 'Babe, *I'm* sad. Can you believe this year's over already?'

I frowned. 'Yes. Well. I'm worried my dad might have a date tonight.'

'Oh yeah, parents shagging. Grim.' She looked around. 'I told James to come tonight, but I haven't heard back . . .' She turned back to me. 'Oh babe, I'm sure it's not a date.' She took my hand and squeezed it. 'He's probably just going to see a friend. Someone who will take his mind off the fact this is the first year in decades he's spending without your mum. God knows, New Year's Eve is tough enough at the best of times. Trust me: you Kennedy women are special. You don't just move on from one of you that easily.'

I smiled and squeezed her hand back. 'Thanks, M.'

The front door opened.

'Tommy,' she squealed.

Tommy ran over and picked her up, slinging her over his shoulder. This type of thing happens a lot to Maria.

'Happy New Year, guys.' He smacked her bottom for emphasis.

'Take me to the drinks. That way,' Maria shouted and he galloped off to the kitchen, carrying her away.

I rubbed my temples and walked into the lounge, where people were standing and talking. Most of them, I noticed, were holding green drinks. I went up to Sophie and Lou, who were bent over and fiddling with the music.

'It has to be eighties pop,' Lou was saying, shoving a row of bangles up her arm.

'Can't we at least start with some Britney?' Sophie said.

I slipped my arms around their waists.

'Hannah,' Lou said, squeezing my hand. 'Ollie made me a green drink. Is it safe? I mean, I don't really care: I'll be drinking it either way.'

'We're quite drunk already,' Sophie said, staggering slightly in her court shoes. 'These are really strong. I should probably eat something.'

I raised my glass. 'Good. It's New Year's Eve; we're supposed to be.'

Lou put her drink down and took my face in her hands. 'You don't look drunk enough,' she said. 'We're going to need more drinks.' She turned her head. 'Maestro, drinks,' she shouted.

'Who is maestro?'

She waved me off. 'Someone will have heard me. Now, we are going to have a lot of fun tonight, Han. And then, we're going to have a good year.' She squinted at me. 'We should dance.' She bent and turned up the music.

Ollie walked in holding a tray. 'More drinks,' he said.

144

'Me,' Lou said, skidding towards him and almost taking out Ollie and the tray in the process. 'Your girl-friend needs one, too, Ols. She's not drunk enough.'

Ollie handed me a glass. 'For you.'

I waggled my Prosecco at him.

'Don't care,' he said. 'You can drink both.' He looked at me sternly. 'That's an order, Kennedy.'

I decided at that moment to have a good time. It was what Mum would want. And if I decided at some point that I had had enough, I could go to bed. Mum would probably want that, too.

I emptied my glass and took the new one. Then I drank most of that one, too. I coughed and put my hand over my mouth. It was somehow both sweeter than I had expected and strangely tangy. It was also a lot stronger than I had thought it would be. I felt a bit light-headed.

I took a deep breath. 'A good year,' I said.

'A good year,' Lou and Sophie chanted back.

I put my arms around my friends and we walked the two steps to the centre of the room that was serving as the dance floor.

As the night wore on, surrounded by my friends and people I loved, I was imbued with a deep feeling of well-being. I had also had a lot of Ollie's cocktails by that point. I can't tell you exactly how many, because I lost track after I'd had four, but trust me: it was a lot.

In the lounge, Sophie kept trying to get Mark to dance, while he strategically pointed out that they couldn't: there wasn't space. There were already a lot of people spinning around the floor.

Across the room, Lou was doing karaoke, using a bottle as a microphone. When the doorbell rang again and someone dropped a glass, she looked affronted.

'I'm in the middle of a set,' she shouted.

I didn't even care that Tommy had already broken three shot glasses playing Ring of Fire to warm up the room, or that someone else had managed to get locked in a cupboard and had then taken the hinge off the door, trying to force their way out. 'Offering to the party gods,' I said to myself, in that way that you do when you're very drunk and think there actually might be party gods and they need to be kept happy.

I walked out and sat on the stairs. 'So what if it is a date. It's a church woman,' I said to someone (I don't remember who). They kept darting looks over their shoulder. 'She's probably a good, honest woman. And those women don't have sex, anyway.' I patted their arm. ' 'S fine.'

Ollie ran over. 'It's almost midnight. Quick, you're going to miss it,' he said. He grabbed me and dragged me into the lounge for the countdown.

We skidded into a circle of people. We all gathered together, our hands held, Jools Holland playing in the background. 'Ten, nine, eight,' we shouted. Our spirits were high, filled with expectation for this New Year.

'Seven—'

'Wait,' someone else shouted. They pointed a finger

at the muted television screen, which showed the time. 'We've missed it. It's twelve oh one already.'

We looked at each other, unsure what to do. Then someone shrugged and we continued.

'Five, four, three . . .'

A party horn blew. Everyone cheered and hugged. Ollie kissed me.

'Spend New Year's Eve together; spend the year together. That's the superstition,' I said. 'You're stuck with me now.'

Ollie laughed. 'I planned to, anyway.'

I squinted at him. I wondered what he would say if I became horribly depressed, lost myself in my grief and went into a downward spiral, until I couldn't even get out of bed in the morning.

He wrapped his arms round my waist. 'You're having a good time, right?'

Before I said anything, I was grabbed from behind and someone else pulled him away into a celebratory hug.

I broke away and walked back into the kitchen to get a glass of water and held on to the sink for a moment, staring out of the window at my reflection. It was a new year and I was fine. I was enjoying myself. 'A good time,' I mouthed at myself and winked.

A good deal of truly terrible dancing ensued, which more and more people got sucked into, like some snowball of the Mexican wave and hip thrusting, until it climaxed with a conga line snaking round the house to the sound of The O'Jays' 'Love Train'. It only ended when someone in a baseball cap tripped on a stair and took three other people out in the process. They slid down the stairs, knocking over others as they went. A green drink was thrown into the air and onto our previously white wall. This was all caught on camera by some other guy I didn't recognise, who was cheering.

'Yuss, YouTube,' he yelled, pumping his fist in the air. I wondered who had brought him.

It's unfortunate this only happened early; there isn't really anywhere for a party to go after a moment like that.

I collapsed onto the sofa next to Mark. Mark is someone I always seem to find on sofas at parties. I mean this in a good way. It's important to know your role at parties.

I put my head on his shoulder and watched as Maria danced on top of our coffee table. 'A good year,' I said.

'I think Olivia ripped my trousers,' Mark said.

Olivia came up to me.

'Hannah, Sophie's in the bathroom. I think she needs some help.'

I went upstairs. Sophie was spread-eagled on the bathroom floor, her silk dress fanning out from her body, a wet flannel folded over her eyes. She lifted it slightly as I walked in.

'Everything's green,' she said. 'I'm dying.'

'The green drinks. What did Ollie put in them?' I said. I sat on the floor next to her and put a hand on her forehead. 'And why the flannel?'

'It always seems to work in films.'

There was a knock on the door.

'Hannah?' Ollie called. 'Maria's here and she needs you. Can you let her in?'

I got up and opened the door and Maria burst in, sobbing noisily.

She threw herself at me. 'James didn't come,' she said.

I patted her back. 'He still could,' I said. 'It's early . . . ish.'

'He missed midnight. What's even the point any more? If he can't be bothered to see me for the most important night of the year, then why should I care about him?' She pulled away and went to the mirror, taking her eyeliner out of her pocket. 'I mean, what's so wrong with me? Am I so unlovable?'

Maria is the only person I've ever known who can expertly reapply a cat eye, while still appearing to cry.

Someone knocked on the door, again.

'It's busy,' Maria snapped.

'Soph, how are you feeling?' I said.

She pulled herself up. 'I have transcended this life.' She burped and lurched towards the toilet.

There was another knock.

'Can't people wait?' Maria said. 'Oh my God, don't be sick, Sophie. It's so tacky.'

'Han, it's me,' Ollie said. 'Is Maria in there? James is here.'

Maria flung the door open and stormed down the stairs, her arm outstretched like she was trying to ward off an evil spirit. 'No,' she hissed.

I glanced at Sophie. 'Right. Well, I guess that was the end of that moment we were having, anyway.'

I could hear James's voice. 'Maria, I told you. It's my brother's birthday. I was the first to leave . . .'

I went to the door, leaning out and looking down the stairs.

Maria was planted in the middle of the hallway. 'It's not good enough, James.' She took off her shoe and threw it at him. 'Everybody else made it on time.'

'But Maria,' James said.

'It's too late. Everyone agrees with me. You.' She pointed to someone who took a step backwards and pressed themselves into the wall. 'You told me earlier you thought James was in the wrong, didn't you. No, look at me. Didn't you tell me you thought James was in the wrong? Come back and tell him.'

I shut the bathroom door and looked at Sophie. 'I should probably go back down.' I said. 'Can you move?'

She nodded. 'I'll be down in a minute,' she said.

I slipped out and went downstairs. Ollie met me at the bottom.

'Is Maria okay?' he said. 'She seemed really upset.'

'She's just fulfilling her role at parties,' I said. 'God, here she comes.'

The front door slammed and Maria stomped back in.

'Your neighbours are so rude. They told me off for making too much noise. I was having a conversation.'

Ollie and I exchanged a glance.

'Maria,' I said.

'They have quite young kids,' Ollie said.

'People can be so bourgeois,' she said. She stuck a cigarette in her mouth.

'You can't smoke that in here,' I said.

Ollie pointed her towards the kitchen. 'Back door.'

Tommy came in. 'The bathroom was full, so I peed in the garden,' he said. Then he saw me. 'Hannah, don't worry. I did it through the hedge.'

In the next room, something smashed.

'YouTube,' someone shouted.

Ollie looked at me again, a bit guiltily, this time. 'Don't kill me,' the look said.

I clenched my fists. 'Ollie, the neighbours are going to kill us. I don't want to have to deal with that. I didn't even want this party in the first place.'

'I know, I know. Look, it's fine,' he said. 'It's New Year's Eve. People expect a bit of noise.'

I took a deep breath and exhaled, then went back into the lounge. Mark was still on the sofa, only now with Lou passed out on top of him.

'The green drink.' He nodded, sagely.

I nodded back. 'Another victim. Can I get you anything?' I asked.

'Maybe a beer?'

I went into the kitchen. Maria was holding forth, talking at one of Ollie's friends, Josh, who had the look of a man who regretted his choices.

'I just don't understand where the good men are, you know? Like, what is so wrong with me?' She punctuated this question with her cleavage. 'Why is it so hard for me to find men?'

Sophie came into the kitchen. I poured her a glass of water and gave it to her.

151

'Didn't you sleep with that guy from that boy band, once? What were they called, Hand? You said he was nice.'

Maria turned on her. 'Fist,' she said. 'He was the thumb. And so what? I'm allowed to have sex, Sophie.' Here, her voice started to quaver and she dabbed under her eye with a finger. 'But, you know, people just use me for my body then leave. Thanks for bringing that up, Soph. You know, that's a really hurtful memory.' She tossed her hair and walked out of the kitchen. 'I can't even believe you right now.'

Sophie looked at me. 'Maria's on form then. I think it would be good if I stayed away from her now.' She walked out, too.

I gripped the kitchen counter. I thought about the days when I was little and New Year's Eve had involved wearing pyjamas and watching a film with Evie, while downstairs, our parents were having a party. Every now and then, Mum would bring us up some smuggled canapés, which had felt like stolen loot. We'd usually be asleep before it got to ten o'clock, but sometimes, around midnight, I would wake up to Mum or Dad kissing me on the head and whispering 'Happy New Year'. Then I'd go back to sleep again and wake up in the morning to a house that looked battered and Mum and Dad, who looked even worse. I felt a deep longing for those days.

Josh cleared his throat. 'That James guy. He sounds like he really messed her up.'

Ollie came back into the kitchen. 'Han? Maria looks upset again. Maybe you should go look after her.'

152

I tightened my grip on the counter. 'No,' I said. 'No, I think I'm done.'

'But Han, that James guy has really hurt her,' Ollie said.

I threw my hands up in the air. 'They've only been on two dates. And he left his brother's birthday party to come here.' I was almost shouting. 'And you know what, I don't care. There are bigger problems in the world right now. My mum died. She is dead.'

Josh looked as if he wished he were the one who was dead.

'And my dad might be shagging some slutty nun, right now.' This I did shout. I know this, because quite a few people reported having heard me later on. They also asked how my dad was getting on with the nun.

Ollie cleared his throat. 'Hannah,' he said.

'I know, I know,' I said. 'Don't talk about death at parties. Don't worry, I think I'm done with this new year, now, anyway. If you'll excuse me, I'm going now. Possibly forever.'

I swept past the people that were standing in the doorway, evidently trying not to show they had been listening and into the hallway, pushing past someone I didn't recognise.

I pulled my phone out of my pocket and fired off a text to Laura. 'IS DAD SHAGGING,' it read.

I looked up just in time to see the front door bang open and our next-door neighbour walk in. I took a step back. He had the look of a new parent. He pushed past the scrum of people and came up to me.

'Look,' he said. 'I know it's New Year's Eve, but this has been going on long enough. The noise levels are insane. If you don't do something, I'm going to call your landlord.'

I stared at him. 'Ollie,' I shrieked. I smiled at the neighbour. 'Goodbye.'

Ollie came running through. 'Hi,' he said. 'Shit, hello.'

I squeezed past them just as Mark came out of the lounge.

I looked at him. 'You're not on the sofa,' I said.

He frowned at me. 'No?' he said.

I gestured towards the front door. 'I'm leaving.'

'This is your party.'

'I know. I'm still leaving.'

Mark scratched his cheek. 'Okay. Want some company?'

'Sure,' I said.

I grabbed my keys from the hook by the front door and walked out. Right into Maria, who was wrapped around James. She had one leg hooked around his waist. I noticed she was missing a shoe.

Maria opened her eyes and saw me. 'Hannah,' she said. She grabbed my dress. 'We made up. He came back.'

I glanced at James. I was sure I'd seen his butt on a Hollister advert. I uncurled Maria's fingers from my dress and pulled her hand off me. 'That's nice, Maria. But I don't care, actually. About any of this.'

'Babe,' Maria said.

I smiled and walked off with Mark trailing behind me.

Mark cleared his throat. 'So, where are we going?' he said.

'I don't know,' I said. 'I haven't worked out the specifics.'

'Okay.'

We walked in silence for a bit. Every now and then, Mark glanced at me. I ignored him. I was concentrating on the aggressive power walk I was doing.

We got to the end of our street, where another house stood with its front door open, like ours was. Other drunken people were stumbling out in their party hats, spilling out onto the pavement and heading towards the next bash. The beat from their music was registering in my chest, like an extra heartbeat. Mark looked at me.

I opened my mouth and screamed. I mean it: I really screamed. It was the kind of howl that people in films usually do at the sea, or into the wind, which, admittedly, I could have done. But we were in the middle of town and besides, no one actually wants to go to Brighton beach on New Year's Eve, unless they want to wade through a crowd of the paper lanterns that people insist on letting off there. So instead, I screamed into the sound of drunk parties and New Year celebrations. This lasted for at least a couple of seconds. I gathered my breath and opened my mouth again. 'I really bloody HATE NEW YEAR'S EVE,' I yelled.

Then I stopped and sat down on the pavement. Mark looked around, then sat down next to me.

I settled the skirt of my dress down around me and

155

put my head in my hands. 'Have you ever lost someone?' I said.

'Yes,' he said.

I looked up. 'I'm sorry,' I said.

'It's okay. It was a hamster. I was eleven.'

'Ah, so you know what I'm going through.'

'Sort of. I did find the hamster again, though. It was in my sister's doll's house.'

'What was it doing there?'

'She was having a tea party.'

'Right.'

'It died after that. Not straight away. It was probably another six months.'

'That must have been hard: finding it, only to lose it again. What a rollercoaster of emotion.'

Mark nodded. 'It was. So. What are we doing here?'

I sighed. 'I don't know,' I said.

I wanted to go home. Not the home that I had just walked out of (the door to which our neighbours would be knocking on again, in a few short hours, to complain about the noise level in general and the drunk woman in particular who had been screeching 'James' outside their bedroom window). Home, home. The one I had grown up in. I wanted to put on pyjamas that were worn thin from use, get into my childhood bed and cry. But I couldn't do that – there were nuns being defiled there. In fact, at that moment, I was fairly sure I'd never be able to go home again. Home was dead.

I looked up at Mark, who was watching me.

He smiled and looped his arm around my shoulder. 'It'll be okay.'

I closed one eye and assessed him. 'You're good at being there, Mark. You were at the funeral, too. That was nice of you.' He felt like a safe port in the storm away from the madness of the night. He felt like someone who could be there for me. Unlike Ollie, who had brought the storm to my house. He felt like what I needed. I looked at him, my eyes dropping down to his mouth. I half-closed my eyes and leaned in towards him.

He reared back in surprise so quickly he almost fell backwards onto the pavement and grabbed my shoulders. 'Woah.'

I looked at him, then straightened up, mortified. I grabbed my head. 'Oh my God.' I had no idea why I had done that. I was with Ollie. I loved Ollie. And Mark was looking at me like I'd grown another head.

He scrambled to his feet. 'What was that? Ollie . . .'

'Shit. Nothing. I don't know. I'm sorry.'

'We're friends. Only friends. And Ollie's my friend, too. I'm sorry if I gave off a signal? I was just trying to be there for you. As a friend.' He pushed the air down with his hands for emphasis.

I staggered to my feet. 'No. No signals. I don't even know why I did that. I don't know what came over me. Can we just forget it?'

'Yeah, of course. Nothing even happened, anyway.' He wiped his mouth with the back of his lips, which honestly, felt slightly insulting. I hadn't even touched him.

I nodded and turned, walking quickly back home, clutching my head. Mark followed behind me, hurrying to catch up. When we got there, I pushed open the front door and walked inside.

Ollie saw me and ran up. 'Han, there you are. Don't worry, I've sorted it out with the neighbours. Where did you go?' He looked at Mark. 'Hi, Mark.'

I felt sick. I pushed past him and raced upstairs. I crawled into my bed, fully dressed and with all my make-up on and cried. There's a lot to be said for not entering a new year with an old year's make-up on, but at that moment, I chose to forgive myself, because I knew that someone would be crying in the bathroom or someone else would be sick and either way, I didn't have the energy to deal with it.

I thought about the night and what I had almost done with Mark. I thought about Mum and the New Year ahead, which she wouldn't be in.

I decided I needed a change and that change needed to be me. I decided this a lot on New Year's Eves and so far, it had never resulted in actual change. But this time would be different. I was going to make myself into a different person. I would no longer be the old, messy Hannah, the Hannah that made resolutions she forgot about by February. I was going to be better than that: an adult, together Hannah. It was going to be a new year and I was going to be a new me.

I wondered if I could get that embroidered on a pillow.

How to Be a Sister

'I think Dad's having an affair.'

I stared at my phone. It was a text from Laura confirming something I had long suspected: nothing good ever came from reading her messages.

'He's been emailing someone in secret. He keeps the door closed,' she wrote. 'Suspicious.'

Like any information you don't want to receive and wish you never had, I didn't know what to do with this. I thought we had got over the hump, so to speak. I had seen Dad after New Year's Eve and had subtly interrogated him about his plans.

'How was your New Year's Eve?' I said.

'Oh, fine,' he said. We were standing in the kitchen and he was making coffee. 'I had dinner with a woman from church called Susan and her husband.'

'Husband?' I looked round at Laura, who was also in the kitchen and raised an eyebrow. She just shrugged and sipped her tea.

'Father Ray was there, too. Yes, it was fine.' He handed me a mug of coffee. 'Nothing like the New Years' Eves I had with your mum.' He chuckled. 'Remember the year

Barry almost died? Well, I suppose you were too young. He's a deacon now . . .'

The point is, I thought we were past it. So this text was particularly troubling.

I made a mental note to stop reading Laura's messages and stuffed my phone down the side of a sofa cushion so I wouldn't have to look at it. I didn't have time to dismantle Dad's new dedication to private correspondence. I had something else to think about: Mum's upcoming birthday.

When it comes to all the firsts that you have to do without them, their first birthday, you find out, is a particularly wretched one.

It's as if the day has been set up to mock you and what you no longer have. What was a period of celebration in the calendar has become yet another one that signals that great gaping hole in your life. All at once, you realise how vindictive something as simple as the greeting-card display at a supermarket really is, showing off birthday cards that you no longer have a need for. Balloons, in particular, become hostile and passive aggressive in a way you never thought possible from inanimate objects. All the people pushing their trollies along without noticing this seem wilfully blind and stupid to you. But just as you're feeling emotionally superior, you realise you're equally blind and stupid, because you didn't realise any of this when you were happy, either. In fact, you're even blinder and more stupid, because even now that you're aware how on certain days, the birthday cards can be malevolent, you're still largely oblivious to this the rest of the year. And you haven't even thought of the effects the other cards, the ones specific to grandparents, sisters and children, could be having on other people.

This makes going to the supermarket even more complicated than it already is when grieving, which I realised while in the supermarket. I then proceeded to monologue all of this to Ollie, until eventually, he turned to me and said, 'Hannah, we're in the bloody vegetable aisle,' which was true.

'Fine,' I said. 'But what do I do about Mum's birthday?'

Ollie suggested I ignore it; Evie asked if I wanted to go to brunch. Neither felt right or what I really wanted to do, which was be morose, eat and wallow a bit, while everyone around me acknowledged that this day would never be the same, the world would never be the same. And also my insightful point about birthday cards.

In the end, I decided there was only one thing we could do. We all needed to go and see her grave. It was the closest we could come to being with her.

'It's what you do when someone has died,' I said. I was standing in the kitchen of my family home, holding a pack of seeds. 'We can plant something colourful. Mum would like that.'

Laura nodded. 'I can't bear the thought of her alone on her birthday,' she said.

'Iris is at the front door,' Dad said.

I looked out of the window. 'Someone left irises?'

'No,' he said, through clenched teeth. 'My sister Iris

is here.' He huffed. 'What the bloody hell is she doing here?' He looked at me.

I held up my hands. 'It wasn't me this time, I swear. I didn't invite her.'

Dad looked away.

'I did invite Cathy and Dan to meet us at the grave, though,' I said.

Dad glared at me.

A fingernail tapped on the window. It was Iris. 'Are you going to let me in or should I stand out here all day?'

Dad grimaced and went to open the front door. 'Iris. What are you doing here?'

'Don't be stupid, Patrick. It's Jennifer's birthday. Family should be together at times like this.' She eyed him. 'Even if you didn't think to invite me yourself.'

Dad sighed. 'We're going to visit her grave,' he said.

'Well, what are you waiting around here for?'

As a family, we had been big on birthdays, mainly because Mum was big on birthdays and always made them special for us. I had the feeling that if it had been someone else who had died, we wouldn't be trudging to their grave with flowers. Mum would have said that graveyards are too depressing for birthdays, even if the person of honour was buried in one and would have come up with some far better tribute or celebration than that. But Mum wasn't there to plan something. That was the whole point. So we went to her grave, the four of us trudging over damp grass, while Ollie waited in the car.

'It's not my place,' he said.

'She loved you,' I said.

'I think you should spend this moment together as a family,' he said.

'That's silly,' I said.

He was already on his phone, scrolling through Twitter. 'Get out of the car,' he said.

So I got out and followed Dad, Iris and Laura to Mum's grave. This is where we came across a problem. We had forgotten where we had buried her.

It turns out, you have to wait after you've buried someone before you can put the headstone in, which takes a lot longer than it does on television and in films. In the meantime, we had become collectively confused on the exact location.

'It must be here. It's the next along in this row,' Dad said.

I pointed behind him. 'But they've started a fresh row, there.'

'The ground's been recently dug up, here,' Laura said.

'That's a molehill,' I said. 'I really think it was over here.'

'Honestly, Patrick. Have you forgotten already where they buried your wife?' Iris said. 'How careless of you.'

'This is ridiculous,' Dad said. 'There must be some record. They have to plot these things out very carefully.'

I frowned. 'Yes, but that doesn't help us now.'

'What do we do now?' Laura held up her bouquet. 'Where do we put our flowers?'

'I bought seeds.' I shook my packet to demonstrate.

163

'You can't plant them just anywhere,' Laura said. 'What if you got someone else's grave? They might not like flowers or they could be allergic.'

I stared at her.

Dad waved his hands. 'This is absurd. It's obvious: she's buried right here.'

'Good Lord,' Iris said. 'She's here?'

'Mum? Where?' Laura said. But Iris was looking towards the entrance of the graveyard.

We looked up. Dan and Cathy were making their way towards us. Dan was carrying flowers. Cathy was wearing a veil.

Dad glanced at Iris. 'As you said, Iris. Family should be together.'

'Hi, everyone,' Dan said, when they made it to us. He shook Dad's hand and hugged Laura and me. 'Iris,' he nodded.

Iris nodded back.

Cathy lifted her veil. 'Patrick, girls. A once-blessed day has turned sour. Iris. What are you doing here?'

Iris took a step closer to Laura and me. 'Well, Cathy, I thought family should be together on a day like this.'

Cathy put a hand to her chest. 'How wonderful that you continue to show up, even though you never liked Jenny in life.' She looked at Laura and me. 'Take this as a lesson, girls. Regrets about the fences you refused to mend in life can be painful, I know. But I'm sure she appreciates the effort from beyond the grave, dear.' She patted Iris's hand, which Iris quickly withdrew.

Iris forced a pursed smile, which was made more

164

difficult by the fact that her lips had almost disappeared into her teeth.

Cathy looked around at us. 'Where is she? Where is our Jenny?'

'Ah,' Dad said.

'Well,' I said.

'We can't remember,' Laura said.

Cathy put a hand to her brow.

In the end, we decided to hedge our bets and each stood at different places in the graveyard, having separate chats with Mum. At least this way, she'd be able to hear one of us. Iris hovered behind Dad, glowering at Cathy.

I squatted down. 'Happy birthday, Mum. I know you're not really here. Well, you're almost certainly not here, here. I think Laura might have been closer with the molehill. I meant more in the metaphysical sense. But I hope wherever you are, you can hear me and it's somewhere where birthdays are celebrated. I know this isn't how you would have done today. Well, obviously. You would have made sure no one was sad and moping around a graveyard. You'd at least have remembered exactly where the grave was. You would have made a cake and ensured it was a day worth celebrating, like you always did. I miss you, so much. I'm doing my best to take care of everyone, though. I really feel like that's my role now that you're not here. At least it's something I can do for you. I hope you approve.' I was silent for a moment. I stood up.

Iris marched over to me. 'Hannah, is your aunt intending to spend the rest of the day with you?'

I glanced over at Cathy, who was on her knees, beating her chest over what I was fairly sure was someone else's grave. I looked back at Iris. 'Well, we haven't really spoken about it, but . . .' I shrugged. '. . . I think she might want to.'

Iris sighed. 'Honestly, how inconsiderate of her implanting herself on you on this day of all days. Has she no thought to what you might like to do today? It might not involve her.'

Dan and Cathy walked over to us.

'I really felt like I got in touch with her, you know. I feel she heard me,' Cathy said.

Iris looked at her. 'I believe that was someone else's grave, actually, Cathy.'

Cathy wiped under her eyes. 'Oh, I know that. I like to visit the ones that are a bit neglected, too, when I can. It's so sad to think of those who don't have anyone coming to visit them.' She looked at Iris. 'Perhaps one day, I can even do it for you, dear.'

Iris's lips disappeared again. She looked at me. 'Hannah, I have a train to catch. I don't want to intrude any further on this day of yours. I understand needing your space.'

'Do you need a lift to the station?'

'It's fine. I'll take a taxi.' She patted my hand, then marched over to my dad.

Dan and Cathy watched her go, then turned back to me.

166

'We should get going, too,' Dan said. 'Thanks for inviting us today.' He hugged me.

Cathy squeezed me, then lowered the veil back over her face.

On my way back to the car, I scattered some seeds around the edge of the site. That way, everyone could enjoy them, I thought to myself.

I got back in the car while Dad and Laura finished their talks.

'Iris has left,' I said. 'And we need to go buy a cake. For Mum. A birthday cake.'

'Okay,' Ollie said. He was still looking at his phone. 'Why weren't you all standing together?'

'We can't remember where Mum's buried.'

He looked up. 'You've forgotten already? It's right over there, next to that last grave. There's a marker in the grass,' he said and pointed at a fourth location none of us had been standing at.

'Oh,' I said. I bit my nail. 'Do you think I should tell them?'

Dad and Laura got back to the car. 'Strap in. We're going to get cake,' I said.

They both looked at me blankly. 'Why?'

'Because it's Mum's birthday and birthdays have cake. It's like presents at Christmas. There has to be cake.'

'I was going to go to bed,' Laura said.

'It's a bit of a waste. She's not here to eat it,' Dad said.

Ollie put his hand on my shoulder. 'Hannah, maybe we should—'

'Cake,' I said. 'It's what Mum would do.'

I made everyone come to the supermarket and choose a cake, and then when we got back, I cut it into slices and dished it out. I felt like a benign hostage-taker, who ultimately hopes to win her captives over to her cause with kindness and good will. I felt like Marie Antoinette. Dad and Laura, on the other hand, were beginning to look mutinous.

'I'm not singing,' Laura said.

'Sing? We're not going to put candles on it, are we?' Dad said.

'No,' I said.

'Well what do we do now?'

Let them eat cake, I thought.

'We eat cake.'

This would bring us together. This would make the day less bone-achingly sad. This would start a new tradition, which we could take comfort from each year. We could tell our favourite stories about Mum and remember her how she would want to be remembered.

'We could tell our favourite stories about Mum and remember her how she would want to be remembered,' I said.

'No thanks,' Laura said. She held up her empty plate. 'I'm going to go to bed, now.'

'Wait,' I said. 'You can't. Not yet.'

She sighed and crossed her arms. 'Why not? We did the cake like you wanted.'

'Because that's not what Mum would want. Mum wouldn't want you to be sad. She'd want us to be together. She would make this into a nice day for us all. We still have time. We can make it fun.' I started to chuckle. 'Remember that time when—'

Laura stood up. 'No, we can't. Mum's not here, Hannah. That's the point. And nothing you're doing is making any of this any better. You're not her. You can't fix this, so stop trying.'

I stood up. 'Laura.'

'No. I'm sick of your desperate need to keep things exactly as they were before. They're not the same. They never will be the same again. Stop trying. You're just making everything much worse.' Her voice was rising. 'She's my dead mum, too.'

She marched out of the room.

I followed her out. 'What does that mean?'

Laura was halfway up the stairs. She turned. 'I want to grieve, too and I can't because you're making us eat cake. I wanted to be sad today, from my bed. But when your eyes go wide like that and you start to smile with all your teeth showing, it's very hard to say no to you.' She flapped her arms. 'God, you weren't even there when it happened, Hannah. I was. I'm the one that saw that happen.' She wiped her nose, roughly, with her hand.

I leaned forward. 'Yeah, you were. Which means you got to see her before she died. You got to hear her last words. I don't even have that.'

Laura clutched at her head. 'This is exactly the kind of thing my counsellor doesn't believe really happens when I tell her about us.'

I frowned. 'You're having counselling?' Why hadn't she told me she was having counselling?

169

'Of course I'm having counselling. Look at me.' She gestured at herself. 'Do I look like I'm doing well?' I looked at her. She did not. She was openly crying, her cheeks bright red and stained with tears and her voice had begun to shake. 'But you.' She glared at me. 'You're even worse. You're monopolising all the grief. You are a grief hog.'

I blanched. 'I'm not hogging the grief. I don't even want the grief. You can have it. Here.' I started wafting air at her. 'Take it. Take the grief.'

'It's too late,' Laura said. She pulled at her earlobe. 'I'm dressed now. And I lost an earring at the grave earlier. And it's all because of you.' She stormed upstairs, sobbing, slamming her bedroom door behind her.

I marched downstairs and back into the lounge, where Ollie and Dad were sitting, trying not to look anywhere.

There was silence.

'Shall we put the TV on?' Dad said.

A few days later, I stuffed my laptop in my bag and went over to Dad's again. I told Ollie I was working there so I could check up on him and keep him company. I told myself the same thing, but in reality, I wanted to know if what Laura had said, about his secret email correspondence, was true. I wanted to find out for myself if something was going on.

Dad opened the door to me. 'You're here. Again.'

I pushed my way in. 'Internet at mine is down. Got a deadline. Working here today. Can I use your desk?'

'Have you made up with Laura, yet?'

I stopped on my way towards the stairs. 'Do you actually want to know?'

Dad shifted his weight. 'Yes.'

I crossed my arms. 'Really? You really want to get involved?'

He sighed. 'No.'

'I'll be in your study.'

I walked upstairs and shut the door behind me, opening my laptop as an alibi in case Dad walked in.

I sat in his office chair and stared at the blank screen, shaking the mouse to wake it up. When it did, I saw that there was an email open on his screen.

I'm lying. I opened his email and I scrolled through the list of his most recent ones until I found something that stopped me.

There is an argument here that I shouldn't have done that. In fact, that I shouldn't have been there at all, snooping through my dad's private correspondence. It's a good one, about privacy and genies and bottles. It's an argument I have delivered to my friends when they're considering reading their partners' texts. You should never do it and the reason is that if you do find something you don't like, you can't say anything about it without revealing you've been snooping. Then, it doesn't become a discussion about why they have been asking their best friend's ex for sex photos and becomes instead about the fact that you've irreparably violated their trust and privacy. This is another one of those things I have experience with. As good as that argument is, I wasn't thinking of it at that moment. I was too busy reading Dad's emails. Specifically, this one:

From: jessopb@aol.com
To: patrickkennedy@easynet.com

I'm here for you. We'll get through this. Together.
With love,
B

Then I reread it. I thought about that word 'together' and what it meant when it formed its own sentence, as it did in the email. I wondered who B was and what she would be getting through with my dad. Together. There was that word again. And I hadn't even touched on the fact that it was signed 'with love'. I felt a bit sick. I was beginning to think that Laura had been right about my dad having an affair, even if she had been wrong about New Year's Eve. Maybe he had met someone else already. I was barely talking to Laura: I didn't want to admit she could be right about anything at that moment, let alone this.

I thought about the man who had been grieving for my mum. Who – and not too long ago, I might add – had had a tampon wedged up his nose. Was there such a national shortage of unattached men of a certain age that single women had to jump on anything, because I'd always assumed that was an urban myth they told unmarried women over the age of thirty-five.

I thought about talking to Dad about it, but then

172

he'd know I'd read his email. There was also the very important fact that I didn't want to know. No one wants to think about their parents having sex, but it's even worse when that sex isn't with each other.

I took a deep breath and thought about the fact that no matter how much it might bother me, my dad was a grown man and entitled to meet someone else he might want to date, someday.

I'm lying again. I was too busy wondering how long this had been going on for.

I closed the email before I could read it a third time.

I heard Dad's footsteps on the stairs and turned off his computer.

'Hannah,' he said opening the door.

I threw myself onto my laptop and pretended to type frantically.

'Since you're here again, instead of at your own home, where you now live, could you make us some lunch?'

'Sure,' I said. 'Let me just send this email.' I stopped typing and clicked randomly on my desktop. 'And done.'

I didn't listen to a word Dad said as I stuck cheese and lettuce between slices of buttered bread that day and handed them to him on a plate. I couldn't, because all I could think about was the time a man had mysteriously slipped me his number in a pub one night. I had then googled it, feeling like a techy Miss Marple. This turned out to be a stroke of genius as I found it linked to two adverts: one looking for someone who would come over to watch *X-Factor* and then have sex with him and the other selling his TV. This is the kind of information you always want to know before you contact a complete stranger, but rarely do until you're already on a date and wondering if you're going to be murdered by this man who's quietly shredding beer mats and suggesting you go back to his in time to catch *X-Factor*.

I was fairly sure I could replicate my success. In fact, I left Dad's fully intending to retreat to my bed with my laptop and spend the weekend furtively googling B's email address to see what I could uncover. Ideally, there would be something that proved her to be a virtuous woman who would never think about having an affair with someone else's recently bereaved husband, and also a lesbian — perhaps in an interview she did with her local paper or her Women's Institute group's blog. The only thing that stopped me was that I had heard from Charlotte. She wanted to go to lunch with Laura and me. I told myself I had to go. That she was Mum's best friend and I should spend more time with her. That this would be good. That it would stop me from googling the definition of 'together' for possible hidden subtext.

'I ordered Prosecco,' Charlotte said, as Laura and I sat down. We had met outside the restaurant, nodded at each other and walked in, which was as close to an apology as either one of us was willing to go.

'How was it the other day, your mum's birthday? I was thinking about you all. And Jen.'

Laura and I glanced at each other.

'Really hard,' Laura said.

'Pretty terrible,' I said.

Charlotte took our hands. 'I don't think it's ever going to be easy. People say it gets easier, but this is always going to be something you have to get through. I know I found it horribly hard, not being able to talk to her.'

'We tried to talk to her,' I said.

'We lost Mum's grave,' Laura said.

I raised a finger. 'Then we found it again.'

'And Iris was there.'

'And Cathy.'

Charlotte looked from one to the other of us. 'Okay,' she said. 'Maybe we should order.'

After that, we moved on to 'safer topics', like Charlotte's taxes. We had almost finished eating by the time we circled back to discussing anything serious.

Charlotte put down her cutlery. 'Right. We've avoided it for long enough. How have you both been coping? Really?'

She said this without the furrowed brow squint that you get a lot when people ask you this question.

Laura drained her glass. 'I think Dad's having an affair,' she said.

I lowered my glass and took a deep breath.

Charlotte looked alarmed. 'What makes you think that?'

'He's been talking to some woman named Betty.'

I thought of the email.

'He's been sending her emails.'

'Well,' Charlotte said. 'That doesn't necessarily mean—'

I leaned forward. 'She's right. I saw it for myself. I read Dad's email.'

They both looked at me.

'I know I shouldn't have done, but I saw an email. It was to someone named B. Or Betty, thinking about it. Betty makes sense.'

Charlotte frowned. 'Guys . . .'

Laura leaned in, her hands on the table. 'What did it say?'

'That they'd get through this. Together.'

'Together?' Laura said.

'Together.' I nodded.

'So . . .' Charlotte said.

'And she signed it with love.'

'With love,' Laura whispered.

'With love. What do you think it means?'

'He's having an affair.'

I nodded. 'He's having an affair.'

'They've been talking on the phone, too,' she said. 'I think they're planning to meet up.'

'What?' I said. 'You didn't tell me this.'

Laura shrugged. 'I didn't want to upset you. And it didn't seem like you wanted to know after the whole New Year's thing.'

'New Year's thing?' Charlotte said.

'Dad spent it with a woman,' Laura said.

'Yes, but also with her husband and a priest,' I said. 'I don't think that one counted.'

Charlotte cleared her throat. 'Okay. Well, this doesn't mean anything. They could just be friends.'

Laura raised an eyebrow. 'He calls her with the door closed,' she said, with a meaningful look.

Charlotte sat up, straighter. 'It doesn't mean he's having an affair. I'm sure it's nothing,' she said. 'Like with the priest. Even if it was something, it would probably just be a comfort thing, a distraction . . .'

I grabbed my drink and swiftly necked it.

'But it's probably nothing,' she added. 'Let's change the subject. Laura, it's almost your birthday. Are you doing anything special?'

I froze.

Laura fiddled with her glass. 'I don't know. Without Mum here, I don't know if I feel up to it.'

'Nonsense,' Charlotte smiled at me. 'I'm sure your dad and Hannah have something planned. Birthdays are important.'

She probably said a lot more than this, but I wouldn't know because I had stopped listening. I was too busy mentally berating myself and panicking. We had forgotten Laura's birthday.

Charlotte picked up the empty bottle, calling me back into focus. 'Shall we have another?' she said.

'I have to go,' I said, too loudly.

'Okay, we'll just get the bill then,' Charlotte said.

'Yes,' I nodded. 'Great.' I stood up and grabbed the waiter that was walking past our table. 'The bill, please.'

Charlotte and Laura looked at each other.

'I didn't realise you were in such a rush, Han,' Charlotte said.

On our way out, Laura pulled me back. 'Han, if what I said about Dad upset you, then I'm sorry.'

I shook my head. 'I'm not upset. And you heard Charlotte. There might not be any reason to be upset. We're probably overreacting. Like we did with New Year's Eve.'

Laura didn't say anything.

'And I'm sorry for the other day, too. Forcing cake on you. But I just want you to remember that whatever else happens, I did bring you birthday cake once. I have to go.' We hugged goodbye and I charged off in the opposite direction.

As soon as I was alone, I called Dad, tapping my foot while I waited for him to pick up.

I didn't know how we could have let this happen. Yes, we were distracted trying to get through Mum's birthday, but that wasn't much of an excuse: Laura's birthday was always right after Mum's. Mum used to say Laura was the best birthday present she could have ever asked for, even if she was a few days late. This used to make me irrationally jealous when I was little. Forgetting about the day entirely, twenty-three years later and right after our mum had died, though, felt like a particularly cruel revenge.

Finally, Dad picked up the phone.

'We forgot Laura's birthday,' I said.

'What?'

'We were so busy worrying about Mum's birthday that we forgot Laura's.'

'We couldn't have done,' Dad said. 'When is it?'

I clenched my fist until my nails disappeared into the flesh. 'Tomorrow,' I said.

'Didn't you buy her anything?'

'Me? Why me?'

'You bought all her Christmas presents. How could you let this happen? She's your sister.'

'She's your daughter. You helped make her.' I said this deliberately; Dad finds acknowledging even fundamental biology crass.

'There's no need to bring that into things,' he said. 'That was mainly your mother, anyway.'

'What are we going to do?' I said. 'It's *tomorrow*.'

'Maybe she's forgotten, too?'

'Of course she hasn't forgotten. She was just talking about it at lunch. How do you think I remembered it?'

Dad sighed. 'Can't we just ignore it? Make it up to her next year. She's an adult, now.'

'Dad,' I snapped, 'it's her first birthday without Mum. We can't ignore it. Mum would never let that happen.'

'Well, what do we do then?'

'For starters, you're going to have to buy her a present. I'll make her a cake.'

'We have cake here. Can't we use that?'

'Mum's cake?' I sighed. 'You can't give someone left-over cake from someone else's birthday, Dad, no.'

'I don't see what's wrong with it. It's a very nice cake. Sainsbury's finest: it says it right on the box,' he said.

'I'll be round tomorrow after work,' I said and hung up.

I fired out a quick text to a few of Laura's friends.

'Don't know if you remembered . . .' it said. I decided to leave out the fact that her own family hadn't. 'But it's Laura's birthday tomorrow. Do you have any plans for tomorrow night? Might be nice to do something for her.' To which I got a few replies, the gist of which was, 'Of course we remembered. Didn't you?' Which quite frankly, felt a little snotty. Who forgets their own sister's or daughter's birthday, apart from us (and they didn't know that)? They also let me know they had already planned to take her out for dinner at the weekend, which was a relief. This meant I could just focus on the family.

I raced over to the house the following day, getting in before Laura got home from work, which gave me time to set up. I didn't have much to set up. Feeling slightly fruitless, I whipped the tin foil off the cake I had made. This took half the icing off with it. I swore. I had a strong feeling that, this being the first, it would set the blueprint for all future birthdays without Mum. I really didn't want that blueprint to involve bald cake. I stuck some sugar flowers back on and covered the rest with candles.

Dad walked in.

'How did you get in?'

I got the impression that Dad would rather no one had a key to the house but him. That way he could control whom he let in. Even Laura, who lived with him. I got that impression a lot.

'I used my key. Did you get the present?'

'I did.' He looked at the cake. 'Is that the cake?' He slowly pushed the Sainsbury's cake towards me.

I stuck another candle into my cake, like a flag in a battleground. 'What did you get her?'

'Here, you can see for yourself.' Dad passed me one of those gift bags you buy when you don't want to have to do any actual wrapping. There was a velvet box in the bottom of it. It was the kind of box that screams expensive; the kind that can sometimes say 'anniversary' or 'milestone birthday', but can equally say 'made a huge mistake with the person I'm dating'. In this case, I supposed what it was saying was 'man buys daughter birthday present for the first time', or to be more concise, 'man in over his head'.

I looked up at Dad and then back at the box. I opened it.

'The woman at the shop asked if it was for someone special. I said my daughter. She suggested a bracelet.'

'Are those real diamonds?'

'I'm not going to buy fake diamonds, am I?'

I nodded. 'Right. So the pearls: they're probably real too, then?'

'I'd bloody hope so. Why? What's wrong with it?' Dad crossed his arms. 'I didn't know what to get her. That's where I'd get your mother's presents. She always seemed to like them.'

I smiled. 'It's breathtaking, Dad.' I looked up as Laura's car pulled into the driveway. 'Quick. She's here.'

We dashed into the hall and waited to present ourselves.

'Happy Birthday!' we shouted as she opened the door.

'Thanks, guys. Han, I didn't know you'd be here.' She looked around. 'No one else is here, though, right?'

I shook my head. 'Ollie sends his love.'

'Come, come into the lounge and sit down,' Dad said. 'We have presents. And there's cake. Two kinds.'

We sat on the sofa while Dad went to get his present.

'Mine's on the way,' I said. 'They promised it would get here on time, but the delivery . . .' I shrugged and pulled a 'what can you do' face.

Dad raised his eyebrows at me as he came back in. 'Some of us are more organised. This is from me,' he said, handing Laura the bag. 'I chose it myself so I hope you like it. The lady at the shop said you can exchange it if it's not right.'

'*You* bought me a present?' Laura looked at me, uncertainly.

'*He* bought you a present,' I nodded.

'Of course I bought you a present.' Dad looked exasperated. 'Here, open this first, though.' He handed her a card.

'You got me a card?'

'You got her a card?'

'I'd imagine there's a lot to be said for having sons.' He flapped the card at her until she took it.

'Dear Laura, Happy Birthday. With lots of love, from Dad,' she read. She looked up at him. I could see she was welling up. Dad could, too.

'Well, go on, open the present,' he said.

She pulled out the box and opened it. 'Oh,' she said. 'Wow. It's . . . Are these real?'

Dad threw up his hands. 'Of course they're real. Why do you two keep asking me that?'

'It's beautiful, Dad, thank you so much. I love it.' She got up and hugged him.

'You're welcome. Oh, I left the wine in the kitchen. Who wants a glass?'

As he left the room, Laura looked at me. 'Can you believe it?' She gently stroked the bracelet.

'I know,' I said.

'I'm never going to be able to wear it outside the house. It doesn't go with any of my clothes and I'd be too scared of losing it.'

'I know.'

She put it gently back in its box. 'Dad got me a birthday card.'

'Yeah.'

We both stared at it.

'And he signed it. Himself.' She looked up at me. 'I don't think that's ever happened before.'

I hugged her. 'Cake?'

We stood up.

'You know, this birthday hasn't been as awful as I thought it would be.'

I felt a wave of relief. We had pulled it off. She would never have to know we had almost forgotten about it. I smiled at her. 'I wasn't going to let you down.'

I knew I was a good sister.

How to Clean a Ceiling

A few days later I was standing in Mac, pondering karma. Specifically, whether spending a small fortune I didn't have on make-up at Mac for a present for my sister's birthday could cancel out any bad karma I might have accrued by forgetting said birthday in the first place. And then lying about it and saying the present was just delayed in the post. It would have been a lot cheaper to just go to confession, followed by Primark (which is really one of the advantages of being Catholic), but I didn't feel like being judged by a priest. A man would never be able to understand the nuances of being a sister, especially not one who had dedicated his life to avoiding women as much as possible in the first place. Of course, if going bankrupt could be seen as bad karma exacting itself then this whole thing was a moot point.

I looked at the saleswoman who was rearranging the lip liners. 'I need a present for my sister,' I said. 'The kind of present that will make me look like a good sister: a really expensive one.'

*

I clutched the bag to my chest and banged on the door of my family home.

Laura answered it, wearing a dressing gown.

'Oh good, you're home,' I said, walking inside. 'How was work?'

'It was fine,' she said. 'It was work. I was going to take a shower.'

'Cool,' I said. 'Great. Well, look what arrived.' I waved the Mac bag at her. 'It's your birthday present. Let's go upstairs. You can open it in your room.'

I bounded up the stairs and jumped onto her bed, crossing my legs underneath me.

Laura followed me in. 'Thanks, Han. You didn't have to.'

'Of course I did. It's your birthday. What kind of a sister would I be if I didn't get you a present?' I thrust the bag at her and patted the bed next to me.

She sat down and looked inside. 'Oh wow, is that the palette I wanted? Oh my God, Han. Thank you.' She looked back inside the bag. 'And a brush set?' She looked at me and raised her eyebrows. 'Wow, Han. You shouldn't have.'

I waved a hand. 'It came as a bundle. That the saleswoman specifically put together for me. After I asked her to. It's from Ollie, too. Happy birthday. Thank God it finally arrived.' I rolled my eyes. 'It's such a shame it wasn't here for the actual day.' I fiddled with her duvet cover.

Laura smiled and opened the palette. 'Oh it's fine. That wasn't your fault.' She inspected the brushes. 'I really wasn't expecting anything like this. You and Dad really overdid it this year.'

I waved a hand, again. 'Please. It's nothing.' I looked down. I had another reason for being there: Mother's Day. It was coming up and as much as I was dreading the entire thing, I also felt that it was my duty to make sure Laura was coping with it properly. After the revelation that she was seeing a counsellor I hadn't known about, I was beginning to feel like I was slipping slightly on my responsibility to look after the family. Uncle Dan's comments at the funeral had a nasty way of ringing in my ears whenever I felt this way.

Laura stood up and put the make-up on her dressing table. 'Well, I need to have that shower before dinner. I want to wash the smell of work off me.'

'Yeah. Cool. So. How have you been?' I said.

She frowned. 'Since I last saw you on my birthday, you mean? Not much has changed.'

'Right. Right.' I cleared my throat and tugged at the corner of her bedding. 'Because you know, Mother's Day is coming up. I don't know how you feel about that. But you can talk to me about it if you're feeling upset.' I twisted towards her and patted the bed next to me, again. 'I'm here. Any time.' I widened my eyes at her, meaningfully.

'Um. Yeah. Thanks, Han. I'm fine, though.' She shrugged. 'It is what it is.'

'Sure,' I said. 'Well, I was going to have some friends around on the Saturday night. For a girls' night. You know, hang out, have some drinks. Not discuss anything about any Sunday roast plans . . .'

This was part of a carefully thought-out strategy I had to get through the weekend. I was going to cram in as many distractions into as short amount of time as possible. After the girls night, Ollie and I would spend Sunday doing something gentle but fun together. We hadn't exactly discussed this, but I knew we didn't have to. He would get it. Ideally, the whole weekend would be so busy, it would pass in one frantic blur.

'If you want to come, there'll be alcohol.'

Laura nodded and shrugged. 'Yeah, okay. Why not. It will probably be better than drinking here with Dad and listening to him sing "Danny Boy". Again.'

I beamed. 'Great,' I said. I leaned back on her bed.

Laura looked at me and raised her eyebrows. 'Hannah? Can I shower now?'

I jumped up. 'Oh right. Of course. Shower away. I'll talk to you later.' I paused. 'Is Dad in, by the way?'

'I think he's in his study. Why?'

'No reason.'

I made my way back downstairs. I did have a reason, of course: I wanted to see if I could find any more evidence of his possible affair.

I walked into the kitchen and found his phone lying on the counter where he always left it. For a man who had taken to clandestine emailing, he was remarkably relaxed about leaving his phone around unattended. If it had been anyone else, I might have found this reassuring: a sign that maybe he really didn't have anything to hide. But this was Dad. He probably didn't think anyone else knew how to unlock his phone, mainly because he barely did. He'd forgotten his passcode so many times, he kept it written down on a Post-it note next to his phone. This really gave me an edge.

I quickly typed it in and opened his text messages.

There wasn't much there, apart from what Laura and I had sent him and an occasional message from Nigel about sport. Plus something from Iris telling him he needed to get a handle on his daughters' upbringing and suggesting she come to stay to help him. I was relieved to see he had ignored her. I couldn't find anything from a Betty, though. Then I stopped: there was a message from Susan. Church Susan with the husband and the priest, as I now thought of her. That wasn't the problem. The problem was what she had sent him: 'I'm so glad you and Betty connected. She's great. I think she could really help you move on.' I swayed on my feet, slightly. I was really going off Susan.

'What are you doing here?'

I jumped. Dad was standing behind me.

'Is that my phone?'

I locked it and put it back on the counter. 'Yes.' I cleared my throat. I tried to think of something plausible I could say. 'I was just checking your data usage.' This felt like a safe answer: I was fairly sure he wouldn't know what that meant.

He narrowed his eyes and crossed his arms. 'Why?'

'Because. Older people can be taken advantage of.' I crossed my arms. 'By people who don't have their best interests in mind. Who might have found them at a vulnerable time and could be taking advantage of that. Like their mobile network, I mean. They get sold all types of things they don't need, like roaming, minutes, internet . . .' I scratched my head. 'Data stuff. I just wanted to make sure you're not one of them.'

He snorted. 'I've never had any problems with BT.'

'That's your home phone, Dad. Anyway, I should be going. It's late and I need to cook dinner.' I glanced at him from the corner of my eye. 'You know, Mother's Day is coming up. How do you feel about that?'

Over the span of my life, I have discovered a series of societal truths. This makes me sound very old and wise, when in fact, I'm neither, but I do know a few things and one of them is about Mother's Day. Mother's Day, you see, is not about mothers. You might think it is, but it's not. Mother's Day is about posting flattering pictures of mothers from when they were younger on the internet and buying them a small tree from the garden centre. This is so widely known and accepted that that first year, I even got a text from Evie about it. 'Are you going to post that photo of your mum?' she said. I knew exactly what photo she meant. I posted it online most years. It's of my mum when she was in her twenties, on a beach, in a bikini. I am also in the picture. I am eating sand. This photo is infamous in my family. It hangs on the wall in my family's home and I have a copy on the wall in mine. We are all very proud of this photo and draw attention to it whenever we can – except for Mum, that

189

is, who never did and who was the only one actually in the photo (the only one that's worth looking at, at least). It doesn't matter that it's not any of us looking radiant in a bikini; we are connected to her and there is that glow by association. 'If not,' Evie's message continued, 'can I have a copy of it? I need some motivation to give a shit about what my own body looks like now I've got Harry.' I emailed her a copy and turned off my phone.

I didn't want to post a picture of my mum. I didn't want to see photos of other people's young, hot mums. It was like the birthday card display at the supermarket all over again. I wanted to get through the whole weekend blindfolded and at a sprint. Then I could wake up on Monday and it would be over. Hence my plan: see my friends on Saturday, spend Sunday with Ollie forgetting about it entirely.

The night before my friends were due to come over, I had a dream. It was about Mum, but of course it was about Mum. I'm not going to tell you about the time I dreamed that the Mona Lisa was trying to kill me. I was in Mum's bedroom and then I saw her (Mum, not the Mona Lisa). She was wearing a beautiful dress and glowing. Not in an ethereal, ghost-like way, but in a healthy living and really good yoga-session way. I felt infused with love. She came towards me, smiling, with her arms outstretched and then I pushed her away and started yelling at her for borrowing my make-up and making me late. I told her she ruined everything and just had time to see her look very hurt, before I woke up and started to cry.

I started crying again later on, when I tried to hand wash some delicates and reached for my phone to ask Mum how to do it properly, before realising I couldn't do that. This isn't the lasting tribute she'd probably want, but it is part of the day-to-day minutiae of grief: wishing the person you lost was still there to tell you how to do things you don't know how to do yourself. I walked around for the rest of the day feeling off-kilter.

By the time people were due to arrive at my house that evening, I just wanted to stop having to think. I poured myself a gin and tonic, thinking briefly about how the counsellor had asked me if I was using alcohol as a coping method. This was something I could really have talked about, I thought. Then the doorbell rang and Laura arrived.

She took the drink out of my hand. 'Thanks,' she said.

The doorbell went again. Ollie came downstairs and then turned and went straight back up as Sophie came in. She grabbed Laura and me by our shoulders, like a general briefing his soldiers.

'We're going to have a good time tonight, girls,' she said.

Lou and Maria arrived together next. They would get me through it without acknowledging there was anything to get through.

I parcelled out drinks, waved them benignly to the coffee table, where I had put the hummus I had prepared and put music on in the background.

Sophie stood up. 'I'm so glad we're doing this. I really need a chat. I walked in on my boss peeing yesterday. Do you think it looks bad that I've asked him for a promotion?'

Laura looked round the group. 'Did you ask while in the toilet?'

'No, no, of course not.' She sighed. 'I was standing outside. I wanted to get things back on a professional level.' She looked around the room. 'Is Ollie here, actually? I could really use his opinion on this: what it's like to be walked in on in the toilet. As a man, I mean.'

It felt like it was going to be one of those nights when nothing really happens, but you know you'll all remember it as a good night. Lou told us about the latest in a series of bad dates she had had. Once she had had enough to drink to be able to think about it, Sophie told us more about walking in on her boss in the toilet.

'I saw it,' she said. 'IT. Can I respect a man whose penis I've seen?'

'I hope so,' I said.

'No,' Maria said.

Maria told her story about sleeping with the guy from the boy band Fist, which, when she tells it properly, is a truly great anecdote. She even manages to work in some dance moves that go with it.

Then she put on a playlist, tipped her glass at me and squinted. 'Bowie, babe,' she said. 'It's always Bowie.' She picked up a bottle of vodka and topped up our glasses with it.

'Remember that guy I dated last year who looked

like Bowie?' Lou said. 'He was even called David.' She nodded round at the group.

Sophie drank from her glass and winced. 'He didn't exactly look like Bowie, Lou. He just had those silver boots he was always in and wore eyeliner. The only people who thought he actually looked like Bowie were you and him, and you only thought that because you liked him so much.'

Lou looked hurt. 'What are you talking about? He even had different coloured eyes.'

'He had a lazy eye,' Sophie said. 'Why do you even care? That was a year ago.'

'Because,' Lou said, 'he's just added me on Instagram and he messaged me suggesting we get a drink.'

Sophie and I looked at each other.

'What?' Lou said.

'I just don't think that's a great idea,' Sophie said. 'You can do better. He was always a bit of a dick.'

Lou frowned. 'What do you mean?'

Sophie sighed. 'There are just some things we heard about that we didn't want to tell you about at the time. We didn't want to upset you.'

'Oh my God,' Maria said.

We all turned to look at her.

'This is my song.' Blondie's 'Maria' started to play. She started singing along, at least to the bits with her own name in it. She never bothered learning the rest of the lyrics. She raised her arms in the air, her drink still in her hand. 'Blondie, babe. It's always Blondie,' she said to me, ignoring the vodka that landed in her hair.

193

'I thought it was always Bowie,' I said.

'It's both,' she said.

'I see,' I said. I didn't see.

Lou waved at her. 'Maria, shut up. I want to hear this. Sophie? What do you mean?'

'Um,' Sophie said.

Maria snorted. 'Oh please, babe. He came on to everyone he saw. He was doing it the entire time you were seeing each other. He came on to all of us.'

I stood up. 'Who wants to play a drinking game? I'll start.' I poured myself a shot of gin and downed it. I felt it curdle with the vodka in my stomach.

'What's the game?' Laura said.

I clamped my mouth shut and shook my head.

Lou looked as if she might cry. 'Why didn't you tell me this at the time?'

Maria shrugged. 'It was hardly a secret. It was obvious to everyone. You just didn't want to see it.'

Sophie glared at Maria, then turned to Lou. 'We didn't want to hurt you. You liked him so much.'

'I can't believe this,' Lou said.

Maria walked over to her and topped up Lou's glass again, then her own. 'Forget him, babe. You were far too good for him. You can have any man you want. Don't waste your time thinking about him.' She tottered back towards the drinks.

Lou looked down. 'Okay.'

There was a silence.

Sophie clapped her hands. 'So what's everyone doing tomorrow?' She looked at Laura and me. 'I mean . . .'

Lou looked up. 'Did any of you sleep with him?'

I frowned. 'Lou, how can you even ask that?'

'Who wants a cocktail,' Maria said, waving a bottle of vodka.

'I don't think straight vodka counts as a cocktail,' Laura said.

Sophie nodded. 'Yeah and maybe you should slow down, Maria.'

Maria rolled her eyes. 'Oh God, Sophie, you're always such a killjoy.' She turned back to the drinks, knocking over the bottle and spilling vodka all over the floor.

I glanced at the photo of Mum on the wall. This was not going the way I had thought it would.

It took us almost an hour to get Lou to stop analysing posts on David's Instagram for signs that he'd changed and we only stopped her doing that because Destiny's Child came onto the playlist, which started a heated discussion about who we'd all play if we had been cast in the original *Charlie's Angels* movie.

Lou raised a finger. 'Okay, but can I just – exactly how bad was David around you guys? I mean, do you think he cheated on me?'

Maria rolled her eyes. 'Oh my God, we're back on *this*? Of course he did. And while we're at it, so did that broiled ham you dated at university for, like, two years. You need to pick better men, babe.'

Lou opened her mouth. 'Louis?'

Sophie glared at Maria.

'I need another drink,' Maria said. She pulled herself

up from the sofa and dropped her glass. It smashed on the floor. She looked down. 'Oh thank God it missed me. I thought it'd spilled on my shoe. Han, babe, I'm getting another glass.' She staggered out of the room.

My stomach clenched. I stared at the mess on the floor. 'That was expensive,' I said. 'It was part of a set Mum gave me when we moved in here.' I got down on my hands and knees and started picking up the broken shards. I wondered if I could glue it back together again.

Lou moaned. 'David . . .'

I glanced at her. 'Lou, why do you care so much?'

'Because I lied earlier. We already went out and we slept together.' She put her head in her hands. 'Now I feel like an idiot.'

'I'm going to the loo,' Sophie said.

Laura moved over to Lou and squeezed her hand. 'It could be worse. At least you're having sex.'

I looked at the photo of Mum, again. I was beginning to seriously regret the entire evening. Nothing was going to plan. Instead, I was tired, the gin was making me feel irritable and I could feel the next day's hangover making an early appearance. I considered getting Ollie to pretend there was an emergency so everyone had to leave.

Sophie came back downstairs. 'Guys, Maria's been sick.'

I cut my hand on a piece of glass and swore. 'Okay.' I stood up. 'Could you pass me a tissue?'

Sophie shook her head. 'No, it's not okay. It's not even in the toilet. It's everywhere. It's all over the stairs. It's all over the hallway carpet. Hannah, it's all over the hallway walls.'

I think I went white. I can't be sure because I didn't have a mirror to hand and who actually knows what going white feels like. It's the kind of thing you really have to rely on other people to tell you. For the sake of this story, though and to properly express how horrified I was at this moment, let's say I went white.

I went white. 'You're joking,' I said. 'Please tell me you're joking. This can't be happening. This especially can't be happening today.' I sat down. I put a hand on my chest and tried to concentrate on my breathing, which suddenly felt like something I had to think about.

'This is typical,' Lou said. She stood up. 'Don't worry, Han. I'll deal with Maria. I have some more questions for her, anyway.' She pushed her sleeves up and went upstairs.

'I'll help.' Sophie followed her. She jogged up the stairs. A few seconds later she came back. 'She told me to fuck off. So, I did. I thought it was best. We need to get her home.'

'Shall I call her a taxi?' Laura said.

'Uber might be better,' Sophie said. 'We can track her on it and make sure she gets back okay. Have we got her phone?'

'I think she'll have it on her,' I said.

Sophie nodded. 'I'll go get it.' She marched back upstairs.

Laura grabbed my arm. 'Oh my God, Han. Do you think it'll stain? Are we going to have to clear this up now? What if she won't leave?' Laura's voice was trembling. 'I can't believe this is happening before Mother's Day, as well.'

I put my hands into my hair. 'I . . .' I said.

I didn't say anything else because at that point, my vision started to blur and I felt a wave of dizziness. Then it hit me: I was going to die.

My heart started racing, pounding so hard in my chest that it was painful. I tried to take a breath, but I realised I could barely breathe at all. I began to feel frantic. The pressure in my chest was growing and it wouldn't allow any air into my lungs. I knew what was going on with a deep dread: I was having a heart attack. I got down on the floor on my hands and knees. This is it, I told myself. I'm going to die here, in a house that smells of Maria's sick. I thought about my family, who had just lost Mum and were now going to have to cope with losing me, as well. I thought of Ollie, who would find me on the floor, next to the crisp crumbs and half-eaten hummus. There's no way he'd get our deposit back after this.

I was vaguely aware of Laura fanning me and saying my name, loudly. Then asking if I was also going to be sick. She emptied the last of the Doritos from one of the bowls on the coffee table and stuck it under me.

I don't know how long it lasted for, but then it was over and I could breathe again. My heart stopped feeling like it was trying to physically break through my chest. The panic subsided.

Laura eyed me. 'Are you okay?' She picked up the bowl and held it, warily, near me.

I waved it away and moved back onto the sofa.

Sophie came downstairs again. 'She'll be gone soon. Han, are you okay?'

We heard the bathroom door swing open and Maria's voice.

'No one understands how hard it is to be me sometimes. Where's Hannah? Jus' lemme speak to Hannah. Hannah doesn't understand, either, but I wanna see her.'

I have to say, her Princess Margaret was impeccable.

'Hannah's busy,' Lou said. 'Okay Maria, your Uber's here. Your housemate is going to keep an eye out for you, so you'll be fine.'

'You guys are so mean. I hate my housemate. She doesn't get me. You're all so small-minded.' I heard her spit on the floor.

Laura winced.

I took a deep breath, which still felt like a novelty and stood up, shakily. Once I was sure my legs weren't going to collapse underneath me, I stormed out into the hallway.

Lou looked alarmed. 'Han. Are you okay? You look a bit grey.'

Maria turned to me. 'Hannah,' she said. She opened her arms. 'Babe.'

She started walking towards me. I can honestly tell you the sight of her was worse than any zombie film I'd seen.

'I'm just so—' she said.

I held up a hand. 'Maria,' I said. I wanted to shout at her but I couldn't. My chest felt too tight. 'I've had enough,' I said. 'You have been a complete bloody nightmare recently. And now. Now.' I laughed, a little bit hysterically. 'Now, on the weekend of Mother's Day . . .' I held up a finger. 'My first Mother's Day since my mum died. *Died*, Maria. When all I wanted was a nice night to distract me. You . . .' I pointed the finger at her. 'You, get wasted and throw up all over my house.'

Maria was standing there looking at me, slightly slack-jawed. I realised I'd never shouted at her before. Not that I was actually shouting at her then, either, which was probably for the best: the neighbours still hadn't forgiven us for New Year's Eve.

'You have just no idea what you've done.' I hugged myself, tightly and shuddered. 'I'm going to have to clear up your vomit. God, Maria, you just don't care about anyone but yourself, do you? You're so self-absorbed it's laughable.' I laughed again, to emphasise my point. 'We're not teenagers now, Maria. We're not at university. We're adults. So bloody start acting like it for once, will you?'

Maria waited for a second, staring at me as if working out how best to react. I'd seen her do this before, when on the verge of not getting her way. Then her lip started to wobble. She flapped her arms, flicking more sick onto the floor. Lou pulled a face and took a step away from her. I didn't blame her: the smell was stifling. I wondered if I could open the door for ventilation without spoiling my momentum.

'Hannah,' she said.

'No,' I said. I threw open the door and pointed at

the car that was waiting outside. 'Just get out, Maria. Seriously, I have had enough. I've had enough of this.' I waved my arms around me. 'I've had enough of being the audience to your drama. Literally. I went to all your events at university. Even the weird play you did with masks you only did because you got to have sex on stage. And you never even once came to one of my poetry readings. That's the way it always goes. I am always there for you and you are never, ever there for me. Well not any more. I'm done.' I stepped aside (quite far to one side, in fact) to let Maria walk past me.

Lou followed her out to the car, closed the Uber's door after her and walked back inside.

'Thank God. I'd really had enough of that smell,' she said. Then she hugged me.

We walked back into the lounge.

'She's gone,' Lou said. 'But the bathroom is a mess. It's on the towels, the mirror . . .'

'The mirror?'

'Maybe she was watching herself,' Laura said.

'I think there's some on the ceiling. It looks like *The Exorcist* came here for the wrap party,' Lou said. 'Where are your cleaning products?'

Sophie jumped up. 'Yes, we've got this.'

'It shouldn't take long,' Lou said. 'We just need to throw everything away and start again.'

I waved them off. 'Thanks, guys, but I can't let you do that. This is my house: it's my responsibility. I need to be the one to clear it up.'

In the end, we decided we'd all do it together. And

this is how I ended up, at two in the morning, scrubbing someone else's sick out of the hallway carpet, while in the bathroom, my friends wiped down surfaces and my sister aimed a mop at the ceiling.

'This isn't even my worst bathroom story of the weekend,' Sophie said.

I eventually crawled up to bed that night around three. Ollie lifted up the bed cover and let me in.

'Maria was sick everywhere,' I said.

'You're joking,' Ollie said.

'We cleared it all up,' I said.

He yawned. 'I thought I heard you swearing.'

'And I think I had a panic attack,' I said.

Ollie sat up a bit. 'What? Han, why didn't you come and get me? Are you okay?'

I nodded. 'Yeah. I'm fine now. I just want to forget tonight ever happened.'

He put his arm round me and pulled me into him.

I huddled down into my pillow, taking my phone and opening Instagram. Laura had put up the bikini picture of Mum. I posted a heart and turned my phone off.

How to Behave at a
Dinner Party

I started thinking of the words panic attack in bright, neon lettering. I braced myself for more. I felt slightly panicky every time I thought about it, then panicked that that would be enough to bring another one on. Then, once the shock had worn off, I stopped feeling panicky. Not only that, I started feeling surprisingly fine. I didn't have another one. I didn't even feel all that upset about the one I had had. The neon lettering faded away and became normal lettering and then even that faded away to the point I barely thought about it.

I didn't feel that upset about anything, in fact. I was beginning to think the whole episode had shocked the grief out of me. I had reached the pinnacle and now, I was on the mend. It wasn't just the panic attack I felt fine about, it was everything. I felt emotionally even-handed, mature and rational. This was quite new for me. I was fairly certain I had become an adult.

I thought about this as I sat in a café on the seafront, having brunch with Ollie, staring out across the sea. I didn't expect to feel that way, but I did. I was coping. I even felt fine about everything else that had happened on Mother's Day and the semi-permanent stain on my bathroom ceiling. I was still furious with Maria, of course (I was beginning to call that my righteous anger); she was the one that left the semi-permanent stain. But otherwise, I really felt fine. I didn't feel like a lost child floundering without my mum any more. This was quite amazing, when you thought about it. And I did think about it.

I looked at Ollie. 'I feel fine,' I said.

Ollie didn't say anything. Clearly he didn't grasp the importance of what I was saying.

When I imagined grief, I saw myself spending every day in a robe, my hair unwashed and the last vestiges of mascara I had put on months ago flaking off. I would sustain myself by eating crumbs I found in my hair and licking food stains off my robe. But now here I was and I wasn't doing any of that. In fact, I was quite proud of how well I was doing: I was looking after Laura and Dad in the way Mum would want me to; I was in a healthy and loving relationship with a man (if we ignored the whole almost kiss with Mark slip, which I was doing my best to); I was even doing well at work. I had started getting dressed for it more often now. I was pretty sure Mum would be proud of how well I was doing without her.

After twenty-eight years, I finally felt like I understood what it meant to be an adult. And it had only taken losing Mum to get there. Admittedly, this wasn't a great trade-off, but I was coping with it. Because I was definitely fine.

I watched as Ollie shoved some of his garlic mush-rooms onto my plate and took my beans. I took hold of the hand that wasn't transferring food. 'You know, you're my favourite person,' I said.

I stopped and dropped his hand. I had always thought of Mum as my favourite person. But there I was, telling Ollie he was. Had I replaced Mum with Ollie? Should I be more upset than I was? Was it possible I was too fine?

I frowned. 'Do you think I'm too okay?' I said. 'Mum's just died and I feel okay. I really expected to feel worse than this. Should I be feeling more upset?'

Ollie bit into his fried toast. 'I think you just feel how-ever you feel. You're coping.'

'Right.' I chewed this over. 'You don't think it's an insult to Mum's memory I don't feel worse?'

Ollie frowned at me. 'No?' He put his cutlery down. 'I think she'd be glad you're feeling okay.'

'Fine,' I said. 'I feel fine.'

'Right.'

'Right.' I picked up my cutlery. 'You're right. It just means I'm well adjusted. I think this is just what being an adult is, you know. I'm just an adult now.' I cut into my sausage.

It was around this time that the inquest happened.

'Why?' I asked when Dad called to tell me a date had been set.

'She didn't die of old age. This is what happens in those circumstances. They need to make sure that no one did anything wrong,' he said.

I mulled this over. 'But, but, but,' I said.

'What?'

'But we didn't even donate her organs,' I said. 'She didn't want to be cut up. And stuff.'

Dad sighed. We had been through this. Well, we sort of had. It had been a question that had come up at the time and we had said no. Mum hadn't said she wanted to donate her organs. So we didn't donate her organs. That was her choice. I had fought to defend her right to that choice. Well, again, sort of. It had been a very hypothetical fight. The kind of hypothetical fight that is the only fight you can have at a dinner party, which is where this fight happened.

Sophie had had some friends round for dinner and she had invited Ollie and me. I hadn't wanted to go at first. I was worried someone would ask me how I was doing, or want to talk about it. But Sophie had assured me that the people going would know better than that or wouldn't know me at all and so wouldn't know to ask. So we went.

When we first got there, Mark had tried to ask me how I was, but Sophie saw and kicked him and then Ollie had asked him about a book they had both read and that was that. Dinner was served and Sophie's a good cook.

I sat across the table from Mark and next to a man I didn't know, called Adam, who Sophie knew from work. I could mainly distract myself with the coq au vin and mashed potatoes and not think about anything other than small talk with Adam.

Then, in a way that felt far too on-the-nose for real life and more like some contrivance in a film plot, which meant it could only ever actually happen in real life, we had got onto the subject of organ donation.

'Everyone should hold a donor card,' Adam said, to the entire room. There hadn't really been any lead-up to this statement. Adam had just had a thought and voiced it. 'It's immoral not to. You're dead. Let someone else live.'

Sophie had looked alarmed in the way only a hostess who can see her dinner party is about to go horribly wrong can look.

Across the table, Ollie shot me a look. It was a look of concern laced with a deep wish I'd let this go.

I did not. 'Well,' I said. 'I think it's an individual choice.' I popped a piece of potato in my mouth.

Adam turned to me. 'Fine, sure, of course. But everyone should choose to. If you were going to die anyway, wouldn't you want someone else to be able to benefit from your heart, or your kidneys?'

'Yes,' I said. 'But not everyone feels the same way about it. Some people don't like thinking about that happening to their body. Even after death. It's still a choice.'

Adam spread his hands in a way that included the whole table in a conversation that so far, only the two of us were having. 'Look,' he said. He laughed. 'No one's stealing organs.' He grinned round the table. 'I'm just saying the people that don't want to donate their organs are being fucking selfish. And probably a bit stupid. I mean, say your husband, or parent, or kid was dying and down the ward, there's some brain-dead vegetable who is going to kick it. Nothing anyone can do. Very sad, etcetera. But they decided when they were alive that they wanted to hang on to the organs that could save your husband's, dad's, kid's life and probably a few other people. What then?'

I carefully cut up a piece of chicken. 'Well then I'd have to respect their wishes,' I said.

Adam snorted. 'Okay,' he said, in a way that actually said, 'You're clearly too stupid to reason with.'

'Okay,' I said. 'Let's say we didn't have a choice. That organs were just taken from dead people without their say. Because they're dead: they don't have a say. Universal donor cards for everyone.'

Adam pointed his fork at me. 'That would be a better system. More lives would be saved.'

I nodded. 'What about Hitler,' I said.

Adam narrowed his eyes. 'Really? The Hitler argument?'

'I think it's applicable here.'

'Okay, so you're going to say what if Hitler came along and started harvesting organs to give to the people he deemed worthy. The master race. Eugenics. Really?'

'No,' I said.

Adam watched my face.

'What if Hitler wanted an organ? And by not giving him one you could save thousands of lives. But because of universal organ donor cards, Hitler lives.'

'You realise he could still get an organ, probably, from someone else who volunteered an organ card.'

'What if I was a Jehovah's Witness?'

'Are you?'

'No. But I could be.'

Adam sighed. 'Give me one good reason why you wouldn't donate your organs. You can't because there isn't one.'

I put down my knife and fork. 'My mum just died and we didn't donate her organs. She didn't want us to,' I said.

There was a bit of a hush as the other people round the table looked to see how Adam would react to this. It might not have been the most logical argument, but it's hard to argue with a grieving person.

Adam kept eating. 'Look, I'm sorry that your mum died. But I still think it's a selfish decision not to donate when you can. You chose to not help other people that could have lived. Or your mum did.'

I wondered if I could throw mashed potato at him or if that would invalidate my argument. It would probably make me the 'overly emotional' one. That was true, but it still wouldn't help my argument.

Sophie was staring at me. She shook herself and loudly changed the subject. Mark and Ollie enthusiastically joined in.

I waited for a moment, then went to the loo, where I stared into the mirror and tried not to think of Mum on her hospital bed and then tried not to cry.

When I came back, Mark was sitting in my seat.

I had looked at Sophie, who smiled apologetically at me. I had smiled back. She had disrupted her table plan for me. I had sat down next to Ollie, instead.

Now, that all felt like it was for nothing.

I took a deep breath. 'Do you want me to go to the inquest?' I said.

'No. I think it would be better if you didn't. No point you sitting through that.'

'Does Laura have to go? She was there, at the time . . .'

'No. Your aunt and uncle will be there, though. Dan called me. They've suggested we all go for lunch after.'

'The pub would be better.'

'That's what I said.'

I didn't want to think about what this inquest meant or what it could potentially find.

'What if the judge – do they have judges? What if the judge tells us Mum could have lived if we hadn't been in such a rush to turn the life support machines off?' I said to Ollie, as I paced the lounge floor. It occurred to me that a lot of our conversations seemed to involve me pacing, recently. He watched me from the sofa.

'You weren't in a rush. You waited; she didn't make it. It wasn't your choice, anyway. It was the doctors',' Ollie said.

'What if her brain was actually completely fine and they just got it wrong?' Then I stopped. I had watched enough forensic shows to have a good idea of how they would work this out. This was almost completely unbearable.

'Mum would hate having her skin cut through,' I said. 'She always took care of her skin.'

I thought about someone tearing her open, breaking her rib cage, taking out her organs and sticking them in a bowl. Someone who didn't know her who would be mutilating her. I felt sick. I bitterly regretted watching so much television.

You can imagine the atmosphere in the pub on the day of the inquest. Ollie, Laura and I got there first; they had both taken the day off so they could meet Dad afterwards and hear the results. We called it 'getting there early to secure a table', though as it was mid-morning on a Thursday, this wasn't particularly necessary. What we really meant was having time to drink more. I got to the bar first.

'I'll have a large coffee, please. Black,' I said.

Laura and Ollie looked at me in surprise.

'Is that all—' Laura said.

I held up my hand. 'With an equally large whiskey, please.'

'Ah,' Laura said.

We found a table and huddled round it, waiting for Dad, Dan and Cathy to arrive.

Laura shifted in her seat. 'Do you think—'

'No,' I said, firmly. I knew what she was thinking about because I was thinking about it and I didn't want her to say any of it out loud.

'But—'

'No.'

'But let's say—'

'No.'

'Hannah,' Ollie snapped. 'For God's sake, let her speak. Go on, Laura.'

'No, she's right.' Laura took a sip of her wine. 'It's just so hard to think about it. What if they find that we could have done something, but didn't? What if we could have done something differently and Mum would still be here. You guys weren't there when it happened.'

I looked at her and took her hand. 'Laura, there was nothing you could have done. Nothing. It wasn't your fault.' I tried to look deep into her eyes, so she'd really believe me. 'It wasn't. You couldn't have stopped her from falling.'

She looked down and nodded.

'They're here,' I said. Dad, Uncle Dan and Aunt Cathy were walking over to us. They all looked sombre, which is probably a stupid thing to point out, because how else would you expect them to look?

'I always knew Jenny had a big heart,' Cathy said, dabbing at her eyes with a handkerchief. 'But I didn't think I'd ever hear it from a coroner. They're such ghouls, coroners. Are we eating?'

I gripped Ollie's hand under the table until he had to pry it off. Laura stuck a handful of crisps in her mouth.

Dad told me later that during the inquest, Cathy had put her hand in the air and asked the coroner if, as her sister, this would have an effect on her. 'Be honest with me now: how safe are X-rays really?' she had asked.

When we had all shuffled round the table and taken a seat, clutching our drinks, Dan cleared his throat.

'So,' he said. What he meant was, 'how have you all been coping?'

'Miserable,' Cathy said. 'I'm just so miserable. Life.' She threw an arm out. 'Life is terrible. You really have to ask yourself, what is the point of life at all? One day you're here, the next, you have some grubby little man rooting about in your organs.' She let out a sob and covered her face with a scarf.

Laura and I both dived towards the crisps.

Cathy lifted her face. 'Let me tell you now, I don't want any man touching me when I'm gone, unless I've said so. I want to be cremated.'

Dad frowned. By the look on his face, he would have preferred the inquest. 'You can't let yourself think like that. God has a plan for us all, in the end. Hopefully, we'll all be reunited. On the other side.' He gestured, vaguely, towards the other side.

'Oh God, shmod,' Cathy wailed.

Laura and I looked at each other.

Dan cleared his throat again. 'That's true, Patrick. Yes.' He nodded vigorously. 'I just try and focus on the day-to-day. You really have to do whatever you can to get yourself through it. Whatever helps you to cope, really.'

Cathy sat up. 'That's true. I've been sleeping with a lot of younger men. I've really found that it helps. They have so much youth and vitality; it's like life's blood. It's really very invigorating. It makes me feel so alive,' she said. She turned to me. 'Hannah, how's that friend of yours from the funeral? The nice one with the thighs?'

Dan's face went puce and slowly folded in on itself.

'Yes, well, it's never going to be easy is it?' Dad said. 'None of us ever expected this. Not for a long time. I have felt very alone without Jenny.'

I looked at him in surprise. This was getting very close to *The Archers*' territory. I wondered if he had found someone else to help him get through the loneliness. Like Betty. I glanced at Laura.

'I didn't ever expect to have to do this. Not for my younger sister,' Dan said. 'I thought that was my right as the oldest. I got to do everything first.' He tried for a laugh. 'Yes, it's very sad. Very difficult.' He looked so broken and vulnerable for a moment that I wanted to reach over and give him a hug. Dad patted his arm.

I thought about how well I had been coping and felt a pang of guilt. Perhaps I should have been more upset, like Dan was.

Dan looked over at Laura and me. 'You two girls, though, without your mum.' He spread his hands. 'I know Jenny would have hated not being around for you two.'

Everyone turned and looked at us.

Ollie put his arm round me.

Laura shrugged. 'I don't know if it's all hit me, yet. I feel tired more than anything. I'm sure I sleep a lot more than I used to. It's strange not to feel worse, if you know what I mean. I always thought I'd be much worse than this.'

Ollie looked down at me. 'You've been having bad dreams, haven't you?'

Everyone looked attentively at me.

'Mm,' I said. I nodded my head in a way that I hoped said I agreed with what people had said without actually having to say anything. I coughed. 'Yeah. Dreams.'

Cathy nodded. 'I think dreams are a communication with the dead. It's their way of getting in touch with us, the only way they can, from the spiritual plane. What happens in these dreams, Hannah?'

I cleared my throat. 'Oh you know, I pick a fight with Mum, tell her she ruins everything. Basically, I really upset her, then I wake up.' I paused for a moment and looked at my lap. 'Shall we order some chips?' I said.

We moved on after that. Cathy told us she was setting up a burlesque club with a focus on the over-fifties, which felt like a sinister development on her travelling theatre group.

'Just picture it.' She swept a hand in front of her.

'I'd rather not, Cath,' Dan said.

'We open on a stage. There's soft lighting . . .'

Laura put a hand over her mouth.

Cathy tossed one end of her scarf back over her shoulder. 'It's really just a case of funding, now.' She looked eagerly around the table.

'Ollie,' Dan said. 'How's work going?'

Later, after we had eaten two rounds of chips, left the pub and said our goodbyes, Dad told me that the inquest

215

had come to the conclusion that the accident was a part of a 'medical event' and that nothing could have been done to stop it or save her. That it hadn't been some random accident that could have been stopped if Mum and Laura hadn't gone for a run that day, or if she hadn't tripped. In fact, she didn't trip at all, but had actually had a stroke, which had caused her to fall and had then caused the bleeding in the brain.

Once I was off the phone, I texted Laura. 'See: there was nothing you could have done. I told you it wasn't your fault.'

How to Confront Your Ghosts

After the inquest, I felt like I had been absolved of something. Regret, maybe, or just wondering what could have been. There was nothing any of us could have done. We couldn't have saved her. It almost made the fact that we had to have an inquest worth it.

We had answers now, I told myself. Answers weren't going to bring Mum back, of course. Answers weren't going to make life without her better or significantly different. But answers might help us move on. If we didn't have the 'why' exactly, we could at least stop asking 'what if'.

That wasn't enough, though. I couldn't just accept that I felt fine (which, by the way, I still did) and move on with my life; I had to make sure Laura was fine, too. Or if not completely fine, at least slightly better. It was my responsibility to do so.

So I showed up at my family home and waited to be let in.

Laura opened the door. 'Hi,' she said.

I looked at her. She was wearing her depression pyjamas: the too-small ones with fluffy teddy bears on them that she'd worn almost exclusively in the immediate

217

weeks after Mum had died. She was also holding a half-empty bag of sliced white bread in one hand. This did not feel like a good sign. She was depression eating, too.

I followed her into the kitchen, the surfaces of which, I noticed, were littered with pieces of bread with a bite or two taken out of them. Laura picked one up, bit into it and dropped it again.

She looked at me. 'Dry,' she said.

'Mm.'

'I was making tea. Do you want a cup?'

'Sure,' I said. I looked in the cupboard for a mug; there wasn't one. I looked back at Laura. She was holding a fresh piece of bread and staring into space.

'Why don't we go out for a coffee,' I said.

'Could we have two hot chocolates, please,' I said to the waitress.

'And I'll have a sausage roll, please,' Laura said. 'And a pain au chocolat to go.'

The waitress looked at Laura, then she looked at me.

I nodded.

She walked away.

I looked across the table at Laura. 'You know, you could have changed. If you wanted to. I would have waited. You didn't have to come out in your pyjamas.'

Laura stared out of the window. 'I'm comfortable like this.'

'Right.' I cleared my throat. 'So. How's work?'

She shrugged. 'It's my day off.'

'I know. I meant more generally.'

I leaned back as the waitress returned and deposited our order.

Laura took a bite out of her sausage roll. 'It's fine.'

I nodded. 'Are you still looking for other work? Something that puts your degree to use, like you were talking about before?'

'Sort of. I mean, I was thinking about it and I found some good options, but I just haven't felt up to it, recently. And my job isn't that bad at the moment. It's a bit boring, but at least it's easy.'

I shifted in my seat. 'Cool. But maybe it would be good to have a challenge again. Get yourself out there?'

I watched as she dipped the sausage roll into her hot chocolate and then chewed on it.

'Right. Right . . .' I stirred my drink. 'Well, we don't have to talk about work. Are you dating anyone?'

Laura just looked at me.

I looked at her pyjamas. 'Sure. That makes sense. Dating's hard.' I took a deep breath. 'Well, what about your friends? Have you been going out much?'

Laura nodded. 'I saw them all for my birthday.'

'And after that?'

Laura frowned. 'Sometimes. Why are you asking about all of this?'

I took a sip of my hot chocolate. 'I just want to make sure you're coping. With everything. To do with Mum. And life.'

Laura put a bit of sausage roll in her mouth and chewed it. 'I'm okay.'

'Right. I can see that. But I mean, specifically, after

the inquest. Now we know what happened. How are you doing with that?' I eyeballed her.

She looked vaguely up at me.

I pressed on. 'I know I've found it really helpful. It's like closure. Now we know it wasn't your fault.'

Laura narrowed her eyes. 'Mm.'

'It wasn't anyone's fault. It was a freak medical thing. It was God's will. Probably. You know: part of a bigger plan.' I waved my hands about to demonstrate the bigger plan.

Laura was frowning.

'My point is, you couldn't have done anything differently,' I said, slowly. I wasn't entirely sure she could hear me.

'Right,' she said, equally slowly.

I fidgeted. 'Well, aren't you relieved?'

She sighed. 'I don't know, Hannah. It's just happened. I guess I'm relieved, but I'm still trying to process it. And I just watched an episode of *Forensic Files*. It's hard to think about that stuff happening to Mum.'

'Right. Well, yeah. Maybe don't watch that,' I mumbled.

'Yeah.' She sighed. She took another bite of her food.

'At least this means that we don't have to wonder what could have been any more.' I pressed a hand to my chest. 'It's really been helping me to know that.' I looked at her. 'It's really helped me move on.'

'Okay.' She looked at her phone. 'Well, thanks for that. But . . .'

I took another sip of my drink. 'I just think I've got

220

to a place where I'm coping with that. Honestly, it's a relief.'

'Good for you.'

'Yeah. And it's what I want for you, too. It's what Mum would want. For you to be okay. You know, getting on with your life.'

She stuffed the remainder of her sausage roll in her pocket. 'Yeah, well like I said. I'm fine. You don't have to worry.' She looked pointedly at her phone. 'I should be going, anyway. Don't you have work?'

I pulled my phone out of my pocket. 'Actually, I do have a deadline for this copywriting agency. There's some big campaign coming up for one of their clients.' I looked back at her. 'But you come first. I'm here for you. Always.'

Laura downed her drink.

'Okay, well . . .' I opened the calendar on my phone and froze. 'Shit,' I said.

'What?'

'My ten-year school reunion's coming up. And I'm supposed to be going.'

Laura raised an eyebrow and smirked. 'Well. Don't worry. I'm sure it will be fine.'

I stared at the date in my phone. The college I had gone to after the girls' school was inviting us back. I had had big hopes for it, before I went there. There would be boys there and it's hard to overestimate the excitement that comes with moving to a co-ed school, after a lifetime in a single-sex one. I might finally meet a boy, I thought.

I also wrote this in my diary, several times. I did meet a boy, as it happens, lots of them in fact. Unfortunately, I'm still not entirely sure if any of them ever met me. The co-ed experience, as it turned out, wasn't all that different from the girls' school when it really came down to it: I was painfully unpopular at both.

I had known about the reunion for a while. There had been murmurings on social media from overly chirpy people for months. The people you tell yourself peaked at seventeen. Plus, it had been ten years since I had left and this is the sort of time that ten-year reunions tend to happen. I had even talked to Mum about it, when people first started posting that it had been nine years already and we only had one year left before it was ten. You got the impression that they had been counting down to this moment since we graduated.

I had brought this up with her in a 'quelle horreur' way. 'Can you imagine anything worse,' I had said, laughing. In response, Mum had looked at me sagely and said, 'Han, it's been ten years and you still have nightmares about these people. You need to let it go. You're not the person you were back then, darling. I think you should go. It would be good for you.' I had responded by changing the subject. Mum hadn't let it go, though. A few months later she asked if I had thought any more about it. 'I really think this would be good for you,' she had said. 'It might help you move past all of it. You might even have fun. Do you remember when I first joined Friends Reunited? That was great fun.' It was hardly the same thing. Still, I had messaged my friend Stephanie to see if she was going.

Stephanie had been one of my closest friends at college. Now, she lived in London, working a very demanding job in finance and I did not. Our relationship had progressed to the phase where one of us would suggest a drink, we'd try and find a date when we could both be in the same city and then lapse into silence again until the other one started the ritual all over again. When she messaged to say she was going and begged me to go, too, I finally gave in. I RSVP'd. When I had begrudgingly told Mum this, she had nodded in satisfaction. 'Good choice,' she had said. 'Promise you'll keep an open mind and at least try to enjoy it.'

There was another reason that made me, if not want to go exactly, at least feel slightly more curious about the entire thing and that reason was called Rich. Or Head Boy Rich as I knew him back then.

I had first met him on my second week at the school. He hadn't been the Head Boy then. I had managed to get lost and was wandering through a corridor, looking for my History lesson. I walked up to the third door in the corridor and almost went in, then realised it was the boys' loo. I jumped back so it wouldn't look like I had almost walked in. That's when I saw him. He came out of the loo. I stared deeply into – well, the side of his face. Handsome in that Ryan Gosling sort of way, he had the kind of soulful looks that could convince you he would be deeply interested in fourth-wave feminism and read Simone de Beauvoir in his spare time. I held my breath as he scratched at the illegal blond stubble that covered his jawline (illegal in the sense that the school rules banned facial hair, which doesn't mean much, but meant a lot more back then). I watched as he looked over my head without noticing me at all, partly because he was six foot and so several inches taller than me, but also (mainly) because I was socially invisible. He strode past me, swinging his bag over his shoulder, which narrowly missed my head.

'Sorry,' he said, without actually turning round to see who he had almost knocked over.

My heart started racing. I opened my mouth to say something to him. Then I wondered who I was kidding and closed it again. I gazed after him as he walked down the corridor. Then someone else rounded the corner and stopped him.

'Rich, mate,' the new person said and slapped him on the back. 'What are you doing now?'

Rich raised a shoulder. 'Going for a smoke. Want to come?'

They walked off together.

I briefly wondered if I could ever date a smoker, then wondered who I was kidding, again. That was it. I turned round and walked right back into the boys' loo and into my English teacher, Mr Rosewood. I slammed into his belly and bounced off.

'Oh, ho,' he said. 'Where are you supposed to be, because I don't think it's in there.'

I felt myself go puce. I babbled something about

Mr Taylor's History lesson and waited for the embarrassment to kill me.

'Ah, yes. Wrong corridor,' he said, then marched me to the right corridor, opened the door to the lesson just as Mr Taylor was expounding on the Russians and shoved me inside.

'One of yours, Robert,' he said. 'Found her trying to get into the gents'.' He laughed. And then so did everyone else.

It had taken me years to live that down. The only reason people stopped bringing it up was because we graduated and I never saw them again.

It wasn't that I was still interested in Rich, or at least, not in the same way as I had been then. Of course I wasn't. I had Ollie and was very happy with him, as I planned to tell anyone who happened to ask. Including Rich, if it came up. But there was the new and compelling possibility that he could have lost his looks and become hopelessly pathetic and human and that was something I was very interested in. That was something I really needed to see.

For a while, I felt relatively optimistic about the idea. I even pitched a story about the experience to a women's magazine, which they then commissioned. It felt like fate. Or at least, work. I told myself I was essentially an investigative reporter. Or maybe a millennial Jane Goodall. Plus, I'd watched enough American films that involved the heroine's triumphant return to high school after a life of misery there to believe it could all work out.

Then I stopped feeling optimistic about it and started wondering what on earth I had been thinking. Steph and I could get coffee. Rich, I could google. None of my reasons for going required me to actually go. I could probably even do the article that I had been commissioned to write staying at home and watching those very same high-school movies.

I spent the weeks leading up to it dreading it and actively looking for a way out.

'You've already paid for your ticket,' Ollie said.

'You promised your mum you'd go,' Ollie also said.

'Can't wait to see you,' Stephanie said. 'I'm really looking forward to catching up,' which Ollie then saw and used as another reason why it was too late to back out.

'Your friends are going,' he said.

'My mum just died,' I said.

'Right. And you can't break your final promise to her,' he said. 'Or your editor. This is work, remember?'

'Will you at least come with me? For emotional support? Please? You could be proof someone will actually date me now.'

'I can't. I'm meeting Josh.'

'You're just going to the pub.'

Ollie looked offended. 'It's the pub quiz.'

'Right. Which you do every month.'

'But the jackpot's getting big now. If we win, we could get a lot of money. We've been revising.'

I crossed my arms.

'You'll be fine. You don't need me, anyway. You're blowing this all out of proportion.'

I ground my teeth. 'I'm really going off you,' I said.

So I went. It was only when I got there that I remembered how much I had hated school.

I had dressed carefully, putting on a printed full-length dress with an oversized leather jacket over the top. It was an outfit that said 'edgy, yet smart', while also saying things like 'I have a job. I have a boyfriend. I can look people in the eye now', and a whole lot of other positive things you start to hear when you believe your clothes can talk. When I got to the school hall where the reunion was being held, though, everyone else was wearing jeans with a blazer (men and women alike), which isn't to say they were better dressed, just that they were dressed differently. At school, differently means everything.

I took a step backward and gripped my bag. Mum was wrong about me. I couldn't do this after all. It was nothing like Friends Reunited.

A table near the door had been set up holding glasses of something fizzy and alcoholic, which had clearly been strategically placed there for people like me who needed a reason to actually go in. I took two glasses and drained one, wondering if I could still make an exit.

A girl I had spent at least seven months sitting next to in the same English lesson walked over to me, squinting slightly.

I sighed with relief and raised a hand. At least there was someone there I recognised. 'Hi,' I said.

She looked at me. 'Did you go here?'

My face froze.

227

She tipped her head to one side.

I forced myself to blink. This is a good thing, I told myself. I looked different than I had then, which made sense. I was different. I plucked my eyebrows now. This is what I wanted to show people. I smiled and nodded. 'Yes, I did. You were a teacher here, right?'

She sneered at me and walked off. I downed my second drink and picked up a third, took a deep breath and walked into the room.

I looked around. There was no one there. That wasn't technically true: there were loads of people there, just no one I wanted to see. Most of the attendees, in fact, were the people so popular in school, they probably wouldn't have chosen to ever leave, had that been an option. As it was, it looked like they'd done the best they could in adverse circumstances: they'd simply married each other and continued their lives as if they hadn't left. Half of them seemed to be deep in the throes of spawning the next generation, too. I touched my stomach and wondered if I was behind at life. Then I wondered how it was that they still made me question my own life choices. It was almost a skill.

I craned my neck in case all of the other people who had been unpopular at school were hiding in the corners somewhere, sort of like they had when we were actually at school, but no: it looked like everyone that had had a bad time in school had stayed away.

I started plucking at my dress. 'This was a horrible mistake,' I whispered. This was also a mistake: talking to yourself is rarely the way to ingratiate yourself in a hostile crowd, something I should have known from the last time I was there. As it was, I only remembered this when I spotted two women looking me up and down and tittering.

I sighed and looked away. Across the room, I spotted Mr Taylor. As seems to be the tradition with History teachers, Mr Taylor always looked like he'd stepped out of one of the eras he taught about just in time for our lesson. I plastered on a smile and walked over to him.

'Hello, sir,' I said.

He looked at me.

'Hannah,' I said. 'Hannah Kennedy. Class of . . .' I gestured at the banner on the wall. 'I was in your History group.'

'Ah, yes,' he said, vaguely, looking over my head. 'Hannah, hello. Are you well? How are your parents?'

'Um,' I said. I looked over his head, in return. 'Yes, they're fine,' I said. 'Mum and Dad doing well. Very well. Right, well, I'll let you talk to other . . .' I waved my hand around at the imaginary queue of students also waiting to speak to him and darted off.

I grabbed another drink from a tray that was being carried around the hall by a waiter and skulked at the edges of the room, wishing I were dead. You'd think that would be the kind of thing I'd stop saying, having actually encountered death recently, but you would be wrong.

I pulled my phone out and started texting Ollie. 'Horrible mistake,' I typed. 'No one here I know. Want to die.

Please come get me.' Then I rang him for good measure. He didn't pick up, but he did reply.

'You've barely got there. Your friends will show up soon. Can't talk, at the pub with Josh.'

I clenched my jaw and tried hard not to cry. I rang him again. Then I rang him a third time, when he finally picked up. 'I really don't think I can do this,' I said. 'It's awful here. And I haven't heard from Steph. She might not even come.'

There was a sigh that was somehow still audible, even over the background noise of the pub. 'Hannah, you paid for this. Just stick it out,' he said.

'That's not helpful,' I said.

'You've got to write an article on this. You can't leave. It's for work.'

'It'll be more believable if I don't stay. I can wring six hundred words out of my entrance alone.'

There was another sigh. 'Remember why you went,' he said.

I pursed my lips. 'Because I promised Mum I would. And also because I wanted to show people I'm not the same person I was. I'm better than that.'

'Actually I think what you said was you're better than them. So go show them. Okay, the quizmaster is looking at me. I've really got to go now. Good luck.' He hung up.

I mulled over what he had said. He was right. And even if he wasn't, I couldn't stand here all night on the phone, anyway. That wouldn't show anyone anything — or at least, nothing good. I stuck my phone back in my bag and squared my shoulders. I am a different person now, I thought. I can show them. Mum believed in me.

I looked around and spotted a girl who had once tried to spread the rumour that I had hepatitis. Luckily, this didn't get past the second person she told, as no one believed I had had sex.

I rounded my shoulders. Mum was wrong. I went and hid in the loos.

I locked myself in a cubicle I had eaten lunch in more than once, closed the toilet lid and sat down. Then I pulled out my phone and called Evie.

'I'm at my school reunion,' I said as soon as she picked up.

'Why?'

'I don't know. It was probably something to do with all those high school movies I've seen where it's a good idea. I was indoctrinated. The characters in those always have a dramatic makeover that changes everything about them and then there's a slow-motion walk when everyone realises,' I said.

I could hear Evie nodding. 'It's very believable.'

'I know,' I whispered.

'So leave. You don't owe them anything.'

I knew I should have called Evie first.

I bit my finger. 'I can't. Ollie won't let me. And I haven't even seen Rich-I-used-to-have-a-crush-on yet. He could be fat and bald by now. That's something I really need to see.'

'Mm, you need closure. Well, where are you now?'

I looked at some graffiti on the toilet door that said Jessica Wood was a slut. 'In the toilet.'

'The one you used to eat lunch in?'

I dropped my head. 'Yes.'

Evie took a deep breath. 'Okay, Han, look. You're better than this. And even if you're not, you can't spend all night in the toilet again. People would just think you have the runs. You'd have to go to the twenty-year reunion just to undo that damage. Channel those teen movies. You've had your makeover. Now go walk slowly over to someone and show them.'

I nodded. Evie has a way of marshalling people. It's why she makes such a good mum. 'You're right,' I said. 'I can do this. And I will. Thanks, Evie. I'm going to go.'

'Call me tomorrow and fill me in,' she said.

I walked out and gave myself a hard stare in the mirror. I could do this. What's more, I would do this. I straightened my back, strode out of the loos and back into the hall.

A man I recognised was standing alone, clutching a glass. He looked like a good bet, so I went over.

'Did we go to school together?' I smiled.

He smiled back. 'I think so. Did we play squash together once?'

I shook my head. 'Definitely not me.'

'Oh. Well, what have you been up to for the last ten years?'

'Oh, lots,' I said, nodding fervently. 'I have a job now. As a writer. I'm actually on assignment tonight.' I tossed my hair and smiled in a way that I hoped was winning. 'And I have a boyfriend now.' I nodded some more and took a sip from my glass. 'Then I made the terrible mistake of coming to my ten-year reunion. It all went horribly wrong after that. I might just drop dead, right here.' I laughed.

He did not. In fact, he looked nervous. 'Right, okay. Actually . . .' He gestured at something across the room, mumbled an excuse and strode off.

I watched him go and considered going back to the loo. Then someone tapped me on the shoulder. I turned round and saw my friend Megan.

'Hannah, I'm so glad you came.'

'Megan. Thank God you're here. It's great to see you.' I hugged her. 'Stephanie was supposed to come but I can't see her. I didn't think I was going to know anyone else.'

She smiled. 'Well, I had to come. I helped organise this.'

This made sense: Megan had been Head Girl. She had been the kind of person who thrived in organised social environments. 'Oh. Cool. Right. What are you up to these days?'

'I'm a barrister for a firm in London.'

I smiled. 'Of course you are. You were destined to be brilliant.'

A waiter holding a drinks tray walked nearby. I tried to catch his eye. When that failed, I waved. 'What do you have to do to get a drink round here . . .'

Megan looked at the glass in my hand.

I followed her gaze. 'Right. I'm probably fine. But you: you don't have a drink.'

233

'Thanks, but actually, I'm not drinking.' She passed a hand over her stomach and smiled.

I gasped. 'Oh. Wow, you're pregnant too? Is everyone here? Well, not the men I guess.' I laughed, then cleared my throat. 'Sorry. Congratulations. I'm so happy for you. Children. I want them, too. I thought I had plenty of time to worry about it but looking around here tonight, I'm beginning to feel like I'm behind. Maybe I should get pregnant.' I laughed. 'Why aren't I pregnant?' I laughed again. I willed myself to shut up.

Megan smiled politely and looked away.

I closed my eyes, briefly. 'I mean, congratulations. Congratulations. That's fantastic news. I'm really happy for you.'

'Thanks.' She squeezed my hand. 'What have you been up to? I'm so sorry about your mum. I saw something on Facebook.'

'Oh.' I pulled a face. 'Thanks. You know, these things happen...'

'Right. Look, I've got to go. I need to make sure the staff aren't drinking the cava. The staff are the students the school roped in to help.' She sighed. 'I'll make sure someone comes over with a glass for you.' She winked at me and walked off.

I nodded. I kept nodding even when Megan had left and could no longer see me nodding. I told myself to get a grip.

I looked around for Steph, who I was convinced had abandoned me to spend the entire night alone. I decided

I'd give her ten more minutes then, if she still hadn't shown up, I'd get a taxi.

That's when I saw him: former Head Boy Rich. He was standing at the front of the room, tapping on a glass and waiting patiently for everyone to stop talking to each other and listen to him. I waited for my stomach to drop the way it used to whenever I saw him.

'Thanks for coming, everyone. It's good to see you all, again. Although, some of you I've seen more recently than others,' he said. Then he made a sports reference that I didn't understand. 'And it's good to be back, here, in these hallowed halls,' he continued, arching his eyebrows and smirking.

I looked at him, closely. I was disappointed to note he hadn't spent the intervening years losing his looks. In fact, he looked largely the same. He was, however, wearing tight white chinos and an equally tight white shirt, which is a combination that has always been a red flag for me. Plus, he looked smug. I don't know if he had always looked smug and I'd been too busy adoring him to notice, or if this was a new development, but either way, I was pleased to realise I was no longer in love with him.

I turned away. I realised that as I was no longer in love with him, I no longer found it necessary to listen when he talked, either. It was really quite liberating. I took a sip of my drink and looked around the hall.

Across the room, I saw Stephanie slip inside. Behind her, my friend Mary followed. Mary had been another good friend in sixth form, but as she was one of those people who signed up to every possible club and sports team available, we didn't spend as much time together. She'd also moved to London and we mainly kept in touch by periodically commenting on each other's Instagram posts. The last time I'd seen her was at a house-warming party Stephanie had had a couple of years ago. I sighed with relief and started waving. They looked around, then started waving madly back. Mary gestured at my dress and made a heart shape with her hands, which is essentially what she did on Instagram, but in real life.

They walked up to me and hugged me.

'You look great.'

'It's been too long.'

'Thank God you're here. I really thought you weren't going to come and I'd just be left here, alone.'

'I know. Sorry. There was traffic from the station. How's it been?'

'Terrible.'

'Why are we here?'

'Who knows. Thank God you came.'

'Drinks after?'

'Definitely.'

We smiled at each other.

Around us, everyone had started clapping. I looked up and realised Rich had stopped talking.

'Is it over?' I said.

Mary shook her head. 'No, it's just time for dinner. Apparently, we're eating in the dining hall. That will bring back happy memories. Come on.' She linked arms with the two of us and pulled us through.

Inside, one big table had been set up.

'Last time I was here, I got salmonella,' I said. 'I swore I would never come back.'

Steph looked doubtful. 'I don't think they're going to be serving us school food. Are they?'

I looked down and saw a place setting that had my name on it. 'Looks like I'm here.' I looked around, but Mary and Stephanie had already disappeared over to the other side of the table. I pulled out a chair and sat down.

I looked to my right.

'Oh shit,' I muttered under my breath. I was sitting next to Amber Upton. Amber and I had known each other since we were about thirteen. Our mums were friends, which is not to say that we were. What this really meant was that we'd been forced to spend time together. I would spend this time being very quiet, which made it easier for Amber to ignore me.

'Amber, hi,' I said.

She turned to me. 'Hi . . . Harriet?'

This was someone who had been in my house. Who had looked at the toys in my room and smirked. Who had then repeated every detail about them and my bedroom to the other popular girls in school. I cleared my throat. 'Hannah,' I said.

'Right. How are you?'

'I'm fine,' I said. 'I'm good. I'm a writer, now. A journalist. That's why I'm here tonight, actually. I'm

237

on assignment. I'm writing about what it means to go back to school after you've found success as an adult. For *Vogue*.' This wasn't technically true, in the sense that it was a lie. But on the other hand, it sounded good, which was more important to me. 'And I have a boyfriend, now. He couldn't be here tonight, but he exists. I'm very happy, actually.' I hated myself. I took a deep breath. 'How about you? Did you become a dancer like you always wanted?'

She frowned, slightly. 'Oh, no, the industry, you know?' She waved a hand. 'I do something better, now, anyway.'

Porn, I thought. 'Acting?' I said.

She frowned. 'No. I got married and had kids.' She touched her stomach, even though I was fairly sure she wasn't pregnant. 'They're my main focus. It doesn't leave a lot of time for anything else.'

I nodded.

'I'm on Instagram, now. I have almost four thousand followers.' She tossed her hair and waited for me to be impressed.

I tried my best.

She tilted her head. 'How's your mum? I remember her. She was always so cool and pretty.' She looked at me in a way that implied I was not.

I smiled tightly. 'Actually, she died.'

'Oh, no,' she said, then turned and started laughing with the person on the other side of her.

The man on my other side finished his conversation and turned towards me. 'So, did you go here?'

I closed my eyes.

Plates were put down in front of us. The woman across from me looked at hers, doubtfully.

'The last time I actually ate in here, I got food poisoning,' she said.

I smiled and said a silent prayer that this time, the food would kill me swiftly and thoroughly.

During a lull in the soup course, Amber turned back to me. 'So, how did your mum die?'

I was used to this question. It's a fairly obvious one when someone passes away, suddenly. It used to come up a lot when people rang to express their condolences and then fish around for information – which was fair enough. I'd want to know the details about how a friend died, too. To be honest, I'm quite ghoulish: I'd want to know the details about how someone I didn't know that well had died. So I understood Amber's curiosity.

'The plague,' I said.

She widened her eyes. 'Really?'

I felt a wave of sympathy for her parents, who had paid for her education. I nodded. 'Yes, it was terrible. By the end, she was so far gone. It was . . . Well, have you ever seen *Night of the Living Dead*?'

'The zombie film?' She nodded.

I raised my eyebrows meaningfully and looked away.

'Oh my God,' she whispered. 'How did she get it?'

'Um . . .' I spotted the menu card in front of her plate.

'You know, they say it was from beef. Like a rare strain of mad cow disease. Mum used to eat a lot of red meat.'

Amber looked horrified. 'But I'm having beef tonight!'

'Mm.' I leaned in. 'And you remember what school food was like, right? Why do you think I got the vegetarian option?' I smiled. 'More wine?'

I had never really forgiven her for laughing at my toys, after all.

By the time the pudding was being served, there was a lot less wine.

'Yes, it was a fox-hunting accident,' I said to the man sitting next to me. 'Mum was dressed as a fox.'

'Oh my God,' he said. 'That's terrible.'

I nodded. 'I know.' I flicked my hair back over my shoulder. 'I wrote a big exposé on it for *Vanity Fair*. Where I worked. As a columnist. I'm freelance, now.'

The man next to me scratched his head. 'How does that even happen, though? Fox hunting is banned.'

'Um,' I said.

'Do we have port?' someone shouted from the other end of the table. 'I'm telling you, you've got to get your face in there like it's Jessica's minge.'

Amber leaned into me. 'My mum's such a bitch,' she slurred.

The woman on the other side of her nudged her. 'Amber . . .'

She turned to her. 'What? Just because her mum's dead, doesn't mean I can't have problems.' She turned back to me. 'She's so interested in my life. So smothering.

If I didn't need her to look after the kids while I build up my career, I'd tell her to get her own life.'

'Mm,' I said. 'Right, your career. So where is it you work?'

Amber looked me up and down. 'I told you. I'm on Instagram.' She turned back to the person on the other side of her.

Someone across the table snorted.

I looked up and noticed that the girl who had been sitting across from me had disappeared and former Head Boy Rich had taken her place. He was staring at me. I didn't think that had ever happened before, but here he was, definitely noticing me.

I smiled, slightly. I wondered if now would be the moment I'd been secretly envisioning: the one when he'd reveal that actually, he'd fancied me all along. Or failing that, that he fancied me now. I pictured letting him down gently, telling him he'd missed his chance and that I had a boyfriend now. I'd shrug and smile in a way that let him know I was confident in my life choices, but also slightly sad over what could have been if he'd only said this years before. And then I'd call Evie to let her know the films had been right all along: makeovers really did work. I could be dining off this story for *months*.

He tipped his glass at me.

I waited.

'Weren't you the girl that never washed her hair out of, like, protest or something?' He laughed.

Later, I came up with a comeback to this, a good one, too. It was witty and acerbic and I was almost positive it would have been withering, too. But I'll have to save it for the twenty-year reunion, because in that moment, all I could think of was that this was not the reason I came to my reunion and I didn't think this would have the effect I wanted.

'No,' I said.

Amber giggled.

The guy next to him leaned over. I recognised him, as well. He had been a big deal in the sixth form, which was something we used to say back then.

'No that was someone else. She's a lesbian, now. I saw it on Facebook,' he said. 'Rich, mate, stop hogging the Stilton. You've got to pass the cheeseboard down.'

'Oh, right,' Rich said. He looked me up and down. 'So what was your problem?'

'I'm going to the loo,' I said.

When I came back out, someone barrelled into me and pinned me against a wall.

'Hello?' I said.

'You smell good,' he said, his face in my neck.

I leaned to the side and looked at him. I recognised him: he had once given Amber herpes and bragged about it. I waited for him to ask me if I had gone to school there. Rich came out and smirked.

'Easy,' he said.

At this point, I didn't think a withering put-down would be enough, which was good, as I still didn't have one. I shoved the guy off me and stalked back into the room.

'Vodkaaa,' Amber was moaning.

I downed my wine and picked up my jacket. I had fulfilled my promise to Mum: I had gone. I even had something to write about — enough for a self-help book on doing the opposite, in fact. And now, I was ready to leave and never go back again. I gestured at Stephanie and Mary across the table and signalled at the door. 'Ready to go?' I mouthed at them.

They nodded, got up and grabbed their coats.

'Pub?' Mary said.

'Pub,' we echoed.

'Well, that was fun,' Mary said as we walked down the street.

'I thought Mr Taylor had died during dinner,' Stephanie said.

We made our way to one of the pubs we had gone to when we were still at school. I am ashamed to admit we referred to them as 'our old stomping ground'.

'ID,' Mary said, as we were waved in. 'It makes such a difference.'

Steph shrugged. 'I don't know: I used to come here on our lunch breaks, sometimes. I always got in.'

I rolled my eyes. Not only is Steph beautiful, she has the kind of presence that gets described in magazine profiles as magnetic. It was only her personality that saved her from becoming another Amber: she had one. The point is, she could get in anywhere.

'Weren't you almost suspended for doing that once?' Mary said.

Steph pulled out a chair from a table. 'Almost. It was lucky I was drinking with a teacher. My round?'

As she walked up to the bar, Mary turned back to me. 'That teacher almost got fired for that. He wasn't allowed to be in a room alone with a female student afterwards.'

When Steph came back with the drinks, we caught each other up on what had been going on in our lives. Then we started retelling our favourite anecdotes from our time at school. We also drank. A lot.

A couple of hours in and some of our former classmates lurched through the door, so we quickly slipped out and moved somewhere else.

Eventually, last orders were being called. We were already beginning to slur a bit by this time and retell the same story someone else had told an hour before. Mary groaned and looked at her phone.

'Oh God. I've missed my train back to London. I'm going to have to get an Uber back to my parents. I hope they left a key out somewhere or I'll be sleeping in the shed, again. Guys, this was so great. Let's not leave it so long next time.'

Stephanie stretched. 'I'm staying with my parents, too. I'll have to get a taxi.'

I slammed my hand on the table, almost knocking over a collection of empty glasses. 'No. No taxis. No sheds. I won't allow it. Steph, Mary, you're family. You're my family. And that means something. Trust me: I know. I keep losing parts of it. Come stay with me. We live close by, anyway.'

'Really?' Mary said.

Steph frowned. 'I don't know, Han. I don't want to impose.'

I waved my hands. 'It's not an imposition. That's what old friends are for.'

In retrospect, the tequila had been a mistake.

There were more drinks when we got in. We sat giggling on the sofa, talking about everything that had changed since we left school. I talked about losing Mum and Steph talked about breaking up with the man that she had at one point thought she was going to marry.

'She was just gone,' I said. 'And now my dad might be shagging someone else.'

'He just left,' she said. 'And he's definitely shagging someone else. I've seen her on Instagram. She's a vet.'

Mary wiped away a tear. 'My life has actually been pretty good so far. I'm so sorry, you guys.'

It's hard to say how much we had had to drink at that point.

We hugged each other tightly and promised we'd do more to stay in touch from then on. We all decided that ten years hadn't been long enough to even consider revisiting our school days.

'What had we been thinking?' I said.

'Everyone was married,' Mary said.

I raised a finger. 'To each other, though.'

Steph hiccupped. 'The marriage market starts early. My mum told me that once. She wanted me to marry rich.'

I closed an eye. 'Marry rich or marry Rich?'

'Head Boy Rich? Oh no, he has herpes. Got them from Amber.' She stretched. 'I need to go to bed.'

Mary stood up with her and took her arm. 'Me too. This has been great, though.' Together, they climbed the stairs, unsteadily.

I poured myself a glass of water and then followed them up. I was relieved the night was over and I was finally home. I got into bed and curled up next to Ollie.

I was just beginning to drift off when there was a knock on the door. I jerked awake again.

'Hannah?' Mary said. 'Are you awake? Steph's been sick. In the bed. It's in my hair,' she wailed.

I opened my eyes. 'Oh my God,' I said. I looked at Ollie, who was still asleep. I shook him. 'Ollie, wake up,' I hissed. 'Steph's been sick. In our spare bed.'

Ollie opened an eye. 'Why do your friends keep doing that in our house?'

I shook him again. 'Can you help me? Please? I can't deal with this tonight.'

'Hannah.'

'*Please.*'

He sighed and pulled himself out of bed, while I opened the door to Mary. I recoiled as I smelled her.

'Don't worry. She's in the bathroom. But it's all over me. Can I have a shower?' She pulled out a tight coil of hair and winced. 'This is not good for my hair type.'

'Of course,' I said. I went downstairs and showed her how to use the shower, while Ollie got the fresh sheets.

Steph raised her head. 'Sorry. So sorry. I think it's food poisoning. The beef.' She made a sound that could be described as mooing and reared back towards the loo.

I turned round and went back to bed.

Ten years, I thought. That means nothing.

How to Keep a Baby Alive

The next day, we chucked out our pillows.

'Shouldn't we try and save them?' I said. 'They might still be okay.' I prodded one. It squelched.

'We're not students, Hannah. We earn money,' Ollie said. 'We can buy new ones.'

'Right,' I said. 'We're adults.'

I was standing in the kitchen wearing a pair of rubber gloves, an apron and clutching a bin bag.

Steph and Mary had already left.

'I really do think it was the beef,' Steph had said, as she walked through the door. She looked pale, but more regular-hangover-pale than food-poisoning-pale. 'You wouldn't believe how many times I got ill from that school food. Amber was saying something about mad cow disease. I'm telling you: it was the beef.'

Mary had glanced at me and rolled her eyes as she followed her out. Mary also looked pale, but then, Mary also smelled vaguely of sick that wasn't hers, so who could blame her.

In the kitchen, Ollie pulled a face at me. 'Can you get out of here? Or change? You really stink.'

There might have also been a clothes peg on my nose.

I turned and went back up to the spare bedroom, thinking about what it meant to be an adult.

There's something interesting you find out when you lose a parent: it's not just the present that you lose them in. They take your whole past with them too. Gone are their memories of you when you were too young to do the remembering for yourself. You lose your childhood all over again. Obsessing over this isn't productive though, so you try not to focus on the fact that no one will recall the fact that Proust was your first word and that you said it at an almost unheard-of young age. You try to look forward, instead. That's when you realise it's not just the present or your past that are now riddled with holes, but the entire blueprint of your future is missing. The mirror you had of yourself in twenty-five or thirty, or however many years on, has disappeared. Will you get breast cancer? Will you age well or should you be researching night creams with active ingredients now? Will you live until you are a hundred? Who can say because the person that could tell you has gone. It can all leave you feeling stuck in a present you don't particularly want to be stuck in.

I had come to one clear conclusion, and that was that I couldn't go back. I knew that. If the night before had taught me anything, it was that. You can't go back; you can only go forwards. I repeated this to myself like a grim mantra. I said it while I was changing sheets; I said it while I was looking up Oxfam's policy on donating used bedding; I said it – barely breathing, but still, I said it — when I carried the desecrated bundle of linen downstairs to the washing machine. You can't go back; you can only go forwards.

I slammed the washing machine door shut and looked at Ollie, who was making lunch.

'Do we drink too much? Twice in the last six months, people have been sick in our house. I think this means we drink too much.'

'No, I think it means other people drink too much,' Ollie said. 'Can you open a window?'

'I think we need to rethink how we socialise. We need to be more adult about this whole thing.'

He didn't turn round from the cooker. 'Maybe we need to rethink who we socialise with. My friends don't pee in the garden.'

I waved him off. 'We need to stop getting people so drunk. It's beginning to feel like we're hazing them. Eighteen-year-olds get drunk and throw up everywhere, not twenty-eight-year-olds. We need to move past that. To... Well, I don't know to what, exactly. Maybe dinner parties. But we need to move past it nevertheless.' I pointed to the ceiling. 'Onwards.'

Ollie turned and handed me a plate. 'I made omelettes.'

My stomach lurched.

Looking back meant school reunions and ruining pillows. Looking back meant remembering life when you still had someone that wasn't there any more. Looking forward meant progress. It meant normality. Looking forward probably meant moving forward, which I liked the sound of.

Ollie went out after lunch to help a friend work on his car, which meant I had the day to myself. I decided to spend it on the sofa under a blanket, glued to my computer, searching through my old classmates' social media and feeling morose.

I used to do this quite a lot. Not with my former classmates — my interest in that dried up after university, when I stopped having disappointing sex, or stopped having it with them, at least. I don't know if anyone can really be definitely done with disappointing sex. Sometimes, it's just not up to you. But with anyone new in my life that I was vaguely interested in working out, or anyone that used to be in my life and wasn't any more, when I wanted to know how they were coping without me. I used to think of it as a special skill. For a while, I offered my services out to my friends whenever they met someone new. I even bragged about my abilities for a little bit. Then I stopped, because it came across less like a spy for the internet age and more sad and creepy. Then I met Ollie, started having the actually really good sex, stopped pretending stalking people online was a hobby at all and logged off.

Now, though, I was back on and nursing a hangover while scrolling through holiday photos, updates about promotions that came with important job titles and a series of engagement, wedding and baby photos. I wondered if there had been some kind of mutual consensus that everyone would make a success of their life by twenty-six and if so, why I hadn't been included in the decision. I plucked at my blanket and allowed myself

251

to feel worse about myself. It wasn't the first time I had questioned where I was in my life compared to them, but in the past, this had meant 'am I the only one not dating yet' or 'am I the last person to discover eyeliner' and that had all been much easier to manage.

By the time Ollie got home that evening, I had made a decision. I was moving forward. I knew what to do because I'd seen all my classmates do it before me. I was the last one standing. I just had to grow up. It was time to put down roots. It was time for me to create my own family. I was an adult now; it was time.

Ollie had told me he wanted children on our third date. I had still been trying to work out if I should have left him with Izzie.

'Do you want children?' he had said.

I hadn't known how to respond. Did he want children? Did he want them with me? Did I want children with him? Was I about to walk into a trap when the wrong answer could end things entirely before they'd even started? But he had just said it, simply, like that: did I want children? And I did. I had always envisioned having them. So I responded the same way.

'Yes,' I said. 'I do.'

'Cool,' he said. 'Me too.'

Ollie was making his special sauce when I decided to talk to him about it; it meant he was in a good mood. He turned off the hip-hop playlist, cracked black pepper over both our plates with a flourish and we sat down to eat at the kitchen table. He was still rapping quietly under his breath. I stuck a fork into my pasta and twirled it deftly. I learned how to do this at a young age. I was twirling spaghetti before I learned how to swim. Dad was always very insistent on the fact that I should be able to eat pasta properly. He seemed to have given up on this by the time Laura came round to solids. It was years before she could go to an Italian restaurant and not embarrass herself. She did learn how to swim before me, though.

I raised the fork to my mouth and said, carefully but casually, 'I think we should try for a baby.' Then I popped the fork into my mouth.

I had lost my past, there was a gaping hole in my present, but I could create my future.

Ollie stopped rapping.

'What?' he said.

I put my fork down. 'I think we should have a baby. Now. Well, not right now; these things don't happen right away. But I think we should start trying now.'

He laughed.

'I'm being serious.'

Ollie looked alarmed. 'Is this because of the reunion, again? You've just seen all your old classmates with families and now you want one, too?'

Sort of, I thought. 'No,' I said. 'It's about more than that. I just feel like it's the right time, now. Listen.' I took his hands in mine. 'When I was a little girl, my grandma asked me to write a story about cellos. That's all she wanted: a story about cellos. Then one day she died and I realised I had never written her that story about cellos. So I decided I would write it then anyway and it would be the best story about cellos that anyone had ever written. So then, when Mum died, I thought, I should have a baby.' I said most of this without breathing.

I waited.

Ollie shook his head. 'What about cellos?'

'What about cellos?'

'I thought you were going to say you wanted to write a story about cellos for your mum. Like you did with your grandma. I thought that was the moral of the story.'

'Why would I do that? Mum didn't care about cellos.'

'Fine. But what does any of that have to do with having a baby?'

'Mum loved babies.'

Ollie rubbed his eyes. 'So you want to get pregnant as a weird tribute to your mum? Can't you just write about cellos again?'

'I never wrote the cello story. I didn't get round to it. But this time, Ollie, I really think this will fix everything.'

'How is that?'

I spread my hands. 'I won't have to miss Mum any more because I will become her. She will be me. I will become the mother.'

Ollie looked a bit wild-eyed, the kind of way people look when they're talking to someone who's deeply irrational. He looked around him and raised his hands. 'That's not what having a baby means; that's reincarnation. Or possession or something...'

'No, that's just what happens to women when they age.' I shook my head. 'You don't understand. I have been focused on what I've lost, but I can't get it back. That's gone now, forever. Poof, it's gone. Bye-bye.' I waved. 'There's no point stewing on it. You have to focus on the future or you'll never move on. But if I have my own child, then I get that relationship back again. Plus, my mum loved kids. She would have loved having grandchildren. I want to do this for her.'

'Hannah, you're not blinking.'

I blinked. 'Think about it. I'll never have a sad Mother's Day again because it will become something fresh and new. It won't be about what I've lost; it will be about what I've become.' I stared at him intently, willing him to understand. 'A mother,' I mouthed.

He took my hands and looked into my eyes. 'Hannah, you're acting crazy,' he said. 'Can we just eat dinner?'

I chose not to dwell on Ollie's initial reaction. I was busy. I had realised I could stick a pillow down my jumper and get a better look at 'Pregnant Hannah'. I had always thought that was something only female characters on television shows ever did and never any women in real life, but there I was: admiring my new silhouette. I left it there for most of the afternoon, while I worked.

A few nights later, when we were sitting watching television after dinner, I brought it up again. We were watching some programme about a woman who thought she was pregnant with the devil, at the time. It felt right.

'You know,' I said, watching Ollie from the corner of my eye. 'I really think I would enjoy being pregnant.' We watched as the woman started clawing at her stomach and screaming. 'Our child wouldn't be demonic. Probably.'

'Mm,' Ollie said.

I took a deep breath and turned to him. 'I meant what I said the other day. I really do feel ready to have a baby. Our baby.'

On screen, the woman was vomiting, noisily.

'Hannah,' Ollie said.

'Don't let that put you off,' I said. 'I mean it, Ollie. I want this.'

Ollie sighed and turned to me.

'It's not like we haven't discussed it before,' I said. 'We were talking about maybe starting a family before Mum died. If she hadn't, we might have started already.' This was only half true. When Evie had had Harry, Ollie had seen how much I loved Harry and asked if I had thought about us having children together. I had been thinking about it, I had been thinking about it a lot. But I'd always imagined I'd be married first, which is really another by-product of being raised Catholic and not wanting my parents to know I'd had sex until I was legally married and it became unavoidable.

'Maybe, but . . .' Ollie said.

'You always said you wanted to be a young parent. Well, why not now?'

Ollie paused.

'Life is short,' I said. This could be convincing, given the evidence we had. I tried not to stare at him too intently.

'I thought you wanted to be married before having children,' he said. 'Something about being able to look your dad in the eye.'

'Things change, people die. I'm ready now,' I said.

'Right. And isn't it a bit soon after to make a life-changing decision like this?'

I waved this off. 'Major life-changing things have already happened that I had no say in. Having some control over one might make a nice change. That's all you're worried about: you know you'd want them if you thought I was ready. And I am.'

He didn't look convinced, but at least he wasn't as sceptical as he had been.

I squeezed his thigh. 'It would take us a while to get pregnant anyway. No one gets knocked up first time. The only people that happens to are the ones that don't want it to, like teenagers and Catholics who already have nine children and have been medically forbidden to have another one. That's how biology works: Sod's Law. It would take us at least a year to actually get pregnant, so we'd have time to get used to the idea.'

Ollie shook his head. 'And your parents paid for your education,' he said. 'Hmm.'

It felt like progress. We went back to watching TV. I

257

wondered if I should show him the cushion under the jumper trick. I gently rubbed my stomach, instead, like there was something already gestating in there.

In the end, it took another week of me gently prodding and him gently questioning the state of my mental health before he finally agreed.

'Okay,' he said.

That was it. It was enough, though. We were off.

We had sex that night. I lay back, my legs pinned against Ollie's chest.

'Fill me up, fill me up, fill me up,' I chanted, like an unsexy mantra.

Ollie paused. 'No,' he said.

I sat up. 'Ollie, you have to. How else are we going to get pregnant?'

'Oh. Right.'

He thrust into me, again.

'Fill me up, fill me up.'

'Hannah, can you not?'

'Sorry.'

When we had finished and were lying there, sweating and panting, I threw my legs in the air and rested them against the headboard.

'What are you doing?' Ollie said.

'Gravity,' I said.

Ollie rolled off the bed. 'I thought we weren't going to put pressure on this happening right away. Let nature take its course.'

I waggled my toes. 'I know, but if it happened right

away, even better, right? Think how efficient that would be.'

Ollie turned away and walked out of the room to the bathroom. 'Let's go have a shower.'

I climbed off the bed, but I felt excited. This would work.

I had realised something important: 'mother' could become my new identity. Before Mum died, my identity had been 'twenty-something', it had been 'writer not always satisfied with her career'. It had been 'girlfriend', 'feminist', 'daughter' and lots of other things. Then Mum had died and all my other identities had disappeared and been replaced with 'motherless'. That had taken over everything. All people saw when they looked at me was 'grieving' even when I didn't feel that way about myself. I was lost. I wanted my identity back. I wanted a new one. 'Mother' could be it. And until then, there was 'trying'.

While I had felt smothered and conflicted when it came to talking about my feelings after Mum, I positively yearned for people to ask me all about my new quest for motherhood. I wanted to talk about nothing else. I was ready to gush about multivitamins, nausea and heartburn I hadn't even experienced yet. I threw myself into it.

'We're trying,' I told friends, smugly and conspiratorially, placing a hand on my stomach, then resting it there for the rest of the conversation as if there was already something in there to nurture – which there was not.

259

When they then looked at each other and said things like, 'Wow, that's soon' or 'Are you sure you're ready for that?' or 'Can you take the time off work right now?' I would pretend they hadn't said anything. 'We had sex this morning, before I came here,' I would say, instead.

I even took my performance on the road. In the supermarket, Ollie reached for a packet of condoms and I lightly slapped his hand away.

'Ollie, no.' I laughed. I turned and smiled at the teenage boy posturing over a packet of Durex Comfort XL. 'We're trying,' I said.

Ollie looked down and pushed the trolley on.

In short, I was insufferable. But, I reasoned, insufferable about something you're allowed to be insufferable about. If you can't act that way over your children, someone needs to tell that to parents on the internet.

I had always heard that sex when you were specifically trying to get pregnant wasn't sexy. It was carefully timed, it was planned, it involved taking temperatures and careful ovulation calculations. I didn't want that. I was determined to keep it fresh, exciting and most importantly, sexy. I thought about the rooms in the house we hadn't had sex in, which, when it came to listing them, was a lot of them. Apparently, we only ever had sex in bed. So one Friday, I trussed myself up in matching underwear and stockings and went down to the kitchen to lie in wait until Ollie got home. It was less creepy than I'm making it sound. Because I got dressed far too early and then didn't know what to do with myself, I also made dinner and then put it in the oven to keep it warm for after. Then I draped myself over the kitchen counter and waited for Ollie to come home.

I heard his lock in the key. 'I'm in the kitchen,' I shouted.

I waited for him to take his socks off and leave them by the front door.

He walked through and grinned. 'Did you make a curry?'

I pushed my hands up into my hair and slipped off the counter.

'Hello, big boy,' I said. I don't know why I said this; I think I read it on a car advert, once. It was as if I'd forgotten how to have sex.

Ollie raised his eyebrows. 'Big . . . boy?'

I smiled and kissed him, reaching for his belt buckle.

He pulled away slightly. 'Are we . . . ?'

'Let's do it here,' I said, firmly.

Ollie smiled and kissed me, again. He grabbed my bum and pulled me into him, kissing me harder. I pulled off his T-shirt and flung it over my shoulder. He unhooked my bra and pulled it off. He cupped both of my breasts in his hands and sucked my nipples. I pulled off my knickers, stepping out of them while he tugged off his jeans. I hopped up onto the counter and onto the electric hob. I had forgotten about the curry. A curry I had cooked on the hob. A hob that was still hot. I screamed.

Ollie looked alarmed. 'Han, what—'

I ran to the sink, turned on the cold tap and tried to

angle my bum underneath it. I wished I had bothered going to yoga.

'Grab the yoghurt,' I yelled, gesturing frantically at the fridge.

Ollie finally grasped what had happened. 'Oh shit,' he said. He snatched a pot of yoghurt out of the fridge and practically threw it at my bum.

'I think I've burned off my vagina,' I wailed. 'It's gone. I'll never have sex again.'

Ollie ran towards the stairs. 'I'll get the first aid kit.'

I sank to my hands and knees and stayed like that, trying to blow at my bottom to cool it down.

He came clattering back down, throwing plasters. 'Where's the bloody Savlon? Do you have any moisturiser?'

I moaned.

'Tea,' he said. 'Tea is good for burns.' He took a box of Tetley out of the cupboard and clicked the kettle on.

I glared at him.

'Oh, right. Milk.' He got the carton out of the fridge, soaked a tea towel in it and draped it over my behind. I was just glad we had bought full fat.

When I had calmed down, Ollie inspected my wounds.

'I don't think you've done any permanent damage,' he said. 'It's just a bit red, that's all. It sort of looks like you sat on a really hot plate.' He looked like he was trying not to laugh. I glared at him until he fetched me my dressing gown from upstairs and draped it gently round me. I spent the rest of the evening on my front. I knew there was a reason we saved sex for bed.

It took me a few days of not being able to sit down properly until I felt ready to leave the house, again. Once I was, I met Evie for a coffee in a vegan café in Hove. Evie was one of my few friends who had actual experience of getting pregnant. I thought she might have some tips.

When I got there, she was already sitting waiting for me, sipping tea and reading a book.

'Sorry, sorry, sorry,' I said.

Evie held a hand up as she finished her page. 'That's okay. I got to read something.' She looked up. 'You could have been later.'

I sat down. 'Where's Harry?'

'With my parents. I have a whole afternoon off.' She beamed. 'Go get a drink so I can finish my chapter. No rush.'

When I came back, she put her book away and examined my face. 'How have you been doing?'

I shrugged. 'I'm fine.'

'Be honest,' she said.

'No really, I'm okay.' I smiled and leaned in. 'Ollie and I are trying,' I said. 'For a baby,' I added, when she didn't say anything.

'Why?' she said.

I blinked. No one had asked me that, yet.

'Because we want to have a baby,' I said, although it came out sounding more like a question.

Evie gave me her hard stare. It's a very impressive hard stare. It's where I got mine from: I copied it off Evie.

'I know you want children, Hannah, but why now? You've just had one massive disruption to your life. Why are you so keen to have another?'

I shifted in my seat. 'It's not like anyone's dying this time,' I said.

Evie crossed her arms.

I took a packet of sugar from the bowl, ripped it open and poured it into my tea.

'I just want to make something good come out of this. And starting a family of my own can be that thing. Everyone goes on about how much they love their children. I could have that. The whole special bond between a mother and her daughter.' I smiled. 'Just think about it, Eve. I could dress her up in lots of sweet little outfits. And read her all my favourite books. Then, when she gets older, she'll confide her secrets in me and I can impart my life's wisdom. And we can become best friends. You know, like Mum and me.'

Evie kept her hard stare going. 'And Ollie's okay with this?'

I huffed. 'I'm not stealing his sperm.' I narrowed my eyes. 'Why? Don't you think I can do it? Don't you think I would be a good mum?'

'I think you'd be a great one. I just want you to be sure you're being realistic. It's not easy, Han. Is now the right time to be making such a life-changing decision? Have you thought how you're going to handle this without her around? And what if it's a boy. What happens to the magical mother/child bond then? Or does it have to be a girl for that to work?'

I crossed my arms. 'Of course I have.' I hadn't. 'It's not like if I wait long enough, she's going to come back. I don't have a choice in this. I want to get on with my life and make something good happen. I want to have a child before any more of my relatives up and die.'

Evie went quiet. How dare she make me question this? So what if it was a boy?

'Okay,' she said, eventually. 'Do you want some practice?'

I looked at her, suspiciously. I wasn't expecting to win her over so quickly. I also wanted to talk about it, though and this urge won out.

'We have been practising,' I said. 'A lot. The other day, we had sex upside down.' I nodded.

Evie sat back in her chair. 'Upside down? What, both of you?'

'No, just me. Ollie was upright. I had burned my bum, you see, so normal positions were off.'

'Oh. How did that work?'

I leaned forward. 'You sort of have to do a handstand, but with your legs open, of course. So I did that, then Ollie sort of dipped himself into me.'

'Dipped?'

I reached for her tea. 'Imagine I'm the mug,' I said. I took the teabag by the string and lifted it. 'And the teabag is Ollie. Sort of like that. We couldn't do it for long, though. I began to feel faint.'

Evie nodded. 'Sure. Jake and I usually just do it lying down, now.'

'Well, I didn't want to make this whole trying to get

265

pregnant thing boring. How did you get pregnant with Harry?'

'Accidentally.'

I nodded.

'Anyway,' she said. 'I meant do you want to practise with an actual baby? You know, see if you like it before you commit to it? You and Ollie could take Harry for a day.'

'Are you actually being supportive or do you just want someone to babysit for you?' I said.

'Both,' she said. 'That's allowed, though.'

I considered this. A whole baby to practise on. One that I knew and liked already. This would definitely be more useful than the pillow down the jumper – there was only so far that could take you. I probably needed the practice.

'Okay,' I said.

For some reason, we shook on it.

I practically bounced through the door when I got home afterwards.

When Ollie got home, I accosted him at the front door.

'Where do you want to have sex now?' he said, a bit wearily.

'I found us a baby,' I said.

He looked alarmed. 'What have you done?' He looked around, as if I was hiding one in the house.

'We're babysitting Harry for Evie and Jake,' I said. 'Next weekend. They need a babysitter and we get to practise having a baby before we actually have one.'

Ollie pulled off his shoes and socks. 'Did Evie convince

266

you to do this because she needs someone to look after Harry?'

'No. Well, maybe sort of. But it works for us, too. We get some practice in.'

'Hmm,' Ollie said.

I waited for a moment. 'Speaking of babies, shall we have sex on the stairs?'

I spent the days leading up to babysitting reading parenting blogs and articles to prepare myself. Then I would text Evie to ask if she had heard of whatever I was reading about, like co-sleeping or a new study that had definitely decided that breast really was best. She never replied.

By the time we were due round to look after Harry, I felt ready and capable. I knew not to feed him grapes and I was well versed on the effects of screen time on hand-eye coordination. I knew what to expect.

'This will be great. I really feel like I'm ready for motherhood,' I said, every few minutes, until Ollie had to tell me to shut up.

I put on a jumper that had animals on it. Harry had once had a violent bowel eruption on it while I was wearing it, which I took as a sign of approval.

When we arrived, Evie flung the door open, holding Harry and grinning. There was a strange glint in her eyes that I couldn't immediately work out. Jake stood behind her, looking a bit uncertain, but mainly relieved to see us. 'New parents,' I thought. He and Ollie shook hands while Evie smiled knowingly at me.

'How do you feel?' she said.

'Excited to be spending the day with my favourite kid.' I waved at Harry. 'Look, Harry, I wore the jumper you like.' I pointed to a sequin tiger. Harry didn't look as impressed as I was hoping.

Evie hugged Ollie with one arm.

'I think this is going to be a really good experience for you guys,' she said. 'Get an idea of what parenting's really like, before you have one of your own. Right, Harry?' She smiled, then turned back to me, that glint in her eye again.

Jake rubbed his neck. 'Evie.'

'We're looking forward to it,' Ollie said. 'What have you two got planned for today?'

'We're going into town,' Jake said. 'Have lunch, do a bit of shopping.' He took Harry's hand and wiggled it. 'But if you need us, we'll have our phones.'

'Oh no, Jake. They'll be fine,' Evie said.

I narrowed my eyes at her. She had the eyes of a shark.

'Well, we should go,' she said.

I smiled. 'Come on, Harry.' I reached for him and Evie handed him over.

'It's okay, it's okay,' she shushed him.

Jake clapped his hands together. 'Okay, we shouldn't hang around in case he gets upset.'

Evie grabbed her jacket and kissed Harry. 'Instructions are in the kitchen. Everything you need is in there or in the sitting room. Good luck.'

The door closed. I smiled at Ollie and jiggled Harry. 'It's just us now, little man.'

Harry looked at me. I looked at Harry. I realised this was the first time we had actually been alone together. Harry looked as if he was realising it, too. He narrowed his eyes. I could almost feel him sizing me up.

I swallowed. 'It will be fine,' I said.

Harry frowned. Then I felt a spreading warmth.

I sighed. 'Ollie, get a nappy.'

The real problems started with the mashed banana. I can't imagine much good ever starts with mashed banana, but in this case, it was the start of a complete nightmare. Up until then, our biggest problem had been stopping Harry from eating soil out of the house plant's pot and that had almost been a welcome distraction. Babysitting, it turned out, could be very dull. That was before we tried to feed him, though. I told myself we would have to deal with worse with our own children and that was the whole point of babysitting. We looked at each other knowingly, in a 'babies, eh?' way and started pulling the kind of tricks adults do to try and get babies to eat things like mashed banana. But they didn't work. Harry refused to eat. We looked at each other again, this time a little less knowingly and a little more anxiously. I consulted Evie's list of instructions, which included the now unhelpful phrases like 'Harry's a good eater' and 'Try the mashed banana'. I shrugged at Ollie. He went back to pretending Harry's spoon was an airplane.

When that didn't work, he stood up. 'Your turn.'

I took the spoon and leaned over Harry, smiling madly. He looked at me for a long second and then picked up his spoon. We stopped despairing. We started to cheer him on, championing the mashed banana. Then he threw the spoon at me. Mashed banana spattered my jumper. I swore.

Harry had clearly decided he was done and started trying to clamber out of his high chair.

I grabbed him and he started to grizzle. Then this turned into a howl.

I gave Ollie a world-weary look but waved him off.

'Don't worry,' I said. 'I've got it.' I thought I had. I had done so much reading. I was basically the horse whisperer of babies. I was Mary Poppins. I was Wonder Woman.

Ollie sat down and started eating the mashed banana as I walked Harry round the kitchen, jiggling him gently and singing a nursery rhyme. The crying didn't stop. It got louder. I jiggled some more and started singing more loudly, too — I had to, he wouldn't have heard me, otherwise. The howl then became a screech.

I looked down at him. His face was red and scrunched up, streaked with tears. His eyes were firmly shut. I had never seen him like that before. I wondered if it was me.

'Harry, Harry, please don't cry any more,' I said. 'You don't have to eat the banana.'

I was beginning to panic. At the decibels Harry was reaching, I half expected him to splinter his vocal cords. Or alert Evie, who at any point, would come running in, proving to me that I was incapable of doing this. I didn't know which was worse. I wasn't Mary Poppins or Wonder Woman. I was Mommy bloody Dearest.

Harry opened his eyes and shot me a look of pure hatred I didn't think babies were capable of.

I looked at Ollie, desperately. 'This isn't working,' I cried.

Ollie stood up. 'Okay. Let me try, again,' he said, gently extricating Harry from my arms. He walked off into the sitting room. I braced myself against the sink. At first, there was no change, then the wails started to get quieter. When I walked in, Harry was lying on the floor on a changing mat, sucking on a toy.

'I think it might have been trapped wind,' he said when I walked in. 'And his nappy needed changing. Again.'

Harry looked at me from the floor and laughed in a way that made it feel it was personal.

My phone pinged. It was Evie.

'How's it going,' it said. 'Ready for parenthood yet?'

I sent her back a series of random emojis and put the phone in my pocket.

Ollie got Harry up, sat him down on the sofa and turned the television on. He flicked through channels until he found cartoons, then sat down on the sofa with Harry and pointed him in the direction of the screen.

'There you go,' he said, bouncing him on his lap.

I was aghast. 'Ollie, no screens. It's bad for babies' development. He should be playing with wooden toys, only.' I grabbed the controller and switched off the television.

Both of them looked at me, aggrieved. Harry scrunched his face up.

'Hannah,' Ollie said.

I turned it back on.

'Thank you.'

I sat there with my arms crossed while Harry pointed a chubby finger at the animals on the screen.

I didn't say anything else for a while.

Eventually, Ollie glanced at me. 'What?'

'Nothing,' I said. I continued to glare at the TV.

'Hannah.'

I huffed. 'If you must know, I was just thinking that I'm clearly terrible at this. You might as well just leave me now before we have kids of our own and it gets messy.'

'Oh my God, the melodrama,' Ollie said.

I looked at him, mutinously.

'You're the one that wanted to do this, Hannah. It was your idea.' He smiled at Harry who was bouncing enthusiastically. 'That's right. It was, wasn't it Harry.' I didn't know if he meant looking after Harry or having our own.

I didn't say anything.

My phone pinged.

'I need air,' I said. 'Let's go for a walk.'

I strapped Harry into his pushchair (a pushchair Ollie had managed to construct quite simply, after I had shut my finger in a join and almost lost a nail).

'Hove Park isn't that far away. Harry loves it there. He likes it when I take him on the swings.' I smiled into Harry's face. 'Don't you? What do you think Harry? Swings?'

Harry just looked at me.

I stood up. 'He has his mother's eyes.' I grabbed the nappy bag. 'This will be great. It's just what he needs. We can take him on the miniature steam train. No more relying on screens just to pacify him when things get a little bit tricky. This will be great.'

Harry waited until we were on the street until he started complaining, squirming in his seat and pulling at the straps that were fastening him in.

I looked down at him. 'What is he doing? He loves the park. He's usually so happy when we go. It's almost like he's reacting to the fresh air and sunlight. It's like he's been replaced by a vampire child. That would certainly explain a few things.' I paused. 'How plausible is that?'

Ollie didn't bother replying.

A bus trundled past us and Harry threw himself towards it in a deep lunge, rocking the pushchair, which swayed to the side, threatening to fall over.

I jumped. 'Harry, no!' I gripped the pushchair handles tighter. 'You can't do that. It's dangerous,' I told him. Danger, I was beginning to notice, was everywhere. I slightly regretted exposing him to more of it by leaving the flat.

We walked along in silence. I noticed people were looking at Harry, who was trying to shove a pink fist up his nose and then at us. Except, they weren't looking at him the way they usually did, when Evie was with him, which was to say, lovingly. They looked a bit disapproving. I wondered if anyone could tell how unprepared I was now feeling. How a small child was

273

mentally besting me. This was supposed to be my chance to prove my maternal instincts. I was supposed to be a natural. Now, I was beginning to feel like I had a neon sign over my head that said 'imposter'.

I bent over the pushchair and laughed. 'Now Harry, don't do that,' I said, gently removing the fingers he had pushed up both nostrils and smiling at passersby. I turned back to Harry. 'Stop acting like I've taken you hostage,' I whispered. 'We're going to the park. You love the park.'

Harry responded by trying to take off his shoe.

I leaned into Ollie. 'I feel like everyone's judging me. Like they know I'm not doing this right.'

'No one's judging you. Apart from maybe me, that is.'

'What if people realise he's not ours and think we've stolen him?'

'No one's going to think that. Unless you keep saying that.'

Then I heard a shout. 'Excuse me.'

It came from behind us.

'Excuse me!'

I looked round. A woman was running towards us, waving.

I grabbed at Ollie. 'Oh my God, Ollie. It's happening. What do we do? Do we run?'

Ollie looked at me. 'Why would we run?'

'I don't know. Stranger danger. What if she sees I don't know what I'm doing and tries to take him off us?' I protectively blocked the pushchair with my body.

Then the woman caught up with us. 'Excuse me. Sorry, but the baby.'

I grabbed the pushchair. 'He's fine. I'm allowed to have him. You can't take him away from me.'

Ollie and the woman stared at me.

Ollie smiled at her. 'We're babysitting for a friend,' he said.

'Um,' she said. 'Okay.' She handed me a block. 'You dropped this. He threw it out of his pram a little while ago. I just wanted to give it back. I thought he might miss it.' She stooped down to look at Harry and cooed.

Harry obliged by smiling and waving.

Traitor, I thought.

Ollie smiled at her. 'Thanks,' he said. 'That's very kind of you.'

She nodded and we walked on. When I turned round, she was standing there, watching us.

'Ollie, look. She's still there. She must be suspicious. She blatantly thinks we've taken him.'

Ollie looked at me and raised an eyebrow. 'You're acting like a lunatic.'

'That's what I'm worried about. Do you think she noticed?'

A siren went off in the distance and I jumped, again.

'Oh my God, she called the police on us. Ollie, they're coming to get us. What do we do?'

Ollie stopped walking and turned to me. 'Hannah, will you get a grip? No one's as interested in us as you think they are.' He pointed towards the park. 'Look: we're here.'

We wheeled Harry through the park and into the playground. Once inside, I reached down to unstrap Harry. 'Okay, let's get you out of this pushchair and onto the swings, eh?' I said.

Harry obliged until I picked him up. Then he started squirming and reaching towards Ollie.

'Fine,' I said. 'Why don't you take him to the swings?'

'Are you sure?' Ollie said, taking him off me.

'Sure. Sexism is clearly internalised much younger than anyone thought,' I muttered. I followed them to the swings in silence.

Miraculously, things then perked up. Harry stopped acting like this was the Lindbergh kidnapping and started to smile, again – sometimes at me. He even let me take him down the slide, even if he did then make a lunge towards Ollie and the swings again, afterwards. Other mothers started nodding and smiling at us, stopping to tell me how good Ollie was with Harry. And I started thinking of them as 'other mothers' and not just 'mothers'. I told myself that everything up until then had just been the warm-up; the day was back on track.

Until, that is, I put him down on the grass to get a snack and he instantly started trying to eat a line of ants. I swept him back up and offered him a piece of cheese, which Evie had also assured me he loved. He took it and threw it.

I looked at Ollie in despair.

Ollie looked at his phone. 'He's probably overtired,' he said. 'We should get him back.'

I nodded and picked Harry up. When I tried to get

him back in his pushchair, though, he went rigid. He stiffened his legs and refused to bend them, his feet burrowing into the seat.

He started shouting, 'No, no, no.'

People started looking again.

'Come on, Harry. We've got to get home. It's your nap time,' I said.

He wouldn't listen to me; he was doing his best impression of a log of wood.

I could feel more eyes on me.

'Harry, if you're good, I will give you chocolate. I swear,' I said, quietly.

Harry tried to bite me.

'That's it,' I said. I tickled him behind the knees until he bent his legs, then hoisted him into the pushchair. He started crying, but I had stopped caring. I grabbed the pushchair's handles and walked determinedly out of the park, leaving Ollie to run to catch up with me, and marched back. I ignored my phone, which was pinging, again.

When we got back, I got Harry out of his pushchair, kicking at it until it sailed across the floor and banged into the front door. 'Harry, it's nap time,' I said.

Harry shook his head.

'Harry,' I said. 'We're going to put you in your cot and you're going to sleep.'

Harry took a deep breath and opened his mouth, clearly preparing to scream. Then he shut it again. This was new and unexpected. I looked at him suspiciously.

He was sitting very still in my arms. He stared into my eyes. I stared back. There was a hint of a smile, then his face went mauve and he grunted. There was an overwhelming smell and I felt something damp on my arm. Harry grunted again and there was a fresh wave of damp. Poo was soaking through his trousers. It was running down his leg and into his shoe.

'Ollie,' I shouted.

'I'm right behind you,' he said.

'Get a nappy,' I said.

I rushed Harry into the lounge and got him onto the changing mat, tugging his trousers off. Green liquid faeces covered his legs and was settling into the chubby folds of flesh. I retched at the smell that was filling my nose. I could almost taste it.

'Ollie, bring all the nappies,' I shouted. 'And a towel.'

I got the old nappy off and tossed it onto the carpet, desperately trying to clean Harry off.

Harry lay there, calmly watching me. As I turned to get another wipe, he let rip again. I screamed. There was poo everywhere, now. It was seeping down the mat. It had gone up his shirt and was coming out of the neckline. It was in his hair. It was all over my trousers.

'How are you doing this?' I cried. 'You didn't even eat the mashed banana.' I swiped my hand across my forehead and left a smear of poo across it.

Ollie came in with the nappies. When he saw what was going on, he threw them at me and ran back out. I started whimpering. Harry was looking at me coldly. He

278

smirked. Then he threw his head to the side and started to scream. My phone pinged again.

I lay down next to him and started crying, too.

Ollie came back in, brandishing a cloth.

'I can't do this,' I moaned.

Harry was still crying in what I was beginning to feel was a carefully planned performance. I couldn't see any real tears.

Ollie grabbed me by the wrists and pulled me up. 'Now is not the time. I'm not doing this alone.' He looked at his phone. 'How long does a lunch out take, anyway?' He looked at Harry, who had started grabbing his own faeces and smearing it down himself. 'That's it.' He picked Harry up and carried him into the bathroom. 'Who has carpet in their bathroom?' he shouted.

I followed him through. Harry was sitting in the sink. He had stopped crying, I noticed.

Ollie pulled the last of Harry's clothes off and threw them in my direction. 'Can you deal with these?'

They hit me in the chest and dropped onto the floor. Harry pointed and chuckled. I was really going off him.

Ollie started hosing Harry down. He grabbed a bottle from the side of the bath and liberally dispensed it over Harry.

I gasped.

He glanced at me. 'What?'

'That's Evie's favourite bubble bath. It's discontinued.'

Ollie glared at me. 'Just get him some clean clothes. And another. Bloody. Nappy.'

By the time we had him cleaned up and dressed again, I was beginning to suspect Evie had set me up. She had clearly fed the child something noxious before we arrived. That was the least of it. The bathroom walls were somehow wet, Harry's dirty clothes were in a stinking pile on the floor and the smell was indescribable. I shut the door on the mess in the bathroom, firmly.

We went into the lounge, but the same unholy smell had followed us in and I could already see a stain on the carpet where I'd left the nappy.

Then we heard the key in the lock.

We looked at each other in panic. I grabbed a cushion off the sofa and chucked it onto the dirty nappy, saying a quick prayer that Evie wouldn't notice it or go into the bathroom before we left.

Jake and Evie walked in.

'Hi guys. How did it go?' Evie said, rushing over and picking up Harry. 'We missed you.'

'We missed you too,' I said. Ollie nudged me.

Evie turned to me. 'Hannah, you've got something on your face. And your clothes . . . And what's that smell?'

'Harry farted,' I said. I glanced at Harry, who was giving me evil looks.

Jake walked across the room and opened a window.

'Right,' Evie said. 'So, Hannah. How did you find it? Ready to do it yourself?' She grinned.

Ollie looked at me.

I smiled vaguely. 'We should really get going.'

I propelled Ollie through the door before anyone could start crying, again. Mainly me.

When Ollie turned to me in bed that night, I rolled away.

'Too tired,' I said. 'Tomorrow.'

It would be puerile to suggest one bad babysitting experience had put me off having a baby (even if I was becoming convinced that was Evie's plan all along). I told myself this: Don't be puerile, I said. Some of it was the extensive research I had done, too. I became convinced I was going to feed my baby a grape and that would be it: I'd be thrust in front of a grand jury and become one of those women you see in the tabloids. I couldn't manage with Harry for one day and nothing that bad had even happened: we hadn't killed him, after all and that felt important. What if I couldn't really do it at all full time? And what if it *was* a boy? Could I be a mother to a boy? This was a roundabout way of avoiding the real question: could I be a mother? I had been relying on a mother's love to carry me through a lot of this, but that was beginning to feel like a bit of a gamble. I'd also been reading about postnatal depression. I was scared I would be postnatally depressed. I was prenatally depressed.

If you were thinking this means that I slowed down on my plan, though, you would be wrong. I ploughed on. But something had shifted.

One evening, I was on top and moaning a bit performatively, because I was thinking more about what we needed from the shops than concentrating on what we were doing, Ollie grabbed my hips and stopped me.

'Hannah,' he said. 'I don't think you're really enjoying this.'

I tried to not look guilty. 'What? No. Yes, I am.'

'You seem a bit distracted. I can tell, you know. Plus, you've said broccoli twice, now.'

'Oh,' I said.

'We don't have to do this. I don't like feeling like you're only going through the motions.'

I snorted. 'Don't be silly. I want this.' I rolled off him and onto my back, pulling him on top of me. But Ollie just moved away.

'I'm not into it if you're not into it, Hannah. That's just weird. I'm not your sperm donor. I'm beginning to feel like that's all I am to you, now.'

'Ollie. No. I'm into it, I'm into it,' I said. I pouted and tried to seductively squeeze my breasts together.

Ollie shook his head. 'That's not going to work. Look, I'm tired, anyway.'

'But,' I said.

But Ollie was already standing up and turning off the light.

'Goodnight,' he said, firmly.

We didn't have sex for a few days after that. Ollie kept saying he wasn't in the mood, or was too tired. But it turned out, it didn't matter, because I missed my period.

How to Test Your Relationship

I don't want to sound like I was being crazy about this, but I did have an alarm set on my phone for the day my period was due. I also had a reminder that popped up saying 'period due' with three exclamation marks after it, which was particularly unnecessary when you consider the fact I was also using a period tracking app. The point is, I knew when I was due and so when my period didn't arrive, I was instantly aware. I obsessively checked my underwear every time I went to the loo, while sternly telling myself that this was probably no big deal; I had been a day or two late before. This could all be a false alarm.

When a couple more days had passed and it still hadn't arrived, I knew: I was pregnant. My heart jumped and my stomach dropped. Despite everything, my first instinct was still to call Mum. I even reached for my phone. Then I remembered. I sat on the bathroom floor, next to the bath, clutching my phone to my chest. I was pregnant. I whispered it to myself. I was pregnant and I couldn't share it with the person I wanted to talk to the most. I was pregnant and she wasn't going to see it. I was going to have a baby she would never know, who would never know her. I was pregnant and I would have to do all of this without her. I was pregnant and I didn't know what to do.

Still, I was pregnant. I had got what I wanted. I sat on the floor for a while.

When Ollie got home that night, I told him.

He found me in the kitchen.

'I'm late,' I said. 'I'm pregnant.'

He dropped his work bag onto the kitchen floor. 'Oh.'

I frowned. 'Oh?'

'Oh! Well. This is good news. Right?'

'Right,' I said. But we both looked away.

'Should you do a test? Should I go and buy a test?'

I shook my head. 'It's probably too early. But I'm late. I'm pregnant.'

We stood there for a moment, facing each other, then Ollie came over and gave me a tentative hug.

He clapped his hands. 'I'm going to have a beer. Do you want a beer?'

'No, I can't drink.' I gave him a hard stare.

'Right. Just for me then.' He walked over to the fridge, then stopped and turned to me. 'Should I touch your stomach?'

'Sure. I suppose.' I lifted up my top and Ollie tentatively rubbed my stomach. We looked at each other.

'Dinner's ready, by the way. If you want to eat,' I said.

'Yeah. Great.' He dropped his hand and I turned back to the hob to serve up the food.

After we finished dinner that night, Ollie looked at his phone. 'I said I'd meet Josh at the pub. Might be one of my last chances before, you know . . . Parenthood.' He stood up. 'Is that okay, though? Do you need anything?'

I shook my head.

He nodded and hovered for a minute, before leaving the room, the front door slamming behind him.

I touched my stomach.

Getting what you want can have a funny way of making you wonder if you still want it. To be honest, I have always been a bit like this. I was determined to be a hairdresser, until I finally got to practise on Laura's Barbie. Then I was over it. This wasn't like that. I wasn't suddenly sure that I didn't want to have a baby after all. 'Mum, mum, mum' had been a rhythmic pounding in my ears since I conceived of the idea of conceiving: a joyful war cry of my future as one. That hadn't changed. But I also wasn't completely convinced that I did still want it, either.

I needed to talk to my mum.

I didn't go to the grave, this time. I didn't see much point if I couldn't be sure I'd even find the right one. I got in the car, instead, put on some loud music and went for a drive with all the windows down, which felt as good a way as any of getting in touch. I thought briefly about the fact we'd need to get a car seat for the baby, then I wondered if we'd need a more suitable car altogether. It was a tiring thought.

I drove around for a bit, until I hit a bit of empty road.

'Mum, I really miss you,' I said.

She, well, she didn't say anything because she's dead. But I did imagine her telling me she missed me too, which made me feel a bit better, even though I was basically talking to myself and doing both sides of a conversation.

'I think I'm pregnant. I haven't done a test yet, but I'm a week late. I know how much you wanted grand-children, so I hope you think this is good news.'

Nothing.

'I hope I can be as good a mum as you. I always thought you'd be here to help me when the time came to have my own kids. And now you won't be, obviously. You know that. I don't really know how I'm going to manage it without you, actually.'

Still nothing.

'Ollie's very good, though. It's not the same, but it could be a lot worse. And I still have Laura and Dad. That's important. I want one of you to be around to know your grandchildren. You know, in the flesh.'

Silence.

I pulled up to a light. 'Sorry, I know you hate this song.' I turned down the radio. 'I really wish I could know what you think. I could really use some motherly advice. Do you think this is a good idea? Maybe you could give me a sign, if you could do that. People always get those in films.' I took a deep breath and stuck my head out the window. 'Give me a sign,' I shouted.

'Oi.'

I turned. There was a horn blaring behind me and in the rear-view mirror, I could see someone gesturing.

'Pay attention, will you. It's green.'

This wasn't Mum, but the guy in the car behind me.

He revved his engine, pulling out and coming up beside my car. 'Stupid cow. Get off the road if you can't drive, you dozy bitch,' he shouted into my window, before flipping a final finger at me and speeding off in a cloud of exhaust.

I looked at the sky. 'That wasn't the kind of sign I meant,' I said.

I was sitting at my desk, trying to write something more inspiring about pine furniture and trying not to think about what might be growing inside my uterus when my phone buzzed again. I went to turn off another reminder about my period I had set when I still felt excited about not having it. Then I saw it wasn't a reminder after all, it was a text from Laura.

'I've got some bad news about Dad,' the text said.

I stopped working and called her immediately.

'Oh my God, what is it?' I said. 'Is he dead?'

'Of course he's not dead,' she said. 'Do you really think I'd text you to let you know he's dead?'

'That's how you let me know about Mum,' I said.

She huffed. 'She wasn't dead, then.'

'Okay, fine,' I said. 'So what's wrong?'

'I don't know if I should tell you,' she said.

This is one of the most stupid things people can tell you after they have already told you they have something important to tell you. For some reason, though, they always seem to. Either tell them straight away or don't

287

tell them at all but don't tell them you have important news and then prevaricate over whether or not you can tell them what the important news is.

'So why did you text me, then?' I said.

'I don't know if you're going to want to hear it,' she said.

I sighed. 'So why,' I said, 'did you text me?'

'You don't like hearing about this stuff.'

'What stuff?'

'Dad dating other women.'

I sat up a bit straighter. I imagined Dad telling Laura about Betty. I imagined Dad telling me about Betty. Then I imagined us all having to meet Betty. Betty, who my unborn child might call Grandma Betty. 'What's happened now?'

'So I should tell you, then?'

'Laura,' I snapped.

'It's bad, Han,' she said. I heard her take a deep breath. 'He's being going out at night, sometimes,' she said, meaningfully.

'That's it?' I slumped back in my chair. 'I thought you had something concrete. That could mean anything.' I stopped thinking about Betty and went back to thinking about what I had barely stopped thinking about: the baby I might be carrying that I might also have been having very conflicted thoughts about.

'He's clearly meeting someone, Hannah. Probably this Betty woman.'

'Sure,' I said. 'Or he could be seeing Father Ray. Or Nigel.'

'Wait. That's not the most important part.'

I sighed. 'Then why didn't you just tell me the important part?'

'I was leading up to it. He takes her lasagne. Hannah, he's been *making* lasagne.' There was a weighty pause.

'So?' I said. I was trying to sound casual, but I was being facetious. This was in fact rather shocking. Dad can cook precisely one thing: a jacket potato. It has to be a regular jacket potato, too. He once got cocky and tried to bake a sweet potato for variety. He left it in the microwave – he didn't even make it to the oven – and it shrivelled to the size of a plum and smoked. When he tried to cut it open, it flaked, hissed and deflated even more. So the fact that Dad was cooking a lasagne really was a big deal. It was significant and we both knew it.

'Come on, Hannah,' Laura said.

'Maybe it was a ready meal,' I said. 'Or one of those nice frozen meals.' I thought about it. 'Where would he have learned to make a lasagne?'

I could almost hear Laura rolling her eyes down the phone line. 'It's not about the lasagne, Hannah. The lasagne isn't the point.'

I disagreed. The lasagne seemed to be a big part of it.

'The point,' she continued, 'is that he's preparing food for someone. And taking it to them.' She waited for a moment. 'That,' she said, 'is the point.'

I chewed on a nail.

Laura sighed. 'He's clearly dating someone,' she said, like I was being especially thick and refusing to accept basic facts. Which was partly true.

I cleared my throat. 'I can't keep going on like this. We need to know for sure. You've got to ask him.'

'I did.'

I clenched my fist. 'What did you say?'

'I said, "What are you doing with the lasagne?"'

'What did he say?'

'That children should be seen, but not heard and preferably neither.'

'You're not a child.'

'I'm his child.'

'Mm.' I picked up a pen and started doodling on a piece of paper. 'That does sound like Dad. But still, it's not proof.'

'I agree,' Laura said. 'We clearly have to get some.'

'Trust me, I've been trying.' I sighed and put down the pen. 'How?'

'I think we should follow him next time he goes out.'

I snorted. 'Right. And I'll bring my night vision goggles.'

'Hannah, this woman could be our stepmother. We have a right to know. We have a right to find out what's going on.'

'Don't you think following him is a bit extreme, though? Have you checked his emails recently? Can't you just do that instead?'

'I did. I couldn't find anything.'

'Right, well.'

'Which just means he's either deleting them or has moved to doing whatever he's doing in person.'

We were back to Grandma Betty. I was beginning to

feel dizzy. This was all getting a bit overwhelming and I didn't feel like I had the capacity to deal with any of it. I dug my fingernails into my palms. 'I really don't have time for this right now. I have to go. I have work to do. I need to write about pine furniture.'

'Furniture? Hannah—'

I hung up the phone.

I was sitting in the car counting grandmas. There was Grandma Betty and then there was Ollie's mum, Grandma Anne, who we were on our way to see. She and John were celebrating their wedding anniversary. It was an important one, though I had no idea which one, so they had hired out the village hall and invited the whole family.

I hadn't wanted to come; I hadn't felt up to it, which I blamed on hormones and also on the fact that coming meant having to talk to all of Ollie's relatives I hadn't seen since Mum died about how I was doing. I put a hand on my stomach, which was beginning to hurt. I imagined my anxiety seeping through to the baby and gently rubbed it.

Ollie glanced over at me and squeezed my knee. 'You okay?'

'I was just thinking about grandmas,' I said.

'Okay. Well, we're here.'

Anne greeted us as we walked into the hall, her arms open. 'Ollie. Hello, dear.' She kissed his cheek. 'Hannah. Still not sleeping well?' This seemed to have become her customary way of greeting me.

'She's just wondering how you're coping,' Ollie whispered.

Anne walked us further into the hall. 'So glad you could both make it. John and I are so thrilled you can celebrate with us. Ollie, your sister's already here. Make sure you say hello to everyone. And do help yourself to the buffet, both of you.' She strode off, back into the midst of guests that were milling about.

I looked around. It looked like all of Ollie's relatives were already there, including his great aunts, who have no business still being alive. Most of the guests seemed to be wearing some combination of cashmere and tweed. I tugged at my skirt, which now felt inappropriately short.

Ollie squeezed my arm. 'Buffet?'

We were sitting eating beige food on the kind of beige chairs that you're never entirely sure about sitting on, because they always have ambiguous stains on them, which make you wonder what the people who sat on them before you were doing at the time.

Ollie was eating something that looked like it might once have been chewed by someone else. He pointed at it. 'You know, the potato salad isn't as bad as it looks. Can I try some of your pasta?'

My stomach lurched. 'Please do.' I handed him my plate.

'Oh, here we go,' he said.

I followed his gaze to the group of aunts and middle-aged cousins who were making their way towards us, looking for somewhere to sit.

Ollie stood up as a woman on crutches approached. 'Here, Maggie. Take my seat.'

I smiled at a man leaning on a walking stick and panting, who had been circling us. I went to stand up, too, but then I felt it: a hot wave surged through my stomach. 'No,' I whispered.

The man with the walking stick looked at me, expectantly.

I looked back at him.

He looked at the chair, then at his stick.

I slowly shook my head. I couldn't stand up. I couldn't even move. I was pretty sure I was going to die right there in that chair. My period – the period that had been missing for days, the period I had stopped thinking of as a late period and started thinking of as a baby – had chosen that moment to come after all. I was fairly sure I had ruined the chair.

He huffed and walked away.

Before I could worry about seriously offending a man who looked worryingly close to death, I felt another gush surge through me. I gripped the arms of my seat. This couldn't be happening. I looked at Ollie, but he was caught in another conversation with someone about the quality of the cold pizza slices. I couldn't even make a graceful exit: we were surrounded by his relatives, who seemed to be multiplying by the minute.

'Ollie,' I mouthed, willing him to turn round. He didn't. 'Ollie,' I whispered. Ollie didn't notice, although a couple of other people had started looking at me, which made sense: I was beginning to sweat, heavily.

'Ollie,' I mewed.

Finally, Ollie turned round and looked down at me. He smiled. 'You okay?' he mouthed.

I shook my head.

He frowned.

'Period,' I mouthed.

Ollie looked blank.

I gestured at my stomach and made a sweeping gesture with my arm. 'Whoosh,' I mouthed.

Ollie looked confused.

I gritted my teeth. I was almost certain I would have better luck with a golden retriever at this point. I started acting out a series of gestures evoking tampons, rushing water and at one point, the fall of Adam and Eve, until finally, I did the only thing I could think of that might actually work: I stuck my hand down and when I pulled it back, there was blood on my fingertips.

Ollie went pale.

I glared at him. 'Help me,' I mouthed.

Ollie looked around and then back at me. He nodded and walked off.

I was fairly sure he had abandoned me to my fate and that I would be stuck on the chair, in the hall forever. Then I saw him lift up a glass at the front of the room and tap it.

'Everybody,' he said. 'Hi. If I could get your attention, please.'

I watched as the people that had been sitting around us looked over at him.

'If you wouldn't mind gathering round,' Ollie said.

'I'd like to make a toast. To my mum and dad on this special day.'

Anne and John smiled at each other and held hands.

I inched my chair backwards, towards the door.

Ollie cleared his throat. 'Um,' he said.

Everyone was now looking at Ollie. The hard-of-hearing were even making their way over to him.

I continued pushing my chair backwards, wincing with every squeak of the shiny floor.

'What is love, really?' he said. 'Who can know? Well, Mum and Dad seem to know, that's who. They have been a constant example to me in my relationship.' He smiled at me, which made other people start to turn and look at me, too.

I froze. I was still about three feet from the door and more importantly at that point, several feet from everyone else in the room. I crossed my legs and tried to look nonchalant.

'But today isn't about me,' Ollie said, in a rush. 'It's about Mum and Dad. Over there.' He gestured in their direction. 'So, if we could all be on our feet, for a toast . . .'

I made it to the door. I picked up the chair as best I could with my bum still firmly attached to it and scuttled out of the hall. I didn't let go until I made it to the toilet, where I cleaned myself up. I rinsed my underwear out in the sink, drying it under the hand dryer, while I clenched a wedge of hand towels between my thighs.

I dragged the chair out into the car park and hid it behind the bins, squatted down and started crying.

At first, I was crying because I was mortified. Then, when I was done crying about that, I cried because I had realised I wasn't pregnant, after all. I had secretly thought that we would be the fertile ones and would get pregnant straight away. But we weren't. It hadn't happened. And I cried because I wasn't sad at all: I was relieved. I wanted children, I wanted them with Ollie – desperately – but I was also realising that I wasn't ready to have them right now. That everyone had been right when they said it was too soon after losing Mum to start thinking about it. I cried because I was beginning to realise that I wasn't okay after all. That I probably wasn't as much of a functional adult as I had thought I was, either. That this entire plan to have a baby had been a ridiculous and misguided attempt to pretend I was doing better than I actually was.

I cried because my dad might be having an affair and I wasn't ready for him to be moving on when I still felt so hopelessly stuck.

Mainly, though, I cried because I really missed my mum and even after all these months, months when I thought I should be better, I still wasn't and I didn't know what to do with that.

I wiped my face, smearing mascara over my hands. This was perfect. I still had to go back into the party and now, I'd have to do it with my back against the wall and make-up down my face. Anne was going to have a field day with this.

*

I sat in silence as Ollie drove us home that night, staring out of the window.

Ollie glanced over at me. 'Mum and Dad really seemed to like my speech. You missed the applause, but there was an encore.'

I didn't say anything.

'I don't think anyone noticed. Plus, those chairs always have weird stains on them. Now we know where they come from. Some of them.'

I grunted.

'You know, something really similar happened to my sister one time. It's probably really common.'

I closed my eyes.

He sighed. 'Are you okay?'

'I'm not pregnant,' I said.

'Oh,' Ollie said. 'Well, we didn't expect it to happen that quickly, anyway. A year for most couples, we said. This is normal. We'll just keep trying.'

'Mm,' I said. I didn't tell him I wasn't sure I wanted to keep trying. I didn't know how to. I had been the one who had convinced Ollie I was ready to get pregnant. I had said I was fine. And here I was: not fine and no longer ready to have kids, either. Not at that point. And Ollie was ready. He wanted them for the right reasons. Not only was I going to have to tell him that the last few weeks had been for nothing, but I was going to disappoint him. What if this all proved too much for him? What if I was too much for him after all?

I spent the rest of the drive home pretending to be asleep. When we got home, I went straight to bed.

I was still in bed the next morning when Ollie went to work. And when he got home from it again. In fact, I stayed there for the next few days, moving to go to the toilet, get food and Ibuprofen for the cramps. When Ollie questioned when I was planning on getting up, and made sensible comments about work and deadlines, I clutched my stomach and said I couldn't move.

By the fourth day, though, he had had enough. He pulled back the covers.

I squinted up into the light.

'Okay, Han,' he said. 'You never usually go to bed like this. Don't you think it's time to get up?'

I squeezed my eyes shut and curled up in a ball. 'I'm not ready,' I said.

Ollie sighed and sat down on the side of the bed. 'Hannah, it's a period. We haven't even been trying that long. Don't you think you're making too big a deal about this? You knew it would probably take time. It's not like you lost the baby. You haven't lost anything.'

My whole body tensed. 'Oh really,' I said.

He sighed. 'You know what I mean,' he said.

'Yes,' I said. 'Mum died months ago. That's old news. I should be fine now.'

He sighed. 'Hannah, don't be ridiculous.'

I sat up in the bed. 'Oh, so I'm being ridiculous, am I? My God, Ollie, I just lost my mum. My mother. Don't you think you should, I don't know, give me some time to deal with that instead of constantly forcing me to be okay, to be normal? Oh, better not show any emotion or it might be too much for Ollie.'

Ollie looked at me like I was being deeply unfair. Now, I can absolutely confirm that I was. I was projecting. Still, in the moment, I wasn't going to let that stop me. It was easier to be angry. I ploughed on.

'Better move on, quick, quick, quick,' I clapped my hands with each 'quick'. 'Better have children right away because that's what Ollie wants: children.' I threw my hands up. 'I mean, maybe, Ollie, if you'd actually given me some time to process losing my mum rather than just pushing me into becoming one myself the second I expressed the slightest interest then I would be more ready for it.'

Ollie had gone red. 'What *I* want? Hannah—'

'Then maybe I would actually be ready for it and not having all these doubts about it.'

Ollie was frowning and shaking his head, opening and closing his mouth as if he was speechless in the face of such irrationality. Which, again, wasn't a completely unfair reaction.

But still, I didn't stop. 'Maybe,' I said. 'Maybe this is why I kissed Mark. At least around him, I don't have to pretend.' I sat back.

Ollie had stopped opening and closing his mouth. Instead, he had gone very still, which was a lot worse.

'You kissed Mark?' he said. 'When?'

I regretted the words as soon as I'd said them. I wanted to stuff them back into my mouth and swallow them, but it was too late, so I shrugged. 'At New Year's

Eve. When you were forcing me to have a party I didn't want, because I had to be totally fine right away. And no, we didn't actually kiss. I almost did, but he stopped it. I could have done though.' I looked up at him from under my hair.

I saw the shock register on his face, then turn to anger. We didn't usually fight. Not really. We bickered, but that was usually when we were hungry. He stood up without looking at me. 'Fuck this. I've had enough. I've tried really hard, but I'm done. I'm going,' he said. 'And for the record, Hannah, I have been having doubts about having kids right now, too. But I was doing it for you. Because I thought it was what you wanted. Not me. You.'

I clambered up onto my knees. 'You've been having doubts?'

Ollie grabbed at his head. 'Of course I've been having doubts. The way you've been acting recently? But I just hoped it would take a while and we'd both have time to get used to the idea more.' He looked at me. 'But clearly, I was right to doubt. I can't be here, right now. I need some space. Go be with Mark.'

He left the room and I heard him stomp down the stairs. Then the front door slammed behind him.

I slowly pulled the covers back up and over me.

I told myself I was glad I'd said it. I told myself I was glad he had finally shown his true colours and left. If he wasn't going to stick around through this, the worst time in my life, it was better I found out now.

To be honest, I still expected him to come back. I thought that I would apologise, we would talk about the baby thing and maybe agree to postponing it for a while and then we would move on. But when a couple of hours passed and he hadn't returned, I began to worry.

By midnight, when he still wasn't back, I was getting frantic. I envisioned him going out and having sex with someone else – someone who was, patently, more normal. I envisioned him stepping out into the road in his fury and not noticing an oncoming car. I envisioned him lying in the road, dying. I envisioned losing him, too.

I did get up then and started pacing. I called his phone and when he didn't answer, I left a near-hysterical voicemail, apologising effusively and begging him to let me know he was all right. Then I sent him a flurry of texts. Eventually, I received one back.

'Staying at Josh and Olivia's. I'll be back after work tomorrow.'

I curled into bed and sobbed until I fell asleep.

When I finally heard his key in the lock the next day, I ran downstairs and threw myself at him.

'I thought you might be dead,' I said.

'I'm not,' he said.

Then I started crying. Well, I started crying harder than I already was. 'I'm sorry, I'm so, so sorry,' I wept. 'I didn't mean it. Nothing even happened with Mark. I regretted even thinking about kissing him immediately after it happened. You've been so kind and patient with me. It was me: I felt I needed to be normal and adult and okay right away. But I was just so sad and angry. I'm

always sad and angry. I don't know how to be normal,
any more. I feel broken.'

'I know,' Ollie said.

I tightened my grip on him. 'Are you hungry?'

How to Ride a Tandem

There were many times when I felt like I was just sitting around waiting for the shoe to drop. Or rather, the next shoe. Shoes seemed to be dropping everywhere, all the time. It was exhausting. Even when Ollie and I had resolved our fight, he had learned about Mark and my doubts over the baby and hadn't immediately broken up with me, I was still waiting for the next shoe.

Then another one did drop: my birthday.

'What are we doing about your birthday?'

It was Dad. I was sitting at my desk again wearing an old dressing gown and eating a bowl of cereal I had started on two hours before. I was also still working out how to write about furniture and bitterly regretted picking up the phone. I didn't want to talk about my birthday. I didn't want to have a birthday at all, to be more precise. A birthday felt like a lot of effort and I barely had the energy to get out of bed in the mornings – as it was, I was taking a lot of naps in the middle of the day just to get through it. A part of me (a big part that was most of me) also felt like I didn't deserve a birthday. Besides, there wasn't much to celebrate.

I didn't say any of that to Dad, though. 'You remembered?' I said.

There was a pause. 'Laura told me,' he said, begrudgingly.

'She really is the better daughter.'

'Takes after your mother. You're more like me.'

I grimaced. 'Well. I don't know about that. I think I'm quite like Mum.'

'No. You take after me. Always have.'

'People say that Mum and I are very similar.'

'No, that's Laura.'

'I have her eyes,' I said, under my breath.

'Well,' he said. 'What about your birthday?'

'We're not doing anything about it. I don't want to celebrate this year.'

'Really?' Dad sounded suspicious but keen, like a child that's been offered ice cream in lieu of dinner. 'What about your present?'

'You got me something?'

'I wasn't going to forget, was I?'

'You did for Laura.'

'Exactly. I could hardly do it twice. Your mother would never have forgiven me.'

'We didn't celebrate your birthday.'

'That's different.'

'Why?'

'Because I said so.'

I wiped at the milk I had spilled down my front. 'Fine. I'll come round the day after, on Sunday, for my present and cake.'

'Cake?'

'We're not going to have cake?'

Dad sighed. 'Fine. I better go to the shops, then.'

'Okay.' I paused. I thought about what Laura had told me. 'Have you been cooking lately?'

'Cooking?'

'Yeah. Like spaghetti or a lasagne . . .'

'Lasagne?' He said, cagily.

'Yes, it's a meat and pasta dish.'

He huffed. 'Not this again. Have you been talking to Laura? She's been strangely interested in my eating habits, recently.'

'I . . . Never mind.'

'Fine,' he said. 'I'll see you on Sunday.'

I repeated this to Ollie while I made dinner that night.

'I told Dad I'd go round there on Sunday. For my birthday. It's no big deal. You don't even have to come.' I said all of this without looking at him. 'But that's it. I only said yes to get him off the phone. I don't want to do anything else.'

We had moved past our fight. We had even agreed to wait before we started trying for a baby, again; that perhaps neither of us were quite ready after all. But that didn't mean that things were magically fine between us, either. There was still a vague feeling of unease. We were both so keen to prove everything was okay again, we were being especially careful and considerate of each other, which only made things feel even more stilted. I wasn't sure I wanted to add the extra pressure of a

305

birthday celebration. More to the point, I wasn't sure he would want it, either.

'Why wouldn't I come?' he said. 'And why wouldn't we celebrate? It's your birthday. We always celebrate.'

'Right.' I looked at him from the side of my eye. 'I just didn't know if you'd want to do anything this year. For me.'

'Why wouldn't I?'

I concentrated on dicing a tomato. 'No reason,' I said. 'But you know, I still don't feel like celebrating.' Actually, what I felt like doing was going to bed and staying there. I looked away. 'There doesn't feel like there's much to be happy about this year.'

He shook his head. 'I think you're being defeatist. You love birthdays. You love having a day that's all about you. You once told me off for not being excited enough about my birthday.'

I made my mouth as small as I could. 'So?' I said.

Ollie raised his shoulders. 'So, don't you want a party?'

I shook my head, firmly. 'I'm not drinking.'

'You can have a party and not drink.'

'Not a very good one.'

Ollie crossed his arms. 'So that's it? You're really not going to celebrate this year?'

I made my best prim face. 'Ollie, there are bigger problems in the world than me letting a single birthday go by. People are starving. Children are dying. Dying.' I threw the tomato into a pan.

*

I woke up on the morning of my birthday to a bang. Literally. This isn't my way of telling you it got off to an exciting start. My present fell over.

I sat up in bed. Ollie was no longer in the bed, I noticed. He was now at the end of it, trying to prop my present upright, again. When he saw that I was awake, he looked a bit guilty.

'Happy birthday,' he said. He let go of the present to do jazz hands and it fell over again. 'Did I wake you?' he said.

'No,' I said. I pointed. 'That did. What is it?'

Ollie beamed at it. 'That is your present,' he said. 'Do you want to open it now or after your birthday breakfast?'

I looked at it. Ollie picked it up again. It looked a bit like a bicycle, but a bicycle that had been weirdly extended and that had big boxes instead of wheels. I felt a rush in my stomach and my eyes began to well up. Ollie had bought me a present. After everything I had put him through, he had still done this for me.

I beamed. 'Now,' I said.

'Now, this was very hard to wrap,' Ollie said, as I clambered down the bed. 'So feel free to take a moment to appreciate the presentation before you rip it all up.'

I ripped into it. I have never been very good at being patient.

Ollie looked pained. 'What did I just say?' he said.

'Sorry,' I said. I tried to slow down a bit, but I've never been very good at pacing myself, either. I pulled off a piece of tape.

'Oh, just open it,' Ollie said. 'I took a photo of it after I wrapped it anyway.'

I grinned and pulled off the remaining paper. It was a bicycle, but weirdly extended with boxes for wheels.

I looked at it, then at Ollie.

'It's a tandem,' he said. He beamed.

'Oh,' I said. 'It has square wheels,' I said.

Ollie bent down. 'No, I just put boxes on it to disguise the shape so you wouldn't guess what it was. I didn't want the shape to give it away.' He pulled the boxes off. 'It's very hard to wrap a bicycle.' He stopped and looked at me. 'Well? Do you like it?'

I looked it over. It was bright red, its two seats covered in brown leather. On the front, it had a wicker basket that Ollie had filled with flowers and a miniature bottle of champagne.

'I thought we could take it out for a picnic,' he said. He watched me, his face falling slightly when I didn't react.

'I love it,' I said.

'Really?'

'Are you joking? Yes.' I clapped my hands together. 'I love these things. My ex and I rented a tandem once on holiday. We cycled everywhere on it – all over Butlins. We had so much fun. I've wanted one ever since, then.' I launched myself at Ollie. 'Thank you,' I said.

'Great,' Ollie said. 'This one's particularly good, too. I did loads of research.' He started talking about gears and tyre pressure. I stopped listening and stared at it in admiration, instead. It was beautiful.

'I thought we could take it on adventures,' Ollie said.

Ollie is always talking about having adventures together, but apart from the time we almost drowned in a canoe together, we never seem to really have any.

I placed my hand on his heart and smiled.

He jumped up. 'Your breakfast.' He ushered me towards the bike. 'Go on, sit on her. Have a go. The kickstand's on so she won't fall over again, now. Try her out. I'm going to get your breakfast.'

He walked out, then stopped in the doorway and turned.

'I thought we could call her Bo Peep,' he said.

I frowned. 'Why?'

'Because she's red.'

I stared at him for a moment. 'Do you mean Little Red Riding Hood?'

Ollie rubbed his mouth. 'Oh, yeah. Well, your present. You should be the one to name her.' He ran out and went downstairs.

I climbed onto her from the bed and swung my legs about.

'You are going to be much better than Moby Dick,' I said. We really should have known better than to call our canoe that. We were just asking for trouble.

I looked up at the ceiling. 'Hi Mum, it's my birthday, today. Twenty-nine years since you birthed me. I know, who can believe it? I wish you were here. It's not going to be the same without you. Which you know, because I keep telling you. Because nothing is. I miss you. I wish you were here to celebrate with me. Although I'm not actually celebrating this year, so you won't be missing much. So ... Thanks for making me.'

When Ollie came back upstairs, balancing a tray, I had it.

'Bertha,' I said.

Later that morning, Ollie produced a picnic basket. 'I thought we could take Bertha to the park and then have our picnic,' he said.

I thought about what would have happened if we had actually got pregnant. Then, we'd be dreaming of doing all of this with our baby, instead of our bike.

'It will be a good place to try her out,' Ollie was saying. 'Then, when we're used to her, I thought we could plan a trip to Paris.'

'As a reward?'

'No, we'd cycle there.'

I imagined cycling down the Seine, me in an A-line dress, Ollie in a pair of chinos, maybe a beret. 'Definitely,' I said.

It was one of those lovely autumnal days when it's warmer than it has been for most of the summer, which makes you worry about climate change, but you're mostly glad you don't have to wear tights. We wheeled Bertha out to the kerb.

'Are you ready to give her a go?' Ollie said.

'Of course,' I said, although I was feeling a bit doubtful. Now I was standing next to her, she looked a lot bigger than she had upstairs.

I tried to get on. I couldn't. I couldn't get my leg up

high enough. I tried again. My leg got stuck and I almost fell over.

'I can't get on,' I said. 'I think she's too big for me.'

'She's not, I measured it,' Ollie said. 'You just have to angle it. Look.'

He showed me how to lean the bike over to get on. I managed to get on. Ollie nodded and got on in front.

When we were both on it, he turned and looked at me. 'Right, feet on pedals and off we go.'

I put my feet on the pedals. He kicked up the kick-stand and pushed off. We wobbled. I panicked and put my feet down again.

'I thought we were going to fall over,' I said.

'We're not going to fall over,' he said. 'We just have to get going. Try again.'

I put my feet back on the pedals. He pushed off again. We wobbled. I put my feet back down.

'Hannah,' Ollie said.

'Sorry,' I said.

'It's going to wobble a bit at first,' he said. 'We have to get going. Once we do, it will be fine.' He looked ahead. 'Let's try once more.'

We tried again. I tried not to put my feet on the floor. We wobbled. We wobbled a bit more. Then we started veering towards the road. I let out a long, drawn out scream.

'Hannah,' Ollie said. 'Hannah,' he shouted. 'We're not moving.'

I opened my eyes. 'Oh,' I said. People walking past were beginning to look at us.

'Will you just trust me?' Ollie said.

'Maybe we should walk it to the park,' I said.

This is just a hiccup, I told myself. When we get to the park, we'll be fine.

We got to the park. It still wasn't fine.

'Let's try it on the grass,' I said.

'That will make it harder,' Ollie said.

'But it will also make it less dangerous,' I said.

'Stick to the path, Han,' Ollie said.

'Let's ride next to the grass, then,' I said.

We tried again. This time, we got a bit further before Ollie realised I wasn't pedalling.

'Why aren't you pedalling?' he said.

'I was waiting for us to get going first. Then we got going and the pedals were going too fast for me to put my feet on them. Are you sure this is the right bike for me? It was much easier before, with my ex.'

Ollie stared into the distance for a few seconds. He cleared his throat and turned round to me.

'Han, you can ride a bike, can't you?'

I crossed my arms. 'Of course I can ride a bike, Oliver.'

'Okay. When was the last time you rode a bike?'

'I told you. On the tandem with my—'

'Yes, I know. Your ex.' He took a deep breath. 'And when was that, exactly?' The words were coming out slower, now.

I thought about it. 'Seven, ten years ago, maybe.'

'And how long . . .' he was speaking very slowly now. '. . . was it since you rode a bike before then?'

'Five years, maybe.'

Ollie sighed. 'Okay,' he said.

'What?' I said.

'Nothing, you're just a little bit out of practice.'

I scoffed. 'It's a bike, Oliver. You can't forget how to ride a bike. Everyone knows that. It's a saying.'

Ollie didn't say anything.

I tried to get back on, then almost fell off on the other side. 'Oh my God,' I said. 'I've forgotten how to ride a bike.'

'Let's take a break and have our picnic,' Ollie said.

We ended up in the playground, on the soft tarmac bit next to the slide. The parents eyed us suspiciously at first, then they saw how bad I was and started giving Ollie sympathetic looks, instead.

'I've been there, mate,' one man said to Ollie, nodding to his tiny daughter who was circling the park at speed on her bike. 'You'll be fine, love,' he said to me. He gave me a thumbs-up.

Ollie eyed me. 'Okay, let's start again.'

I pointed at the child. 'I'm so behind in my life. I'm twenty-nine and I can't even ride a bike. Little children can do what I can't. This is exactly why I wanted to get pregnant.'

He shook his head. 'You're just out of practice. You're not that familiar with bikes any more. It can be tricky, at first. For some people.'

I didn't say anything.

'It's fine, Han. Now, if you fall—'

'I don't want to fall.'

'You won't fall. But if you do—'

'I don't want to fall.'

'If you do . . .' he said. He was mainly speaking through his teeth now, which were clenched. '. . . you'll have a soft landing, so you won't hurt yourself. Okay, now, let's try again.'

It was still no good. In fact, it was even worse in the playground, because now we had children to dodge. After a particularly nasty kid on the swings seemed to take deliberate aim at Ollie's head, narrowly missing, we called it a day. Ollie seemed in a hurry to stop, which was understandable. It was probably because the bicycle adventure was going almost as badly as the canoe adventure had although no one had almost drowned yet.

I tried for a joke to lighten the mood. 'Shall we cycle back to the house,' I said.

Ollie didn't say anything.

The mood was still tense coming home. Ollie was marching forcefully back with the bike, meaning I practically had to run to keep up. As we got home and I waited for Ollie to find his keys, I looked mournfully at my beautiful red bicycle that I was resigning myself to never being able to use.

'I think I might have permanently damaged myself on the bike seat,' I said, as we walked through the front door.

Ollie snorted. 'You weren't on it long enough.'

I walked into the lounge. There was a shout and from the corner of my eye I could see something rushing at

314

me. Oh my God, it's a burglar, I thought. This is how I'm going to die. My heart was racing. I screamed.

'Happy birthday, Hannah.'

I looked up. Lou, Maria, Sophie, Evie and Laura were standing there, holding up a banner and waving it at me. Maria was even holding a cake. I looked round. Ollie was leaning in the doorway, grinning.

'But I didn't want a birthday party this year,' I blurted.

'Hannah,' Ollie said.

'Oh, sorry. That was so rude of me. This is lovely. Thank you. All of you. Sorry. Would you excuse me for a moment? I just need to pop to the loo.' I turned and scurried out, ran upstairs and into the bathroom. I shut the door firmly behind me and sat on the loo.

The door burst open. I screamed, again.

Lou, Sophie and Evie were standing in the doorway.

'Oh, you're actually going to the loo,' Sophie said.

I huffed. 'Yes. Do you mind?' I waved at the open door. I could just about see Ollie hovering around the bottom stairs. This is an example of one of many times I should have locked the toilet door.

They quickly shut the door behind them again.

'We thought you might be sulking,' Evie said.

'Well, I sort of was doing that, too,' I said. 'I just needed a moment.' I gave them a pointed look. 'I'm going to get up now.' They turned away.

'What are you all doing here?' I said. 'You almost killed me.'

They glanced at each other.

'Well, we were coming to help you celebrate your

birthday,' Lou said. 'But maybe that wasn't such a good idea.'

I didn't say anything. I washed my hands, instead, staring into the sink.

'What's going on? You love your birthdays,' Evie said.

I carefully dried my hands. 'I didn't feel like celebrating this year.'

Evie crossed her arms. 'That's not good enough.'

I blinked. 'I thought it was.'

Evie shook her head. 'No. Continue.'

I spread my hands. 'What is there to celebrate? What is a birthday, really, but a reminder that time's passing and we're all one step closer to death.'

Evie raised an eyebrow. 'I've been saying that for years and it never stopped you before. Keep going.'

I crossed my arms. 'Okay. Well how about the fact that I'm almost thirty and my life is a complete mess. What's fun about that?'

'You're twenty-nine,' Evie said.

'Right, which is almost thirty.'

Evie shook her head. 'It doesn't work that way. You can't freak out about thirty yet. You need to save something for the year ahead.'

I waved her off. 'Besides, my parties never end well, or have you forgotten Mother's Day. It's just another year my mum won't be around to see, anyway.'

Lou stepped forward. 'Speaking of that, Maria insisted on coming. She wants to apologise.'

I stared at her. 'But she never apologises. I didn't think she knew how to.'

Lou nodded vigorously. 'I know.'

Sophie touched my arm. 'Should we go?'

'We're not going,' Evie said.

Sophie looked at Evie and nodded.

Sometimes, you really need someone to tell you to get over yourself and Evie is usually there to be the one to tell you.

Evie turned back to me. 'Jennifer would never have let you get away with this crap. She would have said you have to live your life. You don't know how many birthdays you have left.'

'She would know,' I said.

'Now, you have guests downstairs, so stop being silly and get out there. You can't miss Maria apologising. You'd regret it forever.'

I nodded. I probably would.

Evie swung the door open and waved us out.

We walked back into the lounge, where Maria and Laura were huddled, talking to Ollie. They looked up as we came in.

'Should we say happy birthday again?' Laura whispered.

I smiled. 'Thanks so much for coming, you guys. I really was going to the loo just then. I wasn't just having a strop.'

'It's true,' Lou said. 'We walked in on it.'

There was a pause, during which we all looked at our feet.

'We brought wine,' Laura said.

I smiled again. 'Thanks, but actually, I'm not drinking for a bit.'

Their eyes widened.

Sophie grabbed my arm. 'Oh my God. Are you pregnant?'

I cleared my throat and glanced at Ollie. 'No, no. We're putting that off for a bit.' I raised an eyebrow in Evie's direction. She raised both of hers back.

'Oh, thank God,' Lou said. 'We all thought you were crazy to be trying, but we didn't want to say.'

'Oh,' I said. 'Cool.'

'Well. I'll just open this for everyone else,' Ollie said, taking the wine off Laura and disappearing with it into the kitchen.

Sophie gestured at the coffee table. 'We also brought party food,' she said.

I looked over. 'This is genuinely really great,' I said. I meant it. 'I always wanted a surprise party.'

'We know,' Sophie said. 'You've been dropping hints for years. But you always plan something for yourself before anyone else can. This was our first real opportunity.'

Ollie came back in with the wine. He looked around at us.

'Why don't we all sit down?' he said. 'I'll put some music on.'

Maria sidled up to me.

'Hannah, babe, can we talk?' she said.

'Sure,' I said. We walked into the hallway. From the sofa, Lou raised her eyebrows at me. I shrugged at her.

Maria fluffed her hair in the mirror then turned to me. 'Look, babe, I just want to say sorry for getting so sloppy drunk at your girls' night. If I'd known how much that weekend meant to you, I would never have drunk so much vodka. It just does stuff to me, you know?'

I didn't know what to say. Maria had never apologised to any of us before. Not even to Sophie, when she had pushed her off a stage in a club we had all been dancing at, because she thought Sophie was blocking other people's view of her. That was something to be sorry about. Sophie hadn't made an issue out of it, though, mainly because she couldn't remember much of it. We chose to put this down to the drink instead of the fall. This felt like an important moment.

She looked down. 'Anyway, I really am sorry.' She looked up. 'I can go. Lou told me not to come, but I've missed you and we haven't talked. And I brought you a birthday present. It's a really nice one.'

I still didn't know what to say, but now it was also because I didn't know how to forgive her without it looking like I just wanted the present. Maria had access to sample sales. Good ones. Or so she said, anyway; Maria says lots of things about her work. She once told us she slept with a client who happened to be an A-list celebrity and the only reason she didn't get fired is because he said he'd go to another PR firm if she did. When she finally told us who the celebrity was, it turned out to be a news journalist from ITV.

I smiled. 'It's okay. And not just because I want the present. I was having a bad weekend, anyway.'

Maria raised a hand. 'That's what I said. I said it wasn't really my fault.'

I chose to ignore this.

We went back into the lounge.

I sat on the arm of the sofa, next to Evie.

'I really hate it when you're right,' I said.

'Everyone does,' she said. 'But I always am.'

Later that evening, Laura pulled me to one side.

'About Dad,' she said.

'Has something else happened?'

She took a sip of her drink. 'He's made another lasagne,' she said.

'Oh God,' I said.

'And he's told me he's going out tomorrow night.'

'What?' I said. 'When he's supposed to be celebrating his daughter's birthday?'

'You didn't want to celebrate it. It doesn't matter, anyway, because it will be after that. I think we should follow him.'

'That's stupid.'

Laura looked impatient. 'Why? We need to know what's going on. We have a right.'

'Do we, though?'

Laura tapped her fingers against her glass. 'Okay fine, we don't. But we should.'

I sighed. 'What if we find out something that we don't want to know? What if he really is having an affair? We couldn't do anything about it. Maybe not knowing is better.'

Laura shook her head. 'I have to know.'

Then Ollie walked in holding the cake and singing, which will bring an end to any conversation and did to this one.

I was relieved when Ollie shut the door after everyone left that night and no one had stained any more of our carpet or ruined another pillowcase.

'I thought about inviting Steph and Mary, but I didn't know if the timing was right,' he said. 'We've just got the smell out . . .'

Now, I just had my dad to contend with.

I wanted my dad to move on and be happy again, with someone else. Except that's a lie, I didn't. I wanted him to mourn Mum forever and live out his life as a committed widower, who would tell stories in his latter years of his one great love and why he could never so much as look at another woman again in his life. I realise this makes me sound selfish and a bit crazy, but – well actually, that's it. It makes me sound selfish and a bit crazy. There's really nothing else I can say to defend myself. It would be different if this was something new that he had come to in the months after Mum's death (and was preferably largely platonic and asexual), but I had strong evidence – well, I had evidence – that this could have been going on when Mum was still alive and that was much harder to accept.

This is the state of mind I was in when Ollie and I went round there the following afternoon.

Dad opened the door. 'Where's Laura?' he said.

Ollie and I looked at each other. 'Isn't she here?' I said.

'No,' Dad rubbed his chin. 'I haven't seen her since she left for yours last night. Are you sure she isn't with you?'

He stared at us. We stared at him. Ollie spread his hands as if to say, 'Look, she's not hiding in these.' I could feel my chest tightening. Not again. Please God, not again.

Then Laura walked out holding a cake and Dad's face broke into a grin.

'I'm joking, of course. I just didn't want to ruin the surprise.' He gestured at the cake.

I sucked my teeth.

'Let's get inside, shall we?' Ollie said, pushing me in.

We went into the lounge and sat down. Laura gave me her present: a jumper that was very similar to one of hers that I liked to smuggle out of her room whenever she wasn't paying attention.

'This is for the good of our relationship,' she said.

Then Dad handed me a long box in plush navy velvet.

'Oh, Dad,' I said. 'You really shouldn't have . . .' I took it and opened it slowly, thinking of Laura's bracelet. I gasped. It was a medallion. A gold medallion, to be exact. I don't mean this in a good way, either. If it's even possible for there to be a good way to receive a gold medallion that doesn't involve winning a mayoral election. It was also heavy – surprisingly heavy – and sat on an equally heavy gold chain. Plus, it glinted. I wondered if the jewellers had had to wrestle it directly off Joan Collins' neck while she was between scenes in *Dynasty*.

I glanced up.

Dad was watching me, intently.

I looked back down. 'Oh. Wow,' I said. I lifted it out of its box, my hand snagging slightly under its weight, and hefted it up. 'Would you look at that, guys?'

'Yeah, it's nice,' Ollie said.

I glanced at Laura. She looked horrified, then delighted. She was clearly trying not to laugh.

'Oh, Han,' she said. 'That will go so well with your black leather waistcoat.'

Dad looked at her. 'Excellent. You have something to wear with it,' he said. 'Does that mean you like it?'

I looked back down. 'Of course, Dad. Thank you. I'm just going to put it back in its box. It's a bit heavy . . . Hurting my hand, actually.'

There was a snort followed by a cough from Laura's direction.

Dad beamed. 'Oh good. A different woman helped me this time. It wasn't the same girl that helped me find Laura's present. This one was a bit older. I think she might have been the manager. They think you're both quite spoiled.'

Laura and I glanced at each other.

I smiled. 'It's really something, Dad,' I said. 'You shouldn't have.'

He waved me off. 'Don't forget your card.'

I held my breath as I opened it. There it was: *To dear Hannah, Happy Birthday, Love, Dad x*. It was in his handwriting and everything. I exhaled slowly.

Ollie squeezed my knee.

323

'Thanks, Dad,' I said.

Dad stood up. 'Right, shall we do the cake, then? Hannah, you don't want to stay for dinner, do you? I've got to pop out later.'

Laura looked at me and raised her eyebrows.

'No, Dad, that's fine,' I said. 'Where are you going?'

'Just to meet a friend. They're not very well, you see.'

'Ah. And will you be eating? Maybe a lasagne,' I added under my breath.

'If they feel up to it, perhaps,' he said. He looked slowly from me to Laura.

The phone rang. 'I should get that,' Dad said. He looked back at us. 'Upstairs.'

I waited a beat. 'Just going to the loo,' I said.

I crept upstairs to Dad's study. The door was closed, which was not a good sign. I tiptoed up to it. Inside, I could hear him talking. I leaned into the door and pressed my ear against it. I prayed that this was nothing. That he was talking about work and needed his privacy, even if he was retired. Or maybe he was talking to Nigel or Father Ray. A telephoned confession, even. I leaned in closer.

That's when I heard him say Betty.

'No, Betty, I'd really like to come today,' is exactly what he said.

I clenched my teeth. There was no denying it, now. Laura had been right: he really was sneaking off to see some other woman. Betty. Betty the shagger, as her friends probably knew her. Then it got worse.

324

'How many people will be there this time? Will there be a lot of us all getting into it?'

I blanched. I almost laughed. I would have laughed if there was any denying what I was hearing. But there wasn't. Not only was my dad sneaking off for illicit sex, he wasn't even bothering to confine it to one person. My dad was a bit player in *Eyes Wide Shut*.

'And there will be other men? It won't just be me and a group of women this time?'

My vision was beginning to swim. I didn't know how much more I could feasibly withstand. I stood back for a moment and stared at the door, leaning a hand against it. I wondered what the implications were of being fathered by Don Juan. I leaned back in. There was nothing. Then the door swung open and I went with it. I staggered into the study, where Dad was standing, staring at me.

'What on earth—' He watched as I hit the floor. 'For God's sake, Hannah.'

I jumped back up. 'I just came to get you. For cake.' I tossed my hair and tried to appear nonchalant. 'Who was that on the phone?'

He narrowed his eyes. 'Why? Were you listening?'

I snorted. 'No. But who was it?'

Dad huffed. He put his hands on his hips. 'Nigel,' he said.

I clutched my throat. 'Nigel?' For one horrifying moment, I thought of Nigel at a sex party. It was hard to think about anyone wanting to have sex with Nigel. Certainly not anyone who had ever seen him in the salmon pink shorts that were a couple of inches too short that he wore from March through to October.

'Yes. His wife's having one of her Tupperware parties.'

Nigel's wife's Tupperware parties were legendary, mainly because she still threw them, several decades after everyone else had stopped. That didn't mean Dad ever went to one, though. I narrowed my eyes. He hadn't been talking to Nigel; I knew that: I'd heard him say Betty. He was lying to me. He'd probably been lying to me for months, or for however long this affair with Betty had been going on for.

Dad was staring at me. 'Well? Are we having cake or not?'

'I don't know,' I said. 'Do you deserve cake?'

'What?'

I looked away. 'Nothing,' I said.

'Are you just going to stand there?' he said.

I crossed my arms. 'No,' I said.

'Well come on then: cake.'

We stood there for a second longer, eyeing each other, then we both turned, slowly and walked down the stairs.

As the day wore on, Dad began getting fidgety. By half past six, he had stopped engaging in conversation and had started watching the clock, his mouth moving as he counted the seconds until it was six thirty-one. I know he was doing this, because I was watching him, counting how many seconds he had been doing it for. When six thirty-one came and we were all still sitting there, he began huffing a bit. He pulled out his phone and started fiddling with it.

I turned to Laura. 'Do you remember that time on your birthday, Laur—'

Dad sighed noisily.

Ollie leaned into me. 'Maybe we should go,' he said. He nodded at Dad.

I put a hand on his arm and turned to Dad. 'Dad, you can go see your...' I paused for emphasis, '...friend. We can stay and hang out with Laura for a bit.'

I waited for him to say that it was my birthday, he wouldn't leave for some random woman he had been making lasagnes for and lying about for months on my birthday. Even if she did have her own swingers' collective, which, to be honest, I was beginning to doubt. It seemed too ridiculous to be true.

'Okay,' he said. 'Happy birthday. I'll call you soon.' He kissed me on the cheek and left the room.

'I can't believe he left. On my birthday,' I said.

'You told him to,' Ollie said. 'Besides, his friend is ill. It's nice that he's going to visit them.'

Laura snorted. 'There's no friend, Ollie. He's seeing a woman.'

'Maybe several,' I muttered.

'We're following him,' Laura said.

Ollie laughed. 'Oh, you're serious? You can't do that. Well, you can, I suppose. I can't. He'll never speak to me again.' He took my hand. 'Hannah, if we go home now, we can have another go on Bertha.'

'I bet that's what Dad will be doing, too,' I said. 'Having a go.'

Laura grimaced. 'We're following him.' She turned to me. 'Come on, Hannah. Dad is not a young man any more. The elderly are very vulnerable.'

'He's sixty-five,' Ollie said.

Laura ignored him. 'This woman could be anyone. She's probably some scam artist that preys on the lonely.'

'I did just watch a documentary on black widow killers,' I said. 'They target widowers, you know. They're easy game.'

Ollie sat back in the sofa. 'Or maybe he's going to see a friend and you're making this into something it's not.'

'Well then isn't it better we find out and stop torturing ourselves?' Laura looked behind her. 'Look, he'll be leaving any second. We haven't got much time.'

I picked at my legs. 'He did pretend you were dead, earlier, Laura,' I said.

Ollie looked at me. 'What has that got to do with anything?'

'Well, nothing, really, but it's annoying.'

Dad stuck his head through the door. He had changed his shirt, I noticed. 'Right, I'm off. Laura, I'll be back later. Good to see you, Ollie.'

His head disappeared and a few seconds later, the front door slammed.

Laura stood up. 'I'm following him.'

I stood up, too. 'We're following him.'

Ollie sighed and stood up, as well. 'I'm going home.'

We jogged into the hallway.

'We should wear tights over our faces, so he doesn't see us,' Laura said.

I picked up her car keys. 'Whose tights?'

'Well, yours, obviously. I don't want to cut holes in any of mine. I need them for work.'

I gestured at my legs. 'These were expensive. They're M&S.'

We stood facing each other.

Ollie looked from one to the other of us. 'This is going to end really badly. He's going to see you and then he's going to want to know why you're following him.'

'I'm not cutting up my tights,' I said.

Ollie took the car keys off me. 'I'm going to drive you,' he said.

'Thanks, Ollie.' Laura opened the door and looked out. 'He's at the end of the drive. He's indicating right. Quick.'

We dashed to the car. Or rather, Laura and I dashed, then we jumped in the back. Ollie walked deliberately slowly, rubbing his eyes.

'Ollie, hurry,' Laura said. 'We're going to lose him.' She bounced impatiently.

'It's fine,' I said. 'He turned right. It's just houses for ages that way. We'll see his car if he parks. Oh God, it's just houses. Houses that probably have beds.'

We caught up with him by the time he got to a set of traffic lights.

'There,' Laura shouted, leaning forward between the front seats.

'Jesus.' Ollie put his hand up. 'We're going at thirty

in a residential area. This is not a high-speed car chase. You both really need to calm down.'

The lights went green and we pulled off again. Ollie made sure he kept a couple of cars between Dad and us.

'You're good at this, Ollie,' Laura said.

'Well, I wanted to be a spy when I was younger,' he said. 'And now here I am: stalking my girlfriend's father on a Sunday evening.' He looked at me in the rear-view mirror.

I pointed at the road and gave him a meaningful look.

Ollie has a knack for making some of the things I do sound ridiculous, but on this occasion, he was the one in the wrong. I thought about all the 'women who kill' documentaries that I like to watch when I have PMS. Ollie always refuses to watch them with me; he says they make him too nervous when he goes to the supermarket. The point is, single widowers practically had their own victim subgenre.

The question, though, was how were we going to prove anything was going on? I hadn't thought about what we would do when we got there. Did we watch through the window? I didn't want to watch. What if Betty had curtains? What if she lived in a flat on one of the upper floors? What if she lived in a flat on one of the upper floors and there wasn't a ladder around? We could get caught by Neighbourhood Watch. Unless they really were swingers, in which case, Neighbour-hood Watch might be in on it. This was beginning to feel complicated.

Then it got more complicated: Dad disappeared.

Laura shrieked, causing Ollie to almost do an emergency break.

Ollie swore. 'I will crash.'

'He's gone,' Laura said.

'He can't have gone far,' I said. I looked around. 'There: car park.'

'That's the town hall car park,' Ollie said.

We pulled in anyway.

Laura pointed. 'There's his car.'

Ollie drove into a parking space.

I felt a glimmer of hope. Maybe he wasn't secretly dating, after all. Maybe he was secretly an alcoholic and was going to an Alcoholics Anonymous meeting. The alcoholism wasn't even that much of a stretch; it was the compulsion to stop that was the real surprise.

'Maybe he's in a local club?' Ollie said. 'Or the choir?'

I nodded, enthusiastically. 'Or Alcoholics Anonymous.'

Laura glanced at me. 'He's had a drink every night this week.'

'Exactly,' I said.

Ollie pointed. 'Look.'

Another car had driven in while we were sitting there. A man had got out and was making his way round to the entrance. Then, a woman followed. She looked around, checked her face in a compact she pulled out of her handbag and then went inside.

'See,' Ollie said. 'There are other people here. It's a club night.'

'Or they're swingers,' I said. 'I heard him on the phone earlier. He was talking to Betty. About seeing her. And multiple other people. I didn't think it could be true, but . . .' I gestured, then groaned and clawed at my face.

Laura already had the car door open. 'I'm going in,' she said.

I grabbed at her. 'Laura. What if he sees you? What if they are swingers?'

But she was already out of my reach. She dropped low, her back to the car and scuttled towards the hall.

I sighed, opened my door and got out, too.

'Hannah,' Ollie hissed.

I ran inside. Laura was lurking near the entrance, by the toilets. In front of us were a set of double doors and then a corridor leading further into the building.

'Where's Ollie?' Laura said.

'Oh, he's definitely reached his limit with all of this. He's in the car,' I said.

'I heard voices.' She nodded down the hall. 'That way.'

'How did they sound?' I said.

'Horny,' she said. 'Come on.'

We tiptoed down the corridor, sliding along the wall until we found the source of the voices.

'Who has group sex in a function room?' I whispered.

'The middle class,' Laura said. 'This must be where they hammer out the logistics.' She looked at me. 'Hannah, I don't know if I can cope with Dad being a swinger. Does this mean he was cheating on Mum with loads of women?' Her face fell. 'Was Mum one, too?'

My stomach dropped. This was all getting to be a bit too much.

The door to the function room was still slightly open. Laura craned her neck and peered in.

'Do swinging parties usually involve fold-away plastic chairs?'

I leaned over her. Inside, there was a group of mainly middle-aged and older people sitting around in a circle. There was a table set up to the side that was covered in plates and dishes.

'The lasagne,' Laura said.

'Sustenance,' I said.

As we watched, two people stood up and hugged each other.

'Here it goes,' Laura said. 'This must be how it gets started.'

'I feel sick,' I said.

Then someone came up behind us. 'Excuse me.'

We jumped and turned round. It was a woman.

She looked at us and smiled in a way I'll admit I interpreted as predatory. 'Are you coming in?' She pushed the door open. 'There's no need to be ashamed or afraid.'

As far as recruitment tactics go, it felt fairly basic, but maybe she wasn't that into us.

We stared at her in horror. She looked benignly back at us.

'Our dad's in there,' Laura blurted.

She nodded. 'Okay,' she said. She looked into the room.

Then it got even worse. Dad saw us. He stood up and came towards us.

'No,' Laura said. She put her hands up and shut her eyes. 'I don't want to see anything. I'm sorry I came.'

I glanced at her. 'Laura, he's not naked. You just saw him.'

Dad, for the record, looked furious.

He put his hands on his hips. 'What are you doing here? Did you follow me?'

We looked at our feet.

'Well. That's very nice, isn't it,' he said. 'Am I not allowed any privacy?' He glared at us.

I toed the floor.

Dad turned to the woman who was still standing there, watching all of this unfold. 'Sorry, Betty. These are my daughters. Their mother raised them.'

I gasped and looked at the woman. 'You're Betty?' I said.

'Yes,' she said. She looked uncertainly at me.

'What is it now?' Dad said.

It didn't feel like the right time to tell him I'd been spying on him, so I stayed quiet.

Betty cleared her throat. 'Patrick, why don't you come back inside? Do you two,' she said, gesturing at Laura and me, 'want to come in, too?'

'No,' Laura, Dad and I all said in unison.

'Thank you,' Laura added.

'You're welcome to join,' Betty said. 'It might help, even, Patrick. We do encourage family members to come and share.'

Laura went white. I went red.

I mustered up a voice. 'Thank you,' I said. 'And we don't judge. But we're just not swingers.'

Betty's mouth opened.

Dad looked apoplectic, which was the first time I had really understood what people meant when they described people as looking that way.

'Swingers? My dear,' Betty said. 'This is a grief support session.'

In the end, we had had to join the meeting. It was quite nice, actually. Once Dad stopped sharing why he was so disappointed in us and let someone else speak. Still, we hadn't exactly hung around afterwards. In fact, Laura and I had run out of it as fast as possible once it ended, jumped into the car and instructed Ollie to drive, who had only done so reluctantly. We didn't think Dad would be in the mood to offer us a lift. We hadn't spoken to him since. Or more to the point, he hadn't spoken to either of us.

A few days later, Ollie drove me to my family's house.

'Does he know you're coming?' he said.

I stared out the window. 'We thought it was better he didn't. He might not let me in. Laura was scared he'd lock her out when she went to work.'

'Right. Well, I'll pick you up when you're done. Just call me when you're ready.'

'You're not coming in?'

He shook his head. 'You need to talk this out as a family.'

I narrowed my eyes. 'You're scared of seeing Dad aren't you.'

He pointed at the car door.

I took a deep breath and got out.

Laura opened the front door.

'I've set up the dining room,' she said, solemnly. I had never heard of her setting up any room before.

I nodded. 'Is Dad in there?'

'No, he's in his study.'

'Then how are we going to get him in there? He's not talking to us. I don't think he wants to be in the same room as us, either.'

Laura shrugged. 'I made dinner. He has to eat.'

'Is it lasagne?'

Dad came down the stairs and saw us standing there.

'Oh,' he said.

'Dad, I made us dinner,' Laura said. 'It's in the dining room.' She sounded like the butler.

Dad looked from one to the other of us. 'Will you be eating, too?'

We nodded.

He looked at us for a long moment. Next to me, I could feel Laura holding her breath, but since Dad hated to cook and, until recently at least, was very limited in what he could successfully make, he didn't have many options when it came to dinner. I waited for him to realise this, too.

He gave a curt nod and walked through to the dining room.

He sat down at the table and we pulled out two chairs in front of him.

'Before I serve the food,' Laura said.

Dad looked pained.

'We wanted to say sorry,' she said. 'We should never have followed you. It was wrong of us.'

'We were worried,' I said. 'I'd watched a documentary on black widows.'

Dad frowned. 'The spiders?'

'No, the women who kill men. We thought you might be a target. Although now, this sounds a bit silly.'

Dad nodded.

'We thought you might be dating someone,' Laura said.

Dad crossed his arms. 'And so what if I was?'

This question had never occurred to me before, but now that it had, it sounded like a good one. A good question we didn't have the answer to. I wasn't going to admit that, though.

I crossed my arms. 'We wouldn't have had to spy on you if you hadn't been so secretive. What were you doing at a grief support meeting? Why didn't you just tell us you were going to one? It would have been nice to know you were struggling a bit, too.'

Dad scowled at me. 'Oh that's rich. You follow me, embarrass me in public, practically accuse me of being a pervert and then come into my house and have the nerve to question me?' He stood up. 'I don't have to listen to this. I can eat in the other room.'

I stood up, too. 'Fine,' I said. 'Blame us. You were the one sneaking about and suddenly learning how to cook.'

'It was a ready meal,' Dad shouted.

'You're always shouting,' I shouted. 'That's how you told us Mum was going to die: you didn't tell us, you yelled it.' I waved my arms around. 'And here you go again. All we were trying to do was protect you. But that's fine. We won't any more.'

'I am your father. I don't need your protection.'

'Fine,' I said.

'Fine,' he said.

'Um,' Laura said. 'I think we've gone off track.' She tugged at my arm until I sat down, again. 'We're sorry. We thought you might have met someone and we got upset. We shouldn't have followed you.' She nudged me. 'Right, Hannah?'

I looked away. 'Right.'

Dad sat down, slowly.

'You could have told us where you were going, though,' Laura said.

Dad folded his arms, again. 'I was forced into going to those meetings, if you must know. Carol made me.'

Laura and I looked at each other.

'Forced?' Laura said.

'Carol?' I said. I nodded, slowly. I knew Dad would never actively choose to share his inner feelings. This made much more sense. Maybe we weren't that far off with our dangerous woman idea, after all. I prepared to feel smug.

'Yes, Carol from church. She thought it would be a

good idea for me,' Dad said. 'Said it helped her after her husband died. She said Betty had helped her get through a lot.'

'Oh,' I said.

'She made me promise to go to one of the meetings,' Dad said. 'I thought it might be worth a go. It would get me out of the house, at least.'

'Right,' Laura said.

Dad snorted. 'Well, all a bit of rubbish really, isn't it? Talking about how you're feeling. Everyone knows how you're feeling: you're upset, obviously. Someone's died. It's sad.' He cleared his throat. 'Still. Been quite helpful. Nice to meet new people. More interesting than sitting around in an empty house,' he said. He frowned. 'Are we eating dinner or not?'

Laura got up and went into the kitchen.

I looked at Dad. 'So you're going to keep going to these meetings?'

He narrowed his eyes. 'Why? Are you planning on coming? You should. They'd be more useful than that quack you saw. Don't know why you ever went there. Have you spoken to Father Ray, yet?'

I closed my eyes and sat back in my chair as Laura came back in with plates of spaghetti.

'I fancied Italian,' she said.

How to Channel the Dead

Back when Harry turned one, Evie and Jake threw a party with a few friends and family. There were some games and balloons and Harry sitting in the middle of it all, totally oblivious to the meaning behind any of it because he was too young to understand. Still, a year is a big milestone. Even my friend Louise – the one who really believes in the Law of Attraction and dated a blow-up doll she pretended was her boyfriend – decided a year was long enough to wait for the law to start working and for the actual boyfriend to come back. She held a small ceremony to mark the occasion of her officially letting go on a rooftop in London by letting the inflatable boyfriend go – she blew him up and let him float off into the night sky like an adult balloon. I know this because she filmed it and posted it on Instagram; it was very moving.

But how do you mark the occasion when it's a year of grieving? When what you've been carrying around for twelve months isn't a growing child or even a misappropriated sex toy, but an empty space?

In the days leading up to the first anniversary of Mum's death, I'd been spending a lot of time at my family home. I didn't know what else to do with myself, so I went there. You'd think after a whole year, I would have more of a handle on things, but there you go. Dad walked into his bedroom one afternoon and found me with my face in one of Mum's drawers. I got into her bath and rubbed myself with all of the soaps and lotions she used to use and just breathed myself in. I think I was delayed: I hadn't let myself do it when she first died; I had been too busy pretending she hadn't.

Dad never said anything, because we were barely talking. Not because Laura and I had followed him and accused him of being a swinger. Actually, things were a lot better on that front. Laura had even decided to go with him a few times and she seemed to find it useful. She had started seeing more of her friends and was even looking for a new job. Apparently, the stalking had made her realise how much she needed a life. We weren't talking because no one wanted to talk about the anniversary, which we had all sort of agreed to pretend wasn't happening, but that was still all any of us could think about. What exactly are you supposed to do with that kind of anniversary?

I really felt like I was done with grief. If you say that to people, they say depressing things back to you, like, 'Oh, but you're never *done* with *grief*. It stays with you forever.' I knew that, logically, but I didn't want to listen to them. I felt like I should be the exception to the rule.

I was ready to have my mum back as a reward for how well I'd done. And by that I meant that I had got through it — I had lost my mum and survived a whole year after that. I had had emotions and I had dealt with them (sort of). I had seen a counsellor. I'd even had an evening in a grief support group, even if it had been a total accident.

But the only reward you get for all of that is that now, you're allowed to make a big decision, which you're not supposed to do in the first year after you've lost someone close to you. Big deal: I have never been any good at making decisions in the first place. It was quite relaxing having a year off.

And I'm sorry to tell you this, but the first anniversary of a death is the unholy of all unholies when it comes to first anniversaries, of which that first year felt like a random collection. It makes crying in Tesco look like a fun day out.

The first anniversary of the day someone you loved died is like being sucked into a giant vacuum of pleasure, happiness and good will. It takes all the enjoyment you might be getting out of life and rips it away from you, spitting a bit of depression back out at you. You're left there on the outskirts, desperately clinging on to anything you can that could cheer you up to prevent yourself from losing it completely and becoming a quivering ball of sadness. If vacuums could laugh, this one would. It would cackle at your pain, while it sucked the light out of life. That book you just read the night before that you swore used to be able to bring you some pleasure now won't. Everything is miserable. This has become a slightly confused metaphor, but that is basically what the first anniversary of a death is like.

So I went home, where I could be surrounded by Mum's things and feel closer to her. I would just take my laptop round and pretend I was working. Which is what I was doing the day Nigel came round and started banging on the door: standing in the kitchen, pretending to do some work, putting bits of nearby food into my mouth.

Dad opened the door.

'Patrick, I have some news,' Nigel said, marching through to the front room.

'Bloody hell, Nigel, what the hell is it?'

'I think you need to sit down,' Nigel said, pointing at the chair he was by this point standing in front of.

I froze. Naturally, my first instinct was that someone else had died. For what it's worth, this is what anyone who is recently bereaved will think as soon as someone tells them they have news. Which is exactly what happened to me. Oh God, I thought, who is it this time? I stopped what I was doing and pressed myself into the doorjamb, watching Dad and Nigel through the crack in the door. I hoped it wasn't someone I liked.

Nigel pressed his hands together in a steeple, raised them to his mouth and took a deep breath. 'Barbara went to her psychic meeting last night,' he said, pausing. 'The psychic came through with the letter "J".' He waited while his words sank in, eyeballing Dad significantly.

Dad didn't react.

Nigel dropped his hands. 'It was a woman. Who died suddenly. About this time last year.'

Still nothing.

343

'A woman named Jennifer. Married to a man named Patrick.' Nigel stopped, practically panting at this point and looked at my dad, who still wasn't reacting.

Dad sucked in his cheeks. 'Okay. What exactly did my dead wife have to say?'

Nigel cleared his throat. 'Well. I don't know, exactly. Barbara didn't put her hand up. You have to put your hand up if you know the person, to claim the message. And she didn't really know Jennifer, you see,' he said.

Dad raised a hand to his mouth. His shoulders started shaking.

Nigel looked ready to dive in and console him, should he be needed. Which he wasn't, because Dad wasn't upset: he was too busy laughing.

'Bollocks,' he said.

Nigel looked confused, then slightly crestfallen. 'But, Pat—'

'Bollocks,' Dad said again. He said it several more times. He added two extra syllables to it. He practically sang it, in fact. Then he stood up, ran upstairs shouting Laura's name and told her the whole story.

I went to the bottom of the stairs.

'Your mum's not dead after all,' I heard him shout.

'No, she is dead, she just came back with a message,' Nigel said. 'Through a psychic.'

I couldn't hear what Laura said back to this.

Then Dad came running back down the stairs and I had to dart back into the kitchen and pretend I hadn't been listening all along and had in fact been making a sandwich.

'Hannah,' Dad said. He practically crowed. 'You'll never believe this. Barbara . . .' he threw his thumb back at Nigel, '. . . says your mum came through at her psychic meeting. Tall woman and everything.' He laughed. He was beginning to look a bit hysterical.

I looked at Nigel. Nigel looked slightly agitated. I gave him a small smile.

Dad pointed at me. 'See, she finds it just as funny as I do.'

Nigel shifted his weight onto the other foot. 'You've got to admit, Patrick,' he said. 'It's an amazing coincidence.'

Dad snorted. 'That's not a coincidence. I'll tell you what that is: it's a scam. She obviously read through the obituaries on *The Argus* from last year, found the ones that have an anniversary coming up and threw them out there to see if anyone responded.' He spread his hands. 'This isn't that big a place. Odds are, someone will recognise one. And if they don't, I'm sure she's got plenty more where that came from.' He shook his head and chuckled. 'Bloody ridiculous, isn't it?'

Nigel looked put out.

I cleared my throat. 'Nigel, do you want a sandwich?'

Dad and Nigel looked down at the chopping board, where I had wedged a piece of ham between two pieces of cheese, with an olive on top.

'I'll have one, too,' Dad said.

I tried to find this as funny as Dad did. I didn't believe in psychics. I drew the line at Catholicism. Besides, even if Mum was trying to get through to us, she knew us all well enough to know not to try through a psychic. That wouldn't help her cause at all. Just ask Nigel. So I started to laugh about it, too. I told all my friends about it.

'What nonsense,' I said. 'Can you believe it?' I said. 'A psychic,' I said. Then I waited, grinning expectantly at them, encouraging them to find it equally as absurd.

My friends would then look back at me and say, 'What if it was real, though?'

I'd scoff some more. 'Oh please. That was just a dramatic reading of the obituary. I should know: I wrote it.'

Then I'd go home and repeat all of this to Ollie, while he watched me, looking a bit worried.

'I really don't think this is anything, Hannah,' he said.

'I know it's not,' I said. 'That's what I'm saying.'

'I think this woman's probably a bit of a con,' he said.

'Right,' I said. 'A huge one.'

'So best to just forget about it altogether. Don't let it get to you.'

'Oh,' I said. 'It won't.'

But it did.

I had meant everything I said. But on the other hand, what if I was wrong? What if she really did have an important message and we would never hear it? What if this was her only way of communicating with us? What were the chances?

'What if she was right?' I said one night. I was back to pacing while Ollie sat on the sofa and tried to watch television.

'Who?' Ollie said, leaning to look past me.

346

'The psychic. What if Mum really was trying to come through?'

Ollie looked away from the television. 'Han, I thought you were going to ignore this?'

I stopped pacing. 'Come on, Ollie. I think we both know better than that.' I resumed walking.

'Hannah, it's ridiculous. You know that. You don't believe in psychics.'

'I know, I know. But what if I'm wrong? She knew details.'

'Details you wrote,' Ollie pointed out. He stood up. 'Han, your dad was right. She looked up the obituaries online. It's just a coincidence someone you know was there.'

I started nodding. 'You're right. She is a con artist. How dare she. How dare she intrude on my grief?' I thumped my chest for emphasis. 'At a time like this. It is the anniversary of my mum's death. My mum. This isn't a joke. She has forced herself into my life and made me question everything.' There was a quaver in my voice now. 'I actually thought that my mum – my mum. My dead mother – had come back with a message for us.' I raised my hand. 'A message I will never get to hear because Barbara – Barbara – didn't know Mum well enough. Well, thank you very much, Barbara. And fake psychic.'

Ollie took me by the shoulders and pulled me into his chest. He stroked my hair, soothingly. 'Do you know what you should do?'

'Kill her,' I said.

'What? No. You should try not to think about it any more. It will make you crazy. Look, why don't you go have a bath? Try to relax a bit. Take your mind off it.'

'Okay,' I said.

I tried to do that, really I did. But I couldn't get it out of my mind. I was plagued by the thought that I had missed a message from my mum. I was furious. I was furious and upset and confused. Mainly, though, I was furious. I was right back to where I had started: angry.

The next day, I went back to my family home.

Dad opened the door. 'Do you not work any more? You keep telling me you have a job but I never seem to see you actually working.'

Dad has never been able to understand the fact that I work for myself. I produced my laptop and waved it at him. 'I thought I'd work here today.'

Dad frowned. 'Fine. I've cleaned the bathroom if you're planning on using it again, today. I'll be in my study. Do what you will.'

I walked through to the kitchen and took Dad's phone off the counter. I called Nigel.

'If you're calling to laugh some more, Patrick,' Nigel said, when he picked up.

'Nigel, it's Hannah,' I said.

'Oh,' he said.

'I was wondering if you could give me the details for Barbara's psychic? I'd like to go along to the next meeting.'

'Oh,' he said, again. 'So you think there's something to it, too? Funny isn't it, how much she knows? I'll get the details off Barb.'

When he came back on the line, I jotted down the name and website and hung up.

I looked at the website, scrolling past a picture of a woman in a turban. I clicked on the page that listed her upcoming meetings, or 'spiritual communions', as the website put it. I was lucky: there was another one coming up. I already knew the building. It was a horrid, squat modern build that was mainly used whenever the antique coin fair came to town. The stamp club also hired it out for their monthly meetings. I knew this because there was a semi-permanent banner outside advertising both events. We had also had our prom there. I didn't expect this to be any more enjoyable than that had been, but I needed to go. I had to see it for myself.

I was going to go alone, this time. Laura's espionage days were behind her. She had made that very clear. I didn't think she would be up for this, anyway, now she'd rediscovered her social life and her days had taken on some more purpose and meaning, again. I very deliberately didn't tell anyone else what I was planning, either. They probably wouldn't understand; they almost definitely wouldn't approve.

As I left the house, I shouted to Ollie, 'I have a thing. Bye.'

I was gone before he answered.

*

I pulled into the car park, which looked busier than I had ever seen it. I was beginning to feel nervous. I contemplated not going in, then I remembered what I had been going through and I was back to being angry again.

I marched into the building and found my way to the psychic meeting room. The chairs were arranged in a horseshoe around a small stage. They had even managed to erect raised seating, so everyone had a clear view of what was going on.

There were about twenty other people in the room. I climbed the stairs and found a seat near the back.

Then the psychic walked on stage. She was dressed in an ankle-length kaftan and was wearing a turban. She looked around the room and beamed.

'Hello, my children,' she said. 'Some of you have been before, and . . .' She raised a hand to her temple and squinted, slightly. 'Some of you are new.'

I tried not to snort.

Another hand went to a temple. She moaned slightly. 'Yes, the messages are clear tonight.' She clapped. 'Shall we get started?'

Someone came out on stage behind the psychic and produced a chair. The psychic nodded. The person whispered something to her and went out.

The psychic sat down. She started breathing deeply and waving her hands about her head.

I looked around. Her audience was rapt. I rolled my eyes. If these people wanted mystical pomp and

350

ceremony, they should come to a Catholic Mass. It was far more dramatic.

Then the psychic opened her mouth. 'P752 VPN,' the psychic rattled off.

A man in the audience stood up.

The psychic looked at him. 'You're parked in a reserved spot.' She glanced off to the side of the stage. 'Is that right? Yeah? Yeah.' She looked back at the man. 'You just need to move your car, love.'

'Thanks, Linda,' the man said. The psychic's name was Linda. He scuttled out.

Linda put her hands back to her temples and closed her eyes. She hummed. 'W,' she said. 'W is coming through.'

Everyone looked around at each other. Then a thirty-something woman in the audience raised her hand. 'Whiskers?' she said.

Linda looked at her. 'Face or feline?'

The woman cleared her throat. 'Whiskers was my cat,' she said. 'He died when I was ten.'

Linda nodded and inhaled. 'Yes, that's it,' she said. She meowed. 'He's happy,' she said. 'He wants you to move on. Love other pets.'

'Well, I do have another cat,' the woman said.

Linda had moved on. Her hands were back in the air. 'I'm getting the letter P.'

I stood up.

Linda opened one eye. 'Yes, I thought it was for you. It's a girl,' she said. 'She's showing me the colour pink. Pink is important to you.'

'No,' I said. 'I'm not here for that. That's not for me.'

Linda opened both eyes. 'Oh. Well, then. Anyone else. P. P.' She put both hands on her temples, again and closed her eyes.

'Oi,' I said. I won't lie and tell you this was my most articulate moment. It wasn't.

Linda opened her eyes, again. She sighed. 'Yes,' she said.

'You said my mum had a message for me. And that's not okay.' This sounded a bit lame, but I didn't really know where to go with it after the 'oi'.

Linda held up her hand. 'I can't control the messages I receive. If you didn't like the message, you'll have to take it up with her.'

'She can't though,' someone across the room said. 'If her mum's dead.'

I ignored this. 'I never got the message. I wasn't here. Someone else was and they didn't ask for the message.'

There was a sympathetic murmur at this from the crowd.

'She never even got to hear the message,' a woman in a purple hat sitting next to me said.

'That's not the point,' I said.

Purple hat woman looked up at me in surprise. 'It's not?'

'The point is, I never asked for the message in the first place.'

Purple hat woman shuffled in her seat. 'Ungrateful.'

On stage, Linda sucked her teeth.

I balled my hands into fists. 'The point is, I never

asked for any of this. But you,' I said, pointing at Linda, 'intruded on my life, anyway. You came along and said my mum wanted to talk to me. And I got all worried that I had missed the last message from my mum that I'll ever get. But it wasn't my mum. How could it be? It was just you, reading the obituaries and hoping you'd find a target. Do you have any idea the pain I was already in? Well, it was a lot. And you made it worse. You read old obituaries and used the information you found there to pretend that my mum had a message for me. You are a fraud.'

There was a gasp from the audience. Everyone looked at Linda, who was rubbing her temples as if she were receiving an incoming message from the Great Beyond, or maybe a migraine. Then they looked back at me.

I took a deep breath. 'You don't hear messages from the dead. You just scam the living and use their pain against them. You're sick. Totally sick. Well, I'm not going to let you get away with it any more. None of us are, right, everyone?' I looked around for support, which I was sure would start kicking in at any moment. I was helping these people, freeing them from the shackles of Linda's bullshit. Or something more erudite than that. I wasn't going to let her take advantage of anyone else's pain. 'Say it with me people. She's a fraud.' I took a breath and started to chant. 'Fraud, fraud,' I said. I clapped my hands to go along with it. 'Fraud.' I tried to stand on a chair, but it was plastic and felt a bit rickety, so instead, I started wafting my hands to the ceiling in that way people do at sports games, political events and concerts when they're trying to garner support. Then I pointed at Linda. 'Hear us, Linda,' I said. 'We won't be conned by you any more. You need to leave us be.' I stopped and put my hands on my hips, waiting for the noise of the crowd agreeing with me. It didn't come. I looked around. No one else was chanting. In fact, they were being unusually quiet. People turned to look up at me. A lot of them looked very sad and also very scared, like I might at any point turn this session into tomorrow's news headline. I crossed my arms. I was beginning to wonder if the psychic had a protocol for times like this. Was someone going to take me out? At any minute now, would security grab me? I decided I would go kicking and screaming. That's really your only option when you've started a chant that no one else has picked up on.

'So,' I said. 'What are you going to do about it?' I was finding out I wasn't great at making dramatic speeches in the moment.

Then someone stood up. He was about six foot tall and three feet wide. I wondered if he was Linda's bodyguard, here to protect her from anyone that made a scene, like I was. I wondered if he ever crushed people with his biceps, which looked entirely possible. I wondered, if he hadn't, if I'd be the first. I braced my arms across my chest. 'I won't go easily,' I whispered.

'Look,' he said. He spread his arms.

I flinched.

'Sorry about your mum, love. But some of us come here to get in touch with our relatives. This is the one chance a week I get to hear from my son. I've been waiting months for him to come through.' There was a quaver in his voice that was all too familiar to me from the quaver I'd heard in my own voice. 'If you don't believe in it, that's fine. We all have to get through losing someone in our own way. But this is how we grieve. I need to know I can hear from my son again. Don't try and take that away from us.'

There was a murmur of assent from the crowd to this, which really proved they could rally in support of a cause, just not mine.

He turned to the front. 'Now, Linda,' he said. 'Have you had any Bs come through?'

Everyone turned to Linda. She opened her mouth. Then looked at me. Everyone looked back at me.

I sat down, slowly and quietly. I nodded at Linda.

She turned back to her audience, touched her turban and closed her eyes. 'Daniel,' she announced. 'Does anyone know a Daniel?'

I looked at the man who was trying to communicate with his son. He looked slightly crushed.

A woman raised her hand. 'My dad was called David,' she said.

Linda nodded. 'He loved to watch you paint.'

The woman's mouth fell open. 'I'm a graphic designer,' she said.

Linda nodded some more. 'He loved to watch you on Microsoft Paint. He says he misses you.'

The woman had begun to quietly sob. 'She couldn't know that,' she told the person next to her. 'He must really be here.'

I stood up and shuffled out.

In the car park, I fumbled in my bag for my car keys. When I couldn't find them, I upended my entire bag on the ground, with a scream of frustration.

I looked up at the sky and gave God my hard stare, which had gone a bit fuzzy around the edges, because I was crying.

'All right, God. I am losing faith. You took the most important person in my life away from me and left me with an emotionally repressed father and a sister who sleeps a lot, who I should look after, because I'm the oldest and that's what we're supposed to do, but I can't. And then you give me Linda? Bloody Linda?' I closed my eyes and scraped my nails against my scalp. 'How could you? I've been good. I might have had sex, but that's it. If that's what you're so upset about, then you should have punished me, not her. You took the wrong person.' I was shouting now. 'And you know what else? It's not just me you're upsetting, here. There's a whole load of people who Mum was important to, besides me. That should mean something. But you don't care do you? You stupid bloody deity,' I shouted into the sky. 'You bloody arsehole. What kind of a useless god are you, anyway? Give me Jesus. At least he had some compassion and could bring people back from the dead.' I started pounding the ground with my feet. 'Give her back. Give her back, give her back, give her back.' I sat down on the ground. 'Just give her back. I'm not moving until you do. I will sit here until you give her back to me.' I waited for a beat. 'You can't do it, can you?' I stood back up. 'Or you can and you choose not to. Well, I'm done with you. We are *breaking up*. From now on, I only believe in the Ancient Greek gods. At least they did stuff. They brought people back from the dead. What are you doing? Well?' I stood there, my arms open staring into the sky. 'You vindictive prick!'

It was only when I noticed a woman pop her head out of the doors of the building, holding a phone she was talking into, that I stopped shouting. When I heard her describing my outfit, I gathered up my things, climbed into my car and drove away.

I drove home and quietly let myself into the house. Ollie walked out into the hallway.

'Where have you been?' he said.

'I went to see the psychic,' I said.

'Psychic? Oh no.'

I took my coat off. 'I interrupted the meeting to yell at her.'

Ollie walked over and put his arms around me. 'What happened?'

'I yelled at her,' I said. 'I called her a liar and a fraud.'

'Uh oh,' Ollie said.

'Then I realised that there were people there that really rely on Linda. That's the psychic's name, Linda.'

'Sure,' Ollie said.

'They really believed in her and I was spoiling it for them. So I left.'

'I see.' Ollie pulled me into a hug.

This was necessary as I had started to cry.

'I'm just so—' I said.

Ollie pulled away slightly. 'Hey, you have nothing to be embarrassed about.'

'Angry,' I said. 'I'm just so angry.' I started crying harder.

'Oh, right,' Ollie said. He stroked my hair. 'I know.'

'I'm just so pissed off that she died.' I wiped my face on his T-shirt.

Ollie looked down at me. 'What can I do? We could get a takeaway and eat it in bed?'

I cleared my throat. 'I think I need to stop pretending that I'm fine.'

How to Live Without Her

I sat in the hospital, waiting to meet my new counsellor.

I had told Dad I was coming back to counselling.

'For the love of God, why are you going back?' he said. 'It didn't work the first time. Why won't you go and see Father Ray? If you'd just gone there, you might be fine by now.'

I had had to promise to go to Mass on Sunday before he had reluctantly agreed not to call him.

I settled back in my chair and looked at the form in front of me. 'On a scale of one to ten,' it said, 'have you ever had violent feelings towards other people?' I thought of the psychic and circled a two.

Across the room, I saw someone I thought I recognised from the last time I was there. I waved.

A door buzzed and a woman called my name, while a teenage girl was ushered out. She was wearing, I noticed, the uniform from my old girls' school. I sympathised.

'It gets better,' I whispered as I walked past her signing out on the visitors' form. Then I realised I was at the same hospital she was, only thirteen years later. I didn't blame her for the suspicious look she gave me.

My new counsellor was waiting patiently at the

door for me. This one wasn't wearing a kaftan, either, although she was in a pair of chic, lilac wide-legged trousers that I took as a good sign. She was also older than me and experienced. I had made sure of that when I asked to come back.

She walked me through to a room and gestured towards a chair.

'So, Hannah,' she said. She smiled. 'What is it that made you seek out counselling?'

'My mum died,' I said.

She nodded and looked at her clipboard. 'You've had some counselling sessions before?'

'Yes, but I decided I needed to come back.'

She looked up at me. 'And why is that?'

I clasped my hands together. 'I didn't feel like I was coping properly.'

She made a note. 'Have you been using drugs or alcohol to help you cope?'

I shook my head. 'Actually, I've stopped drinking for now, which really goes against everything I was raised to believe in. I'm Irish Catholic: drinking is a big part of how we feel close to God. It's really the only way my dad and I have ever really been able to relate to each other. But recently, it's only ever made me feel worse. And then two of my friends got drunk and vomited all over my house. On two separate occasions.'

She cleared her throat. 'Okay, well what made you feel like you weren't coping properly?'

I took a breath. 'Well, I thought I was doing fine, but then I decided I wanted to get pregnant and I convinced my boyfriend it was a good idea. But then I decided I didn't want to after all and the thought of what could have happened is a bit terrifying. I've been scared I'm going to lose my boyfriend – that if I fall apart, it will be too much for him and we'll break up. Plus, I almost cheated on him.' I bit my lip.

She waited.

'I also thought my dad might be having an affair and that he might be a swinger, so I followed him and it turns out, he was just going to grief support meetings. Oh, and there was a psychic who I yelled at.' I stopped and took a breath. 'I've realised maybe I haven't been as completely fine as I thought I was.' I paused. 'I had a panic attack, once, too,' I offered.

The counsellor put down her clipboard. 'Okay, why don't we start with your dad,' she said.

I nodded.

I went to see Dad. This had been Sally, my counsellor's, idea. It had come up as part of a long conversation about Dad's right to an independent life, boundaries and why I felt the need to cross them so often. She thought I owed him an apology – a proper one – and an adult conversation. I had eventually agreed with her; it felt rude not to.

He answered the door. When he saw it was me, he sighed. 'Did you ever actually move out or does Ollie live alone?'

I gritted my teeth. 'Can I come in?' I said.

Dad turned and walked back into the house. 'I'm surprised you ever left.'

I wondered whether I really needed a relationship with my dad. I followed him in.

He was sitting in the lounge with the television on, watching the golf.

I took the remote and turned it off. 'I wanted to talk to you,' I said.

He eyed me, suspiciously. 'Why?'

I took a deep breath. 'Well. I feel like I owe you an apology. A proper one. And to explain myself. I should never have followed you when I thought you were having an affair. You have a right to an independent life.' I gritted my teeth again. 'And to another relationship. As and when you want one.'

Dad raised his eyebrows. His fingers edged towards the remote.

I snatched it and sat on it. I took a breath. 'So I thought we could have an adult conversation about it,' I said.

Dad looked pained.

I probably did, too. I tried to remember what else Sally had said. She hadn't let me take notes at the time. 'It's just that you never tell us anything about how you're feeling. I didn't even know if you really missed Mum. And then suddenly, there was this other woman in your life and I just felt like you were replacing Mum with her. I realise that doesn't justify the way I acted; I probably didn't handle it in the best way.'

Dad snorted. 'Of course I bloody miss her. Best woman I've ever known. I could never replace her.'

I bowed my head.

'It's hard enough trying to get used to not having

her here any more, without having to get used to a new woman.' He chuckled.

'Right,' I said. 'Well. Glad we cleared that up.'

He looked at me and sighed. 'You girls and your obsession with talking. That's what your mother always wanted to do. I don't know why: what good does talking about death do? It doesn't bring her back. It just reminds you she's gone. I was always told you've just got to get on with it. And you do.'

I nodded. 'Right.'

Dad brought his hands together. 'Besides, it's not like we'll never see her again. We'll all be reunited one day on the other side.' He pointed at the ceiling. 'Assuming we all get into Heaven, that is. There's no doubt that your mum's up there already. And with the amount I put in the bloody collection box each week at Mass, I better get let in, too. Not nearly as much as I had to donate to get my mum in, of course. Could have built a new church. Woman would be rotting in purgatory forever if I hadn't. Probably still is.' He shrugged.

I bit my lip. 'I'm sorry, anyway, for questioning that. I should have known how much you loved her.'

He nodded. 'That's all right.' He looked pointedly at the television.

I ignored this. 'I've also realised,' I said, slowly, 'that I've been meddling in your life a lot recently. Laura's too. And I think that was because I was denying how upset I was over losing Mum. I was trying so hard to be okay, that I needed to make sure everyone else was okay, too.

363

And that's not right. It's not my responsibility to look after you all.'

Dad picked at the folds of his trousers. 'Did your counsellor tell you that?'

'Yes.'

'Hmm. Maybe I misjudged her. She seems to have helped you.' He looked up at me.

'She has,' I said.

'Yes, well, I appreciate you saying that.'

I nodded.

There was a pause. I wondered if we should hug.

Dad cleared his throat. 'You don't want to hug, do you?'

I snorted. 'No,' I said. 'Anyway. I want to see Father Ray, too. I think it would really help me. So I was wondering if you could set up an appointment for me.'

'Well. It's about bloody time.' He stood up. 'I'll call him right now.'

A few days later, we received an actual message from Mum. It wasn't via a psychic this time. In fact, it was thanks to Dad that we found it.

He was making Laura and me go through Mum's papers. He wanted to move her bureau out of their bedroom and put in an exercise bike.

'It's been a year,' he said. 'And we still haven't touched her clothes. It's time we went through some of her things. And I've wanted an exercise bike for years.' He crossed his arms. 'Your mother would never let me have one. She said they were ugly.'

Laura and I looked at each other. We were standing in Dad's bedroom. We had volunteered to go through the bureau. Mainly because we suspected that if Dad did it, he would just shred everything. He had shown us his new shredder.

'What?' Dad said. 'She's not here to see it now. You've got to make the best of these things. Life goes on.' He pointed at the bureau. 'Come on then. I want to take it to the charity shop tomorrow.' He walked out of the room, and then turned. 'Oh and Hannah, I made that appointment with Father Ray.'

I nodded.

Laura ran a hand over the bureau. 'Wasn't this Grandma's?'

I sat on the floor. 'Yes, but on Dad's side, so it doesn't matter.'

'Ah.'

I pulled out the first drawer and we peered in. It was full of unused greeting cards. Mum would always pick a few up whenever she was shopping. She had yet to be caught unawares by a surprise baptism with nothing to show for it.

I grabbed them. 'Mine,' I said, snatching them away.

'Why do you get them?' Laura said. 'You never send cards. I haven't had a birthday card from you in the past five years.'

'That's because I never have any when I need them. Now I will.'

Laura poked about in the bottom of the drawer. 'Fine.

But I'm having the stamps,' she said, producing a few booklets.

'Fine.' I narrowed my eyes. 'Why do you want stamps?'

Laura raised an eyebrow. 'That's for me to know.'

'You'll never use them.'

'Yes I will.'

'For what, then? If you can't tell me, you clearly don't have a reason.'

'Loads of things. Like sending cards.'

I thumbed my stack of cards. 'I'll give you five of my cards for a pack of stamps.'

'No. They're mine.'

I huffed. 'How am I supposed to send birthday cards without stamps? I never have stamps.'

Laura smiled. 'Well, you should have thought of that.'

I stood up. 'I'm having Mum's red jacket.'

Laura stood up, too. 'What? Why? Red's not even your colour.'

'I'm the oldest. It's my right.'

We glared at each other.

Dad walked in. 'How's it going?'

We sat back down, slowly.

'Great,' I said. 'I've got all the birthday cards.'

'And I've got all the stamps.'

Dad eyed us. 'Right. Are you almost done?'

Laura looked at the bureau. 'We've done a drawer.'

Dad sighed and turned. 'I can always bring up the shredder and we can just put everything in there,' he said as he walked out.

I opened another drawer. 'Let's just take a drawer each,' I said.

'Fine.' Laura opened a drawer and pulled out a photo album. She smiled, smugly.

I pulled a folder out of mine. 'Insurance,' I read.

Laura smirked. 'Have fun sorting through that.' She opened the photo album. 'Look how cute I was as a baby.'

I sighed and opened the folder, flipping through its contents. And that's when I found it: the letter. It was towards the back of the folder, tucked in alongside a copy of her will. It was in Mum's handwriting and it was addressed to Laura and me. I pulled it out.

'My darlings,' it read.

Your daddy and I updated our wills today (we have split everything equally between the two of you, so please don't squabble) and it has got me thinking about what would happen if anything should happen to us. There's something about updating a will that makes you feel dreadfully morbid. Funny that. We also had some wine with lunch, which maybe didn't help. How I hope we are both around to see you grow up, marry and have children of your own (which I hope happens sooner rather than later) but just in case something should happen and you find this before I get to the ripe old age I hope to see, I wanted to take a moment to remind you how much I love you both. I am so proud of my two girls and the women you are becoming. Today, you are both teenagers. Soon, you will be all grown up. But you will be my babies, always, whether I am still

around or not. Never forget that. And even though I can
hear you now, bickering over something, I hope that you
will always be there for each other, especially if Daddy and
I aren't around to make sure of it. Anyway, I shall now
stop being so maudlin and get back to you in the present,
my darling girls. All my love, now and always,
  Mummy X

PS If tragedy should befall us at a young age, please try
to be sensible and don't squander all of your inheritance
straight away. And remember to share.

I looked up. Laura was looking at me, suspiciously.

'What?' she said. 'What is that?'

I handed her the letter.

When Dad next came back in to check on our progress, we were both on the floor, our arms around each
other, crying.

'Oh for God's sake,' he said. 'I'll do it myself.'

I wish I could tell you something profound at this point.
That, after a year, I had learned something fundamental
about life, death and grief. That the next time someone
I knew went through it, I'd be able to offer them something that I had wanted when this first happened that
would have helped. But I can't. The only thing that
had really changed was that I had a couple of decent
anecdotes. That and the nagging feeling that it had been
a year: I probably couldn't use my grief as a reason to
cancel plans at the last minute, any more.

This was unfortunate because as far as the definitive markers of passing time go — the new calendar year, a birthday ticking off a new year of life — the anniversary that shows you've been through a whole twelve months without someone is really the big one. No other annual anniversary after that really compares, because you've already done the first year. It felt like an ending. And I hate endings. I don't even want to end this. But you know what they say about good things, or just about things, really: they come to an end. Just like that year did.

A few days after we found the letter, I got another text from Laura. 'Dad's booked a ticket on a singles cruise for the over fifties,' it said.

At least this time, no one had died.

How to Be a Mum

Sometime after all this happened, something else happened. I realise that's not my best opening gambit, but bear with me.

It was months after Dad got back from his singles cruise, complaining about the buffet.

'Just dreadful. Awful things, buffets. Everything's half cold and the food always looks orange. Doesn't matter what it is. Still, wonderful weather. Most of the time. Terrifically calm seas. Hardly felt a thing. Although the boat did still rock, sometimes.' He winked and I had to block my mind from the thought of the over fifties having it off.

'The swell of the ocean's probably very sexy,' Laura said. She was trying hard to show she had accepted Dad's new life. 'I mean, it's a natural rhythm.'

'Stop talking,' I said.

'Your mother would have hated it,' Dad said.

'You on a singles cruise?' I said. 'Well, probably.'

Anyway, this was months after that. It was a weekend and Ollie and I were both at home, and I was staring at a pregnancy test.

370

'Holy shit,' I said. 'Fuck,' I also said. Then I said a lot of other swear words. It had gone pink.

I don't know why this was such a shock. We had been trying for months. Properly this time, and not with Ollie the reluctant hostage to my mental health. Every time my period had started had been a small disappointment and a slight worry about when it actually would happen for us, before we tried again the following month. Still, when it actually came to it – the test going pink – it was all a bit overwhelming. Let's call it the hormones.

I skidded into the lounge, where Ollie was sitting, watching TV.

'What?' he said, rather stupidly, I thought: I was waving the test in the air, after all.

'It's gone pink,' I whispered. 'I'm pregnant.' And I burst into tears.

Ollie jumped up, almost knocking his cup of tea out of his own hand. 'Pregnant? You? Pregnant?'

I shoved the stick in his face.

'Okay, you peed on that,' he said, gently extracting it from my hand.

'I know,' I wailed. I sat on the floor and hugged my legs. 'I don't think I can do this after all, Ollie. I don't know why I ever thought I could. Not without Mum. She was going to babysit. She was going to help me. I can't do it without her. I won't do it without her.' I started rocking.

Ollie dropped to his knees and held my shoulders. 'Hannah, we talked about this. We planned this. This is what we've wanted for ages.'

I stuck my nose in the air. 'I have changed my mind.'

'It might be a little bit late for that,' he said, looking at the test.

'Well then you do it.'

Ollie waited a beat. 'You need to stop panicking. You're going to be a great mum, just like your mum. She might not be here to help, but she's shown you what to do by raising you and Laura. And we have other family who will help. We have your dad and Laura. And there's my mum.'

I hadn't even thought about Anne. This felt a bit too much to bear.

I let out a sob. 'It's not the same.'

'I know. But just because she's not here, doesn't mean she's not watching over us right now. Think about how happy she would be at this moment. She'd be thrilled. She'd be getting out the champagne. In fact, we need the champagne. Where's the champagne?' He jumped up, ran into the kitchen and ran back with a bottle. The cork popped.

I snorted. 'I can't even drink! Oh my God, I can't. Even. Drink.'

'I'll get the fizzy water.' Ollie ran back out again. 'Han, it's going to be okay. We'll do this together. We'll work it out,' he said. 'We're going to have a baby.'

I stopped rocking and sat very still as Ollie dashed off to get the glasses he had forgotten. I tentatively touched my stomach and thought about all the times I'd experimented with touching my stomach when there was nothing actually in there.

I was going to bring something into this world that was at the end of a line of women it would never know. The women that shaped me weren't there any more. My grandma was gone, my mum was gone; it would only know me. I hadn't thought about any of this when we had decided to start trying again, but now that I had, it felt like an extremely raw deal for the baby.

But Ollie was right. I wasn't in any position to admit this to myself, but he was. We wanted this. There had been a real plan that hadn't involved me lying in wait to surprise him with a new angle of my vagina. Getting pregnant was no longer a solution to a problem. Time and counselling meant that I could see around the edges of grief. I'm sorry to tell you it was still a part of everything (those very earnest people at the beginning had been right, after all: it doesn't ever go away), but it wasn't the only thing, any more. It was about us, our family and creating one together. Only, now it had actually happened, I was having very serious doubts about my ability to do it at all. I wasn't a mother; I was barely a daughter, any more.

I took a deep breath. It didn't matter: it was clearly going to have to do. I was going to have to do.

Ollie came back in with the glasses, pouring frantically and gibbering at me about calling our parents and buying a pram.

Holeee shit, I thought, with two additional syllables to really emphasise my point. I was going to be a mum.

Acknowledgements

There are so many people I owe thanks to.

This book wouldn't be here without Hannah Schofield and Amanda Preston, my agents, who have been brilliant champions of this story and who have provided me with much-needed feedback, encouragement and support.

I am very lucky to have Olivia Barber as an editor, who has made this story so much better with her spot-on insights and edits. A huge thanks also goes to the rest of the team at Orion. I am so grateful Hannah found a home with you.

I wrote the first draft of this on the New Writing South creative writing programme and a lot of thanks go to my friends there and tutors, Rosie Chard and the true sage that is Beth Miller, who has done so much. Every writer should have a Beth.

Thanks to the Friday Society, editors, readers and all-round support system: Sevi Lawson, Isabel Scott-Plummer, Lynsey Evans, Sonia Yeandle, Fran Beckett and Lindsay Gillespie.

Thank you to Isabel, Jonathan Palmer, Jade Clements and Emily Spence for reading early drafts and giving notes.

Thomas Dearnley-Davison, you knew about this book before I even started writing it and we both know you'd never forgive me if you weren't mentioned here. Thanks for being enthusiastic about the idea.

I owe so much to my family. My dad, Peter, for everything he has done for me; Sinead, who spent a lot of our childhood reading things I had written and who has refused to do so ever since; Matthew, I may never write about brothers, but I'm very grateful I have them; Anthony; Penny; Tanya; Rebecca and all of the rest of you. Thank you for everything and for not being Hannah's family.

On the subject of family, thank you to Peter and Tina: this is what became of that notebook you gave me.

To my friends, who have patiently listened to me talk about this (sometimes, in the form of a dramatic reading). I'd love to name you all, but I'll have to thank you in person instead.

Finally, thank you to my husband, Francis Hart. None of this would have been even slightly possible without you.